INSPECTOR KETCH OF NORWICH

Collected Short Stories about a Norwich Detective

By

Kelvin I Jones

CUNNING CRIME BOOKS

CONTENTS

THE SINS OF THE FATHER

Shortly after midnight father Geoffrey Collins woke, startled by a noise. He switched on the bedside lamp. Youths again. The third time in just over a week. Hurriedly, he pulled on his dressing gown and made his way downstairs, remembering to collect his hawthorn walking stick from behind the front door.

When he had first moved to Norwich's Earlham Road district some 15 years ago, there hadn't been a youth problem. The most he'd had to endure was noisy carousing when the pub directly opposite threw out its Friday night clientele, but over the past few years, his peace and quiet had been eroded. There was the late-night joyriding which these days extended from the weekends to occasional midweek occurrences. Only last week, the corner shop had been ram-raided by a gang of hooded youths. More disturbingly, his back garden, a long strip of land stretching from the conservatory at the back of the property and abutting the rear of the Cathedral, was now frequently invaded by marauding yobs late at night. In the mornings, it was not uncommon for him to find bottles of vodka, used syringes, and condoms strewn along the lawn.

As he opened the back door, a blast of freezing November air hit him. He switched on his torch and paused for a moment. He could hear the chickens in their coops sending out their alarm signals. Someone was out there in the dark, hidden somewhere among the dense canopy of hawthorn bushes and rhododendrons. "Who's there?" he called, aware of the futility of his utterance. Suddenly, he realised he had forgotten his carpet slippers. His feet were frozen. He plunged ahead into the inky darkness, the feeble torch throwing its pale light into the gloom. He had cleared the lawn and was almost up to the chicken coops when a hooded figure stepped onto the path. He turned and caught the glint of the blade as the figure raised its arm. There was a sharp pain in his chest, then he gasped and fell forwards, coughing blood.

It wasn't often that Detective Chief Inspector Ketch indulged in a recreational Saturday, but today was a rare exception. Usually, his idea of recreation consisted of a lie - in with the weekend newspapers, followed by a liquid lunch at the Grapes pub. But today was somewhat unusual. In fact, he had been looking forward to doing something different with his weekends for quite a while. So when he saw a poster for the event in the Millennium library, he made a note in his diary. 'Secrets of the Norwich city cemetery,' it had read. 'A conducted tour by blue badge guide and local historian Neil Shelley.' Ketch had never much been interested in local history, but this event fascinated him. During his long career at Bethel Street police station, he had often passed the Victorian cemetery on the Earlham Road and wondered how it came to be in such a state of neglect and dereliction. He had read an article in the local newspaper, explaining that the burial ground, opened in 1856, housed some remarkable celebrities of the Victorian age, including members of the Coleman family, manufacturers of the famous English mustard.

10 o'clock on a cold November morning found him standing alongside a small expectant crowd, surrounded by beech trees, oaks and a profusion of ornate gravestones. The guide had stopped in front of a large marble monument depicting a horse. "Here," the guide was saying, "is the gravestone of one Richard Able, horse dealer, and entrepreneur, and just over here, is the family tomb of the Coleman family. To my right, beyond the trees, lies the Jewish plot and to my left, between those overgrown sycamores, is the Roman Catholic sector. Let us proceed."

The company pressed onwards, their footfalls ringing like pistol shots on the frozen asphalt path. Ketch glanced inquisitively at some of his elderly companions, wondering why they had turned up to the guided walk. Morbid curiosity perhaps? Beyond the sycamores, the guide paused to allow his retinue time to survey the scene. Most of the gravestones were mildewed or partly illegible through erosion. However, one very ornate tomb caught his eye. Depicting a tall figure in priestly robes, it read: 'To the memory of Father Francis Ebenezer Doyle, author of 'The Dark Night of The Soul,' born 1858, died 1910. May the light of The Saviour Burn in Eternal Splendour.' The Dark Night of the Soul. It rang a bell. Something he had read in his father's study, in Wales, a Victorian tract, a ghastly piece full of hellfire, damnation and suffering. He had been 10 at the time and it had left a lasting impression on him. Doyle... Wasn't he a Jesuit?

His mobile rang, breaking his reverie. The eyes of his graveyard companions turned on him accusingly. Ketch walked three paces into a clearing. It was D.C. Watkins. "Sorry to disturb you on your day off, sir. There's been a murder."

By the time Ketch arrived on the scene, the barrier tape had already been erected and SOCO were in the early stages of their operation. Ketch, who didn't drive, had decided to walk the length of Earlham Road to the large Victorian villa which had once been the residence of father Geoffrey Collins. He hadn't counted on his morning comprising both the long and the recently deceased, but today it was Hobson's choice he told himself. He met Watkins at the top of the garden where SOCO had erected a temporary plastic tent, screening of the body from passers-by.

"Housekeeper found him early this morning," Watkins told Ketch. "Came round to do the cleaning and found the back door open." He pointed to a small, grey haired woman in her late 60's, sitting on the garden bench, being consoled by a young WPC.

Ketch donned shoes and surgical gloves, then pulled back the tent flap. The priest lay on his back, his left arm raised to his face in a defensive manner. His throat had been slashed and there were cuts to his upper torso. "Looks like he put up quite a fight," Watkins observed.

"Any forensics yet?"

"Too early to say, sir, except for a single footprint just to the left of the body. Clearly not the victim's."

"Time of death?"

"Around 11 pm last night, according to Dr Hennessy."

"Where *is* Carol?"

Carol Hennessy, the young pathologist, had known Ketch for some five years. Ketch harboured a secret liking for her and on occasions, they had shared a meal together.

"Inside, on her mobile, when I last saw her."

A tall, striking brunette appeared at the back door of the property, swathed in white.

"Bad luck. Your day off, is it?"

"No rest for the wicked. What can you tell me?"

"Victim in his 60's. Cause of death, massive blood loss. A long-bladed knife, cutting straight through the jugular. Initially, he was attacked from behind though. There is a long initial cut to the back of his neck. Then he must have turned around to face his attacker. Tried to defend himself with his right hand before the killer blow felled him.

7

Attacker was most likely taller than him by a few inches."

"Anything else?"

"Time of death..."

"I already know that."

Ketch nodded in Watkins' direction.

"I'll let you know more when I get him on the slab."

After Hennessy had disappeared once more, Ketch and Watkins went back indoors to the study. The walls were lined with theological works and among them, Ketch found a history of the Jesuit order, several volumes of the lives of the saints, plus a small collection of Irish poetry. There was a musty, bachelor tobacco smell to the place.

"What do we know about Father Collins?" asked Ketch.

"A quiet man, according to his neighbours. The old woman who does for him told me he'd had some trouble with local youths lately."

"What kind of trouble?"

"They kept breaking through the fence into the back garden. On one occasion, they stole one of his chickens. The creature hasn't been seen since. Lithuanian kids, according to old Mrs Robinson. Collins confronted a gang of them about a week back, but they threw stones at him. There had also been an incident of dog shit through his letterbox. That was about a month ago."

"You got a description of them?"

"I'm onto it, sir. The ringleader is already known to us. A boy called Stefan Leibovitch. He lives in one of the terraced houses off the Earlham Road."

"Neighbours? Acquaintances?"

"WPC's Taylor and Evans are doing door to door. And we've contacted Father Murphy. He's at the Cathedral offices. He was a close friend of Father Collins. Known him for 20 years."

Ketch had passed the imposing edifice of the Catholic Cathedral many times on his way to the Bethel Street HQ. Built in mock Gothic style in the 19th century, its dark red brick dominated the skyline of Norwich. Father Collins' office was a small, dingy room at the rear of the Cathedral, lined with books but barely furnished with a chipped Formica desk and two chairs which had seen better days. Father Murphy was in his mid-30s, pale-faced, lean and with penetrating, close-set eyes. He spoke with a strong, lilting accent which Ketch immediately identified as being from the west of the Republic. He rose to shake hands with the Chief Inspector.

"A tragic business. I heard the news about an hour ago. What happened exactly?"

Ketch explained without going into too much detail.

"Would you care for some tea or perhaps coffee?"

When Father Murphy had returned, Ketch said: "I understand from DC Watkins here that you knew Father Collins very well?"

"Indeed. We went way back. Attended the same seminary in Cork. I suppose you could say he was my mentor."

"You knew about these youths who'd been vandalising his property?"

"He was very distressed about it. We knew the parents of one of the boys. They come to the Cathedral. The parents both work at a wholesale book distributor on an industrial park here in the city. So there's no one at home to supervise their kids. It's the old story, I'm very sorry to say."

"Do you know why they decided to persecute Father Collins in particular?"

"Good heavens, no. He had a great concern for young people. Ran a youth club in Cork for many years. That's where I met him."

Back in his flat off the Earlham Road, Ketch treated himself to a fish and chip supper and sat afterwards with a glass of whiskey, watching the lights of the traffic flickering beyond the lounge window. He put on a CD and listened to the soaring lyrics of Elbow's 'Seldom Seen Kid' before finally retiring around midnight. About 2 am he woke suddenly and lay, listening to the sounds of mayhem emanating from the Earlham Road. It was the usual Saturday night debacle involving hordes of drunken teenagers. These days his colleagues rarely sent a unit to deal with the problem simply because they were inundated with problems in the centre of the city.

Unable to get back to sleep, he pulled on his dressing gown and got out his laptop. Then he googled the name, Francis Ebenezer Doyle. Within seconds, he had hit Wikipedia where he found a short biography of the man whose gravestone he had glimpsed that morning in the cemetery. 'Born 1858, died 1910,' the entry read. 'Francis Doyle, leading figure in the Irish Jesuit movement, author of the book "Dark Night of The Soul", and influential Jesuit tract on the nature of suffering.' Below was a separate entry from the book. He clicked on a PDF of the entire work. His eyes scanned the text. One entry, in particular, caught his attention. Headed 'The Abjuration of The Flesh,' it read: 'The flesh being weak, a portal to daemonic infestation, must, therefore, be abjured on a regular basis. I recommend the wearing of a cilice and hairshirt. In addition, the daily application of a scourge applied on the back and buttocks to guard against sexual urges and thoughts of an unseemly nature.'

The text went on, but Ketch stopped reading and disconnected himself from the net. For some while, before he drifted back to sleep, he lay and pondered the day's events. Collins was a celibate. Was it possible that he might be a paedophile? It might explain the harassment by the youths. He put his brain to rest, turned over, and drifted off into a troubled sleep, involving dark, oak-lined rooms and a priest wielding a count of nine tails.

The following morning dawned fair and bright with a light covering of snow to the rooftops of the city houses. As usual, Ketch walked the length of the Earlham Road into the heart of the city, reaching the Bethel Street HQ just after 9 AM. He found DC Watkins in the Ops room.

"Stefan Leibovitch and the father are in interview room number three, guv. The boy was picked up near Castle Meadow late last night. One of a gang of 10. They'd steamed their way through the express Tesco. The security guard phoned HQ around nine o'clock."

Stefan's father was lean, muscular man in his early 30s with tattooed arms and a scarred face, who looked like he'd lived for 100 years. He spoke in short, faltering sentences and was clearly unhappy about being present. Stefan Leibovitch, who bore a close resemblance to his father, sat back in the chair, hands behind his head, nonchalant, careful to avoid eye contact.

"I want to talk to you about this man, Stefan," began Ketch, pointing to a photo of Father Collins. "You knew him, I believe." Silence. Ketch looked at Mr Leibovitch who prodded his son in the ribs.

"Answer the policeman," he snapped. Stefan nodded.

"You'd caused him some trouble, I believe?"

The youth nodded again.

"And why was that?"

Stefan smiled, then looked at Ketch directly for the first time.

"Because the old man was queer."

"Meaning?"

"Meaning that he preyed on children."

"Where did this take place exactly?"

"At the Sunday School and sometimes at his house."

"And how do you know that this is true, Stefan?"

"Because he showed me photographs on his computer. And because he paid me money to keep my mouth shut about it."

Mr Leibovitch stared at his son with incomprehension.

"And when exactly was this?"

"Lots of times it happened. He used to invite boys back to his place for what he called Bible studies. That's when it used to happen."

"And did he also molest you, Stefan?"

"He tried, but I refused."

"So you what? You threatened him then?"

"I told him I wanted money to keep my mouth shut about it."

"And he refused so that's why you killed him?"

"No. He said no after a while so, me and a few of my friends started to make trouble for him."

"What kind of trouble?"

"We used to break into his back garden. It was fun. Once we killed one of his chickens. We stuffed shit through his letterbox. Why not? He was a disgusting little man."

Stefan's father looked incredulously at his son and licked his lips nervously.

"Stefan, where were you on Saturday evening?"

"Out with the gang."

"Until when exactly?"

"Until late."

"And can anyone vouch for that?"

Stefan shrugged. "Went to a couple of places. Prince of Wales Road. Places nearby. Dan-"

"Who's Dan?"

"My best mate. Dan gets us all some booze. He's 18 so he can."

"Then afterwards, you went down the Earlham Road to Father Collins' house?"

"Thought about doing it, but decided to give it a rest. Let the old man sweat a bit. I took 50 quid off him last week. I had enough to see me through the week."

There followed a long silence. Ketch stared at Stefan. Somehow he believed what the youth had been telling him.

Ketch left HQ late that evening. Preliminary results from forensics offered no match with Stefan being at or even near the scene of the crime. There were no DNA traces and even the enigmatic footprint didn't match his shoe size or type. When Watkins visited the Leibovitch residence later that day, he found a stash of £20 notes in the boy's wardrobe which could have corroborated his story. Ketch instructed Watkins to conduct a trawl of the CCTV cameras operating on the Prince of Wales Road for the Saturday night. Then around nine pm, he made his way back to the flat, his mind mulling over the affair. In the morning he would get the IT boys to check out Father Collins' PC files and make a thorough search of the priest's house to see if the boy's account held true. On his way back to the flat he dropped in for a pint and whiskey chaser. In the corner of the saloon bar, he spotted Father Murphy, sitting alone with a half consumed pint of Guinness. Ketch thought he looked nervous and somewhat preoccupied.

Ketch spent some of the Monday morning liaising with two DCs at Collins's house where his computer was removed for further investigation. As the men busied themselves with their task, Ketch perused the bookshelves in the priest's study. Books by Cardinal Newman, St Augustine and here, curiously, on top of a shelf, a red, leather-bound copy of Doyle's 'Dark Night of The Soul.' He opened it. On the fly leaf was the inscription: 'To my mentor and guide, Geoffrey, with all best wishes, Christmas, 1987. Father Murphy.'

Ketch pocketed the book and made his way out of the back of the property, pushing under the barrier tape into the garden. It was a long, well-cultivated stretch, bordered by tall pine trees and rhododendron bushes. A narrow path snaked up towards the chicken coops at the far border, but these had been emptied by the RSPCA the previous day. He stood for a while, breathing in the cold winter air. To his left was a pile of compost and just beyond it, an area of what looked like freshly dug soil. He took out a packet of cigarettes from his coat pocket and lit one, drawing in the acrid smoke.

Ketch returned to the Collins' residence around seven pm that same day. It had been a productive afternoon. Father Collins' PC had yielded a stash of information regarding his online activities. Once the password had been cracked by the IT boys, no less than 1000 indecent images had been accessed by them and it appeared that Collins had links with a paedophile ring operating in both Europe and America. All of which provided no further evidence as to his assailant.

By the time he reached the house, it was raining hard and Ketch, who had omitted to bring his umbrella with him, was soaked through. Revisiting the scene of the crime solo was a practice he frequently adopted. He believed that the absence of other people often sharpened his own senses and gave him an opportunity to marshal his thoughts. Although nothing might come of this exercise, it was always worth giving it a try. A clue, a single detail, perhaps overlooked, sometimes would emerge, throwing fresh light on the circumstances of the crime.

Once inside, the sky cleared and a full moon had risen low on the horizon. He decided not to put on the interior light for a few moments and sat in the leather captain's chair for 20 minutes as he slowly began to dry out, trying to figure things out. The curious volume he had plucked from the bookshelves that morning kept coming back to him as if it were the key to the mystery.

As he was about to stand up and switch on the table lamp, he heard the sound of footsteps outside. He rose and concealed himself behind the door. Within a few seconds, the light had been switched on and he saw the figure of Father Murphy enter the room. Through the crack in the door, he caught glimpses of his face which bore a strained, haunted expression. He went to the bureau and producing a long bladed knife, broke open the lock, taking out a packet of envelopes. He was about to exit the room when Ketch revealed himself. Murphy gave him a startled look and moved his left hand behind his back in an attempt to conceal the documents.

"Looking for something, Father Murphy?" Ketch enquired.

"A book I left here. Needed it for my sermon."

"So what's that behind your back then?"

In a split second, Murphy had produced the knife and lunged at Ketch, cutting him on the cheek. Ketch reeled back, letting him flee. He had no intention of risking his life. He was too near to retirement.

Father Murphy sat opposite Ketch and DC Watkins, pale and haggard looking, fumbling with the small rosary which hung from his neck. He was unwashed, dishevelled, and bore a large bruise on the side of his face, evidence of his recent resisted arrest. Ketch turned on the audio equipment to record.

"Interview with Father Richard Murphy, 10:30 AM, November 15. Officers present DCI Ketch and DC Watkins. Father Murphy, you've already told us about the reason why you visited Father Collins' residence."

"To get the letters back."

"Letters which you'd written to him over a number of years, prior to your incumbency here in Norwich."

"Letters in which on several occasions, I pleaded with him to confess his continued addiction to child abuse. And to put a stop to it once and for all." Father Murphy sighed.

"How long had this been going on?" asked Ketch.

"For years. In some ways, it wasn't his fault. We both attended the same school- a Jesuit school in Cork. Father Collins was three years older than me. He endured a regime of punishment there in his later years. He was also abused by one of the brothers. It was also there that he became tainted by this cursed addiction. It was he who initiated me into that disgusting world. When I left Ireland 10 years ago, I took counselling and was able to stop abusing others. I also ceased being a catamite."

"But you applied for the job in Norwich. When was that? About four years ago?"

Father Murphy nodded. "I had heard through a young man William Blaker that Father Connelly had continued with his awful practices. I wrote to him on several occasions. I pleaded with him to stop. He wrote back to me, such terrible things he had done. Including the murder of a young boy. He claimed it had been an accident, the results of a 'sex game.' That was how he described it. He had constricted the boy's airways to heighten his sexual pleasure but things had then gone too far. That was when I applied for the posting here in Norwich. I knew something had to be done to vanquish the demon within him. I tried talking to him, reasoning with him. All to no avail. Do you know of a work by the Jesuit priest called The Dark Night of The Soul? We both had read it at the seminary. There is a passage in that work which describes how we all, at one stage in our lives, face a choice: whether to take the road up into the light or down into the darkness. Father Collins had taken the latter and there was no return to

14

the land of the living. Oh, I debated long and hard about my proposed solution to the problem, believe me. All along I believed that there was some hope for him. Three nights ago, I went round to see him and found him with the boy."

"Stefan Leibovitch?" Ketch interjected.

"Yes. They were in flagrant. Collins had a cord round the boy's throat. Of course, he had paid him for the 'pleasure.' I knew then that I had to act, I had to stop the abuse. So on the Saturday evening, I came back and lured him into the garden."

"Where you then murdered him?"

Father Murphy lowered his head. Tears welled from his eyes.

"I prefer to describe my actions as a mercy killing. Now the fiend is no longer sleeping but dead."

Ketch took a short cut through the Norwich Cemetery when he had finished his business with Father Murphy. It had turned bitterly cold and a north wind was blowing snowflakes into his face as he made his way into the Catholic portion of the graveyard. Here it was, at last, the grave of Ebenezer Doyle, the author of The Dark Night of the Soul. He stood in silence before the elaborate gravestone for a good long while, ruminating on the day's events, wondering why, if there truly was a God, he would allow such unspeakable acts of perversion to exist, especially among the representatives of his church on earth. Perhaps that was the greatest unsolved mystery of them all. Taking out a packet of cigarettes and lighting one, he moved on through the deserted graveyard, pausing at the exit to button up his overcoat. A pint and whiskey chaser might just do the trick.

EASTERN ECHOES

The call came around nine pm. For the third time on a blustery, autumn evening, DCI Ketch had turned from the window of his flat and returned to the chess board in a vain attempt to solve the puzzle set by Richard Reti, the Czech chess player in the year 1921.

The only pieces remaining on the board were the black and white kings and two pawns. The puzzle was simple but also quite incredible. It looked impossible to draw. The black king was too close, the white king too far away. White must take the black pawn or promote his own. But if the white king moved diagonally, being ready to fight on two fronts... well then. It was an endgame puzzle and it was driving him to distraction.

He took another sip of malt and sat, hunched over the board, his mind ticking like a Geiger counter. Outside the flat window, the wind howled as if trying to gain access and it had now begun to rain. The whisky dulled his senses. The synapses refused to yield the solution. It was no good. He would have to admit defeat...again...

The phone call, though unwelcome at this hour, provided his exit route. It was DS Tim Mackenzie. Reliable, thorough, stolid Mackenzie. Ten years his junior, Mackenzie was set to go places. But probably not until Ketch retired as DCI unless he put in for a transfer. And that was unlikely, for Mackenzie was both conservative and cautious regarding his career.

"Mackenzie here, sir."

"I know who it is!" snapped Ketch. His son had bought him a new mobile for his birthday and set it up so he could see at a glance who was phoning. Ketch, a natural Luddite in such matters as digital technology, had been unusually grateful.

"Of course you do. Sorry."

"Where are you?"

"Swadlington. The churchyard, to be precise. Body of a middle-aged man. Looks like he's been poleaxed."

Swadlington. A once prosperous Georgian town, now slightly gone to seed. He hadn't been there since a few years back. He recalled the occasion. He'd visited a Bulgarian restaurant with Carol Hennessy, the Norwich pathologist. The food had been good, though for his taste, slightly heavy.

These days Swadlington was multi-ethnic, with a large Eastern European population and, on the edge of the town, a traveller's site.

"SOCO there yet?"

"On their way, sir."

"What about Dr Hennessy?"

"Tried her mobile but I got voicemail. No answer on her landline, either."

Ketch remembered now. Carol started her annual leave yesterday. She'd emailed him a reminder.

"No matter. Try Stoppard instead."

"Will do."

"Give me half an hour. I'll get a cab."

The journey took over half an hour, a detail which thrust Ketch into a foul mood. Or maybe it was really his inability to solve the chess puzzle. Or perhaps he was just getting old and tetchy. Whatever the reason, the cab had arrived late and the driver was uncommunicative.

Ketch sat watching as the vehicle snaked its way along roads lined with ancient trees until eventually the lights of the town appeared and with them the familiar sight of the broad main high street with its Georgian market portico and Victorian shop fronts interspersed with occasional twentieth-century fascia's.

A huddle of youths drinking and devouring takeaways gathered at the centre but otherwise, the place seemed like a ghost town. Then he remembered. It was a Sunday.

He instructed the cabbie to stop next to Asda, paid him, then walked briskly down the narrow path that led to the church. Two SOCO lights and the familiar plastic tent denoted the murder scene. As he approached, he caught sight of Dr Michael Stoppard who, in his white forensic suit, looked not unlike a beached whale.

"What's the verdict?" Ketch asked him.

"Wait and see. In other words, business as usual," Stoppard replied in non-committal terms. He stepped inside the tent. The body of a tall, grey-haired man, probably in his sixties, lay face down on a gravestone. The back of his head had been split open like a grapefruit and there were gouts of blood on his shoulders and arms. He wore an expensive dark suit and patent leather shoes.

Ketch turned as Mackenzie entered.

"How was he killed?"

"My guess is it was some sort of axe," said Stoppard. "In layman's terms, cause of death, a single blow split his cranium. Death instantaneous. Attacked from behind as he walked here down the path. Attacker was probably waiting for him in the trees over there."

"Time of death?"

"Around seven pm I would say."

Ketch thought Stoppard looked distracted.

"You look as if you'd rather be some place else, Mike."

"Correct. I was half way through a Rotary dinner. Hence the monkey suit beneath this plastic shroud." Stoppard offered a creased smile. "We'll get a more accurate time of death when I get him on the slab."

"What else can you tell me?"

Victim early 60s, well preserved, overweight, scar to his left cheek, expensive dentistry, and affluent, if his clothes are anything to go by. Oh, and here's his wallet."

Ketch opened it and found a driving licence. 'Javor Marcovic, The Cedars, Grantham Road, Swadlington.'

He turned to MacKenzie. "Found out anything about him yet?"

"Yes, guv. One of the local PCs knows him. He owns a couple of restaurants, one here in the town."

"Which?"

"The Bulgarian restaurant in Fore Street. Took it over a couple of years back. He also owns an off-licence in Thetford and is a small-time property developer. Part of his portfolio consists of some properties here in the town."

Ketch rummaged in the wallet and found a small address book. Inside was a home address and phone number.

"Okay then. Give this number a ring and let's see if there is a next of kin."

The Cedars was a tall, impressive building set back from the main road and concealed behind a row of copper beeches. A Georgian style structure with late Victorian additions, it boasted mock Grecian stucco pillars. The place reeks of opulence, Ketch thought. As he and Mackenzie made their way up the gravelled drive, a large security floodlight lit up, almost blinding them. The door opened, revealing a short, swarthy man who looked like a bouncer. He stepped forward, his arms folded.

"Can I help you?" he said in a pronounced Eastern European accent. Ketch showed him his warrant card. "Is there a Mrs Marcovic at home?" he asked.

Agaeza Marcovic was a tall, elegantly dressed woman in her mid-40s. She led Ketch and Mackenzie into a large, oak-panelled drawing room which was full of sculptures and antique paintings. Ketch broke the news to her, and she turned away from the two officers, her shoulders shaking as she wept. After a long silence, she went over to a small coffee table and rang a bell. The swarthy manservant appeared and tea was ordered.

"Have you any idea who might have wanted to murder your husband?" Ketch asked her. Mrs Marcovic put down her bone china cup. She spoke in a subdued, halting voice.

"No, I do not. Javor knew many people through his business contacts. But I cannot think of anyone in particular who would have wanted to do such a thing."

"What about his life before he came here to the UK?"

"We met two years prior to our move together to Britain. After the troubles had ended. I know very little of what happened in his earlier life. He rarely talked about it to me."

"Maybe you could supply us with a list of his contacts Mrs Marcovic. And there is also the question of identifying the body..."

She lowered her head. "Of course."

By Monday morning, the rain which had persisted throughout Sunday evening finally relented. But it was too late for SOCO to salvage much more from the scene of the murder. Stoppard's detailed investigation of the body yielded nothing of further significance. The victim had enjoyed a large meal an hour before his death and a great deal of alcohol. He had also had sex an hour before the fatal blow was struck. One curious detail surfaced – a small tattoo on his left arm, showing a dagger and skull and cross bones.

The briefing session kicked off at 11 am. Ketch had given the reins to DS MacKenzie. The latter stood before a large display board showing photos of the deceased. 20 years younger than Ketch, he looked lithe and confident as he addressed the ten-strong team.

"So far," he was saying," SOCO is unable to give us anything useful in the way of leads. We've not found a murder weapon, though we figure it's probably a small hand axe. At present, no witnesses have come forward and our door-to-door enquiries have thrown up nothing. It seems there were few people about at the time – which is confirmed by Dr Stoppard as seven pm. From the angle of the blow, we can assume the assailant was approximately 5'6". Javor Marcovic was a Croatian immigrant who had lived here for a number of years. It transpires that he was extremely wealthy and had made a small fortune through property speculation in Swadlington and Thetford where he owned no less than 20 properties. He also ran a building firm in Swadlington with his partner, Henrik Horvat. There were two life policies to his name, each amounting to £100,000. His wife is the sole beneficiary of his will." MacKenzie paused to sip some water. "Any questions?"

"What about the wife?" someone at the back of the room asked. "Does she have an alibi?"

"According to the statement, she spent the evening watching television. Which admittedly is not an alibi."

"So she has motive and opportunity then," observed Ketch. "And what about the business partner – Horvat?"

"He's coming into see us later this afternoon."

The session ended shortly after noon. Since they were interviewing Marcovic's business partner at two pm, Ketch decided he'd take a stroll through the city and drop in at the Grapes, his favourite watering hole. Before he left, he asked DC Willis to check out the tattoos found on Marcovic's body.

"Google it, or whatever you usually do," was his laconic instruction.

The depression had cleared and a fine day was now in progress. Ketch made his way down towards Castle Meadow and sat for half an hour on a bench adjacent to the castle before dropping into The Grapes.

A young woman with a child in a pushchair sat on the next bench. The woman was dark and spoke in an eastern European accent. Might be Serbian or Latvian he thought. His mind drifted. He wondered about Marcovic's background. Why had he come to Britain? Why did anyone bother to come to Britain anyway? If the chronology his wife described was right, though, he would have arrived a year or so after the conclusion of the Serbo-Croat wars, the late 1990s. Maybe that needed some investigation. Then there was this fellow Horvat...

According to MacKenzie, Horvat had something of an unsavoury reputation in the town. And according to one of his informants, he had been involved in running a brothel in Swadlington some years back which had since been closed down. He also had a record for GBH - an incident at a nightclub on the Prince of Wales Road a year ago.

The woman put her small child back in the pushchair and for a moment she looked at him, smiled and said something in a language unfamiliar to him. He stood up, lit a fag, and then began making his way towards The Grapes. It was a world without boundaries, a world of shifting uncertainties, he was certain of it.

Henrik Horvat sat at the table in interview room 6. Over six feet in height, he seemed to fill the room. A large, brutal looking face with close-set eyes, encountered Ketch's own weary atlas of past decades. He spoke in low, whispered tones when addressed. Ketch took the polystyrene coffee cups from MacKenzie, then resumed the interview.

"You say you worked with Javor for the last 15 years?"

"Correct. As business partners. I also assisted with the maintenance of his properties."

"Which are principally rented out to your own countrymen?"

"It makes sense to do so. Many come here and work in the building trade. Many are skilled tradesmen. They stay for six months or maybe less. The money helps their families back home. It is logical that they should stay somewhere where they know other members of their community."

"Naturally. And what about the women who you have working here?"

Horvat's face tightened and the livid scar down his left cheek creased.

"What girls are you referring to?"

"I am talking about the sex workers you employed in a house on Praed Street in 2009."

"That was a long while ago. They did this on their own. I merely charged them rent."

"Not according to one of the girl's statements."

"Then she lied. I knew nothing of what they did."

"Let's move on then. How would you describe your relationship with Mr Marcovic?"

"Excellent. We worked well together."

"I understand from a conversation with Mrs Marcovic that two days ago you visited his house and that there was a dispute between you. She says you came to blows over the matter. What exactly took place?"

Horvat shrugged. "It was nothing. A minor disagreement."

"About what?"

"About the accounts. Some rent which was unaccounted for. It was a mistake. An error in accounting. I told you, we were good friends. Occasionally friends disagree."

"Can you account for your movements on the Sunday evening between six and eight pm?"

"I was in a bar with my girlfriend Milica."

"Where precisely?"

"In Blazes. It's a nightclub in Norwich. We had a meal, then several drinks and we did not leave until late that evening."

"I shall need her contact details."

The Limes, Burgh Road, Swadlington, was a tall Victorian villa situated on the southern perimeter of the town. Fronted by elegant Ionic pillars, and surrounded by an ornate garden, it reeked opulence. Observing the CCTV system above the main door, Ketch pressed the electronic intercom and a large male face appeared on the screen. "Police. We'd like to speak to Milica Milosevo."

The interior of The Limes was no less plush than the outside. No expense had been spared and the formerly elegant Victorian interior had been stripped out, giving way to a high-end contemporary finish. Everywhere Ketch and MacKenzie looked they were confronted by steel and black leather. The two policemen sat in uncomfortable chairs and waited. After a short interval, Milica Milosevo appeared. Stunning looking, with long black hair, she was expensively dressed and richly perfumed. A manservant bought them coffee.

"You've come to ask me about poor Jorvat?" the woman asked, pre-empting Ketch's first question. "Poor Jorvat. Who could have done such a terrible thing?"

"You were friends?"

"He was Henrik's closest friend and a good friend of mine also. Have you any idea who might have killed him?"

"We are following up a number of leads. Miss Milosevo, I

understand that you are Henrik's girlfriend?"

"That' s right."

"And can you confirm that you were with him on Sunday evening?"

"That's also right. We went to Norwich – to a nightclub. Didn't get back until late."

"This is your place?" She nodded.

"And Henrik's. We bought it together. We are most happy here."

"And what do you do for a living?"

"I run two businesses, one in Norwich and one here in Swaddlington. I'm a beautician. Here is my card."

MacKenzie's phone rang He got up and left the room. Ketch glanced at the card.

"So you run a massage parlour?"

"You may call it that, inspector. We offer a number of services for clients. We have quite a reputation in this area. Perhaps I can persuade you to make an appointment?"

The door opened. "Guv, I think you should take this," said MacKenzie, giving him his mobile.

Stoppard turned the body of Henrik Horvat over and as he did so Ketch noted the tattoo on his left upper arm depicting a knife and skull and cross bones. The back of his head had been cut through and his dark hair was matted with blood.

"Found in his car, you say?"

"About half an hour ago. In a small woodland area north of Swadlington. SOCO are going over the car right now. Some interesting details for you."

"Tell me."

"The car seat was down and the victim's trousers were at half-mast."

"What a way to go."

"From the angle of the blow, I figure that someone inside the car must have wound one of the car windows down and the blow was struck through the open window. Not an easy feat."

"What about the weapon?"

"Same MO as before. A small hand axe. But there's something else which you will be pleased about."

"Oh?" Stoppard held up a small plastic evidence bag. Inside it was a long red hair.

"Found this attached to the victim's pubic hairs."

Ketch smiled with relief. "Let's get the DNA tested pronto," he said.

It was a lucky break. The only break in an otherwise frustrating case. The DNA provided a match with one Dragoslava Slankamen who already had two convictions – one of attempted burglary and one of GBH, the latter having occurred in an area of Norwich known as Hellesdon only six months previously. And Dragoslava Slankamen was registered at an address in Swaddlington.

Ethelbert Terrace was a row of shabby terraced houses situated on the northern edge of the town. Ketch and MacKenzie arrived in the early hours of the following morning, accompanied by a young WPC. There they discovered three flats, the top flat being occupied by Slankamen who had been entertaining a client since the previous evening. The house, which had been elegantly refurbished as a high-class brothel, was owned by Henrik Horvat, a fact which came as no surprise to Ketch. He was glad that the young WPC spoke Serbo - Croat, it made matters a great deal easier. Dragoslav, a tall, elegant blonde in her 20s, offered little resistance but it was only after several hours of interrogation she revealed the identity of her accomplice, Milica Milosevo.

It transpired that Milica was also a prostitute, managed by Horvat and Marcovic, and one of five girls operating on the southern side of the town. Through the interpreter, Milica and Dragoslav told Ketch their story.

They had been recruited by Marcovic five years ago and brought to England to work in the "tourist industry." When they arrived, however, they found that the services required of them were altogether different from their expectations.

Dragoslav and Milica had not taken long to discover that Horvat and Marcovic had both served as part of a special Croatian police unit serving under the infamous General Cervenko. They had been instrumental in the massacre that occurred in Knin, a village in Serbia during the 90s. On that day, etched forever in the girls' memories, their parents had been taken from their houses. Some were shot at point-blank range but others, like their parents, had been axed to death and, still living, buried in a mass grave. Between them, they devised a plan.

It would not be difficult. Each of the men was in the habit of visiting brothels on a regular basis. The girls curried favour with them and became their favourite choice. Alfresco sex soon became a regular event for the two men.

"Javor had this thing about doing it on the gravestones," said Dragoslav. "Milica was his favourite. When he fixed the date with her, she sent me a text and I waited behind the church until I heard them at it. I killed him like I would kill a pig in an abattoir, with one well-aimed blow to the back of the head. He lay there moaning and bleeding. Milica and I stood there, laughing at him. Then we went back to the house, cleaned up and drank a lot of vodka."

And what about Horvat?"

"That was more tricky. Cars were his thing. He liked doing it with the windows up and seats down. Milica had left her phone on, so I was able to hear them. She asked him to wind down the window to get some fresh air. That's when I knew to hit him. Killing Horvat was less risky. There was no one about. He took a while to die. He kept trying to get up but Milica held onto him tight until finally, he gave up struggling. I recorded it all on my phone, just like I did with Javor. Here. You can see it for yourself if you like."

Ketch stared at the chessboard. It was still no use. Two kings, two pawns and no way to resolve the puzzle. He thought of Dragoslav and Milica going about their butchery with cool detachment. Rather like chess players. Two carefully planned executions, recorded for posterity. A grotesque but fitting revenge.

Outside in the Earlham Road, he could hear a gang of youths fighting. What used to occur only at weekends now took place every night of the week. What were they fighting about? Maybe they didn't need a reason. Black against white, Serbian against Croatian, it was all the same in the end. Like the pieces on the chessboard. Man's age-old inhumanity to man.

Maybe he was just getting too old, too weary. He put the pieces back in the box, folded the board, downed the rest of the malt whiskey from his glass and then walked slowly into the bedroom. Maybe in the morning things would look a lot different. Or maybe they'd be just the same.

SUFFER THE LITTLE CHILDREN

By the time Paddy Fury reached his caravan at the camp on the outskirts of Thetford, it was already well past midnight. At 11:30 the landlord of The Shuttle had closed the doors and the fraternity of Irishmen continued carousing well into the small hours. Much of the evening, Paddy had sat drinking whiskey chasers with his old pal Francie Keenan, a man who had given him innumerable hot racing tips over the past few years.

The two men had discoursed long into the night, sharing common ground – women, politics and horse racing. Both were hard-bitten travellers, survivors, scrap merchants of the old school: semi-literate but also highly numerate. Both had also excelled at prize fighting in their youth.

A light rain was falling. Paddy reached into his leather jacket for his key, blaspheming beneath his breath. As he opened the door he paused momentarily, conscious that something was not quite right. Then, slightly befuddled from the alcohol, he plunged into the interior, reaching out for the light switch. It was at that moment a dark figure stepped from behind him, out of the shadows, and pulled a wire across his neck. Paddy gasped, then struggled to loosen its grip as slowly, inexorably, the life was choked out of him. His hands flailed either side of him but to no avail. He gasped and gurgled, then keeled over, his lifeless body crashing onto the floor.

Detective Chief Inspector Price, alias Ketch turned and looked at the digital clock next to his bedside. It read 4.34 AM. A few hundred yards from his flat off the Earlham Road he could hear the discordant voices of the youths as they marauded in their drunken frenzy, venting their anger, urinating in gardens and careering across the road. This was no different to any other Friday night. He really must move, put the flat up for sale, get a place somewhere in the country, somewhere where he'd be woken up by cockerels or cows. Anything would be better than this. But a terrible lassitude possessed him. He was getting too old, too set in his ways to uproot himself. Besides, in this God awful recession, he wouldn't get much for the flat, especially since it needed, in the estate agents' jargon, "considerable updating." If he had taken his son's advice years back and had the double glazing fitted, he wouldn't hear the cacophony he now had to endure.

But it wasn't just the noise which kept Ketch awake into the small hours. He was an insomniac. When he'd been married, it hadn't been quite so bad. The presence of a warm body next to his lulled him to sleep. But now the single bed he occupied was cold to the touch He'd tried everything over the years – meditation, counting sheep, the BBC World Service, even as a last resort, acupuncture. Nothing did the trick. And the sleeping pills prescribed by his GP had turned him into nothing short of a zombie. No, facts had to be faced. There was no real cure for insomnia.

He got out of bed, switched on the lamp and went to the window. A sudden female scream penetrated the morning air, then there was silence save for the passing of a car. Then, unexpectedly, his mobile phone rang. It was DS MacKenzie.

"Sorry to disturb you, guv, at this early hour."

"As a matter of fact, you didn't, Tim. I was already up."

"Late night?"

"Early morning, more like. What's up?"

"A murder."

"Where are you?"

"Norton Farm."

The traveller site near Thetford. He remembered. He'd had dealings there a couple of years back. Lead stripped from church roofs by the Connolly brothers.

"I know it. Send me a car will you?"

"Already onto it. Should be with you within 10 minutes."

Ketch switched off the mobile. A second, more prolonged scream pierced the silence of the night. Didn't sound much like murder he reflected, but these days one could never be sure of anything.

Ketch reached the travellers' site shortly after 5:30 AM. Norton Farm hadn't changed a great deal since his last visit but if anything it had grown much bigger. One side of the site was taken up by a scrap metal recycling plant, the other consisted of a collection of approximately 70 mobile homes and large caravans. Some of the mobile homes were clearly designed as permanent structures, despite the fact that the travellers had never been granted planning permission for permanent residency.

By the time Ketch's squad car had arrived it was already starting to grow light and a pale sun illuminated the scene. SOCO had constructed arc lights around the caravan where a large crowd of travellers and their offspring had gathered. A couple of dogs barked and ran amok, much to the consternation of the PCs on duty who were making largely vain attempts to keep the crowd under control. A large, dark haired looking man was having an argument with DS MacKenzie close to the barrier tape.

"I tell you I'm a friend of Paddy's," he was saying. "Why don't you just tell us what's happened to him? We've a right to know."

"Sorry sir, you can't enter the caravan. I have my orders. This is a crime scene now."

"So, is he dead or what?"

"We are not permitted to say. I must ask you to step back and allow police officers through."

"Causing my men trouble again, Francie?" said Ketch as he approached the caravan.

"Jesus, it's you, Mr Ketch," said the big Irishman.

"Long time no see."

"Feeling is mutual, Francie." The last time Ketch had seen Francie Keenan was in an interview room after a lead stripping incident. He had suspected Keenan of fencing the material but had not been able to prove it and Keenan had got off scot-free. "Just do as my officer requests, will you? Be a good lad and go back to your own caravan. MacKenzie, I want this crowd cleared. See to it, will you?"

Ketch donned the obligatory gloves and forensic slip on shoes, then pushed open the caravan door where he found the shapely form of Dr Carol Hennessy crouched on the floor. In front of her lay the body of a middle-aged man. A piece of wire had been pulled tight around his neck and his eyes and tongue bulged, giving a grotesque effect as if he was some kind of monstrous ventriloquist's dummy. Carol turned and smiled at him. There was certain chemistry between them. It was yet to bear fruit and so far had amounted to nothing more than a couple of dinner dates. But Ketch lived in hope.

"What's the score, Carol?" he asked.

"Victim's name is one Paddy Fury. Lived here for the past 10 years according to your sergeant."

DS MacKenzie nodded. "That's right sir. Paddy was one of the original travellers on the site. Helped purchase the land here and set things up."

Fury. The name was vaguely familiar to Ketch. He probed the synapses but nothing more came of it.

"Manner of death is much as you see," continued Dr Hennessy. "Victim was attacked from behind with a cheese wire. Violent struggle ensued. See here, the wire has cut through the skin, almost penetrating the windpipe."

"Strength needed to achieve that."

"Yes, most definitely a man and taller than the victim, I should say."

Ketch glanced at the room. A coffee table had been overturned and a number of books and photographs lay on the floor. He picked up one of the photos which showed a few trees in silhouette, illuminated by a deep sunset. Clearly, Paddy Fury had an aptitude for photography. He turned to address DS Mackenzie who now framed the doorway.

"All OK out there?"

"I sent them back to their caravans."

"Excellent. Who found the body?"

"A neighbour returning home from his night shift. He's a security officer on the Thetford industrial estate. He noticed the caravan door was ajar so he looked in. Then he phoned the emergency services."

"What time was this?"

"About 3.45 AM he says. Oh, I forgot to say. One of the travellers is waiting outside. Says he'd like to have a word with us. Apparently, he has something of interest to tell us."

Francie Keenan was a tall, burly man in his late fifties with aquiline features and a Roman nose which had been broken twice during his days spent in the boxing ring. His caravan was both tidy and palatial and contained a number of valuable antiques and oil paintings. Ketch, who had long been interested in art and had collected a number of pieces himself over his years in the Force, recognised some of the collection which crowded the walls of the mobile home. Among them was a small drawing by Rossetti and a large oil landscape by Joseph Wright, the Norfolk artist.

Keenan sat opposite Ketch and Mackenzie, smoking a short briar pipe whilst next to him on the luxurious leather sofa sat his wife Falon and teenage daughter Cadee.

After Keenan had told Ketch about his drinking session with Fury on the night of the murder, Ketch said:

"You had something you wanted to tell us, Mr Keenan?" Mrs Keenan, an attractive, dark haired woman, had a lined face and bloodshot eyes. She smiled nervously at the two officers but maintained a dutiful silence throughout the ensuing conversation.

"Yes, it's been on my mind. I thought you gentleman should know what's been going on here."

"I'm all ears."

Keenan sipped his tea, then put down his pipe.

"There's been an ongoing dispute here at Norton Farm. A bunch of us – Paddy included – bought the land from the farmer some years back. But what we didn't do at the time was to apply for planning permission. Twice the local council have tried to evict us but we've got good legal representation so it has come to nothing. There's a group of locals led by a man called Jack Standing. They've caused us a deal of harassment over the years. Standing's cottage is on the edge of our site. He has a thing about the travellers. He's a BNP member too. Only a month ago there was an incident."

"What sort of incident?"

"Him and a group of his BNP mates got tanked up at the Shuttle."

"The what?"

"It's the local pub sir. About half a mile from the site."

"Go on."

"Me and Paddy were drinking in there with Falon and Cadee. It was Cadee's 15th birthday so we'd had a few. Anyway, when we came out of the pub they were waiting for us. Stood there swearing at us, called us Gypos, diddikoi. The usual abuse."

"So you had a fight?" Keenan nodded.

"Standing and his mates attacked us with baseball bats. They'd come prepared. I had a knife on me and so did Paddy. Fortunately, it didn't get very far before the police arrived."

"So why are you telling me this, Mr Keenan?"

"Because I believe Standing may have killed Paddy."

"And what proof do you have?"

"I know about Standing. We all do. Know what he's capable of. Only last month a friend of ours was attacked on the way back from the Shuttle by someone wearing a balaclava. He was convinced it was Standing. He is desperate, you see. He's tried all the legal channels but nothing has worked. He's desperate."

As Keenan talked, Ketch found himself looking across at his daughter. She seemed old for her years with the same lustrous shoulder length black hair her mother had. Immaculately dressed in designer clothes, she appeared self-possessed, aware of her body. For a 15-year-old she was well developed with large breasts and soft, olive skin. Her short skirt barely concealed her shapely thighs which were swathed in black tights. If I had a daughter like that I think I'd be rather worried he thought. "Is there anything else you wish to tell us?" Ketch enquired.

"No, I don't think so. Just thought you should know about Standing."

"Then thank you for your assistance. We will certainly look into it."

Keenan had been right about Jack Standing's house. It was virtually a fortress. The perimeter, which encompassed both the house and garden, consisted of a ten foot high steel fence. Overlooking the main gate was a security camera. Ketch pressed the video intercom and a lined, pale face appeared.

"Mr Standing?"

"Who wants to know?"

"Police." He flashed his warrant card at the device.

"Just one moment."

Despite the austere nature of the exterior of the property, the inside was high spec and contemporary. Ketch and Mackenzie sat uncomfortably on the sofa as Standing, a wizened, miserable faced man in his late 40's with a haunted look, held forth. Ketch noticed that Standing's forehead was partially covered by a plaster around which showed some recent bruising.

"I'd sell up if I could, but no one is interested in buying the bloody property. Hardly a surprise is it, Chief Inspector? You wouldn't believe the half of what I've had to endure here. People defecating in the garden, rubbish, dog muck, they even tried to set fire to the house on one occasion. Paraffin soaked rags pushed through my letterbox."

"You informed the police?"

"And what good did that do? Sod all, that's what. These days the law-abiding property owner doesn't get a look in. They, on the other hand, have influence and a legal team to back them up. Some smart female lawyer they'd appointed came to see me. On the last occasion when there was an attempt at eviction, they even invited a mob down here to protect them. Anarchists they called themselves. That was a couple of years ago now."

Ketch had a dim recollection of the affair. He reached for his coffee cup and took a sip. The cup was stained, the taste was strong and acrid. "You live alone here?"

"My wife left me last September. Couldn't stand any more of it. She suffers from depression. The village shop closed last year - and the school. They've ruined the community. Let me tell you –"

I'm sure you're right, Mr Standing. As I explained when we arrived here, we are investigating the murder of a man called Paddy Fury. I understand that you knew him?"

"I did. And I can't say I'm sorry that he's dead. He was one of the ringleaders."

"I need to ask you about your movement's yesterday evening."

"I went to the local for a quick pint. Left at closing time. Then, on my way back, I took a short cut down Friedmans Lane. I'd forgotten the street light had packed up there, which was stupid of me. Got halfway down when somebody stepped out of the shadows and did this to me," pointing to his forehead.

"You were mugged?"

"Some bastard stole my wallet. Fortunately, I keep my credit cards in my back pocket so all I lost was a few notes, some loose change and my diary. I got back home, sorted myself out, then I watched TV until late and turned in."

"How would you describe your relationship with Mr Fury?"

"What do you expect me to say? The man was a petty criminal. I admit I've had a few run-ins with him from time to time. Him and a man called Francie Keenan. I suppose you know about the illegal stills?"

"Enlighten me."

"The two of them rent a couple of lock-ups on the Thetford industrial estate. Several of the travellers do. Fury has been manufacturing cheap alcohol there. God knows what else they've been up to. Maybe you should go check it out. "

By ten the following morning a search warrant had been issued. Ketch and a team of five officers arrived at the industrial Park by 10.30 and had no difficulty in identifying the unit whose sign bore the legend:

Fury Enterprises. What appeared to be one large unit from the outside turned out to be two. On further examination, the first unit housed the conversion equipment and several large barrels containing almost 80% alcohol which, it transpired, had been fermented from potatoes. The paperwork seized made it clear that Fury had established distribution outlets all over the East of England through mainly ethnic communities. However, Keenan's name appeared nowhere in the correspondence. At the rear of this unit was a steel door which soon yielded to one of the officer's crowbars. Inside was a photographic studio equipped with high-tech lamps, video cameras and exotic furniture. Several boxes of DVDs were stacked at the back of the unit with titles like Bondage Weekend, One on Three, and Teenage Orgy. Ketch instructed his team to remove these, along with the computer equipment, for further analysis. All in all, it was a very productive morning.

Back at HQ, Ketch had just finished an unappetising takeaway sandwich when DS Mackenzie entered. "Thought you ought to know, sir. Something has turned up in the stuff SOCO got from Paddy Fury's caravan."

"What's that?"

McKenzie held up and evidence bag. Inside it was a small red pocket diary. "Jack Standing's diary. Found under the bed."

Ketch smiled. "Let's get Mr Standing in for questioning. See what he has to say for himself."

By two pm that same afternoon interview room three was already hot and stuffy. Ketch was aware that he was sweating profusely under the armpits. He felt tired and listless, probably due to lack of sleep. Getting too old for this game he thought as he switched on the recording equipment. Twenty years ago I could survive perfectly well on less than three hours' sleep. Not so now.

"DCI Ketch and DS Mackenzie. Interview with Jack Standing. September 20, 2011, three thirty pm. Mr Standing, I have here something which interests me. Would you care to identify it for me?" Ketch held up a plastic evidence bag. Inside it was Jack standing's red pocket diary. There was a long pause, then Standing tapped his fingers on the table nervously.

"Looks like my diary."

"Indeed it is because it has your name and address inside it. Guess where it turned up?"

"I have absolutely no idea."

"In Paddy Fury's caravan."

"What?"

"In the murder victim's caravan."

"How on earth-?"

"I was rather hoping you would be able to tell us that Mr Standing."

"Now look here –"

"No, you look here. You told us in your previous interview that you were drinking in the pub until closing time. We're talking about The Shuttle, I take it?" Standing nodded.

"I left just before 11 pm."

"The same pub where Paddy Fury was drinking. You must've seen him in there."

"I was in the public bar. Yes, I did see him. He was drinking with Francie Keenan in the saloon bar."

"Let me tell you what happened. You waited until the two men left the pub, then you followed him back to his caravan. You attacked and murdered him and in the struggle, you lost your diary. The story you told us about the mugging is pure fiction, isn't it?"

Keenan shook his head vigorously. "I swear to you Inspector, what I told you is the absolute truth."

"Cast your mind back - a month ago."

"What about it?"

"The landlord of the pub has told us you were involved in a fracas outside the pub and that you and Fury came to blows."

"I admit that, yes, but –"

"But what, Mr Keenan? Your hatred of Fury wouldn't extend to murder? That's hardly convincing. I tell you what we are going to do. I'm going to leave you here to think about it. Here's a statement form and a pen. I'll give you half an hour and when I come back I expect from you a true version of what actually happened."

Ketch and MacKenzie stood up. Standing put his head in his hands. "It's not true, I tell you it's not true.," he murmured.

The day had been unbearably hot, so it was with considerable relief that Ketch found himself strolling by the River Wensum. It was a route he often liked to pursue in the city, through Tombland and its cobbled streets, into the grounds of the Cathedral and onto the towpath, past the Courts of Justice where so many of his former clients ended up. When he got to Pulls Ferry he paused and sat down on a bench to watch the ducks and swans foraging for worms and titbits. The scene before him was utterly tranquil. His reverie did not last long. His mobile phone rang. It was MacKenzie. "Sorry to disturb you, sir."

"Think nothing of it MacKenzie."

"Only I thought that you should know we've been going through some of the material from Fury's photographic studio."

"And?"

"And we found three films. In each of them Cadee Keenan is a participant and of those three she is depicted having sex with Paddy Fury- in the guise of a schoolgirl."

There was a long silence. "Are you still there sir?"

"Yes, I'm still here. Have we checked the pub's CCTV readings yet?"

"Whitaker has been doing it. Some of the images are a bit fuzzy."

"Well then, ask him to check through again for the night of the murder. Maybe he can use image enhancement. I want to check out Francie Keenan's movements."

It was just as Ketch had suspected. The CCTV images showed Fury leaving the pub alone after closing time. Some five minutes prior to this, Keenan could be seen emerging a few paces behind Jack Standing. And although he had his hood up, he was quite clearly recognisable. The scenario became clear. Keenan had followed Standing, mugged him, stolen his diary, then five minutes later, he had lain in wait for Fury, followed him to his caravan where he had garrotted him, then planted the diary in an attempt to frame Standing.

Once confronted with the facts by Ketch, Keenan put up little resistance and seemed relieved to put his case.

"When I found out what he had been doing to Cadee, it made me sick to the core," he told Ketch. "She had gone along with the business because he had offered her money, told her he could launch her on a modelling career. When she told me he had raped her and filmed himself doing it, I decided to take action. No one does that to my children without paying the ultimate price for their actions."

"But you knew about the DVDs and you also knew he had been enlisting girls from the site?" Keenan nodded.

"I knew about the girls who were willing participants. But the rape of your own child is in an altogether different league."

Ketch stood staring at the autumn leaves as they cascaded down onto the surface of the River Wensum. On the other side of the bank a group of schoolgirls passed, laughing. They were wearing heavy make up and their short skirts barely concealed their slim thighs. They were clearly drunk. He was only glad he never had a daughter... There, but for the grace of God...

The sun was already low on the horizon now and the heat of summer was gradually diminishing. Soon it would be October he thought, and the slow, inexorable descent into winter would gradually begin. Light, then cold and darkness. It was unavoidable. It was part of the order of things. And assailing the dark was part of his job... He must get back to the flat. It was growing cold.

A HEART OF DARKNESS

Ketch was happier than he had been for some considerable while. This was hardly surprising since Ketch was invariably happy when listening to music. But not just any music. Although fond of the classic 60s bands, he was also fond of the true classics. And there were no truer classics in his opinion than the musical compositions of Vaughan Williams.

It was the perfect setting for his Variations on a Theme by Thomas Tallis. The deep, resonant chords soared into the vaulted roof of Norwich Cathedral, filling him with joy and nostalgia. To Ketch it was music most quintessentially English, redolent of rolling hills and deep green vales. For one brief, tantalising moment, he was back in the mountains of Snowdonia with his father, walking the old cattle track up to the peak of Snowdon itself, the great scree laden slopes stretching away on either side as they trudged upwards into the mist.

His reverie was rudely interrupted by a mobile phone ringing. For a moment, he imagined it belonged to the grey suited man sitting next to him but then he realised with absolute horror that it was his own. Mumbling an apology, he lurched to his feet and pushed his way along the pew until he reached the nave. All eyes turned accusingly towards him as he made a swift exit. He had committed the unpardonable sin.

"Hello. Who is this?"

It was, after all, a Sunday evening and Ketch was an old-fashioned policeman. He didn't mind admitting it.

"DS MacKenzie sir. Sorry to interrupt your Sunday."

Ketch was strolling through the cloisters now which were deserted and lit by golden sunlight.

"What's up?"

"Murder victim. The body was discovered about half an hour ago. A house on Oak Road. Number 67."

Ketch knew it. A row of stately Edwardian villas a short distance from the Earlham Road and not far from his own flat. "Give me half an hour. I'll walk it. SOCO in attendance yet?"

"I called it in. They're on their way. I've got Watkins with me. He's interviewing the next door neighbours."

"Who's the victim?"

"Middle-aged bachelor, worked as a librarian and tutor for the University."

Ketch terminated the call and headed for Tombland. It was a fine July evening and a walk was just what he needed. Somehow the Vaughan Williams had imposed on him a mood of melancholy and since he was on his way to view a body, he needed something to dispel his mood.

Number 67 Oak Road fulfilled his expectations. A tall, detached villa set back from the main road and shielded by ancient cedar trees, its red brick frontage glowed in the evening sunlight. Ketch walked past the SOCO van and up the steps to the imposing front entrance which was swathed in a vast spread of mature wisteria. Inside the hall he found DS MacKenzie finishing a call on his mobile.

"Where's the corpse?" Ketch demanded.

"Just through here in the living room, sir." They entered a large room whose walls were bedecked with Victorian landscape paintings and books. In the centre of the room lay the body of a man, face downwards on a rug. To his left a chair had been overturned and a bottle of half empty whiskey and two glasses lay on the floor about three feet away. Ketch circled the corpse.

"Does he have a name?"

"Norman Loftus."

"And how did he die?"

"Stabbed through the heart, a kitchen knife. It's still attached. Here's the thing though. If you look at the surrounding area, you'll notice the body has been rolled backwards, then forwards You can tell it because of the bloody imprint on his left arm and shoulder. It extends further than if he just simply fell and died."

"Meaning that someone – the attacker – turned him over to see if he was actually dead."

"Exactly, sir."

"Good evening, Huw."

Ketch turned to see the petite figure of Dr Carol Hennessy, squeezed into her unbecoming forensic suit. Few people apart from Carol and some closer colleagues called him by his Christian name. Indeed his surname, Ketch, was not even his real name, merely an appellation which belonged to an ancestor of his on his father's side of the family, Jack Ketch, the notorious 18th-century hangman. But

Ketch it was among his colleagues in the Force and the name has stuck, a kind of macabre joke, oddly perhaps, a name he felt quite comfortable with. Though Huw he also didn't mind especially since he harboured a secret passion for the comely Dr Hennessy.

"Evening Carol. Anything significant to impart?"

"Mr Loftus died of a single knife incision to the heart. There are also some interesting lacerations, one on the back of his left hand and another on his left cheek."

"Meaning?"

"Meaning that prior to the fatal blow, there must have been a struggle. From the angle of the blade however, I would suggest that the victim actually fell on the knife."

"So death was accidental you think?"

"Possibly, though I can't be absolutely certain at this stage. Tell you more later."

"Thanks, Carol." He turned to MacKenzie. "What else have you got for me, Tim?"

"Two whiskey glasses would suggest the victim had a visitor so presumably it was someone that he knew well. No sign of break in, though."

"Where exactly is Watkins?"

"With the next door neighbour, a Mrs Goodman."

"Then let's have a word with her shall we?"

Sylvia Goodman was a small, wizened widow in her late 60s, made incongruously youthful by virtue of her dyed black hair. She sat in a room surrounded by framed photographs of her beloved cats and her late husband, drinking weak tea from a delicate china cup.

"This is Mrs Goodman," said DC Watkins, a young, pale-faced officer who, even after six months in the job, still stood in awe of Ketch. Mrs Goodman smiled nervously.

"You found Mr Loftus, I understand?"

"That's correct. I heard a commotion next door and when I went to investigate I found the front door open. I called out to Mr Loftus but there was no reply so I went in and found him lying there."

"What time was this precisely?"

"Must have been about three thirty pm. I had just started watching Inspector Morse."

Ketch smiled at the reference. "Did you touch the body at all?"

"I spoke to him but when he didn't reply I felt for a pulse. In my younger days, I used to belong to the St Johns Ambulance so I knew that he wasn't alive."

"When you entered the house here did you notice anyone else in the street?"

"I did notice there was a car. It pulled away at some speed."

"In which direction?"

"Towards the Earlham Road, the city centre I mean."

"Can you remember what sort of car it was?"

Mrs Goodman thought for a moment, tapping her moustachioed upper lip. "I'm not very good at cars. It was a red car, bright red, a sports car I believe."

"I don't suppose you noticed the make or the registration number?"

"I think it had the letters Y and P in it but I can't be entirely certain of that."

"So when you realised Mr Loftus was dead, what did you do next?"

"I went back next door and phoned the police."

"How well did you know Mr Loftus?"

"Quite well. We have been neighbours for about 10 years or so."

"Tell me, Mrs Goodman, did he have many visitors, recently I mean?"

"Not that I recall. There was that bother with Mr Speight of course."

"Who is Mr Speight?"

"Mr Loftus's next-door neighbour. Not a very nice individual I am sorry to say. He and Mr Loftus were engaged in an ongoing dispute."

"About what?"

"About noise mainly. And his Alsatian dog. It used to get through the adjoining fence and foul in Mr Loftus's garden. I only mention that because Mr Loftus told me that Mr Speight had threatened him with physical violence on more than one occasion."

"Thank you, Mrs Goodman. You've been more than helpful. And if you do remember any more detail about that car, do let us know."

John Speight, a 50-year-old Hell's Angel with a pot belly and tattooed arms, had been standing behind his bay window when the police arrived to interview him, so their arrival had come as no surprise to him. Speight stood in the doorway, his Alsatian dog scrabbling to get out.

"Do you mind securing that dog, Mr Speight? We need to have a word," said Ketch as MacKenzie sheltered behind him.

"Just a minute."

After a brief moment, they entered the hallway where there was a strong smell of dog urine and stale tobacco. The walls were plastered with heavy metal posters and nicotine stains.

"What's this about?" Speight demanded.

"Shall we talk in the living room Mr. Speight?"

Ketch and MacKenzie sat on a battered sofa across from Speight. The Alsatian dog next to him stood to attention, waiting for a command. Its beady eyes fixed upon Ketch.

"We have one or two questions to ask you."

"What about?"

"About you and your neighbour, Mr Loftus."

"Oh? What's happened to him?"

"He is dead, Mr Speight."

There was a trace of a smile on the man's lips. "Heart attack was it?"

"No. We think someone may have killed him."

The dog whimpered and Speight tapped its flank.

"When was this?"

Ketch ignored the question. "You had one or two issues with Mr Loftus I believe?"

"Who told you that?"

"Never mind who told me, I understand that you came to blows."

"About Churchill, and about the music."

"Churchill?"

He pointed to the dog.

"You attacked him?"

"I went round to sort it out. He'd put in a complaint about me to the police. He wouldn't listen to reason so I gave him one."

"And when was this?"

"Oh about a month ago. Since then he's avoided me."

"I have to ask you if you can account for your movements from this morning onwards."

"I slept till late, then went out to get the paper, took Churchill here for a walk around the neighbourhood."

"And what time did you return to the house?"

"Don't know. Around 1130 AM I would guess."

"When you passed Mr Loftus' door, did you notice anything unusual?"

"In what way unusual?"

"You tell me."

"I don't think so, no. Hang on. There was a red sports job parked outside his place. I noticed it because it was unusual, an old MG classic When I went to put the wheelie bin out around 12 though, it was gone. "

By late afternoon, SOCO had all but finished their analysis of the crime scene at number 67 Oak Road. Ketch declined MacKenzie's offer of a lift back to Bethel Street HQ and decided to take the opportunity to look around the property. It was a strategy he often found remarkably revealing, not least regarding the lifestyle and habits of the victim. And number 67 was no exception. Although the house was sparsely furnished with a variety of what was understandably second-hand furniture, it was evident that Loftus was something of a hoarder. A collection of African ritual masks and Victorian watercolours lined the walls, mainly landscapes of Norfolk from the Cotman school, while the bookshelves were stocked with a great number of leather-bound volumes.

Ketch began rummaging. An embossed 18th-century edition of Bunyan's Pilgrims Progress, a rare book by the Elizabethan astrologer John Dee from 1702 and Spencer's Faerie Queene with woodcuts from 1820.There were other, more recent editions, many of them firsts, several signed by the authors, including Virginia Wolff's To The Lighthouse. Ketch noticed that all of them had a faint mark on the spine where a Dewey classification number had originally been stuck. It meant they were all ex-library volumes.

He continued looking and at the end of the bottom shelf found an A4 book with the word 'accounts' on the spine. He took it down and opened it. A series of entries noting transactions caught his eye. Rare books, first editions, mostly with the selling price and in almost every instance, the name of a Norwich bookshop, "the Rainbow Store." Ketch knew the place well, an antiquarian booksellers just off the Madder Market. It had been there for many years. He glanced at the sums involved. They ranged from £200-£600 per volume. He recalled that Loftus worked part-time as a university librarian. It now became very clear. Loftus had been stealing rare volumes from the University library, removing identity stickers and then selling them on to a rare book dealer. He looked back on the bookshelf where a set of diaries were shelved. He pulled them out and put the lot in a plastic bag for further scrutiny.

The following day dawned hot and humid. By lunchtime, the heat in his office at Bethel Street had become so intolerable that Ketch decided to walk across the city to the Cathedral Close where he found a bench under a shady tree. He had brought with him the autopsy report and Loftus's collection of diaries. After consuming half of an unappetising roasted vegetable sandwich and cappuccino he glanced through the autopsy report. It told him little that was new save that the cause of death was a ruptured left ventricle, and that Loftus had sustained several facial injuries before death. Who had been the assailant then? Speight? Perhaps. Ketch had since learned that Speight had an Asbo which he had earned the previous year for misbehaviour in his local pub. It appeared that the Hell's Angel was prone to drunken rages. Ketch began examining the diaries next, conscious of the cool breeze now wafting across the Close. He was starting to feel less claustrophobic. Sometimes the Bethel Street HQ seemed like a black hole of Calcutta and he was glad of the break.

The diaries, written in a neat hand, covered the last 15 years of Loftus's life. Ketch hoped that they might shed some light on the man who so far had proved something of an enigma. He was a bachelor, had no close friends and his neighbour Mrs Goodman saw little of him. He was employed as a part-time librarian and also a creative writing tutor at the UEA. That was about all.

Ketch thumbed through the diaries. It was dreary stuff in the main, detailing his life as a headmaster of a boys' church school in Nigeria. As far as Ketch could determine, he had left some years ago, but there was no mention of the cause of his departure. Ketch sighed, closed the diary he was reading and slowly made his way back through Tombland to HQ.

Professor Tomkins, the grey-haired head of the faculty of Further Education, smiled at Ketch and MacKenzie. "I can't tell you much about Mr Loftus I am sorry to say. He was very much a private person.

Always punctual, good at his job – he taught the history of crime fiction and was something of a manque writer himself I believe. Sorry to hear he had been misbehaving at the library though. Most regrettable."

"Did he have any friends or associates among other staff in the Department here?"

"Our staff are mainly part-time employees on temporary contracts, so we only see each other for the occasional briefing or training session."

The office door opened and a tall, striking-looking man entered, bearing a bundle of papers. "Sorry to interrupt, Professor."

"No trouble. Are these the moderated papers ?"

He nodded.

"This is Detective Inspector Price. He is asking me about Norman. You knew him didn't you?"

"Only in a professional capacity." The man smiled. "Sorry I can't help you. I have a seminar to attend to gentleman."

"Mr Quaishe is one of our senior lecturers," said the Professor. "He's been with us for about four years now. Joined us about a year after Mr Loftus came onto the team. Now then, is there anything else I can help you with, gentleman?"

Ketch had forgotten the grimness and austerity of the architecture at the University. He and MacKenzie made their way across the road towards the public car park. As they reached the entrance, Ketch noticed a small looking red classic MG parked under some trees. He paused for a moment, then turned to MacKenzie. "That licence number. Get it checked out for me would you?"

Ketch was just about to call it a day when MacKenzie entered.

"Anything?"

"Been checking out Loftus's current account. Several large credit payments over the last few months but also a number of substantial withdrawals, all of them on a regular basis. Maybe he had a gambling addiction."

"Or maybe..." Ketch clicked his teeth. "Any luck with that licence plate?"

"Yes sir. The car belongs to a Benjamin Quaishe. Norwich address."

"Let's get him in for questioning, shall we?"

Benjamin Quaishe looked distinctly nervous. When he had first entered interview room two, he had asked for a solicitor but Ketch had told him he wasn't under caution and that this was merely an informal interview. Quaishe stared at the insipid coffee he had been given, then swallowed hard.

"We've been doing a little bit of digging, Mr Quaishe. And guess what we discovered?"

"I can't imagine."

"That you and Mr Loftus once worked in the same part of Nigeria. The same town in fact. A place called Akure. Mr Loftus was the headmaster of the boys'church school about 15 years ago. You would have been a boy at that time. But I understand that you had an older brother called Thomas?"

Quaishe nodded. "He died."

"That's right. We've also been in contact with the Nigerian police. Your brother committed suicide. Hung himself. He was only 13 at the time. A tragic incident. That must have affected you deeply."

Quaishe nodded.

"There was an investigation of course, and an allegation made against the headmaster of the school. In fact, it wasn't the only allegation made. You knew about that?"

"I knew of it, yes."

"So when Loftus resigned four years ago and travelled to England, you followed on."

"It wasn't quite like that. When I graduated, I came here to work. I met someone – a Nigerian friend – who told me he'd come across Loftus in the East Anglia. I found out where he was living and applied to do my master's degree here at the UEA. Then I got the teaching post."

"So – what? You confronted Loftus?"

"We met and I told him I would inform the university authorities about what he'd done."

"And so you started blackmailing him?"

"Considering the nature of his crimes, I thought it a minor form of reparation."

"And this arrangement persisted for the best part of a year?"

"10 months in all."

"What happened on Saturday evening?"

47

"Loftus asked to meet me. After we'd had a drink he insisted that I stop the demands on him. I refused and told him he must face the alternative. When I also reminded him of how he had abused my brother and the other boys at school, he became very angry. He was drunk and not in control of himself. He picked up a knife from the kitchen table and went for me. There was a struggle and to protect myself, I struck him. He fell awkwardly, then lay still. When I turned him over, I realise that he'd fallen onto the knife and that he was dead. There was nothing I could do for him."

Why didn't you phone the police at that point?"

"I don't know, panic I suppose. And I knew how things would look if I did. To be frank with you, I'm glad to get the whole thing off my chest."

"Okay Mr Quaishe. You'll need to make a formal statement. And you will also need that solicitor."

It wasn't until the following spring that the Quaishe case came to trial, following his release on bail. However, the CPS's charge of manslaughter didn't hold water and Quaishe was found not guilty at Norwich Crown Court. During the intervening months, more information came to light about Loftus's activities at the school in Akure.

Over the period of his headmastership, it was discovered that Loftus had beaten and sexually abused no less than 15 pupils and of these, 10 were persuaded to tell their stories. Moreover, in the six months that followed the Nigerian police investigation, the remains of two bodies of former pupils were discovered beneath the cellar of a brick outbuilding at the school. The victims were thought to have run away from school in the 90's.

Ketch sat on a bench, overlooking the River Wensum. The court business had concluded and it was a cloudless, bright day, sunny but mild. For a brief half an hour he sat there, motionless, undisturbed, staring at the waters of the river, whilst in the background he could hear the cries of the Cathedral School pupils playing rugby, a faint reminder of the dark tragedy which he had had to relive in court. In this job, he needed such moments of quiet reflection. They made him forget and charge his weakened batteries.

You could not forget man's inhumanity to man but at least here, by this quiet and tranquil river, you could suspend your belief in it. A small robin alighted on the bench and he gave it a morsel from the last of his sandwich. Then it was gone, a tiny wraith, lost among the trees.

A TWO PIPE PROBLEM

For once in his life, DCI Price, aka Ketch, was actually enjoying Halloween. For years, he had detested this Americanised reinvention of Nicka Nan night, refusing to answer his front door to the adolescent ghouls and demonic figures who stalked and caroused the streets of the city of Norwich on October 31st, terrifying its elderly residents and wasting police time and resources.

But tonight had been different, a truly sublime occasion he had been anticipating with great pleasure. It was the second time that Dr Carol Hennessy, the petite and highly desirable pathologist, had asked him out on a date. Since Ketch was greatly past his prime and an unlikely choice as an object of sexual desire (his own frank assessment), he regarded the opportunity as a one-off, a gift from the gods who were often, he believed, fond of doling out misfortune and despair. That melancholy Greek view of existence was something he had inherited from his Welsh Baptist antecedents, a theology compounded of sin and redemption which held for the worshipper a bleak and fatalistic vision of humanity.

Carol had chosen the venue, a lively restaurant in Swadlington, an ancient but weary market town to the north of the city whose heyday had been the Victorian age and whose now drab housing stock bore the ravages of unemployment and, in later years, mass immigration. Swadlington had two Eastern European restaurants to serve its ever increasing population, one Bulgarian and one Russian. The Russian emporium had changed its management a year back after a scandal involving prostitution, but the Bulgarian restaurant, a more luxurious establishment, was infinitely more friendly and its menu quite exotic. And Ketch had a liking for exotic food though his stomach did not.

As the waiter brought wine to their table, he found himself staring at Carol. As always, she was immaculately dressed in a classic black number, with a revealing and plunging neckline. Though still in its tentative stages, things had been progressing well between them. Only last week, he had invited Carol back to his dismal flat off the Earlham Road where, after a couple of brandies, some extensive fumbling had ensued. Ketch wished it had amounted to more than fumbling. The truth was that since the death of his wife several years ago, he had had

51

only one, short-lived relationship and that with a colleague who subsequently bedded his own son, a nightmare of a scenario which had acted as a dampener on further amorous feelings.

But Carol Hennessey was different. Bright, intelligent, fine featured and green-eyed, she offered hope in an otherwise bleak landscape of human affairs. And in addition, she was ten years younger than Ketch.

"Something wrong?" Carol quizzed him.

"No, nothing wrong."

"Only you seem distracted."

"Just admiring the scenery."

"Is that what you call it?" She kicked his ankle hard. As the waiter brought their starters to the table, Ketch's mobile suddenly sprang into life. He hesitated. *Goddammit, I have the worst of luck.*

"Hadn't you better answer it?"

Ketch gazed mournfully at his starter, then opened his phone.

The squad car took a full twenty minutes to get to the restaurant, so Ketch was able both to finish his starter and gaze longingly again at the rise and fall of Carol Hennessy's exquisite chest without much further interruption. Carol was off duty tonight and it had fallen to the portly Dr Stoppard to act as the duty pathologist. Ketch disliked Stoppard. Unlike Carol, he was often morose and uncommunicative. And while Carol's work was accurate and thorough, Stoppard had been known to make blunders. His shortcomings were well-known among the Norwich Constabulary but up until now, his minor incompetency's had been accommodated by senior colleagues.

At nine thirty pm, DC Watkins arrived at the restaurant and they drove through tree-lined country lanes via Castle Acre to the small village of Great Missenham. MacKenzie had explained only that the victim was one John Parry and that he had died of a gunshot wound in a cottage on the edge of the village.

The car passed a duck pond and thatched pub whose customers had spilled out onto the picnic tables at its front, wearing Halloween masks, then they turned down a narrow lane until they reached a collection of scattered farm buildings, the largest bearing a dilapidated sign with the legend 'Grove Farm.'

They got out of the car and ducked under the barrier tape, entering a long hallway whose walls were festooned with mounted foxes' heads and framed photographs of thick-set men on grouse shoots. There was a strong smell of pipe tobacco which Ketch immediately identified as Balkan Sobranie from his own pipe smoking habit.

"In here, sir," said DS MacKenzie, who had appeared at the living room door. Ketch entered, slipping on his forensic shoes.

The body of a large man lay spread-eagled on a leather sofa. The head, or what remained of it, was at an angle and behind it were great crimson gouts of blood, spread over the sofa and the wall behind it. Stoppard, dressed in the traditional white suit and looking like a large porpoise, turned to Ketch. "Not a pretty sight is it, but shotgun fatalities never are in my experience? However, feel free to take a closer look."

Ketch leaned over the corpse, then peered at the thin splashes of bloodstains on the wall behind the victim. "Notice anything significant?" Stoppard asked.

"The bloodstains would suggest he wasn't shot at such close range for a suicide."

"Precisely my view. The spread should be much wider if the barrel had been inserted into the mouth. I estimate that the barrel of this shotgun was some six inches from his jaw, the latter taking the initial impact. And you can't angle a shotgun at that distance unless of course, you have exceptionally long arms. And this guy's middle name is not Bigfoot." Ketch grinned at the joke, despite the grim nature of the scene before him.

"Victim's name was John Parry," MacKenzie informed Ketch. "A local farmer and property speculator. His wife found him like this. She says she had come back from a choir meeting about an hour ago."

"Where is she now?"

"With WPC Brown next door." Ketch glanced around the room. On a small table next to the settee was a large ashtray containing a short stemmed briar pipe – a Peterson's with a silver band. He slipped on a glove and smelt the tobacco. Not Sobranie after all, probably Gold Block. He couldn't abide the stuff. A bottle of Irish malt whiskey and a single glass, half full. A copy of the Pink Un and a framed photo of Parry, red-faced and corpulent, sitting on a horse in his red hunting gear. Master of the Hunt and Lord of all he surveyed. To the left of the settee was another occasional table which had been knocked over. Correspondence was strewn on the floor. Ketch began to sort through it. Bills, circulars and a black-edged envelope with the words 'RIP John Parry.' He opened it. In neat copperplate handwriting the message read: 'Vermin, your days are numbered, FF.' There was no other clue as to the author. He slipped the letter and the envelope into an evidence bag.

"Let's have a word with Mrs Parry, shall we?"

Cynthia Parry had been crying and her long face was smeared with mascara. She sipped the tea the WPC had brought her, looking like some strange, dishevelled bird cast up on a storm racked beach. She was middle-aged and conventionally dressed in a neat black trouser suit and despite her lined face and dyed black hair, was not unattractive.

"I'm DCI Price and this is DS MacKenzie, Mrs Parry. Do you feel up to answering a few questions?" Mrs Parry dabbed at her eyes and nodded at them. "You found Mr Parry, I believe?"

"I got in at about eight o'clock and discovered him lying there."

"You didn't notice anyone in the lane – a car, perhaps?"

"No. I didn't pass a single vehicle. But then I take a back road to the church – that's where we have our choir practice. Not many people use the road. Perhaps I should explain to you inspector, that John and I had decided to lead more or less separate lives. In fact, my divorce papers came through about a month ago. Because it suits me to do so, I occupy the bungalow on the edge of the estate. You may have glimpsed it on your way in here. I had dropped in on John just to collect my mail when I found him like this."

"I see. Tell me, can you think of anyone who might have wanted to harm your husband? A colleague perhaps?"

"Now that you mention it, yes, I can."

"And who might that be?"

"John had acquired a number of opponents, some from the animal rights movement. He was Master of the Hunt you know."

Ketch nodded. "Go on."

"Only a month ago, someone poured acid on both of our cars. We have also had to endure a number of threatening letters and phone calls."

"Letters like this one?" Ketch showed her the letter he had found in the living room.

"Where did you find this?"

"By the sofa."

"It must have arrived today – I haven't seen it."

"Do you have any idea who might be behind this campaign of intimidation?"

"Yes, I do. It's a group who call themselves Foxy Friends. The organisers are a couple living not far from here, Peter and Mandy Sloane. I can give you their address if you like."

"May I ask you the reason why you decided to get a divorce, Mrs Parry?"

"John had become impossible to live with. For ten years I put up with his drinking and bouts of violence but eventually I had come to the end of my tether."

"When was this exactly?"

"About six months ago. To make matters worse, I also found that he had been having an affair with a local tart."

"Does she have a name?"

"Penny something. I don't know her surname. She works at the Red Lion pub down in the village."

"Okay. Thank you for the information. Tell me, Mrs Parry, when you entered the room and found your husband lying on the sofa, what exactly did you do? Talk me through it."

"After the initial shock of finding him like that, I moved the shotgun –"

"You moved it? How, precisely?"

"What do you mean?"

"Which part of the gun did you actually touch?"

"I can't recall exactly. The barrel I guess, and the stock, yes that was it."

"What did you do then?"

"I felt for the pulse in his neck to see if he was still alive. Then, of course, I phoned the emergency services."

"And you didn't touch anything else in the room?"

"Not that I recall, no."

"That's most helpful. One more thing, Mrs Parry. Did you notice if there was a smell of pipe smoke in the room?"

"I think so. Yes. John was a habitual pipe smoker."

"You didn't notice if his pipe was still smouldering?"

"I didn't bother to look. I was otherwise preoccupied."

"I can understand that, naturally. But let me return to the smell of the pipe smoke, if you will. Was it a smell you usually associate with his pipe smoking?"

Mrs Parry thought for a moment, then she said: "I can't be sure that it was, no, I can't be absolutely certain about that."

As she uttered these words, there was the sound of an altercation in the passageway outside the room. DS MacKenzie stood up and left to investigate.

"What is it?" asked Ketch on his return.

"Someone claiming to be Mr Parry's brother, sir."

Mrs Parry stood up. "That must be Richard."

"Your brother?"

"He was due to visit me this evening. He's just returned from a visit to the States. He works for a real estate firm there and was due some annual leave."

"Let him in, MacKenzie."

A tall, swarthy faced man stood in the doorway. He was expensively dressed in a pinstriped suit, carried a small leather attaché case and spoke with a slight American accent. "Cynthia, I'm so so sorry. They told me what had happened. Is there anything I can do?" Mrs Parry burst into tears. Richard Parry put down the attaché case and held her hand.

"Ask WPC Brown to bring us some more tea will you, MacKenzie?"

After Mrs Parry had recovered her composure, he resumed his questioning. Turning to Richard Parry, he said: "Can I ask you the purpose of your visit here, Mr Parry?"

"By all means. I had some family and business matters to attend to. I phoned John from the States two days back and told him of my intended visit this evening."

"I see. You knew about this visit, Mrs Powell?"

"I'd been looking forward to Richard coming. Richard was very kind to me and supported me through the divorce. I spent a month with him in LA prior to the settlement, just to recharge my batteries."

"John wasn't an easy man to live with – and that's putting it mildly," said Richard Parry. "Frankly, I was concerned for her safety. It seemed like a good idea that she spend some time away from the farm."

"You mentioned just now you were here on business. Can you be more specific about that, Mr Parry?"

"Certainly. The firm I work for has contacts here in East Anglia. But I also needed to talk to John about the farm. For the past few years, we've been making a substantial loss on the arable."

"We?"

"John and I are – were – both owners of the family business, though admittedly I was very much the sleeping partner."

"I see. And how exactly would you describe your relationship with your brother?"

"We rubbed along together well enough for the most part. Of course, I made my views clear to him about his treatment of Cynthia."

"When do you return to America?"

"This coming Thursday."

"We shall need a contact address."

"No problem. I'm presently staying at the Norwich Travelodge on Boundary Road."

When Ketch and MacKenzie dropped in at the dilapidated cottage on Lynn Road the following morning, they found Peter Sloane. He was alone and answered the door in a stained kaftan. His haggard, pale face gave Ketch a clue to the man's lifestyle and, on entering the dingy hallway, he noted that there was a strong smell of cannabis.

"This had better be good," Sloane retorted. "You got me out of the bath." He led the police officers into a tiny living room, littered with campaign material and stained, half empty coffee cups where an old boxer dog eyed them suspiciously from the battered sofa.

"Mind the dog," said Sloane. "He doesn't much care for strangers - especially policeman." Ketch opted for a derelict basket chair whilst MacKenzie stood awkwardly behind him, ready to take notes. Sloane sat beside the dog, his kaftan falling open, revealing a pair of creased and grubby orange boxer shorts.

"I heard about Parry committing suicide."

"We're not entirely certain that he did," Ketch replied. Sloane smiled.

"Whatever. He's no great loss."

"I gather there was some enmity between you."

"I know why you're here, inspector, but I can tell you that your journey is a wasted one. Me and Mandy spent last night in the pub and several people can vouch for us."

"Those several people being?"

"Members of our anti-hunt league."

"Foxy Friends?"

"Indeed."

"Do you know anything about this?" said Ketch, holding up the letter in its evidence bag. Sloane scanned its contents.

"This isn't my handwriting."

"Do you recognise the handwriting?"

Sloane shrugged. "Not sure. No, I know nothing about it." He handed back the bag.

"Nevertheless, you and your group actively campaigned against the Hunt."

"Peacefully we did, yes."

"And caused damage to two of the Hunt members' cars."

"Don't know anything about those incidents."

"And you deny that you persecuted Mr Parry and his wife?"

"Absolutely deny it. Look, whoever did for Parry had nothing whatever to do with our group. We're a protest movement, not a bunch of assassins." The dog growled menacingly. Ketch stood up.

"Very well Mr Sloane. We will of course check out your alibi, but we may need to question your partner as well." Sloane smiled then yawned loudly.

"Be my guest, Chief Inspector."

The pathology findings and SOCO report arrived on Ketch's desk two days later. Ketch, who had returned at lunchtime from his favourite watering hole, instantly scanned their contents. Sadly, the pathology told him little that was new. Parry had died from a single gunshot wound. The bullet had entered at a point below the jaw and exited through the cranium, death being almost instantaneous. The evidence did indeed suggest that Parry could not have fired the gun. The only prints on the gun were those of Parry and his wife, confirming her account. Significantly perhaps, the glass and bottle had been cleaned of prints. Maybe the murderer had downed a glass of malt whiskey, then removed his prints. There was nothing else of significance and no signs of a forced entry. On Parry's mobile phone was a message from his brother telling him of his intended arrival later that evening. He had just finished reading the SOCO report when MacKenzie entered the room. "Anything new?" asked Ketch.

"Been looking at Parry's bank statements and recent

correspondence, sir."

"And?"

"It appears that the brother was right about Parry's finances. He owed the bank £20,000 and had already remortgaged the house." MacKenzie past Ketch a large manilla folder.

"What else?"

"There are a couple of notes from Mrs Parry about bills not being paid. Notice anything about the handwriting?" MacKenzie passed Ketch a small envelope containing a folded A5 note. The handwriting was quite similar to that of the threatening letter that they had found in Parry's living room.

"Any sign of a will among Parry's effects?"

"Not yet sir. Unless it's with his solicitor of course."

"What about Sloane's alibi?"

"The pub checked out. He and his partner were there until closing time - according to the landlord."

"Then I think we had better pay a visit to Cynthia Parry."

It was early evening by the time that they reached Cynthia Parry's bungalow, a modest two bedroomed property which stood between tall copper beeches at the edge of the estate. Ketch instructed MacKenzie to park the squad car at the end of the drive. "Let's walk the rest," he said.

Standing outside the property was a sleek citron bearing this year's registration plate. Ketch peered through the windscreen of the vehicle. On the passenger seat was a small attaché case with the initials RP. He knocked on the front door. After about a minute Mrs Parry appeared in a dressing gown. Her hair was tousled and she looked flustered. "Wonder if we could have a word, Mrs Parry?" asked Ketch.

As he sat in the lounge waiting for Cynthia Parry to reappear, Ketch examined the kitsch interior. The walls were painted a ghastly green and decorated with cheap Constable prints. There was a stainless steel gas fire and a mantelpiece with small porcelain ornaments garnered from frequent trips to Spain and Italy. On the coffee table next to him, he noticed a large ashtray and a straight briar pipe. He picked it up and smelt it. His nostrils were assailed by the unmistakable odour of Balkan Sobranie. Then the truth dawned on him and he cursed under his breath. Richard Parry had lied when he said he'd just arrived at John Parry's residence those two days ago. "MacKenzie, do me a favour will you? Check out the citron that's parked outside and find out who owns it?"

As MacKenzie left the room, Mrs Parry entered, followed by an uneasy looking Richard Parry, dressed only in a towelling robe.

"I think you two have some explaining to do," said Ketch.

Richard Parry had been in interview room for only half an hour before he gave Ketch and MacKenzie the full story. Initially he claimed that he had visited his brother, that there had been an argument over the financial losses of the farm and that the gun had gone off by mistake after John had threatened him. But after an hour of intense questioning from Ketch, the truth was finally revealed.

"I was in love with Cynthia. Had been ever since we first met at John's wedding. When I was working in the States, we kept constant contact with each other."

"And she stayed with you on more than one occasion?"

"Yes, she did."

"Which is where, no doubt, you became lovers?"

"You've no idea how vile John could be to her, especially after he had had a few drinks. He abused her both physically and mentally. I think the mental abuse was the worst of it. That's why I insisted that she have a break from him and why I urged her to divorce him. The problem, you see, was that she had no money of her own. She had given up work some years ago to help run the farm with him."

"You helped her financially?" He nodded.

"I kept her going, gave her a chance to be independent. Then, when the debts began to mount up, I urged her to take immediate action."

"Very well. Now tell us the real version of what happened to John. We now know from forensic tests that there was shotgun residue both on Cynthia's hands and clothes." Richard Parry wiped the sweat from his forehead. "Okay, let's take this one stage at a time. You lied to us about the time of your arrival at the farm."

"When the gun went off, we both panicked. Believe me, neither of us had any intention of killing John. We tried to reason with him, tried to persuade him to sell the farm. I told him he had a moral duty to support Cynthia. He had been drinking as usual and became aggressive. He picked up the shotgun and told me to leave. "Bugger off back to the states," was his exact phrase. I feared what he might do to Cynthia. I told him I wasn't going anywhere until he changed his mind. He cocked the gun and pointed it at me. By now he was incensed. His eyes were blazing. Cynthia thought he was going to shoot me there and then. She tried to take the gun from him, there was a struggle and – well, you can guess the rest."

"And afterwards?"

"We both figured that I would be the number one suspect, since I am the only entitled legatee, following on from Cynthia's divorce. John didn't make a will, you see. Cynthia came up with the idea and we each concocted our alibis. I didn't mean it to end like this. Neither of us did. You have to believe me."

The Parry Case, as the Press subsequently termed it, came to Norwich Crown Court the following January. Ketch recalled it well, for it was during the Arctic winter of 2010 and on the day he was required to give evidence, he had trudged through ankle high drifts of snow to get to the courthouse.

Richard and Cynthia Parry were both found guilty of involuntary manslaughter and given suspended sentences. They married shortly afterwards and Cynthia settled with her new husband in America. Ketch was never quite sure that he believed Richard Parry's account of what took place that evening at the farmhouse. It just didn't quite tally with the black edged threatening letter which he firmly believed that Cynthia had written in an attempt to frame the Sloanes. But it was a suspicion about premeditation which could never be proved in a court of law and thus would be deemed inadmissable.

During the lunch hour of the day on which the court proceedings were concluded, Ketch sat in his usual place overlooking the river. A flotilla of frozen looking swans floated by and he threw the remains of his unappetising pasty onto the waters to appease them. The swans, not liking the Cornish pasty very much, chose to ignore the offering. How he detested the British judicial system. Its wheels turned exceedingly slowly and proof of guilt was often difficult to establish. But that was nothing to the dislike he felt for the long British winter, he reminded himself, feeling in his greatcoat pocket for his silver hip flask. Thank God for small consolations.

SHEER BAD LUCK

The Haven was much as Ketch had remembered it. Nothing had really changed over the intervening years. He had last visited the place on the occasion of his mother's death and the memory of that time was still fresh in his mind, despite the five-year interval which had elapsed.

The tall, Gothic window frames had been given a lick of paint and the grubby nameplate had been replaced, but apart from these innovations, the buildings stood, gaunt and forbidding as ever, framed between tall pine trees and ancient yews, a Victorian monstrosity.

He and MacKenzie made their way down the dark hallway to reception where they found a tall blonde girl who looked about sixteen, manning the desk.

"DCI Price," Ketch explained, showing his warrant card to her. "Here to see Mr Robinson."

"Just a moment sir. He's on the top floor. I'll see if I can find him."

Price, aka Ketch, looked round at the slightly shabby interior. It hadn't much changed since his last visit. The same high, tarnished ceilings, the dark oak panelling, the selection of oil landscape paintings in their heavy guilt frames, a memory of when this was a private residence, home of Leonard Spixman, the Norfolk pickle king. There was a smell about the place, compounded of stale cabbage and potatoes, which made him feel distinctly uneasy. He glanced at the reception desk where a shining sign boasted the new corporate owners: "ACR Care Homes Ltd."

Such places were always very limited, he told himself. Though expensive, they confined the souls and bodies of their inmates in like manner.

"God, how I hate these places," observed MacKenzie. Ketch grimaced but he didn't reply. An image of his aged mother, lying in a small room, surrounded by old photographs and precious china ornaments, drifted back to him on a thread of intense sorrow. The adolescent looking girl had now returned with a tall, dark haired man in a neat black suit, bearing his name badge. He held out a large hand and gave Ketch a vigorous handshake.

"Paul Robinson. I am the care home manager here."

He spoke in a peculiar, high-pitched tone.

"This is DS Mackenzie", Ketch explained.

"Sorry to have to bother you, gentlemen, but –"

"No, you were quite right to do so. Exactly how long has your resident been missing?"

"The major disappeared two days ago."

"The major?"

"That's the name he is known by here at the Haven. He's an ex-military man – did extensive service in the Falklands War and subsequently in the TA."

"And you've had no word from him since?"

"Not a thing. Look, perhaps we'd be more comfortable talking in my office, Chief Inspector."

Robinson led the way down the dingy corridor to a small, darkly furnished room at the back of the property where he ordered tea for his two visitors. Ketch looked about him as his host poured tea. The bookshelves were lined with titles on social care and histories of the Second World War. On the desk was a framed group photograph of Robinson in army uniform.

"I see you've done service yourself," observed Ketch.

"I'm a member of the TA. All our lot were in the Forces. I'm the baby of the family."

"You were talking to me about your resident, Mr Pearson. Was he happy here at the Haven?"

"Seems so, yes"

"Family visit him?"

"No, his wife had died some years ago. There was a son, John, but he emigrated to Australia, I believe. And a daughter, but she rarely visits him. He was popular here with the ladies though, one in particular, Elsie. Bit of a care home romance you might say." He smiled, showing his teeth. Smoker, thought Ketch.

"Okay. Maybe we should take a look at his room now."

"By all means."

Pearson's room was a large and airy space on the ground floor, cluttered up with his military memorabilia and framed group photographs from his time in the Army. Ketch stared at the strong, ebullient face with its penetrating eyes and hawk-like nose. The pencil moustache barely concealed the cruel lips. There was a hardness to the face, almost a suggestion of menace. "May we take a couple of these?" asked Ketch.

"Certainly," said Robinson, who was hovering in the doorway.

"When exactly was he discovered missing?" Ketch asked.

"One of the staff found his bed empty early on the Monday morning."

"How did he get out? Don't you have a security lock on the front door?"

"We do. However, some of the more able residents like the major, have learned the code."

"You don't think to periodically change it then?"

"Too much bother, I'm afraid."

"Did he take any possessions with him at all? Clothes for instance?"

"Difficult to say. Ah, his suitcase is still here, look."

Robinson had opened a cupboard, revealing an array of dress suits and tweed jackets. There was a smell of mothballs. "He didn't leave a note?"

Robinson shook his head. "No note. Elsie – what are you doing out of your room?" Ketch turned. Outside in the corridor, hunched over a walking frame, was a frail, white-haired woman in a pink dressing gown. She gesticulated at Ketch, almost overbalancing in the process.

"Tell them!" she screeched. "Tell them!" Robinson took her by the arm to steady her.

"Now then, Elsie. Let's get you back to your room, shall we? No point in getting upset, is there?" But the old woman refused to budge, repeating herself over and over again. "Nurse!" called Robinson. From the end of the corridor, a young nurse appeared and together, they escorted the old lady back to her room. Before Robinson returned, Ketch studied the contents of the room once more. Among the framed photographs was one of the major, standing in the gardens of the nursing home, Elsie clutching his arm. He took several of the photographs along with a diary from the bedside table and gave them to MacKenzie.

"Sorry about that," said Robinson. Ketch thought he looked faintly embarrassed.

"They are very close, you said?"

"Elsie is his best friend here."

"Then maybe we could have a word with Elsie?"

"She's had a stroke, unfortunately. But of course, you're most welcome to talk to her, inspector."

Elsie's room, a much smaller and darker affair at the end of the same corridor, also had a photograph of herself and the major, pictured at what appeared to be a charity event.

A less frail looking Elsie stood next to Major Pearson, holding a bunch of flowers. Ketch pointed to the photograph and smiled at Elsie, who was now tucked up in bed.

"You and the major are very good friends I believe?" She reached out and grasped his hand tightly.

"Him!" she shouted. "Him!" She pointed to the door with the other hand and shook her head vigorously. "Him!" she stuttered, her eyes wet with tears.

"Is he in some kind of trouble?" asked Ketch. She nodded. "Trouble – Him! Found out!" Then she slumped back on her pillow, exhausted with the effort.

A week elapsed, but there was no further word about the curious disappearance of ex Major John Pearson. Pearson's daughter Anne was contacted, as was his son in Melbourne, but neither proved at all helpful in elucidating the mystery. Diane Pearson, a large, coarse faced woman with jet black hair, lived in Thetford, but, it transpired, had visited her father on only one occasion since he had entered the Haven. Ketch spoke to her in the living room of her council house, surrounded by fluffy teddy bears and Victorian dolls.

Although it was a humid afternoon, the windows remained securely shut and there was a strong smell of perfume and dog urine. Once tea had been brought to her guests, she sat opposite them on the chintz sofa, her ageing Pekinese dog cuddled up next to her ample form.

"I get the impression that you are not especially close to your father," observed Ketch, returning his cup of insipid tea to its stained saucer.

"And you'd be right to say so. He is a very troublesome man."

"Oh? In what way?"

"Controlling. And violent, especially when he can't get his own way. That's why my mother left him. I was only sixteen when that happened. My brother had come home from the youth club – we were living in Colchester at the time. Dad was stationed there. Anyway, when my brother got in late that evening, he kicked him round the hall into the living room. He had the bruises for weeks afterwards. It was at that point that my mother decided we had to leave him. We went to stay with an aunt in Bristol until eventually, my mother got a job."

"When you visited him last in the nursing home, how did he seem to you?"

"Not very happy, actually. He is always the one to be in charge of his own fate, so to live a passive life like that came as a blow to him. He also had a problem with some of the staff."

"What sort of problem exactly?"

"He wouldn't explain. Let's just say there was no love lost between him and the staff at the Haven. But then my dad was pretty unpleasant to most people that he came into contact with."

For a week there was no sign of ex – Major John Pearson. And despite extensive searches being made in the vicinity of the home, no witnesses came forward to offer evidence as to his whereabouts. It was as if he had simply vanished from the face of the earth.

Thornton Woods was a 20-acre area of neglected woodland which stretched from the eastern perimeter of the Haven Care Home to the outskirts of Norwich. It consisted of beech, ash and oak trees interspersed with coniferous trees, and its dense interior was a favourite trysting place for lovers. In recent years, the southern boundary had become a favourite venue for the exhibitionistic practice known as "dogging", and there had been numerous complaints from nearby neighbours about this. Mandy and Alan Brown were not doggers but ardent lovers. On 16th of December, they had driven their car to a favourite spot, a small copse which adjoins a deep quarry in the south-eastern quadrant of Thornton woods. As was their habitual custom, Mandy had made love to Alan in the back of their capacious Volvo, enjoying the alfresco excitement of the occasion, before dressing and going for a walk in the woods.

By now, the mist had cleared and the morning sunlight had started to penetrate the dense canopy of trees. They had walked arm in arm for only 100 paces when Mandy had spotted something in the quarry below them. The crumpled object turned out to be the body of John Pearson. Although it had been badly mauled by foxes and other denizens of the forest, it was clearly identifiable.

On a cold November morning, Ketch and MacKenzie ducked under the barrier tape and approached the scene. Stoppard the pathologist turned and hail them with his large flabby hand.

"Morning," said Ketch.

"And a decidedly chilly one, Huw."

"Who have we here then?"

"Looks like it could be your care home resident. Judging by his condition, I'd say he's been here for around a month. Fortunately, it's not summer or we'd have much less to go on."

Ketch stared at the body. Part of the left leg had been chewed off and one arm was missing but the head had been left intact. He was pretty certain it was Pearson he thought.

"Any idea how he got here?"

"Judging by the position, I should say he was already unconscious by the time he fell over the edge of the quarry. Or I should say, was pushed. That's the more likely scenario."

"How do you know that?"

"Because of the position of the body. And also the likely cause of death."

"Which is?"

"Blunt force trauma. There is a large depression on the left side of the cranium, too small an area for the head to have made contact on falling, probably caused by something like a small ball hammer, I should say. I'll be more certain when I get the body to the mortuary and take a closer look. Another thing which may interest you by the way. The deceased wore no shoes or socks."

"Let's take a look at the top of the quarry," said Ketch, pointing up to the ridge above them. Ketch and MacKenzie climbed back up the path. At the top, they met DC Watkins. "This is where he must have gone over sir," he said. Ketch knelt and examined the edge. It had rained during the night and two grooves could be seen in the loose earth, indicating that the body had been dragged there.

"A set of footprints," Ketch observed. "Mark that, MacKenzie, and get SOCO to make a cast of the prints. Looks like a size nine trainer. Let's follow the track back."

They did so and, some way into the wood itself, found car tracks. "This track connects to a small service road which in turn takes us back to the B road. That was the killer's route in. Heavy duty tyres. Looks like a 4x4 vehicle."

By the time they had returned to the edge of the quarry, Stoppard had emerged, following a stretcher on which reposed the mortal remains of John Pearson. He wiped the perspiration from his creased forehead and said: "By the way, something which may interest you. There's been another death at the Haven Nursing Home."

"Who?"

"One of the residents - an Elsie Standing. Is that significant?"

"Maybe," said Ketch.

It was not until the following morning that Ketch and MacKenzie returned to the Haven. Ketch decided they would first interview Elena, the care worker who had been assigned to Elsie. A large, big boned woman, she had clearly been crying. Ketch passed her a handkerchief. "You were close to Miss Standing, I believe."

"She was a friend. And how do you say? The life and soul of the party. She was so kind to the other residents here – and she had been improving. It is so very sad."

"How do you mean, improving?"

"She had started to regain her speech, and she had put on weight and was able to walk without a stick." She paused, her face effused with emotion.

"I understand that she was friendly with Major Pearson."

"Very friendly – they were close buddies. She was always in his room, chatting. When I first broke the news of his death to her, she was beside herself. She gave me this and told me I had to keep it safe. I don't know what she meant by it."

Back in Robinson's office, Ketch looked at the photograph again. It was a grainy black and white shot, a group photo showing a number of uniformed soldiers. In the centre of the group was what looked like a much younger version of John Pearson. On the left, someone had ringed a face but there was no clue as to why this had been done.

"Tell me, this photo. She didn't tell you what this meant?"

"No, I have no idea what it meant." Robinson scratched his forehead.

"And you have no notion as to how she came to fall down the stairs?" Ketch asked.

"None. It was approximately nine pm. I'd stayed late to complete the accounts and heard the commotion from my room. When I got to the top of the stairs, I could see her lying there. She'd fallen the full length of the stairs. She'd been getting stronger, had regained her speech too. I guess she just overreached herself."

"You've no idea why she was out of her room?"

"I'm afraid not. We are all terribly upset by what has happened. I've informed her son, anyway. Mr Pearson's daughter is also coming to see us this afternoon. All in all, this is a most terrible business."

"Mr Robinson, can I ask you what kind of car you drive?"

"A Renault Megane. Why do you ask?"

One member of the Havens care home staff owned a 4x4 and that vehicle had been in the car park on the day of Pearson's disappearance. The vehicle belonged to Elena Witgenstein.

Over the next two days, Ketch and McKenzie interviewed all of the care home staff. Three members of staff told Ketch of hearing sounds of a violent row on the morning that Elsie died, but none of them could determine whether the other voice was male or female. SOCO's tests on the vehicle revealed small quantities of earth on the driver's side which matched that of the path approaching the edge of the quarry, but there was no DNA trace, apart from a single hair which proved to be indeterminate, but which might have come from Pearson. Still, no murder weapon had been found, but the autopsy report confirmed beyond doubt that Pearson had been dealt a heavy blow with a pin hammer. His subsequent injuries had been sustained during the fall and a broken neck had been the actual cause of death.

Ketch didn't believe that Elena had murdered Pearson or that she even had a motive for doing so. Someone else at the nursing home had used her car, disposed of Pearson at the quarry, then cleaned the car out.

It was 9 AM. Ketch, who had not slept at all well, sat behind his office desk, staring at the black-and-white photograph Elena had given him. The faces stared back at him inscrutably. Then he opened the office door and called DS MacKenzie.

"Colchester Barracks. And Pearson. Google those names, will you? See what you can come up with."

Ten minutes later, a beaming DS MacKenzie returned, holding a sheaf of printouts from the office PC.

Ketch's hunch had been correct about the link between Pearson and Robinson. It was the news article which had led him to the truth.

Dated 19th of November, 1990, the headline ran: 'Suicide Tragedy At Barracks'. The text read:

"A soldier has been found dead at the Colchester Barracks. Private Alfred Robinson was found in the utility block on Monday evening, where he had apparently hung himself. This is the third death at the barracks in just over six months. Rumours have been rife at the Colchester Barracks concerning allegations of bullying by a certain unnamed officer, but the authorities have dismissed the claim as nothing more than unsubstantiated tittle tattle. Mr Peter Robinson, brother of the deceased, said yesterday that the rumours about bullying were true and that a full independent investigation should be held at the barracks to discover the truth of the matter. Major Pearson said that relationships between senior and junior ranks at the Barracks had been excellent and that there was no reason for the public to be concerned. He added that an investigation would be undertaken into the nature and cause of Private Robinson's tragic death."

Peter Robinson sat with his arms folded, staring straight ahead.

"No, I don't deny it," he replied. "And I'm not ashamed of what I did to Pearson. The bastard deserved it. Fred had told me about the bullying. It was systemic, a way of life at the barracks. They would pick out the younger and more vulnerable recruits and concentrate on breaking their spirits. "Moulding character," was the term they used for the torture. They did it without making a mark, too. They took them into the showers, made them strip naked, then whipped them with wet towels. Told them that if they complained they'd do it twice over. But it wasn't just the physical torture that drove my brother to suicide. It was the psychological torture as well. When I took over the management of the Haven and found out that Pearson was a resident here, I could hardly believe it. I knew what was required – justice for Fred."

"But why kill Elsie?"

"I didn't kill her. It was an accident, I swear to you. Pearson had told her about me, feared for his life. He knew what was coming to him and he told Elsie about it. When she started to regain her speech, I knew it would only be a matter of time before she started telling the other patients about me. I tried reasoning with her and unfortunately, she became very agitated. She ran from her room onto the landing where I tried to restrain her. Unfortunately, she fell backwards on the stairs. It was a tragedy - one which I deeply regret, but I had no intention of harming her."

Ketch sat on a bench outside the Adam and Eve pub, drinking a whiskey chaser. It was early evening and the sun was slowly disappearing behind the weeping willows which skirted the River Wensum. On the bench in front of him was a copy of the Norwich Evening News. 'Care Home Murderer Gets 15 Years', ran the headline. Robinson had no previous convictions for violent crimes, and no previous criminal record. With good behaviour he could hope to be at large within eight years. His defence barrister had called character witnesses attesting to his benevolence and good management at the Haven and the members of the jury had been suitably impressed, judging by their demeanours.

He turned to the back of the paper and looked at the crossword there. 'Dear En Paris, close away, serendipity,' ran the cryptic clue. Sherlock, of course. That was it. Yes, sheer luck... It had been sheer luck Robinson had met Pearson at the Haven, but as things turned out, it had been really bad luck for Pearson. He started to fill in the clue, then cursed as his biro ran out. His mobile rang. It was Mackenzie. He decided to ignore the summons, finished his drink, then began walking towards the river bank. It was going to be a fine evening. Mackenzie and the world could wait.

A QUESTION OF DNA

As DCI Ketch was about to walk through the automatic doors of the Norfolk and Norwich Hospital, he paused, then was greeted by an icy blast of January air. Breathing a sigh of relief, he reached into his jacket pocket and pulled out a packet of King sized cigarettes. At least you could smoke out here and not be surrounded by the smells of cleaning fluid, sanitation and death.

He lit up and stared across the flat, even landscape, down into the valley in the direction of Earlham Park and the concrete monstrosity that was the University Campus.

It was good to be out here. For the last two hours, he had been confined in a small room with DS MacKenzie and the charred, but still living remains of one Pieter Rostropovitch. Rostropovitch had had the misfortune to light a cigarette in a small industrial unit in Thetford where the blast from an illegal still had killed his colleague in crime, Friedrich.

Between them, the two had supplied gallons of black market ethanol, laced with vodka, to half the Lithuanian community in Thetford and the surrounding area for more than a year, an operation of which the police had known absolutely nothing until the explosion which lit up the night sky on Christmas Eve.

Despite extensive second-degree burns, Rostropovich had been helpful in explaining to the officers the nature and extent of the operation, speaking in whispers through the interpretative skills of WPC Shostakovitch. An attractive young woman with striking dark eyes, three decades ago Ketch might have considered the WPC fair game, but her face he now looked upon as a painter might regard his model, dispassionately, purely as a creature of aesthetic excellence.

Ketch's reflective interlude was interrupted by the opening of the automatic doors behind him. He turned to see MacKenzie holding out a mobile phone.

"What is it then?" asked Ketch grumpily.

"HQ, sir. Two bodies discovered at Felthorpe Manor."

"Try to be more precise, MacKenzie. And whoever wants to speak to me, you deal with it just this once." MacKenzie mumbled something into the phone about Ketch being tied up just now, then joined his boss by the stone seat. Ketch ground the expired cigarette under his foot. "Details?" he demanded.

"Some human remains have been discovered."

"Whereabouts? Felthorpe is a big place." Ketch recalled the Tudor manor house and its vast grounds with mixed feelings. Years ago, he and his wife would take country walks there among the 200-year-old oak and beech trees. So huge were they that his wife refer to them as "giant sentinels." It seemed an apt phrase to Ketch, as if these representatives of the natural world were truly alive. After his wife died, however, the woods at Felthorpe had become notorious as the place where the bodies of two young prostitutes had been found, buried in a shallow grave. The discovery had sparked off a major manhunt for a serial killer.

"A workman discovered the body about an hour ago. Two estate workers were carrying out some restoration work on the folly when they came across what looked like a bundle of old clothes." Ketch recalled the Felthorpe folly well enough – a strange, pyramid-shaped monument set in the woods some distance from the old manor house. It had been built in the 1860's to house the remains of Lord Acton's wife who had died tragically of consumption at the tender age of 26.

Her body had been re-interred in the family vault in the local churchyard when her husband had died, leaving the monument empty. It had been inspired by Lord Acton's fervent interest in Egyptology.

"They've secured the crime scene, then?"

"Yes, sir. SOCO are there and the pathologist."

"Which pathologist?"

"Dr Hennessy."

Ketch smiled. It was only two nights ago that he had spent an intimate evening with the delectable Dr Carol Hennessy and he had been pleased with the way things had gone. After so many years of solitary abstinence, it was good to be back on track again. When he was with Carol, he felt 10 years younger.

"Good. Tell them we will be there in about 20 minutes."

After dropping off WPC Shostakovich at HQ in Bethel Street, MacKenzie and Ketch drove on through the city and then north towards the Cromer Road. It was now five pm and already the darkness had closed in on the city's snowbound streets, still busy with early evening shoppers and revellers. The street lamps threw out orange halos and the dark alleyways gave the ancient streets of Tombland an eerie and disquieting atmosphere, thought Ketch, as he wound down the squad car window and lit another cigarette.

As the car passed the airport and headed north, slipping between dark rows of trees, he recalled the circumstances of what, 10 years ago, the press had termed the Felthorpe Murders.

In 2001 a young factory worker of German origin, Hans Gross, had been convicted of the murder of two prostitutes in Ipswich. Gross was a sexual sadist who had lured the girls to their deaths. After paying for their services, he had driven them north into Norfolk to a deserted stretch of woodland and incarcerated them in a derelict shack where he had systematically tortured them before strangling them and burning their bodies in a shallow grave.

For two years their whereabouts had remained a mystery. The first body was discovered purely by accident by a walker and his dog shortly after Christmas. Gross, who was already known to the Suffolk police, was subsequently matched to both murders, mainly on the basis of his confession. He was sentenced to a 20-year stretch. The discovery of Maria Leibovitch and Alice Walker a year later had immediately placed Gross under suspicion, but despite extensive enquiries, Chief Inspector Hubbard and his team had failed to link Gross to the murders, and the DNA evidence had proved to be unhelpful in establishing a link, despite the fact that Gross had no alibi for both of the nights on which the girls had gone missing.

Ketch recalled DCI Hubbard well, a tall, aquiline faced man of the old school of detection, an individual who relied overmuch on the psychological profile of his suspects rather than forensic detail, a tendency which at least once in his career had landed him in hot water. Like Ketch, Hubbard was something of a loner. In fact, as Ketch dimly recalled, he had a place somewhere not far from here.

"Don't use the main car park, drive on, and then take the next on the left," Ketch instructed MacKenzie, who had been staring closely at his Satnav. "It's closer to the woods." He didn't intend to have a half mile walk in the bitter cold of a January evening.

"Okay, sir."

Within minutes, the pyramid shaped folly loomed from the shadows, clearly illuminated by arc lights. MacKenzie parked the squad car. The officers ducked under the barrier tape and approached the white - suited form of Dr Hennessy in the company of two uniformed policeman.

"Good evening, gentlemen. Bodies are inside here." Enjoying the pretended formality, Ketch followed Carol Hennessey as she opened the black Gothic doors. Inside, a couple of large lamps had been erected, illuminating the dusty and cramped interior. In one corner lay what appeared on first sight to be a huddle of black bin liners. As Ketch approached, he saw that these had been slit open, revealing two mummified corpses.

"Remarkably well preserved, wouldn't you say?" said Dr Hennessy. "But that's no surprise given the design of this place. It's dry, relatively damp free and cool in the summer. The building blocks are so tightly interlocked that even rodents don't get a look in."

Ketch knelt down and examined one of the bodies more closely. He was staring at the emaciated, yellowed face of a young woman. The eyes were long gone but the structure of the face was still intact. The body was dressed in a short, skimpy, red skirt and low-cut T-shirt. Around the neck was a gold necklace and crucifix, crudely fashioned. The second corpse was dressed in a short, tight fitting black skirt and red mohair top. Around the left ankle was a narrow gold chain. Ketch stood up. "Cause of death?" he asked.

"Strangulation, I should say. In both cases, the thyroid bone has been broken. Whether they were both strangled manually I can't be absolutely certain – won't be without conducting further tests."

"How long have they been here?"

"Difficult to say precisely, but I would certainly guess it's been a number of years. The insect evidence should give us an idea as to the season. As I say, further tests should provide me with a more accurate chronological picture. What I can tell you, Huw, is that both bodies were placed here within a few days of each other."

"Any ID?"

"You're in luck. At least with one of the deceased. Found this tucked into the waistband of her skirt." Dr Hennessy produced a small evidence bag containing a driving licence. The legend red: "Desiree Ashton, 29 Oak Tree Drive, Cromer." Desiree Ashton... The name rang a bell.

Ketch's memory proved to be reliable. A search through the Missing Persons data at Bethel Street HQ the following afternoon confirmed that Desiree Ashton had gone missing in the summer of 2000. She had been a prostitute working around the Norwich Railway Station where she had been arrested on three separate occasions for soliciting. Another girl, Dawn Liskeard, with whom she often worked, had also gone missing at the same time. So far, Dr Hennessy's search of dental records had not produced a satisfactory match for Dawn, but then, as Ketch knew, these things always took time.

Carol's autopsy, held the following morning, confirmed that both girls had been manually strangled in the July of 2000, and there was also evidence of sexual molestation, including semen stains on their underclothes.

23 Oak Tree Drive was a large, Edwardian building, situated on the eastern fringes of Cromer, a part of what estate agents refer to as the "desirable" section of the once elegant railway town. Ketch, along with MacKenzie and a WPC, climbed the steps to the front porch, then rang the doorbell. After a short interval the door opened, revealing a middle-aged blonde, dressed in an expensive trouser suit. There was a strong smell of musk.

"Mrs Ashton? We are police officers. We've come to talk to you about your daughter."

Mrs Ashton held her hand to her mouth, then ushered them in with an almost inaudible invitation. They passed through an exquisitely restored Edwardian interior, then entered a large drawing room. The walls were papered with a William Morris design but furnished incongruously with large, contemporary style sofas and armchairs. Ketch produced the driving licence and explained to Mrs Ashton the circumstances of its discovery.

"We shall need you to identify the body, I'm afraid."

I don't suppose there's any likelihood someone else might have stolen her driving licence?" She spoke with a strong Essex accent. Nouveau riche thought Ketch, glancing round at the costly furnishings.

"We think that's unlikely, Mrs Ashton."

"I've dreaded this day. Strangely, when I woke up this morning, I had a premonition of your visit. After all these years, not knowing, fearing the worst. And now the worst thing of all has to be faced." She broke off, weeping.

After the WPC had brought her a glass of water, Ketch asked: "I understand that you had lost contact with your daughter some while before she disappeared in the summer of 2000?"

Mrs Ashton nodded. "It started when she was at university. She'd got in with a crowd of girls. They went to raves together. Then it was the drugs. Soft drugs at first, cannabis, ecstasy. Then she met this other girl, Dawn."

"Dawn?"

"Yes. It was Dawn Liskeard who introduced her to cocaine and smack. By then they had graduated and were renting a flat in Norwich. And to pay for their habit, they got onto the game through someone they'd met at a club. A ne'er do well called David Jenkins. When Tom found out –"

"Tom?"

"My husband. When he found out, he washed his hands of her. From then onwards, matters got even worse. She lost the flat because she was behind on the rent, then she ended up on the street. It was shortly after that – a month or so later – that she went missing."

Ketch looked at the large brown box on his desk. Shivering, he pulled his overcoat tighter around him. He had arrived at 9 AM at Bethel Street HQ to discover that the central heating system had failed for the second time in a month. And this on one of the coldest mornings of the New Year. It was January 6 and the room thermometer on his wall read 3°C. Fortunately in his filing cabinet there was a half empty bottle of whiskey and he had taken the liberty of lacing his morning coffee (black machine coffee and it tasted disgusting) to provide himself with a measure of inner warmth. Deciding not to remove his mittens, he took the lid off the box and began sifting through the cold case collection of evidence. Autopsy report on MariaLeibovitch. Cause of death: manual strangulation. Evidence of sexual activity prior to death. Autopsy report on Alice Walker...Report on Desiree Ashton. Same cause of death. He dug deeper into the box. Six audio tapes of interviews with Hans Gross, relating to the Leibovitch case, conducted by Chief Inspector John Hubbard. He'd listen to these later he decided.

What about forensic evidence? Some fibres which might have been related to one of the murder victims, found in the boot of Gross's car, but not conclusive. No fingerprints or semen matches. In fact, no forensic evidence which would definitely have linked Gross to the murders. A confession, signed by Gross. Plus a profile of him written by a forensic psychologist, a Dr Ernest Davis.

He perused its contents. Gross was a persistent voyeur, a sadist and masochist, also a frequent visitor to prostitutes in his home city of Frankfurt. Emigrated to Britain in 1996 with his elderly mother. Arrested for soliciting in Ipswich on numerous occasions and well known to the police. On the evening of both girls' disappearance, he had been seen in two pubs in Ipswich, buying them drinks. The last sighting was at 11 pm. Two independent witnesses saw the women getting into a dark saloon car in the pub car park. Neither witness could confirm the make or registration of the vehicle and there was no CCTV evidence.

Not very helpful or particularly conclusive, thought Ketch. A second report, this time by a German psychologist called Friedrich Knutson, but fortunately for Ketch, who was no linguist, written in English. Ketch studied it with interest.

Gross was the only child of aged parents and had been brought up in Frankfurt. His father, a grave digger and stonemason, had deserted the family when Hans was only eight years old, following a long and abusive relationship with his mother. Hans had proved to be a difficult child and was often violent towards other children. This led to his expulsion from state secondary school at the age of 15. There followed periods of manual labour, interspersed with long stretches of unemployment. At the age of 19 he had joined the German Navy and finally emigrated to Britain with his mother 10 years later. He had a history of consorting with prostitutes and on occasions, stalked them.

Ketch tapped his forehead and frowned. Hardly the profile of a psychopath...

His office door opened. It was MacKenzie.

"Some more details from Dr Hennessy, sir."

"Oh yes? What?"

"Minute fibres, found on both of the Felthorpe victims. Clothes indicate that their bodies were kept in the boot of a car in some sort of blanket. And she's been able to extract DNA from both sets of semen stains on each of the victims' underwear. They make a clear match."

"What about the other victim's identity?"

"As we suspected, it's Dawn Liskeard all right. The dental records have proved positive."

By five o'clock, the central heating had still not been fixed. Frustrated and cold to the bone, Ketch gave up the challenge. Taking the six audiotapes and files with him, he decamped to his favourite watering hole, The Grapes, where he spent an hour demolishing whiskey chasers before finally weaving his way back to his flat off the Earlham Road.

By the time he got indoors, snow had begun to fall again, giving the roads and pavements a light covering of ivory brilliance. 12th night, he recalled. The conclusion of Old Yule. The flat, which lacked central heating, and was furnished only with ancient storage heaters, was cold and unwelcoming. He switched on a small two bar electric fire, poured himself a large glass of whiskey, then reached for his cassette recorder. These days it was usually all digital kit, a subject of which he knew virtually little and with which he had little empathy, but audiotapes were both simple to understand and use. That suited Ketch's Luddite temperament.

He switched on tape number 1. Interview between Gross and Chief Inspector John Hubbard. A Dr Barker also present. Ketch listened as Hubbard ran through the usual questions with his suspect. Gross, who spoke in a slow, faltering German accent, admitted that he knew both Leibovitch and Walker and that he had paid for their services on numerous occasions. He had first made their acquaintance at a massage parlour in Lime Street, Ipswich. He admitted to buying drinks for them in two pubs adjacent to the railway station and claimed to have left them at 11 pm when they decided to wait for a taxi to take them back to their respective lodgings. After that, he drove home.

Ketch refilled his glass, pausing the tape. He got the distinct impression that Gross was telling the truth. Also, there was an urgency in Hubbard's voice, a hectoring quality which indicated that he would not be satisfied until Gross made a full confession. Not unusual of course...

He moved on to the second, then the third tape. Gross's story remained unchanged. All that was different was that Gross was made to reveal more about his sexual urges and practices. Details emerged concerning his masochism, his torture of domestic animals in Germany and his sexual exhibitionism. Only a week prior to his arrest, for example, he had been reported by a couple in a piece of woodland near to the city, sitting naked in his car and performing a sexual act. But none of it makes him a killer, and it certainly doesn't fit the profile of a serial killer, thought Ketch.

He put on tape 5. Halfway through, there was a blank of about 10 min's duration. Curious. Why was that? Tape 6 followed. Here Hubbard was really putting on the pressure, trying again to elicit a confession. Still Gross said the same things, over and over again, his story unwavering. His account didn't change, not one iota.

As Ketch finished his drink a sense of unease pervaded him. He decided that he would visit Hubbard and discuss the case. But first, he would drop in on Gross in Norwich Prison. He picked up his mobile and left a message for MacKenzie, asking him to arrange a meet with Hubbard for the following day.

At around midday, Ketch concluded the interview with Gross, left the prison and started the short journey back to Bethel Street. Before getting into the car, he asked MacKenzie to take a short diversion with him onto Mousehold Heath, that high stretch of common land overlooking the city.

The snow of the previous day had largely diminished with the onset of sleet and rain, but the view from here was fine and the cloud had cleared, revealing an azure sky. Ketch sat on a bench, saying nothing initially, smoking cigarette after cigarette.

MacKenzie, who was used to such silences as a precursor to one of Ketch's "epiphanies", knew better than to interrupt his boss. The unease which Ketch had felt during the previous evening about Gross's guilt had not been dispelled. In fact, following the prison visit, it had intensified. Gross, a short, fat fellow with a birdlike face and a soft, haunting voice, appeared to be educationally subnormal. He protested his innocence to Ketch throughout the interview, claiming that Hubbard had used physical violence to force a confession out of him.

Although there had been no real evidence to support this claim, there was the case of the missing audiotape, something which he intended to ask Hubbard about. And there was another circumstance which troubled him. Prior to their visit to Norwich prison, Ketch had discovered that on the evening that Maria Leibovitch and Alice Walker had gone missing, Gross had been driving a white Metro, not the dark saloon car that had been reported by two eyewitnesses at the pub. It was an inconsistency which troubled him.

As Ketch finished his cigarette, MacKenzie's phone rang,

penetrating the tranquillity of the spot. "I think you should take this one, sir," MacKenzie said. "The DNA from the semen stains. They've made a match."

Ketch stared at the darkening sky where already, a bright full moon had risen above the horizon. How could he have been so dense? The circumstances of John Hubbard's resignation from the Force had been widespread knowledge at the time and he had just not remembered it.

Hubbard and two junior police colleagues had been involved in a fight outside a nightclub in the Prince of Wales Road. The gang who attacked them had been a mob of football supporters and the leader of that gang was known to Hubbard, a drug dealer who he had put away for two years and who was later released on parole.

Hubbard claimed that the gang had made the first move, but no witness had come forward to substantiate this claim. After the melee had concluded, the ringleader, Joseph Sutton, lay dead from a brain injury, sustained when he hit the pavement. Hubbard and the two off-duty officers were initially charged with manslaughter but when the case came to court, all three were found not guilty, since the evidence against them was largely circumstantial. The significance of the case for Ketch was that Hubbard's fingerprints and DNA were then put on file.

Hubbard's house was a large, semi-detached property on the edge of Roughton cum Blickling, a small village adjacent to Felthorpe. By the time the car drew up outside the property, it was already getting dark and the house lights were blazing.

Hubbard lived alone here, his wife of 23 years having died the previous year. Ketch and MacKenzie were in luck. The details of the semen traces had not been made public in the press, so Ketch was relying on the element of surprise.

Since the news of the DNA match had broken, one other link in the chain had been established. A colleague had rung Ketch in the car, telling him that Hubbard had arrested the drug dealer David Jenkins on two separate occasions prior to Maria Leibovitch's disappearance. Ketch figured that Hubbard must have been involved in some kind of drugs operation with Jenkins, an operation which probably involved favours using the services of his prostitutes, no doubt gratis. Of course, all of this was supposition and it would have to be proved.

Fortunately for Ketch, the dealer was serving time at Her Majesty's pleasure, so the truth of the matter could be confirmed in due course.

MacKenzie parked the car, then turned off the lights. The two officers approached the illuminated porch and rang the bell. They waited a good five minutes, but there was no sign of movement from within. Ketch peered through the lounge window where the heavy velvet curtains had been drawn back. The TV was on, but there was no sign of Hubbard. Then, pointing to the adjacent garage, McKenzie said: "What's that smell, guv?" Ketch turned to look. A cloud of black exhaust fumes was rising from inside the closed garage doors.

"Get it open. Quick!" he instructed MacKenzie. Within a minute, MacKenzie had returned from the car and crowbarred the doors open. But it was no use. Hubbard, who had fed a pipe from the exhaust of his Toyota jeep through the driver's window, had been dead some 30 minutes before their arrival, according to the pathologist. A subsequent search of the premises by Ketch and MacKenzie failed to produce a suicide note, but an interesting discovery was made in a large shed located at the bottom of the garden.

Under the floorboards, carefully wrapped in decorative paper, they discovered locks of hair, cut from each of the victims, plus a number of Polaroid photographs which Hubbard had taken of from the dead women.

Ketch's hunch about the drug dealer was proved to be correct. Hubbard had been operating a drugs and vice ring in Suffolk for 10 years, but his obsession with prostitutes finally led him down the dark path from which there was no return.

Gross, whom he had known for some while, was the perfect stooge and had the misfortune to be in the wrong place at the wrong time. Getting a confession had proved easy. At the back of the double garage was the dark Ford saloon which Hubbard had used to transport his victims' bodies and fibres found in its trunk verified his link with them. His suicide had been inevitable, Ketch figured, especially since, with the Norwich victims, he had been more careless in leaving forensic traces prior to the bodies' entombment, and, given the advances in DNA matches, it would only have been a matter of time before the link with him was clearly established.

But why place the bodies in the mausoleum? It was a bizarre touch. Less risky than burying them in the wood, where foxes and dogs might disinter them. Perhaps he realised that the owners of

Felthorpe would not bother to open up the tomb, especially since it had not been interfered with for the best part of a century.

Ketch never walked again at Felthorpe, a place which held too many unpleasant memories for him. However, in the spring which followed the sensation of the Hubbard case in the media, he did return to Mousehold Heath, and on mild evenings, could often be seen sitting on a bench high above the slumbering city, calmly smoking his old briar pipe. For a man prone to claustrophobia, it was the perfect antidote to the job, a place to muse and meditate, a medicine for the misanthropic. What else could you ask for?

THE ICENI CADAVERS

The seaside town of Hunstanton lies on the westernmost coast of North Norfolk. An Edwardian railway town, developed at the end of the 19th century, its wide beaches and glorious sunsets have attracted numerous tourists.

Barely a mile down the coast is the old town, a collection of small fishermen's' cottages, added to by sumptuous 1930s villas and, with them, a golf course for the recreation of its more affluent denizens.

Between the two settlements, and lying some way inland, is a dense, tangled wood which has been here since Saxon times. It forms part of a large estate, owned by the prosperous Sauvage family and was once the backdrop to the mansion which was their pride and joy.

In Victorian times, this landscaped paradise boasted a boating lake and broad woodland walks. Now it is a dense wilderness where great trees live, blocking the old pathways. Sycamores have overtaken the resplendent beech and ash trees, forming a dense canopy which blocks out much of the light. In autumn, the wood is full of bizarre looking fungi, and there is a dank, airless feel to the place, a pervasive claustrophobia which dissuades the unwary walker from entering too far into the area.

The house itself, built here in 1868, is a tall, redbrick Gothic mansion with turrets and lancet windows but there is not much left of its former grandeur.

The lower windows have lost the stained-glass depictions of the Morte D'Arthur and for the most part, are boarded up. The great front door, with its brass knocker, hangs forlornly on its hinges, allowing instant access, while inside, the hallway and downstairs rooms are full of mould.

For 50 years this was the home of the Sauvage family. Then, when the last of the line perished, it became a temporary operations centre for the British Army. After the conclusion of the first war, it served firstly as a warehouse to a local farmer, then a care home.

In the 21st-century it has become a place of rumour and omen. Among local youths, it has the reputation of being haunted and there have been several reports of spectral figures at the upstairs windows and piercing cries which shatter the still night. Fantasy or not, there is about this ruin a heavy feeling of oppression.

There is a theory about certain buildings where dire deeds of iniquity have been perpetrated. It is as if echoes of past horrors seep into the fabric of time and these echoes can be perceived by those who are more sensitive to their surroundings.

So it was with The Haven, for to those who had the misfortune to spend their formative years in this dreary mansion, the very name of the place belied its true nature.

Detective Chief Inspector Huw Price, known to his friends and enemies as Ketch, stirred fitfully in his bed, then sat up and coughed spasmodically. His head felt as if it had received a hammer blow and he was shaking violently. He turned and looked at the bedside clock. 7 AM. Such was his condition, the very thought of turning up for work this morning filled him with abject horror.

For four days he had been in the grip of influenza, contracted, he was certain, from a lowlife called Kevin Smith, whom he had had the misfortune to interrogate about a cannabis factory, found in the attic of a house in the Earlham Road, not 100 yards from his own flat.

Ketch was lying in the small lounge of his partner Carol's bijou flat down by the River Wensum, while Carol and baby Sean (his nine-month-old son) occupied the main bedroom. Rather than infect both of them, Ketch had chosen the punishment of the sofa where he had spent the night in his double sleeping bag.

The door opened and Carol entered bearing a tea tray.

"How are you feeling?" she quizzed him.

"God-awful but I'll live."

She put down the tea tray, perched her pert figure on the edge of the sofa and felt his forehead.

"Bit of a temperature still. You'd best not go in today."

"I may not have a choice in the matter." He extended a hand from inside his sleeping bag to touch her breast.

"Careful, you'll knock the tea tray over," she teased him. "And you'd better not try and kiss me, either."

He took the tea tray and drained the cup. It tasted good. A face appeared at the door, grinning at him. It was Sean and he looked as if he was ready for a game.

"Daddy is not well," said Carol. "Go back in the bedroom Sean and wait for me."

The diminutive figure frowned, then retreated, closing the door behind him with a bang which sent shock waves through Ketch's aching head.

"If someone rings, what shall I say?" said Carol.

"Just give me the phone – it's okay."

"Are you sure?"

"Absolutely sure."

Little Sean had not been a planned event. In fact news of Carol's pregnancy had come as a shock to Ketch. He had known Carol Hennessey, the pathologist, for some years before the relationship blossomed, but had been quite reckless about the possibility of children and the prospect of being a father once again at his age had distinctly unnerved him.

Nevertheless, he had risen to the occasion, struggling through the first few months following the birth, with a kind of grim determination to succeed. This period of sleepless nights had coincided with an investigation into a Latvian drug running gang, a combination of factors which had left him utterly exhausted.

By the time that he had finished having a shower and got to the kitchen, his worst fears were confirmed. The phone was ringing. Carol interrupted her feeding of Sean and handed him the handset, shaking her head.

"Ketch here."

"Sorry to wake you this early, sir." It was DS Tim MacKenzie, the most reliable of his younger colleagues.

"I was already awake as a matter-of-fact."

"How are you feeling now?"

"Never mind that. What's up?"

"We've had a call from the archaeological unit of the University – 15 minutes ago. One Professor Julia Bond. They're at a place in West Norfolk called Ken Hill, doing a dig. It's a site associated with Boudicca, the Celtic Warrior Queen."

"I know who Boudicca was. What's that got to do with us?"

"They found several bodies, but one of them was discovered at a shallower depth than the others and it had 20th-century dental work."

"You've notified Mike Stoppard?" Mike Stoppard was the pathologist who had been operational ever since Carol's maternity leave.

"He's on his way. Do you want a lift?" Ketch avoided driving whenever possible.

"Give me half an hour, will you? I'll meet you at HQ."

Ketch consumed a light breakfast and, cocooning himself in a thick pullover and a heavy greatcoat left the house shortly afterwards despite Carol's protestations. "You'll kill yourself if you go on like this," was her final piece of advice.

He took the shortest route across the city to Bethel Street. He thought the stroll would do him good. It was a cold January morning and the temperature came as a shock to him. For the past five days he had been marooned in the flat and had forgotten what winter in East Anglia could be like.

Hoarfrost clung to the bare trees as he made his way up through Cathedral Close onto the busy main thoroughfare. He increased his pace, winding his way through Tombland on to Princes Street but the extra effort expended triggered a bout of coughing so that he was forced to pause by a street lamp in order to recover his breath. A passer-by stopped and called out to him: "Are you all right there mate?" But he ignored the enquiry and pressed on.

By the time that he reached HQ and pushed open the main doors, he was sweating profusely. The desk sergeant looked at him quizzically before saying: "Welcome back sir. DS MacKenzie's waiting for you in the car park. He left a message. You don't look too good if you don't mind me saying." Ketch did mind. The last thing that he needed to be reminded of at this moment was his state of physical decrepitude. When he reached the car park, a loud horn denoted MacKenzie's presence. He wiped his brow, got in, fumbled for his cigarettes, then opened the passenger window wide. This was a courtesy which he extended to his fellow passenger who was not a smoker.

After some desultory conversation, the two men lapsed into silence and Ketch spent the journey looking out at the countryside. They travelled north west of the city and soon passed into an area of land where the fields were flatter and the skies above seemed vast.

This was the westerly edge of Norfolk, once also the domain of the Iceni tribe, led by the legendary leader Boudicca. Many years ago, Ketch recalled, Ken Hill, their destination this morning, had been the site of the discovery of a stunning Iron Age torc, a copy of which resided in the city museum. He had always believed that the place had once been the stronghold of the rebel Queen.

By the time Ketch had finished his third cigarette, the car had already reached the outskirts of the great royal estate at Sandringham and they were flanked on both sides by enormous oak and beech trees. They cut across the estate and then connected with the main coast road between Kings Lynn and Hunstanton where the early morning traffic was dense at this hour. To his right, Ketch could glimpse the low flat expanse of Dersingham Bog and to his left a succession of small copses. The car climbed the hill.

"This is Ken Hill," instructed Ketch. "Here - on the left. Take the woodland road."

He recalled the layout of the place well. In the early years of his marriage, he and Anne used to walk here frequently. They'd rented a small cottage in adjacent Snettisham. In those days, he'd been a humble DC and had a little more time for recreation than now. He remembered that in the late 50s a considerable hoard of Celtic jewellery had been discovered here and that it was thought by archaeologists to have been a site of ritual significance, probably vacated after the persecution of the Iceni tribe, following Boudicca's sacking of Cheltenham and London in the fading days of the Roman Empire.

The car trundled down the rough track between tall oak trees. To his left Ketch could make out the revetments of the old hillfort and glimpsed the familiar police barrier tape.

"Park it here," said Ketch. "We'll walk the rest."

They got out and climbed over the edge of the mound. On the other side was a long trench surrounded by a collection of what Ketch presumed were archaeology students. A tall woman with long black straggly hair dressed in a flak jacket and combat trousers, approached them.

"Professor Julia Bond. I'm leading the dig here."

"DCI Price and this is Tim MacKenzie."

"The body is this way." She led the way to the far end of the trench where Ketch spotted the elephantine rear of Dr Michael Stoppard who was kneeling down, engrossed in his work. At their approach, Stoppard turned and raised his hand in recognition.

"Most definitely not an ancient Briton," he joked. "Judging by the condition, I'd say that the body has been here about 40 years."

"Male or female?"

"Oh, female."

"Have you any idea how she died?"

"That's an easy one. The hyoid bone has been broken."

"Strangled then."

"Precisely. There are some fragments of clothes which might prove useful to you but no ID, sadly."

"We discovered the body only this morning," Professor Bond offered. "One of my third year students noticed the dental work on the lower jaw. That's what alerted us. Of course, the shallower depth is also a give away. I guess it's a perfect spot to get rid of a body – quite unobserved."

"The nearest dwelling is a large mansion called Woodland Hall, some way over beyond those trees, so whoever buried her here would have been quite unobserved," said MacKenzie.

Ketch knelt to examine the body. It had been placed in the foetal position with the head turned to one side. There were fragments of cloth still clinging to the abdomen and the lower legs but they were well rotted through.

"My guess is that she was about 14 years old," said Stoppard. "Certainly no older than that."

"You mentioned that the body may have been here about 40 years," observed Julia Bond. "I may be of some help to you. The site was last excavated in 1972 and there are a number of photographs of the area as it then appeared. Thought it might be of some use to you."

"Thanks for the offer. I'll take you up on that. Meanwhile, I'm afraid that this is a crime scene and I must ask you to suspend your operations." He gave the professor sidelong glance. She must be no more than 25 he guessed. Suddenly he felt old.

Exhausted and ready to crash, Ketch returned to Carol's flat in the afternoon. To his horror, he discovered that they had visitors. Sitting in the lounge and looking as if they'd been there several hours judging by their relaxed manner, were his son James and an attractive blonde girl who Ketch could only imagine was James's girlfriend. She was tall and intense looking with striking blue eyes.

"Hi dad," said James as if he'd only seen his father yesterday. "Meet April."

Ketch shook hands.

"April is a third year archaeology student," James explained. "We met on a dig." Ketch glanced at Carol who merely raised her eyebrows.

"You didn't think to phone to let us know you were coming today?"

"Thought you'd like the surprise."

"How long are you staying in Norwich?"

"About a week or so. I don't suppose there's any chance of using your flat in the Earlham Road as our base?"

Typical of James, thought Ketch. Utterly egocentric.

"I don't see any other alternative, do you?"

That evening, Carol made a casserole and Ketch got in some wine. April proved to be an intelligent and personable individual with an intense interest in Iron Age history.

"We were hoping to look at the dig on Ken Hill," said April after dinner had been concluded. "It's such an important site."

"I'm sorry to tell you that won't be possible," observed Ketch who, owing to the combination of flu symptoms and the absorption of a great deal of wine, was feeling oddly detached.

"Oh? Why's that?"

"Because it's just become a crime scene." He went on to explain why.

By ten o'clock Ketch was feeling distinctly unwell, so he left it to Carol to take James and his new love round to the flat in Earlham Road while he read Sean a bedtime story, then retired to bed. For some while he lay awake thinking about his eldest son. Much as he liked him, James was something of an opportunist and a cadger, he reminded himself. There had been that incident several years back when he'd had an affair with Mary Prosser, the DC who had been his new partner. He had almost not forgiven James for the indiscretion but eventually found the heart to do so. At least April looked like a strong character. Maybe she could keep him in check. God knows what she made of the flat. It was cluttered and neglected, much like Ketch himself, a faded repository of old memories. Well, they would just have to get on with it. He only hoped he'd feel well enough in the morning to turn into work. If not, MacKenzie would have to stand in for him.

By the time Carol returned shortly after 11 o'clock, Ketch was fast asleep.

The following morning, he felt slightly better. The cough had subsided and he was no longer running a high temperature. It was a fine sunny morning in the city and he decided to take the short route to HQ, winding his way through the mediaeval streets of the city.

By the time that he reached Bethel Street by way of his favourite takeaway coffee stall in the market, he found himself sweating again.

On the way up in the lift, he downed two paracetomol tablets washed down with the coffee. He found DS MacKenzie in his office, clutching a bundle of papers. "Morning sir. How are you feeling this morning?"

"Absolutely fine under the circumstances," he replied. Ketch had learned to be economical with the truth.

"Professor Bond e-mailed these documents through earlier this morning. I've printed them out for you."

Ketch sat down as MacKenzie spread the photographs across the desk. "This excavation was done in the summer of 71," he explained. "They returned in 72 when they cleared a number of small saplings and a couple of mature beeches to get an additional trench dug. This is the eastern end of the bank where the body was discovered yesterday."

"How long did the second dig last?"

"A couple of weeks."

"So it would have been possible for someone to have interred the body just after the time when the dig was finally completed?"

"And when the soil was still loose, making the job much easier to accomplish – yes, that's what I wondered."

"How far did you say the Hall was from the top of Ken Hill?"

"Less than a quarter of a mile."

"And who lives there?"

"Lord and Lady Roughton – the same people who lived there in the 70s. They're now in their 70s according to the professor."

"Let's see if they can be of any use to us. Fix up a meeting for this afternoon if possible. Any word from Stoppard about the dental records yet?"

"No, not yet."

"What about the missing persons list for 72?"

"I've been on to that. There were two young girls who went missing from a care home in Hunstanton in the summer of 72. They were never located. And another teenager in the spring of 73 – she was from Kings Lynn."

"Have you got the files?"

"I've asked archives in Wymondham to dig them out for us. They are pre-digital. You should have them by the afternoon."

By lunch time, Ketch was feeling no better. He spent the next hour in the city centre where he consumed two malt whiskeys at his favourite watering hole, The Grapes, then he dropped into Boots where he invested in three packets of menthol flavoured pastilles to help subdue his rasping cough.

When he got back to Bethel Street, MacKenzie was waiting for him.

"The missing persons file that you asked for. Plus I've set up a meeting at the Hall for three pm."

Ketch smiled. MacKenzie was ultra-reliable and that lifted his mood.

Before leaving for Snettisham, he read the files that he'd been given. The girl who disappeared from Kings Lynn was a 16-year-old called Tricia Cleaver. She'd left in April after a disagreement with her parents and had not been seen since. There was a suggestion in the report that she might have eloped with her boyfriend, a student from Manchester.

Ketch turned to the second and third reports. So far it wasn't looking too promising. Diana Durbridge and Priscilla White were both aged 14. At the time of their disappearance, they were living at a children's home called The Haven, a charitable institution situated just outside Hunstanton in West Norfolk.

According to the files, they both disappeared on the evening of 26 July in 1972. They were part of a group of 50 young teenagers who were classified as 'delinquents.' Their ages ranged from 13 to 16 years. The home itself was a charitable trust, run by a group of nuns called the Sisters Of Compassion. It was believed that the girls had escaped through a dormitory window and made their way to King's Lynn, the nearest town, although there had been no sightings to confirm this theory. Despite extensive searches by the police, they had not been found.

Ketch checked the files for the nearest of kin. Both mothers were listed, one living in Hunstanton, the other in Lynn. He called MacKenzie back into the office.

"Check to see if these addresses are still current will you Tim?"
"I already did."
"And?"

"No luck with Diana Durbridge's mother. No longer the same address. However, Priscilla White's mother is still at the address listed in the file. The phone number is no longer current though."

"Dental records yet?"

"Still waiting. I checked with Mike. Should have something before the end of today. He's conducting the autopsy later this afternoon."

"What about the clothing traces?"

"According to the lab at Wymondham, she was wearing a tie-dyed T-shirt and black cotton skirt."

Ketch looked at his watch. "Let's get over to the Hall."

Just as he was about to leave the office, Ketch's phone rang. It was Wymondham with the dental records. They'd proved to be a match with Priscilla White. Ketch took the file with him and slipped it into his briefcase before heading for the car park.

The home of Lord and Lady Roughton was a striking Victorian mansion, situated on the eastern edge of Ken Hill where its elevated position afforded its occupants sweeping views of the surrounding woodlands and beaches. The Roughtons had lived here since Norman times when the estates extended to the edge of the great royal estate of Sandringham.

Up until the 18th century, they had owned half the properties in Dersingham and Snettisham. The Hall itself was a pompous, Palladian style affair, built from red sandstone which, over the centuries, had weathered none too well and now looked rather worse for wear.

The property was only accessible from the estate drive, whose access point lay off the B road a mile away. Ketch and MacKenzie drove through dense woodland down a long and winding unmade road until finally, they reached their destination. They climbed the steps. Ketch pulled the ornate doorbell and there was a loud jangling sound from within. The door opened, revealing a grey-haired, stooped man in his 60s, immaculately dressed in a black suit. Ketch showed his warrant card.

"Lady Roughton is expecting you. This way gentleman, if you please."

They passed down a long hallway lined with Victorian landscape paintings and were led into an ornately furnished drawing room. Lady Roughton was a tall, grey-haired aristocrats in her early 70s. Her chiselled features and well-preserved figure told Ketch that once she would probably have been quite a catch.

"Some tea for our visitors, Andrews," she instructed, waving Ketch and MacKenzie to two plush armchairs either side of a roaring fire where an elderly greyhound slumbered.

When tea had been dispensed and Ketch explained their mission, Lady Roughton looked thoughtful.

"Forty years ago is a long time," she said. "Lord Roughton and I had not been long married then. What month did you say the young girl disappeared?"

"July."

"We had not long taken over the Hall. Peter – that's Lord Roughton - had been living in a flat in London. That's where I met him, you see. I was working in the foreign office in the same department. Anyway, the option we faced was either to sell the family seat lock stock and barrel, or to raise funds to preserve it. We decided on the latter course of action. One of the ideas that Peter came up with was to lease out Ken Hill to a number of promoters for a series of rock festivals. Initially, I was opposed to the idea, but it made a great deal of financial sense since finances were very constrained at the time. We had two festivals that year, one in the May and one in the July, I seem to recall."

"And I believe the archaeological dig had not long been completed?"

"Oh yes, though of course we didn't get paid for the privilege of allowing them to dig up the place. In fact, we lost some of our oldest trees as a result of the dig, a fact which we were none too pleased about."

Ketch produced the photograph of Priscilla White. "You don't happen to recall seeing this girl at the time anywhere in the vicinity?"

"Hardly likely, inspector. Peter did most of the liaising with the promoters. He'd occasionally check to see if the visitors were behaving themselves but I kept out of it on the whole. The noise that they made was fairly horrendous. After the first few days of it, I insisted that we go to London to get some respite."

"How long did the festival last?"

"Five days or so. This I presume is your missing girl?" Ketch nodded. "What a pity – such an attractive looking girl."

"She went missing from a care home in Hunstanton."

"The Haven?"

"You know of it?"

"I should think everyone around here knew of The Haven. We certainly did. It had a bit of a reputation I'm afraid."

"In what way?"

"Oh, there were certain rumours about The Haven. Let's just say it wasn't the happiest of places."

"So you had a connection with the place?"

"Peter was on the Board of Governors there for a short while. However there were certain financial irregularities which he found unsatisfactory, so he left. That was all a long time ago of course. I presume you know the history of the place?"

"I don't."

"It was founded by a Jesuit priest, one Brendan O'Flaherty. When O'Flaherty died, he left the bulk of his estate to The Haven with the proviso that it was to be run by an order of nuns. They were called the Sisters of Compassion. In the early 1970s, the home was supported by the DJ and fundraiser, Freddie Flint – you've probably heard of him. He was a frequent visitor to Hunstanton at the time."

Ketch recalled Flint, a slightly eccentric figure from the 60s, he was widely known for his work for charities in the county and beyond.

"You said just now it wasn't the happiest of places. What exactly do you mean by that?"

"Oh, there were rumours which circulated in the late 1960s and the early 70s about the nuns' cruelty towards the inmates there – rumours based on what some of the young people who resided there had said. Of course, they were unsubstantiated. Several residents escaped but were subsequently found and returned."

"Did you ever visit the Haven?"

"Once or twice but I never much cared for the place – I found it rather grim and forbidding. The nuns seemed reasonable enough. Many of the young people there had severe behavioural problems. There was a resident psychiatrist to manage that side of things – I think his name was Andrew Collins."

"You mentioned the two festivals on Ken Hill. I don't suppose you remember the name of the promoter of the 1972 Festival?"

"I'm sorry but I don't remember that. I know that Freddie Flint was involved with the festival. Some of the money raised went towards The Haven. I believe that Flint made an appearance there. I'm sure that Peter has some paperwork about it in his files. I can ask him to look it up for you if you like when he returns."

"I'd appreciate that – thanks."

Priscilla White's mother lived on the eastern edge of Kings Lynn in a terraced house which formed part of the old suburban boundary of the town. In former days, this had been a respectable middle-class area consisting of Victorian railway villas but now its former glory had long since vanished and the residents were a mixture of races, many of them originating from Eastern Europe. Arriving at the property, Ketch spotted WP Simmonds standing at the door of number 17.

"Mrs White is in the kitchen," she informed him.

"How is she holding up?"

"She's managing – just."

Ketch nodded. "Lead on then."

Mrs White was sitting on a kitchen stool when Ketch and Mackenzie entered. She was smoking a cigarette, a fact which, judging by the tobacco stains on her forefingers, was a frequent occurrence. Now in her 60s, she possessed a long, lean face, etched with lines and creases. There was a look of perpetual sorrow about her which seem to be part of the general dilapidation of her meagre surroundings. Roughly applied lipstick, rouged cheeks and parallel eyebrows gave her the demeanour of a faded clown, thought Ketch.

He sat on a kitchen stool on the other side of the bar while MacKenzie hovered in the doorway and WPC Simmonds brewed fresh tea for them all.

"This must have come as a great shock to you," observed Ketch, using one of the several forms of address he often employed when speaking to relatives of the deceased.

"I always knew she was dead," came the laconic reply.

"What convinced you that Priscilla might no longer be alive?"

"That place – the Haven. I knew there had to be something in it."

"What do you mean by that?"

"She'd escaped from there before – three times in fact. The third time it happened she begged me not to tell them she'd come back here. I wished to God that I'd taken notice of what she said." She inhaled a deep lungful of cigarette smoke.

"And what did she tell you about the place precisely?"

"She told me lots. Of course, at first I didn't believe her – most of what Cilla told me was lies so it was difficult to know when she was telling me the truth, but I should have listened."

"What did she tell you, Mrs White?"

"About the beatings that the nuns gave out to the girls. And about the solitary confinement."

"This was a regular occurrence?" She nodded.

"Cilla told me they had this cellar beneath the house – they called it the dungeon. There was no light in there and it was unheated with just an earth floor. In severe cases of misbehaviour girls would be locked in there for days without food or water. There was no sanitation either. On one occasion, she told me, she was put down there with her friend Debbie and they'd taken away their clothes – this was in January, would you believe?"

"You didn't think to complain about the treatment?"

"In those days it just made matters worse. She begged me not to make an issue of it. It just meant further punishment for her. There were other things she told me too."

"What were they?"

"I can't bring myself to talk about it. She wrote a diary."

"You kept it?"

"I took it from her dormitory table after she disappeared – you can read it if you want to."

"I'd like to see it."

"Then I'll get it for you."

On his way back from Kings Lynn, Ketch asked MacKenzie to drop him off at the top of the Earlham Road. Ostensibly, he thought he would check to see how James and April were settling into the flat but his real motive, he had to admit, was based on a strong apprehension, an irrational, instinctive feeling that James could not be completely trusted.

The flat was cold and dank from the ice cold January temperatures and there was a quantity of flyers and junk mail behind the front door which James had clearly failed to remove. Disgruntled, he entered the lounge and switched on the lights. Two suitcases lay on the floor by the sofa and there was a familiar smell of cannabis in the stale air.

On the coffee table were two empty glasses, a half consumed bottle of red wine and an ashtray containing a large reefer. He took the ashtray and hurling its contents into a waste paper bin in the kitchen, cursed under his breath. He'd speak to James in the morning.

Overnight it had snowed heavily and if anything, he felt worse now. He seemed to have a perpetual headache and the racking cough had kept him awake most of the night.

Despite Carol's protestations, he showered, dressed and left the flat early. On the way through the city streets, now glowing with white pristine snow, he rang the flat's landline number but there was no reply.

He imagined that James and his girlfriend were still recovering from a heavy night's session. He'd ring later.

Grateful for the early morning latte at his usual marketplace stall, he entered the lobby of HQ where he met MacKenzie who had just returned from the canteen.

"Anything new?" he enquired.

"I've been checking the local news coverage for the summer of 1972," MacKenzie replied. "The festival was called the Rainbow Event and it featured a number of folk and rock bands. It appeared to have been organised principally by three people."

They had now reached Ketch's office by way of the lift. MacKenzie opened the folder and showed Ketch three news cuttings. Attached to one of them was a photograph and a headline which read: 'Three local benefactors give the rainbow blessing.'

"I thought this might interest you," said MacKenzie.

"I recognise Freddie Flint from the TV. Who are these people with him?"

MacKenzie pointed to a tall man, dressed in an expensive grey suit. "This, would you believe, is Lord Roughton. And the other man is Colin Murray. He is described here as a festival promoter. I did some research about him. Nowadays he runs an antiquarian bookshop in the city."

Ketch looked at the photograph carefully. The three men were standing on a raised dais. Behind them was a collection of young girls, dressed in T-shirts and miniskirts. Some of them could only have been 15 or younger.

"This character Murray – where is his bookshop?"

"In Magdalen Street."

"Let's drop in and see him this afternoon. Let me know when the autopsy report is done, will you?"

"I'll chase up Dr Stoppard for you."

When MacKenzie had left, Ketch closed the office door, drank the remainder of his coffee, removed his overcoat, then turned over the pages of Cilla White's diary. A small brown A5 sized volume in bright red, the cover still bore traces of coffee stains and watermarks and had a fusty smell. A page a day diary, entries were long, detailed and written in a neat hand.

He scanned the entries for January and February 1972. Cilla's resentment at her incarceration was palpable and her hatred of the nuns manifest. The only redeeming note in these pages was an account of her friendship with Debbie Durbridge whom she referred to as her 'soul mate.'

Ketch skimmed on through the pages. At June 3, he found the following entry:

'Great excitement. Freddie Flint visiting us today. Even sister Angela is excited – a rare sight! Debbie and me were picked out of the line and told to wait on him at dinner. Afterwards, he took us up to his rooms at the back of the building. He told us he knew someone who ran a modelling agency and that if we 'played out cards right', with him he could maybe wangle a release for us both. I asked him what he meant exactly by this but he was a bit vague.

June 20. Freddie visited again along with two other men. One of them, the older guy, I recognised from earlier in the year when he came on his own. Freddie said he'd like to do a photo shoot with me and Debbie but to keep it a secret from the other girls. Debs and me were really excited at the prospect. Sister Angela very pleased. She said we showed a change of attitude recently and was pleased with the way things were working out for us both.

July 2. Freddie called again with his two friends – don't know their names! After we served them dinner, Freddie took us into his back rooms where he had cameras and spotlights already setup. He told me and Debs he'd like to do two test shots of each of us, and for the second shot we'd need to take out tops off. When I asked about it he said all the top modelling agencies required it these days. He took lots of photographs. Felt a bit uncomfortable doing it, but what the heck!'

Ketch flipped over the next few pages, then stopped at July 23.

'Debbie told me what happened with Freddie and the others. I couldn't believe it. Afterwards, she complained to sister Angela but sister Angela didn't believe her. At first, I didn't either. She told me she wouldn't go near them again but that might be more difficult than she imagines.

July 20. Freddie and his friends called again. Freddie said he'd shown my shots to an agency in Norwich who were prepared to offer me some work. He said they wanted some more outdoor shots and wouldn't it be a good idea to shoot some pictures in the woods. It seemed like a good idea. In the afternoon we went into the woods where Freddie asked me to take my clothes off and pose on a tree trunk. I felt a bit uneasy about doing it but I did it anyway. Afterwards I felt a bit cheap.

July 31. Debbie was asked to do a photo shoot in the woods by Freddie but she refused. Sister Angela was told by Freddie she had sworn at him so she was sent to the punishment room for three days. I saw her that night and she looked ill. There were bruises all over her body where the sisters had beaten her with the pandy bat and she told me that she hadn't eaten for two of the days. She said she's going to write to her mother about what happened but I don't fancy our chances since the sisters always intercept outgoing mail. They're not supposed to but they do it. She called Freddie and his mates a bunch of perverts but she wouldn't tell me what happened in the woods. I'm frightened about what might happen to me but I know I can look after myself. Louise says there were three girls from the Haven who went missing five years ago but it was only a rumour. When I asked sister Angela about it she told me to keep my mouth shut or it might be the worst for me.

Freddie came by this afternoon and asked me to his rooms where he had a folder which had a load of photographs of girls in it. He told me they'd all been members of his 'select club.' Some had had big modelling careers, others worked for him in his club in London where he employs top rock groups. He told me I had a brilliant career ahead of me and that he was sorry that Debbie had said those things about him because they were not true. He said he'd set up a shoot with some other models for tomorrow afternoon after the festival is ended. It'll be at a new location but he wouldn't say where exactly. He gave me some money. I said I'd do it though I feel awful about letting Debbie down. Went to see her this afternoon and she looked a bit better. Now I'm looking forward to the Big Shoot.'

Ketch turned the page but it was blank. Blank also were the remaining pages. His door opened, it was MacKenzie.

"Autopsy report on Cilla White, sir."

He placed a brown folder on Ketch's desk.

"Conclusions?"

"Nothing we couldn't have predicted, no. She died of manual strangulation in late summer 1972 – the date was determined by the insect evidence."

Ketch nodded thoughtfully.

"Any luck with the diary sir?"

"Oh yes. A great deal. Get me an address for Freddie Flint, will you?"

MacKenzie discovered that Freddie Flint had been committed to a nursing home in Cromer by his daughter the previous year. Ketch decided to postpone his visit to Murray's antiquarian bookshop and head straight to Cromer.

The Willows Nursing Home was a large Edwardian villa situated on the outskirts of this once prosperous seaside resort. Its redbrick facade had clearly seen better days and its portico columns bore evidence of peeling paint and long years of neglect.

The manager, a tall young woman with jet black hair and a strong Eastern European accent, greeted them. "Mr Flint is suffering from dementia, so you must make allowances for him," she explained as they made their way down the cheerless hallway and up to the first floor.

They entered a small room, cluttered with cheap furniture and a large display of framed photographs which showed Freddie in his glory days as a DJ and promoter.

There were photographs of him arm in arm with the Rolling Stones and Fleetwood Mac and others whom Ketch failed to recognise. One shot, in particular, caught his attention. It showed a large motorhome parked outside The Haven. Flint stood in front of it, surrounded by a collection of young girls and at their side was a tall woman who Ketch presumed to be sister Angela.

Ketch sat down on the only chair in the room as MacKenzie hovered in the doorway. Freddie Flint was propped up in bed and looked as if he had been there since the previous night.

"I am Chief Inspector Price and this is my colleague Detective Sgt MacKenzie," said Ketch. "We have a few questions that we want to ask you in connection with The Haven. Do you remember the Haven, Freddie?" Freddie didn't answer. He was staring fixedly at the space immediately in front of him. Ketch continued asking questions but there were no answers. After 15 minutes spent in this fruitless exercise, Ketch gave up and they left.

On their way back to Norwich, Ketch rang the Hall and got through to Lady Roughton. "I'm sorry to tell you that my husband isn't in at present," she explained. "He went for a walk with the dogs about an hour ago and I haven't seen him return yet."

"When he does get in could you ask him to ring me? Tell him it's urgent."

"Nothing serious I trust?" Ketch didn't reply to this.

The bookshop which bore the legend 'Rainbow Books: Antiquarian and Second-hand Editions- Books bought and sold' lay at the far end of Magdalen Street, squeezed between a Polish food shop and a furniture shop. As Ketch and MacKenzie entered the shop, a short, overweight man in his mid-60s came through from the back, summoned by the shop bell. He looked apprehensive.

"Yes - can I help you at all?" Ketch showed his warrant card.

"We are here to talk to you about the disappearance of Cilla White," he explained. Colin Murray, who had turned deathly white, sat down on a stool behind the desk and bowed his head.

"I knew something was up," he said.

The bookseller had been eager to cooperate. "It was Freddie's idea," he explained. "Initially he approached me and Peter – that's Lord Roughton - with a business idea. It seemed like a good one at the time. We'd each put a stake into organising a series of pop festivals in Norfolk, Suffolk, and Cambridgeshire. Freddie had the reputation and the clout to pull this off. In return, we'd both get a profit from the ticket sales and some of the money would go to his charity causes."

"Including The Haven?"

"Yes, including The Haven. He also mentioned something about 'fringe benefits.' "

"And what were the fringe benefits?"

"As you probably already know, Freddie ran a modelling agency in Norwich. He was also the benefactor to at least five children's homes in East Anglia, one of which was The Haven. Freddie was very fond of the girls who he often encouraged."

"Young girls in particular?"

"Yes, young girls."

"What was your involvement in all of this?"

"Peter and I were both keen amateur photographers. We belonged to a club in Hunstanton. Freddie told us that a couple of the girls at the Haven were interested in making themselves a portfolio and were prepared to do a couple of photo shoots for us."

"And you were present at these photos sessions?"

"Yes, we took a lot of head and shoulders shots of the girls."

"What about the shots that were done in the woods?"

"Freddie told us to meet him there on the Saturday."

"This was in the July of 1972 I presume?"

"Yes, on the two consecutive Saturdays as I recall. The first girl went with us to an area of woodland some way from the house itself."

"This would have been Cilla White?"

"Yes, I think that was the name."

"And the photographs you took there were in the nude?"

"She took her clothes off – quite willingly I should point out to you. Then, when we'd finished the shoot, Freddie said he had some things to discuss with her so we left him alone with her and both went back to the house."

"What happened with the other girl, Diana Durbridge?"

"It was pretty much the same sort of setup. The other girl was much shyer, she seemed rather nervous about doing it. We spent about half an hour doing the shots. Freddie kept pushing her to do more and more provocative stuff. Anyway, eventually, he asked us to both leave. We made our way back through the woods but we could hear the girl crying out. I told Peter we ought to go back and stop Freddie from what he was doing but Peter said we'd best not intervene and that it was Freddie's business. The following day I phoned Freddie and asked about what had gone on in the woods but he told me to keep my mouth shut and keep my nose out of his business and he said that if I said anything about it to anyone else he had photographs of me and

Peter taking shots of the girl."

So you remained silent and have done for all these years?" Murray nodded.

"When I found out that the body of one of the girls had been identified, my heart sank. We both knew what Freddie was capable of but murder – that's altogether different."

Ketch and MacKenzie arrived at Ken Hill shortly after they had concluded the interview with Murray. The butler answered the door.

"We are here to see Lord Roughton," said Ketch, pushing past him. "Is he in?"

"Lord Roughton left the house shortly after breakfast and he hasn't been back since. Shall I inform her ladyship of your arrival, sir?"

They found Lady Roughton in the drawing-room, standing by the window. She looked tense and preoccupied.

"I don't understand it," she said. "Peter is never usually this long. He's been gone over four hours."

"He didn't ring you?"

"He didn't take his phone with him. He usually does, which is a bit strange."

Ketch and MacKenzie left her in the drawing-room, a pale distraught figure, framed by the French windows. They made their way down the driveway accompanied by the butler until they hit a rough woodland track which they were assured, was Lord Roughton's usual path into the woods. They had not gone more than 500 yards when Ketch heard the sound of a dog barking.

"Over here, to your left," he told MacKenzie. Pushing their way through dense rhododendron bushes, they came upon a small area of open ground surrounded by ancient yew trees.

The body of Lord Roughton lay spread-eagled. Half his head had been blown away and the shotgun he had used to mark his departure now lay across his chest. One gun dog lay across his knees shaking while the second stood some yards away growling at the two officers. The butler looked visibly shocked at the scene.

"Phone for an ambulance," Ketch instructed MacKenzie. "Best you go back to the house," he told the butler, "and inform her ladyship."

Ketch shivered and pulled the lapels of his grey coat tightly about his throat. He was standing in the grounds of the Haven and this was his third day here. Much of the surrounding undergrowth had now gone, the boards had been removed from the mullioned windows and barrier tape marked the perimeter of the building as a crime scene.

A previous investigation in woodland at Ken Hill had failed to yield the body of Diana Durbridge and this was the final attempt to gain a forensic result. Six police officers had been using sonar imaging equipment but so far without effect.

Ketch found the atmosphere of the Haven oppressive. It was as if the burden of human suffering which had once held sway here had impregnated the very foundations of the building.

A shout interrupted his reverie. It was DC Thomas, accompanied by the lead member of the SOCO team. "Think you should come and have a look here sir."

They made their way through an archway and down a flight of stone steps to what was once the cellar, or to use Cilla White's description, 'The Dungeon.'

A rectangle, measuring 5' x 4 had been dug and, protruding from the black soil, was the outline of a human skull.

"There are at least two other bodies," explained Thomas, "according to the sonar imager."

"Then let's get on with it," Ketch sighed.

Ketch was sitting on the old battered leather sofa in his flat in the Earlham Road. James and his girlfriend had left three days ago after an altercation with Ketch and this had been the first opportunity for him to clean up the place properly.

It had taken him a whole morning during which time he had cleared away the bottles, emptied the ashtrays, then cleaned and hoovered through. The stains on the new carpet would just have to wait he told himself, though he felt like sending a cleaning bill to James to compensate for the time and inconvenience it had caused him.

Carol, whom he'd imagined would be supportive in the matter, put it all down to youthful inexperience and there had been harsh words between them. He poured himself a Scotch, sipped, then lay back on the sofa and lit a cigarette.

It had been a nightmare of a case. The DPP had been unable to proceed since the main suspect, Freddie Flint, had been deemed unfit to plead and there had been insufficient evidence to prosecute Colin Murray. In the days and weeks that followed the discovery of the three bodies at the Haven, more information about Flint's abusive career was to be revealed.

One of the bodies buried in the cellar was undoubtedly that of Diana Durbridge. According to the autopsy, she had died of natural causes, probably hypothermia – at least, that was Ketch's theory. The other two bodies were those of two male infants, no doubt the offspring of some of the inmates of the Haven.

It had not been possible to interrogate the sisters since they had all died in the late 90s and the only evidence available to the police consisted of the testimonies of the victims, many of them now in the mid-50s.

As soon as the media got hold of the story, those victims started to come forward. There were ten in all who offered their evidence. During their time at the Haven they had been systematically beaten by the nuns and offered to Flint for abuse. Flint had been a major benefactor of the home and his influence was all-powerful.

No questions were asked when he visited the Haven and no one questioned what went on in his flat in the annex to the building.

Two weeks after the discovery of the bodies, Ketch was relieved of his position as SIO and a new team was assembled to look into the affair. Code-named Flint, twelve officers spent three months collating and cross-checking personal testimonies of the victims.

They discovered that over the course of twenty years as a minor celebrity, Flint had repeated his pattern of abuse at no less than three institutions where he had operated as benefactor to charities. In the end over 150 statements were collected and Flint was discovered to have links with two major European paedophile rings. This, in turn, led to twenty arrests in the UK alone.

For Ketch, Ken Hill was never quite the same after the conclusion of the Flint affair. In February of that year, the archaeological team were allowed to continue their investigations. After weeks of digging, two additional bodies were discovered at the eastern end of the existing trench. Both were females, dating from the period when Boudicca held sway in East Anglia and both were of a high-class status.

In their graves were found coins, gold torcs and a variety of jewellery some of which hailed from Byzantium. Ken Hill subsequently came to be known as 'Boudicca's encampment,' and it may well have formed the centre of her operations against the Romans.

It was not until the late summer when Ketch finally returned to the place. The excavation ditches had now been filled in and the place looked largely undisturbed. He wandered along the woodland path with Carol and Sean. Somehow the hill seemed to be shorn of its ghosts at last and there was an atmosphere of peace and tranquillity.

They found a spot beneath a cluster of beech trees and spread their picnic on a blanket. As Ketch tucked into his pâté he recalled the legend of Boudicca and how she had been inspired to do battle against the Roman oppressors after her daughters had been raped by the soldiers. The parallel with the Flint case was not lost on him. It seemed to him that nothing much had changed over the last 2000 years. Thank God he had never had daughters.

DOWN AMONG THE DEAD

She awoke. It was still dark, pitch dark, darker than any dark she had ever known. She tried to move but her arms were chained. She recalled how she had got here, recalled the face of her captor against the black, foul smelling walls of her prison.

Now her eyes were growing accustomed to the gloom, she saw that she was at the end of a long tunnel. Far off, she thought she could hear traffic sounds. She reckoned that the tunnel must be somewhere under the city streets.

She shivered. It must be near freezing point in here. She was dressed only in a short skirt and thin T-shirt. He had taken away her coat and handbag. He had told her she needed to be punished. "A spot of solitary," was how he described it to her. It would bring her to her senses.

How long had she been here? Days? Maybe longer... She felt an overwhelming desire to pee, and, squatting on her haunches, she gave way to the urge.

She could see more clearly now. About 5 metres ahead of where she was sitting was a large oak door with a grille. The place seemed ancient. The walls were wet, encrusted with yellow lichen. Somewhere in the room, there was a shuffling sound. She wondered if there were rats. She remembered how she had been brought here. He'd told her he'd had no alternative. She'd blown her last chance.

She listened intently. There it was again, the sound of a heavy vehicle moving overhead. She'd guessed where she was now, it was becoming much clearer. He must have drugged her before bringing her down here. Her throat was parched. She was desperate for a drink - water, anything.

From far off came the sound of footsteps. Getting closer now. She recognised the tread. The sound of the key turning in the lock, the door opening. He stood framed in the doorway, one hand held the bunch of keys and in the other was a long cane.

"Let's get on with it," he said, smiling. But though he smiled, his eyes were cold.

Detective Chief Inspector Huw Price, known to his colleagues as simply Ketch, stared at the face in the mirror. The face staring back at him was that of a 50-year-old man with strong aquiline features, dark eyebrows, high cheekbones and thin lips.

The eyes, which were small and dark blue, had often been described as penetrating by women he had courted in his younger days, but now they were weary and somewhat inflamed – a consequence of his insomnia and heavy drinking.

Indeed it was the latter addiction – for he now acknowledged that it was an addiction – which had led to premature ageing and the general decline in his well-being. That was a fact he unashamedly – or was it perhaps shamefully? – accepted. The mere fact that he was standing in the bathroom of an empty flat bore testimony to this circumstance.

For the past fortnight he had drunk heavily, so much so that his partner, Carol Hennessy the pathologist, and their nine-month-old baby, had deserted him. Carol had gone to stay with her mother in Whitby, a town for which Ketch had expressed considerable affection on their last joint visit there only a summer ago. Apart from its romantic setting, he had long been an admirer of the works of Bram Stoker, and the literary connection of the church on the hill and the steps up to it were not lost on him. As a child, the book Dracula had enthralled him and he remembered reading it under his bed sheet by the aid of a small torch.

This time he had not been invited to Whitby. He had become, in Carol's words, almost "monstrous." There had been no suggestion of physical violence towards her but the booze had turned him into a creature of morose moods and sardonic utterances.

It was as if the joy had been extinguished and his soul had retreated into a dark place, beyond redemption.

He turned away from the mirror, unable to look at his reflection anymore. He pulled on a shirt then smelt it. There was a distinct odour of male sweat. He had forgotten how many days ago since he'd changed it. He really was slipping. He went into the bedroom and rummaged in a drawer for a fresh shirt.

On the dressing table was a small card which read: "Alcoholics Anonymous: Norwich branch." There followed a phone number. He thought for a moment, then put on the fresh shirt and placed the card in his wallet before pulling on his trousers. Maybe it was time, he told himself. One day this week perhaps.

By the time he got to the kitchen, his phone was already ringing. He looked at the screen on his BlackBerry. It was DS Tim MacKenzie.

"Sorry to ring you this early, sir ."

Ketch glanced at the kitchen clock. It read 6:40 AM.

"Okay, Tim – what is it?"

"There's been a major incident on the Earlham Road."

"Which bit of it?" The Earlham Road was one of the main conduits of the city. It led from the University of East Anglia at one end to the Roman Catholic Cathedral at the other.

"Just down from the Leaping Hare." Ketch knew the pub well. It was not far from the flat he had occupied since his wife's death, a place he rarely visited now except to pick up some junk mail now and again. He kept it on as a bolthole, a bachelor retreat for when he felt the need to escape the confines of his relationship with Carol. He hadn't been back to the flat for six months now but recently had considered doing just that.

"What kind of major incident? Explain."

"A hole has opened up in the road and one of the city buses slipped down it. The passengers are now off board, the driver is unhurt and the fire and rescue services are in attendance."

"Good – no need for us to attend then. Why bother me with this, Tim?"

"They found a body." Ketch put down the banana he was holding.

"Whose body?"

"Dr Stoppard's here right now. He tells me the body's been here for about ten years. He's certain that it's the body of a young woman but he's no idea as to the cause of death. Not yet, anyhow."

"Let me get this right. The body was in the hole the bus went down into?"

"That's correct. According to the fire officer, there's a kind of tunnel beneath the road – the tunnel collapsed. The body was under some rubble which fell in when the top surface of the road caved in. What's unusual about this is that the body was attached to a piece of concrete."

"Attached? How attached?"

"By means of a chain."

"Okay Tim, thanks for the call. Give me 40 minutes. Who's there with you?"

"Dave Thomas."

"Right – tell DC Thomas to get back to Bethel Street and conduct a search for missing female persons – starting with 2002 and ending with 2006."

By the time Ketch had walked to the Earlham Road most of the emergency services had departed and a large recovery vehicle was towing the bus away. He ducked under the barrier tape and stood by a large hole in the tarmac, measuring approximately 15 feet in circumference.

Someone had erected a long ladder by the side of the hole and at its bottom he saw Tim MacKenzie's face staring up at him. Standing next to him and also squeezed into the familiar SOCO gear was the portly form of Dr Michael Stoppard.

"Careful how you step down," boomed Stoppard. "The ladder has a tendency to drift to the left."

Taking Stoppard's advice, Ketch gingerly descended the aluminium ladder and soon found himself at the base of a large tunnel which had been hewn from the surrounding clay, part of which had collapsed.

A floodlight had been erected and approximately 20 yards away to his left he could discern the outline of a recumbent figure partly covered in rubble.

"What is this place?" he asked Stoppard.

"Not entirely sure of its purpose," replied Stoppard. "According to the chief fire officer I spoke to earlier, there's a whole network of these tunnels which stretch across the city. There's even reputed to be one up on Ketts Hill. He informed me that they may date from the mediaeval period or even earlier. As to their purpose, no one's entirely sure. Boltholes for religious dissidents during Queen Mary's reign of terror – somewhere to hide for King Charles I supporters – who knows?"

Ketch recalled Ketts Hill, so named after its rebel leader who encamped on a hill over the city in an attempt to challenge the Kings authority – a mediaeval insurrection that went horribly wrong and ending in his evisceration and execution. A tunnel may well have served him and his supporters. But why tunnel here, under one of Norwich's most busy roads?

"How far does this lead?" he enquired.

"We haven't yet explored it to its fullest length because some of the tunnel has collapsed, as you can see. It looks pretty dodgy to me. Anyway, let me introduce you to our victim."

Stoppard ushered Ketch forwards and he peered down on what at first sight appeared to be a bundle of old clothes. On closer examination, he could make out the body in more detail. Crouched in the foetal position, the figure was dressed in a short skirt and pink, high-heeled shoes. The trunk was bare except for a black brassiere. The hair, which was stretched around an emaciated, blackened face, was blonde and straight.

Ketch stared at the eyeless sockets of the corpse before turning back to Stoppard.

"Exactly how long has she been in here?"

"My educated guess - and that means it's still only a guess – is approximately 10 years. There are a number of forensic details which persuade me of that fact."

"How did she die?"

"Difficult to be precise though two of her ribs are broken. I shall be able to tell you more after I get back to the lab. Fortunately, due to the part mummification, there's a lot that's been preserved for us. This tunnel has enjoyed a fairly even temperature – ideal conditions for the preservation of the corpse."

"Right – lend me the torch will you?" he asked MacKenzie. So saying, and borrowing a hard hat from Stoppard, he began making his way slowly up the narrow passageway, stopping at intervals to examine the roughly hewn ceiling. After about 20 yards he stopped and called back: "There's a door here or something – solid oak by the look of it. Someone needs to find out what's on the other side of it."

"Well it certainly won't be me, Huw," Stoppard replied. "I suggest you take that up with the fire officer."

Ketch spent the rest of the morning interviewing the suspect of a hit and run accident in Hellesdon. The previous Tuesday, a young mother and her toddler had been mowed down by an old Renault as they were crossing the road close to Hellesdon church. Fortunately, a CCTV camera had captured the incident and the licence plate was just visible.

The suspect was a 23-year-old Polish plumber. When arrested, he was found to be over the limit. In the interview room he seemed strangely unapologetic for what he had done. According to Interpol who had sent an e-mail to DC Thomas, he'd notched up a series of traffic offences in his native country before coming to the UK in search of work. A short, thickset individual with cropped, receding hair, he sat with arms crossed and enquired nonchalantly: "It won't mean prison, will it? I have family in Kraków. I need to see them." Ketch didn't give him the pleasure of a reply.

After a largely liquid lunch at his favourite watering hole, The Grapes, Ketch returned to his desk to find DC Thomas waiting for him.

" I hope this is good news?"

"It's hopeful, sir. There were three missing persons in 2003, all from the Norwich area. The first was an 18-year-old called Diana Wescott, the second was Amy Speedwell. She was 17. The third was Tracey Fishwick, an 18-year-old. All three of them disappeared without trace in the summer of 2003. What may be significant is that the first, Diana Wescott, lived originally off the Earlham Road in a flat in Arthur Street along with the two other girls. The three of them were picked up in the city the previous March for shoplifting."

Thomas opened the file and Ketch stared down at the faces of Diana Wescott, Amy Speedwell and Tracey Fishwick. All three of them had short blond hair and pale complexions, but there was something about the face of Diana Wescott that spelled desperation, he thought. Maybe it was the eyes, they spoke to him of a lost soul.

"Wescott and Speedwell were also picked up in March 2003 for soliciting in the Prince Of Wales Road but they were never formally charged," Thomas went on to inform him.

Ketch knew the Prince of Wales Road in Norwich well – a long stretch near the city centre, full of nightclubs and often the scene of drunken mayhem, especially at the weekends.

"Okay, Dave. Good results, now let's see what the autopsy comes up with."

He spent the remainder of his afternoon re-interviewing the Polish driver but with limited success. This time the suspect had his solicitor with him, a short, cocky individual who intensely irritated Ketch.

As a result, all the suspect could come up with was a series of "no comments." After 20 minutes of this, Ketch gave up in disgust and sent the man back to his cell.

By six pm he was feeling dry and claustrophobic. He phoned Stoppard and discovered that the autopsy had been delayed because of an unscheduled three-car collision on the A147 which had taken place that morning. As a consequence, Stoppard had been busy with the fatalities.

As he left HQ, he discovered that it was still light. A brilliant burst of sunlight had spread over some of the city's tallest buildings and the sharp spring air revitalised him as he wove his way through the mediaeval streets, down towards the river.

Here he stopped off at the Adam and Eve, one of his favourite pubs when he needed to ruminate. He took his pint and chaser outside into the cool air where he sat on a bench and smoked several cigarettes. The face of Diana Wescott drifted back into his mind and the phrase "lost souls" kept repeating itself to him like a mantra.

He had an uncanny feeling about this missing persons case – almost a sense of dread. He finished the pint, then wove his way down the river bank towards the pied-à-terre which had been his main residence for the past few years.

Despite, or more probably because of, the excessive amount of alcohol in his blood, Ketch spent a restless night at the riverside flat. Just before 11:30 pm he had received a text with a photo attached from Carol, showing her and baby Sean sitting at the top of the steep flight of steps which leads up to Whitby Abbey. Both looked well and rested he thought, adverbs which could not be applied to himself. He decided that this morning he would make an effort and, with some instant porridge and a bowl, applied boiling water to it. The result was grey, gelatinous and tasteless, so he heaped two dessert spoons of sugar onto it to give him an early-morning sugar rush. Then, selecting a fresh shirt and a pair of trousers from his wardrobe, he dressed and left the flat, making his way through the city towards police headquarters in Bethel Street.

He took the circuitous route which he often enjoyed especially in springtime, down a narrow alleyway opposite one of the main gates to the Cathedral, then past the old Huguenot Church, stopping off at the tobacconists opposite the multi-storey car park where he purchased a pack of handrolling tobacco and Rizla machine.

He had decided the previous evening that he'd be giving up manufactured cigarettes in favour of something much cheaper and less chemically toxic. When he got to the market he sat and rolled several cigarettes. He had forgotten over the years how satisfying it was to roll your own cigarettes.

By nine he was in the building and by ten the Polish driver had been formally charged in the presence of his obstructive solicitor, then returned to his cell. He met DC Thomas at the coffee machine.

"Autopsy's done, sir. The report is on your desk. Seems fairly certain it is a match to one of our missing girls."

"But which one?"

"Until we get a DNA match or the dental records we shan't be able to tell."

"I take it you've contacted the parents?"

"Did that yesterday evening – Diana Wescott's parents now live in Fakenham but they used to run the pub in the Earlham Road."

"The Leaping Hare?"

"Yes."

"What about Amy Speedwell and Tracey Fishwick?"

"Amy Speedwell's parents are divorced – the mother married a Frenchman and emigrated to France two years ago, but the father still lives in the family home in Aylsham."

"And Tracey Fishwick?"

"The last known address for her is a flat in Swaffham. I checked it out but could find no trace of her."

"And her parents?"

"Father dead, mother still living – remarried. She lives in Norwich. What you want me to do about them – I mean the parents, of course?"

"Nothing – at least not until we get confirmation about the identity of our Jane Doe."

After a mainly liquid lunch, Ketch returned to HQ where he checked his messages. A short text from Carol with a photo attachment showing the waves crashing on the harbour at Whitby. The text read: Both having a lovely time – how are you doing? The second was a brief note from Stoppard. 'Dental records confirm body is that of Diana Wescott – Stoppard.'

Ketch blinked in the harsh glare of the autopsy room lights. As he entered, Stoppard, who had been hunched over the body of a new subject, turned and smiled. Ketch noticed his plump forehead was bathed in sweat. Next to him stood his new female assistant, a tall blonde called Amelia who had been shadowing Stoppard for the last six months.

"To what do we owe the pleasure?" Stoppard enquired theatrically.

"Diana Wescott."

"Yes – what about her?"

"Your report mentioned some abrasions to the wrists and abdomen."

"Several. My hunch is that the abrasions to the wrists were caused by friction with a metallic object."

"Handcuffs?"

"Most probably, yes."

"What about the other marks?"

"Beaten with a blunt object though I wouldn't yet bet money on it. The problem you see is down to the mummification process – it limits the options."

"You mentioned in the report that there had been damage to both the rectum and vagina."

"Indeed – two tears, one in each orifice. She's been tortured I've no doubt of it. Do you want to see the cadaver?"

"Not especially."

"Is there anything else, then?"

"The exact time of death?"

"Quite impossible to determine after this interval of years. I can tell you the month though, based on the insect evidence – undoubtedly July."

"The month of her disappearance..."

"I wouldn't know about that – that's your department. Is there anything else?"

"No, that's it."

Ketch exited the room, aware of his long standing dislike of Stoppard. Why was the man always so bloody arrogant?

That evening Ketch returned to the flat around nine o'clock armed with a Chinese takeaway. Despite a mountain of food in the fridge which Carol had left for him prior to her departure, the routine was always the same when she absented herself. The takeaway was both convenient and appetising to him. Sated with monosodium glutamate and a third of a bottle of 10-year-old malt, he soon drifted into a profound sleep and next morning found he had forgotten to retire to bed. After a brief wash, he phoned MacKenzie and asked him to enlist the help of a WPC before departing to Fakenham to visit the Wescott's.

The journey through Taverham and beyond was as he remembered it. Way back in his youth he had dated a young WPC who lived in Fakenham and he had often travelled there to see her on his trusty Honda 175 cc. It was in the main an attractive and tree-lined route.

Fakenham itself had not outwardly changed much over the intervening years. An old Victorian market town, it had clearly seen better days, its shopping centre blighted by a new and brash supermarket, a true blot on the landscape.

MacKenzie drove the car down the main high street and past the supermarket, then turned up a broad road lined by Edwardian terraced houses bearing nameplates like 'Kenilworth' and 'Fairhaven.' He pulled up outside a large terraced building and the three of them got out. The door opened revealing a short woman in her early 60s with dyed blonde hair, bearing a worried expression.

"Mrs Wescott?" said Ketch, showing his warrant card.

She nodded.

"I'm DCI Price and these are my colleagues, DS MacKenzie and WPC Hughes."

"You've found my Diana?"

"Let's go inside shall we?"

Mrs Wescott led the way down a long hallway lined with small landscape paintings into a comfortable sitting room which had been furnished in mock Victorian fashion, complete with a Victorian writing desk and chaise longue. Sitting in a wide captain's chair was a huge man with a bald head and coarse features. He did not attempt to get up to greet Ketch but merely leaned forward as if he had been somehow glued to the chair.

Ketch grasped his hand which was red and sweaty. After the formalities have been dispensed with and WPC Hughes had done her utmost to console Mrs Wescott and provided them all with hot tea, Ketch asked: "What sort of girl was Diana, Mrs Wescott?"

"She was, frankly, much troubled, Chief Inspector. She used to be such a happy little thing when she was in primary school. John used to call her his little princess, didn't you, John?" John nodded. "Then she went to the secondary school and that's when the trouble began."

"What sort of trouble exactly?"

"Trouble with some of the other girls, the younger ones. They complained to one of the teachers that she'd been bullying them. At first, we didn't believe it. Didn't seem to be in her nature, not our Diana. But then it happened a second and a third time. As a result, she was suspended for three weeks. They said she and two other girls were taking money off the younger kids. She'd also started to self-harm. I found cigarette burns on her wrists. I didn't know she even smoked. I suppose we were a bit naive really weren't we John?" John nodded dutifully. "Anyway, things finally came to a head when she was in year 10. She'd not been doing at all well in her school subjects for a long while. Then we got called into the school. Apparently, she and another girl had attacked a girl in a lower year and left her badly bruised, so they suspended them both."

"She went back to school in the end, though?" Ketch asked.

"For a while, yes, but then we got a call from the police – this was when she moved into year 11. She'd been picked up in the Norwich market with two other girls, shoplifting."

"And after that?"

"She simply disappeared. We were told she was squatting in a flat off the Earlham Road somewhere but when John went round there to find out about it they said that she'd not been living there."

"They? Who exactly were they?"

"Two young girls. One of them John recognised actually. She'd been a friend of Diana's – I think her name was Amy."

Ketch produced a photograph of Amy Speedwell. "Was this the girl you saw, Mr Wescott ?" Mr Wescott extended a flabby hand. There was a brief pause.

"I'm fairly certain it was her, yes."

"Tell me now," said Ketch showing him a photograph of Tracey Fishwick. "Do you also recognise this girl? She was associated with Diana."

Mr Wescott frowned. "The face is familiar to me but I can't exactly place her."

"Do you still keep any of Diana's belongings? Did she keep a diary?"

"She did keep a diary, yes. After she went missing, we kept all her stuff. Everything is there upstairs, exactly as it was when she..."

Mrs Wescott tailed off, eyes brimming with tears. Mr Wescott looked faintly embarrassed by this sudden display of emotion.

"Do you mind if we take a look at Diana's bedroom? WPC Hughes here will look after you."

Mr Wescott heaved himself out of his chair and shuffled out of the room towards the stairs.

"It's the first on the left," he said, ushering Ketch and MacKenzie forwards. "I'm coming up – I need the bathroom – Waterworks not too good."

The two police officers entered a small bedroom whose walls had been painted a vivid, almost psychedelic pink. There were two posters, one advertising an American rap group. The other one had a sign which said 'legalise pot.' There was a small bed with pink sheets and three small teddy bears and a dressing table, crammed with cosmetics. In the adjoining wardrobe was a collection of T-shirts, cheap short skirts and high heeled shoes. MacKenzie leafed through them as Ketch listened to Mr Wescott urinating loudly and intermittently in the adjoining bathroom. Ketch opened a small bedside cabinet. Inside was a packet of cigarettes, a pile of paperbacks, and a small clasp bound diary with a glittering pink cover. He opened the diary. The legend ran: 'Day-to-day Diary 2003' and below this was scribbled the name Diana in childish handwriting. He turned and found MacKenzie clutching a small netbook.

"This might be useful," he commented.

Outside on the landing, the two men found Mr Wescott in the process of zipping up his fly.

"The WPC tells us you found Diana's body not far from here but she wouldn't tell us exactly where. I didn't like to press her further Chief Inspector because of the way my wife is. She suffers badly from her nerves you see."

"Her body was found in a tunnel underneath the Earlham Road."

"Where the bus went down the other day?"

"That's right. Tell me, Mr Wescott, when you were running the pub in the early part of the millennium, were you aware of the tunnel in the area?"

"There were stories of the tunnel, yes, though we imagined those accounts to be nothing more than old wives' tales. The pub is old of course. It dates back to Queen Mary's reign. We had some historian chap from the University come to check it out. He said it was genuine alright."

"But you never found the entrance to the tunnel?"

"No, I think we should have noticed such a thing if it had been there."

"We need to take a look at these items, Mr Wescott. They may provide us with evidence."

"Certainly. Anything I can do to help."

"Oh, one other thing – at the time of Diana's disappearance she was living in some sort of squat off the Earlham Road. You say you've visited it. You wouldn't happen to have the address?"

"Certainly – I can't bring it exactly bring it to mind but I'll dig it out for you."

"Did your daughter ever introduce you to this girl called Amy Speedwell?"

"Yes, as I said earlier, I remember Amy well. She was a friend of Diana's from the secondary school – they used to hang out together – I think that's the modern phrase for it. A tall girl with dark hair – rather full of herself. Bit of a dominating character. I had the feeling that she wasn't an especially good influence on Diana."

By lunchtime, the sky was overcast and a light drizzle had begun to fall. MacKenzie parked the car back at HQ and Ketch passed the next hour with a pint and whiskey chaser in The Grapes before returning to his desk. When he got there, he found DC Thomas waiting for him.

"A couple of things for you, sir. Here's the address for Amy Speedwell's father - and another thing – I checked CRO for 2003. Nothing. But in 2002 the three girls were brought into questioning a prostitution charge. The neighbours had complained about the comings and goings at the flat off the Earlham Road. The case was investigated by two DCs but the girls were let off with a caution. However, I did manage to trace the owner of the flat. She's one Lorraine Birch, a known prostitute who has considerable form. She's still going. And we also have an address for her. She has connections with a nightclub in the Prince of Wales Road. The place is called the Red Dragon."

Good results Dave. Let's find this Birch character and see what she has to say for herself. I take it she was interviewed at the time of Diana Wescott's disappearance?"

"She was, though her statement is only a brief one. You want me to bring her in this afternoon?"

"Don't bother bringing her in. We'll pay her a visit instead – I take it you've contacted Amy Speedwell's father?"

"He's agreed to speak to us this evening. I've set up a meet in Aylsham at six pm today."

"Good. Another thing – I want you to make an enquiry at the University – the History Department. See if you can find someone there who has a knowledge of the city's tunnel system."

"I'll get onto it straight away."

The trip to Aylsham yielded nothing of great significance. Michael Speedwell had divorced his wife two years after the disappearance of his daughter Amy, and was now living in a small flat in Red Lion Street, overlooking a butcher's shop. He showed Ketch and MacKenzie into a shabby, dimly lit sitting room and served them coffee in stained mugs.

"Amy was always something of a tearaway. After she went up to secondary school I must admit we both entirely lost control of her. By the time she was in year 10 she was going to clubs and had developed a booze problem. There was an incident when she was in her last year involving an attack on a student and she was suspended along with Diana Wescott. Then she left us and set up in the flat off the Earlham Road with two of her mates. We didn't see her again after that."

"Were you aware that she had a drug habit?"

"I suspected as much but I could never prove it. She was hyper much of the time and prone to fits of extreme violence. On one occasion she attacked my wife with a knife – injured her quite badly, actually."

"And you reported it?"

"We chose not to – things were bad enough anyway."

"Did you ever visit the flat in Norwich?"

"On two occasions we went there, once to drop off some of her belongings."

"Were you aware of how the three girls were earning a living there?"

"We had our suspicions."

"Did Amy ever mention a woman called Lorraine Birch?" Ketch showed him a photograph.

"I can't be sure – I don't think so. On the second visit, there was a man there – an Asian guy. He was quite aggressive towards us until we explained who we were. We didn't fancy the look of him."

"Would you be able to describe him to me?"

"Hardly – it's such a long time ago. Since Amy disappeared I try to forget. They say that time heals us but it's not entirely true."

By the time Ketch and MacKenzie got back to Norwich it was already getting dark and still raining. Ketch got MacKenzie to drop him off in the city centre and began walking the rest of the way. He always found that walking was an aid to concentration. It helped clear his mind considerably.

As he cut his way through the meandering streets of the old mediaeval part of the city, he tried to unravel the mystery of the girl's disappearance and Diana Wescott's subsequent brutal murder. It seems increasingly likely to him that the three girls were the victims of organised crime and there was no doubt in his mind that the key to this mystery lay in the link with Lorraine Birch.

When he finally arrived at the flat he could see that all the lights were on. Letting himself in, he found Carol in the hallway, dragging a large suitcase towards the bedroom door. She turned and gave him a faint smile.

"You're back then," he observed, clumsily stating the obvious.

"We got back over an hour ago. I put Sean straight to bed. He's exhausted, poor thing. I think the journey was just a bit too much for him. I see you haven't bothered to restock the fridge," she concluded, unable to restrain herself. Ketch frowned.

"Some of it went off."

"It will if you don't use it. Can you give me a hand with this?"

He dragged the suitcase into the bedroom, lifting it onto the bed. "What's in this? Gold ingots?"

"I bought a few things – souvenirs. So how have you been then?"

"Busy," he replied. He rarely unburdened himself about the job. It was an aspect of his personality which Carol found hard to accept.

"I put the beer and whiskey bottles in the recycling bin," she continued. "You could at least have washed them out after you finished them. I take it that you're still drinking heavily then?"

"Yes."

There was a pained silence. "You haven't asked me how the trip went?"

"You texted me about it – remember?" This was going nowhere. Then, at last, he said: "I think I might go out for a walk."

Leaving the flat, he made his way down by the river. The place was deserted at this hour save for a solitary dog walker. Despite Carrol's mini break, nothing much had changed between them. If anything, the gulf appeared to have widened.

Lorraine Birch lived in a row of respectable looking terraced houses next to the ancient parish church in Hellesdon. It seemed ironic to Ketch that a woman of her reputation and background should be living here in polite suburbia. MacKenzie parked the squad car and the two men walked up a short gravel drive adjacent to a well-stocked garden populated by garden gnomes and a priapic Pan figure, cast in black resin, the latter providing the only clue to the owner's occupation as a brothel keeper.

They had almost reached the front door when it opened, revealing a tall, well-manicured blonde in her early 50s. She was impeccably dressed in a well-tailored black skirt and top which sported a generous amount of suntanned cleavage. Expensive but tasteful earrings and an elaborate Egyptian styled necklace completed the overall effect.

"Chief Inspector Price, I presume?" she said. The voice had a strong tinge of Essex and was smooth and almost commanding in its effect. Ideal for a Madame, thought Ketch.

"You presume right," he replied.

"Please do come in – both of you. I took the liberty of preparing some tea for us."

Ketch said a polite thank you as they passed down a wide hallway containing a number of framed erotic lithographs showing fauns and satyrs indulging in abandoned congress.

They entered a spacious lounge containing more framed works along similar lines, an expensive mahogany writing desk, a widescreen TV, black, leather three-piece and 1970s style foldaway bar with overhead lights. They were served tea by a young Asian man in a dark suit who was probably no more than 23 according to Ketch's estimation. He wondered if he was her toy boy.

"How exactly can I assist you, Inspector?" she asked.

"Ten years ago you owned a flat in Dale Street, off the Earlham Road here in Norwich," he said, reaching for his bone china cup.

"I own and have owned a number of different properties in the city and beyond," she answered. "I believe you have to speculate to accumulate – wouldn't you agree?"

Ketch ignored the question. "The flat in question was occupied at the time by three young women – one of them was a girl called Diana Wescott. Did you ever meet her?"

"Not that I recall. I make it a point of having no contact with tenants – in fact, I never have done. I leave that side of the business to my husband Ranjit. He and I run a nightclub in the Prince of Wales Road. The Red Dragon – you may have heard of it?" Ketch nodded.

"I know of it. Perhaps your husband knew of Diana Wescott?"

"Most possibly – I would have to ask him about that."

"You were aware that these girls were working as prostitutes?"

"No, I didn't know that."

"But you admit to having run a brothel?"

"That was some years ago and in a different location – great Yarmouth, to be precise. And that was also before I met my husband. My business affairs these days are strictly according to the letter of the law."

"Glad to hear it. So, to the best of your knowledge, you have never had contact with Diana Wescott or the two other girls who lived there – Amy Speedwell and Tracey Fishwick?"

"The names are not familiar to me – why do you ask?"

"Because the first was a murder victim and the other two have since disappeared."

Outside in the car, Ketch lit a cigarette and wound down the window to exhale. Then, turning to MacKenzie, he said: "Let's check out this Ranjit character. Ask Dave to look into him. And I want you to go through Birch's original statement for me – you noticed the inconsistency I suppose?"

"That she claimed not to have any prior knowledge of the three girls? Yes, I thought that was suspicious."

"It's more than suspicious, Tim. She's certainly hiding something. What time are we seeing Professor Presbury at the University?"

Tim looked at his watch. "In about an hour."

"Then let's drop in first at the Campus canteen. I could murder a fry up."

Professor Bernard Presbury leaned back in his chair, his hands behind his head. A tall, swarthy man in his early 30s, he was, to Ketch's seasoned eyes, the personification of an academic with his corduroy jacket, its leather elbow patches, colourful shirt and goatee beard.

"You ask me about the city's tunnel system, inspector. I can tell you that the city's tunnels go back to at least mediaeval times. Some of them were used for storage of precious goods, others were built much later during the English Civil War, though a few date from Queen Mary's reign and its religious persecutions."

"Were any of these tunnels linked to specific houses?"

"Yes, we believe so, though of course, in many cases those properties have long since vanished. At the moment one of our postgraduates is putting together a detailed map of the tunnels and attempting to link them to certain historical properties and events in the history of this city. It's not an easy task of course. Here, let me show you a map of what he's achieved so far."

The professor opened a filing cabinet behind his desk and produced a large folded map, spreading it out on his desk. Ketch and MacKenzie stared at the web of lines. Ketch pointed to the Earlham Road.

"It suggests here that this tunnel runs all the way down to the pub," he observed.

"The Leaping Hare. Yes. That's correct, though it doesn't anymore and of course, it wasn't always a pub. In Queen Mary's reign, it was the home of one John Wyatt, a religious dissenter. A warrant was issued for his arrest but when the Queen's men arrived to enforce it, they found the house deserted. He was later captured and put to the stake. You'll notice that a number of these tunnels interconnect. Here, for example, the tunnels beneath Ketts Hill – there's an absolute warren of tunnels, probably dug there during the time of Kett's rebellion against the authorities."

"Tell me, have you explored any of these tunnels?"

"One or two, in conjunction with the university's speleological society, yes. The Earlham Road tunnel that you are interested in has an access point from underneath a grotto which lies in the park indirectly opposite from the pub. There's an old doorway which is still accessible."

"I don't suppose you could show us the route – take us there."

"I'd be more than delighted, Inspector. Just name the time."

"How about tomorrow afternoon?"

The professor consulted his mobile phone. "I have a seminar with third-year students at one. How about 2.30 then?"

"Agreed."

"You'll need hard hats by the way – I'll supply the rest."

Back at HQ, DC Thomas had been waiting for his two colleagues to arrive. There was a look of jubilation about him which Ketch knew of old.

"Good news, I take it?"

"That line of enquiry Tim asked me about..."

"About Birch's husband, Ranjit?"

"Yes, about him – the two of them are the proprietors of a nightclub on the Prince of Wales Road."

"The Red Dragon. We already know that. What else?"

"I checked CRO under his full name: Ranjit Hardeep Abdullah. Turns out he was interviewed in 2006 along with two other men, also originally from Pakistan. Their names are Labib Jaleel and Fahid Rodini. All three were arrested under suspicion of grooming two young girls from Norwich. The case would have gone to trial only the victims decided to change their statements. The DCI investigating the case – DCI Roberts at the time – has since retired – thought they might have been got at by a third man whose identity was never known."

Ketch recalled DCI Roberts, a short, stocky Welshman with a severe drinking problem. He had crossed paths with him in the past over a drug trafficking case in Thetford.

"Nothing since then I take it?"

"Nothing on record. Abdullah appears to be extraordinarily wealthy. The nightclub is a successful venue especially since also it has a casino, enjoyed by some of the wealthy residents of the county. Oh – one other thing. The third man, Rodini, was accused of rape by prostitutes working in the Hellesdon area but that charge was also dropped. That was two years ago."

"You have been busy. Good. Let's pay Abdullah a visit. This evening will do fine. It'll also be an opportunity to check out the nightclub. Tomorrow Tim and I are going caving so you can deputise for us."

DC Thomas raised his eyebrows.

"I'm entirely serious," Ketch added.

Friday night at the Red Dragon nightclub was always busy. The inside of the premises was large and palatial. No expense had been spared in providing it with a luxurious, high chrome finish. At one end was a large round stage with three metal poles. Suspended on them were three female dancers clad only in bras and brief knickers. They gyrated with consummate ease, opening, closing and twisting their legs as the deafening music pumped out a rhythm suggesting to its audience both delirium and sexual congress.

Ketch made his way over to the bar as MacKenzie continued to feast his eyes on the trio of pole dancers. A tall black bartender caught his eye.

"Can I help you, gents?"

Ketch showed his warrant card. "Police officers – here to see Mr Abdullah."

"Wait here please – I'll see if the boss is available."

He disappeared through a door behind the bar and 5 minutes passed. Ketch looked around at the clientele. Although many of them were young, the company seated round the casino table at the far end were distinctly middle-aged and prosperous looking. Among them he was sure he could make out the faces of a couple of Conservative councillors and their opulent looking wives. Clearly, the Red Dragon nightclub catered for all tastes.

The bartender said: "This way please," and they passed through a back door and up a flight of red-carpeted steps.

Abdullah sat in a room furnished with full-length mirrors, an art nouveau standard lamp black desk and matching black swivel chairs. On the two walls which were not lined with mirrors hung three paintings which Kedge immediately recognised as the work of a famous Victorian erotic artist. They appeared to be originals and were highly valuable.

Abdullah stood to his full 6'6" and offered Ketch a large, muscular left-hand. "Welcome to my palace of pleasure and entertainment," he said. "How can I help you, Chief Inspector?"

Ketch and MacKenzie sat down and Ketch produced a photograph of Diana Wescott. "This is Diana Wescott – she disappeared 10 years ago. At the time of her disappearance, she was living in a flat with two other women just off the Earlham Road in Norwich. You and your wife were the joint landlords of that flat. Do you recognise her? Did you have any personal dealings with her at that time?"

Abdullah studied the photograph. "I have a vague memory of her. Yes, I believe I did meet her – it was here at the club. I employed her on a temporary basis as a waitress. But she didn't last – she was suspected of pilfering from the bar cash register."

"You knew she was a prostitute?"

"I suspected she had a drug problem so it doesn't come as a surprise to me to learn that."

Ketch showed him the photographs of Tracey Fishwick and Amy Speedwell. "Have you ever seen these girls?"

"Who are they?"

"They were Diana's flatmates."

"I don't recognise either of them."

Ketch had been glad to leave the nightclub. The atmosphere was claustrophobic and faintly surreal. The place oozed opulence. Clearly its success was based not just on ticket sales alone. Several of the pole dancers appear to have assignations with the punters and at the back of the premises was a flight of stairs with rooms at the top leading off. He also recognised at least three well-known drug dealers among the punters by the bar.

He got MacKenzie to drop him by Gentleman's Walk in the city and started to make his way on foot back to his flat. He had just got to the top of St Giles Street when he heard a vehicle behind him accelerating at speed. He turned and saw a large black 4x4 hurtling towards him. It swerved in his direction and, mounting the pavement, attempted to drive straight at him. With seconds to spare, he threw himself into the opening of an alleyway, banging his knees on the pavement as he fell and rolled over, He got up and looked down the road to see if he could glimpse the license plate of the vehicle but by now it was too late. When he stood up he found that he was trembling from shock.

DC Dave Thomas put down the two takeaway lattes and placed the pink covered diary on Ketch's desk.

"Well? Anything useful?" said Ketch.

"Yes and no," replied Thomas. "A great deal of the entries are little more than teenage rantings. Feuds with other girls of her acquaintance, that sort of thing. However, there are a number of cryptic entries referring to names." He picked up the diary and opened it. "Here for example, January 20: 'Waited in for JC but didn't show. Desperate for C and some S.' And here again on February 6: 'FR told us we have a big occasion coming up – the full works. Me and AS providing the floorshow. Insisted we get up front payment – FR agreed.' There are numerous entries of a similar nature."

Ketch scratched his forehead and frowned. "C and S could be cocaine and speed I guess. The big floor show? It could be anything."

"There are also references to someone in the diary she calls Big Daddy. No other name is supplied."

"Could be anyone. What about Abdullah's name?"

"It doesn't occur. I'll leave the diary with you then?"

Ketch nodded. "You've been over Lorraine Birch's original statement?"

"In detail. She mentions the fact that she met Diana Wescott on one occasion when the rent was late. She'd visited the flat with the agent. This was in the June of 2003 – the month prior to her disappearance."

"Just as we thought – clearly she's been lying to us."

"You look as if you'd been in a fight," Thomas observed, pointing to the large bruise Ketch had sustained to his forehead when he'd had to avoid the 4x4.

"Just a brief encounter, nothing more," he joked, but inwardly he was disturbed by the thought that it had been such a close shave. He suspected that whoever had killed Diana Wescott also had friends in the underworld who were prepared to take extreme measures to block the investigation. From now on he must keep his wits about him.

Professor Bernard Presbury met Ketch and MacKenzie at the park gates where a short, middle-aged man in his early 60s, dressed in blue overalls, also waited.

"This is Mr Rowlands, the park keeper," explained the professor. "You may be interested in what he has to say Chief Inspector."

"I was telling the professor here we've had a deal of trouble over a period of years here in the park."

"Oh? What kind of trouble?"

"Complaints from neighbours mostly about cars parking by the road here late at night, slamming of doors and so on. I put it down to local kids. It wouldn't surprise me. I just wish whoever they were they'd take their rubbish home with them. Every week I have to clear out the tunnel with all the stuff they have left behind them – bottles, food wrappings and so on. Recently it's got even worse. I complained to the police about it several times but all they did was send round one of those community officers to talk to me – some bloke with a foreign accent. What use is that to anyone, I ask you?"

Ketch nodded sympathetically but he didn't reply.

"Well, the entrance to the grotto is just over here," said the professor, indicating an elaborate Victorian water fountain to their immediate left. "The door isn't immediately visible as you can see, Inspector."

He stepped forwards and pushed away some thick bunches of ivy, revealing an ancient oak door which he then opened."You'll need this torch," he said, jumping over the base of the fountain. Ketch and the curator followed suit and they entered a long narrow tunnel where there was little headroom. After a few paces, the tunnel broadened out into a large cave whose sides had been decorated with quartz pebbles. "Amazing isn't it?" observed the professor. "This tunnel entrance was started in the early 1800s by a local merchant, one Jeffrey Hawkins, a woollen importer. He used it for masked balls. Then, in the late 1860s, it was sold to a printing magnate and not much used after that. Not, that is, until relatively recently, judging by some of the debris here. I take your point about the rubbish, Mr Rowlands."

"I've even found some condoms here," said the disgruntled Mr Rowlands. "God knows what these youngsters get up to down here."

Ketch shone his torch into the far corner where he could make out the outline of a door. "Where does this lead to?"

"Beyond that door? It's a continuation of the tunnel – it goes straight under the Earlham Road and connects with the other side. That tunnel is much older than the bit that we are standing in now. It dates back to at least the 17th century but I suspect that it's probably much older than that. You won't get the door open – it hasn't been used for many years."

Putting his arm to the door, Ketch shoved. There was a creaking sound, then it shifted and he was covered in a shower of dust. He shone the torch through the aperture. On the other side, he could make out what looked like a set of chains stapled to the tunnel wall.

When they got back to Bethel Street, DC Thomas was waiting for them.

"I've been doing some more digging," he explained.

"Go on."

"It turns out that both Ranjit Abdullah and Labib Jalill were questioned in Ipswich over two years ago concerning the murder of two prostitutes."

"I recall the case. The taxi driver, Stuart French, was found guilty of the murders."

"So he was, but in the early stages of the investigation it was thought that French, Abdullah and Jalill were all running a prostitution racket which also involved supplying cocaine and E's."

"Remind me who was the CIO in charge of that case."

"DCI Briggs."

"See if you can get him to e-mail us the case file contents will you, Dave? I need to check them out."

When DC Thomas had left, Ketch popped out to McDonald's where he armed himself with a large cheeseburger and latte before returning to the office. He opened his laptop and googled: Tunnels, Norwich. There were numerous references to the underground passageways in the old city, mainly from past editions of the Eastern Daily Press. One reference, in particular, caught his attention. It was an article from the university's in-house publication referring to a lecture given by Professor Presbury as part of the Norwich Festival. The lecture was headed 'Norwich's mysterious underground' and provided a summary of his talk given over a year ago. There was nothing in the text which surprised Ketch. The professor described the network of tunnels including those at Ketts Hill and the Earlham Road. What fascinated him, however, was the accompanying photograph. There, in the front row of the audience and unmistakably clear and seated next to each other, were John Wescott and Lorraine Birch. He felt a sudden rush of adrenaline, put on his coat and went next door to fetch Thomas and MacKenzie.

It took just 48 hours to break down John Wescott and Lorraine Birch. Wescott broke first admitting to the murder of his daughter, but it took a while for him to confess to his collaboration with Abdullah and Birch. As for Abdullah and Jalill, they remained obdurate until the last and only cooperated when Wescott and Birch's signed confessions, implicating them, were presented to them. Following a search of Wescott's house, a detailed map was discovered of both the

Earlham Road tunnel and a network of tunnels extending under and beyond Ketts Hill.

On a rain drenched day in late March, Ketch found himself standing on the spur of the eastern end of Ketts Hill, from where he obtained a panoramic view of the city. But today he was not admiring the view. Instead, he was looking at the mortal remains of Amy Speedwell and Tracey Fishwick, two young girls who had been egregiously abused by a gang of men who regarded their prey as little more than to use Abdullah's own words, 'meat.'

The case had far reaching consequences. Among the list of members of the so-called 'Tunnel Club,' who made it their business to attend those nocturnal sessions beneath the city of Norwich, were several well-known local councillors and politicians from across the county and beyond. It was no surprise therefore when resignations came thick and fast in the local and national media.

Ketch's abiding memory of the case was one which persisted in haunting him for years afterwards. It was the moment when Wescott finally admitted to the brutal torture and murder of his daughter. That sly, gloating smile of his was something he could never quite expunge from his thoughts. For nights after the interrogation, he found himself waking in the grip of a fast fading nightmare where all he knew was that he had been trapped underground.

Perhaps it was something to do with the fact that he was claustrophobic by nature, or maybe there was something in the old adage that the evil which men do lives on after them.

At least the case had one positive result. In the September which followed the trial and sentencing of the four, Ketch finally decided to attend AA sessions and began the long and difficult road to his recovery.

DEAD MAN'S SHOES

It was November 5th and it was cold and wet. Ketch had good reason to remember for not only was it the date of the conspirator, it was also his birthday.

DCI Ketch had been born under the astrological sign of Scorpio and, according to popular astrology, persons born thus made good detectives.

Ketch often wondered whether he was a good detective. He lacked the thoroughness of some of his former colleagues, but possessed a dogged determination and staying power which often placed him in good stead. Ketch was also something of a loner, a maverick who had a healthy disdain for innovation for its own sake. In his opinion, the job as he termed it, was too much concerned with paperwork and navel gazing. Experience and intuition had always been his watchwords and at his age, he had no intention of modifying his perspective in the pursuit of crime.

Carol Hennessy, Ketch's partner, held his son Sean in her arms as another cascade of light and colour filled the dark autumnal sky.

"There it goes!" she shouted. Ketch smiled, savouring the moment. At the age of 52, he had dreaded becoming a father for the second time. Since his wife Anne had died, he had condemned himself to a state of melancholy bachelorhood. Finding love with Carol had changed all that. When she had fallen pregnant, he'd doubted his ability to take on the role once more into a nappy changing and doting dad, but when the inevitable happened, he had surprised himself at how easily he had slipped into the part. It had been like putting on an old pair of gloves. True, he regretted the sleepless nights, but it had given him a new lease of life and a means of fulfilment outside the job.

"You take him," said Carol. Ketch obliged as Carol reached into her rucksack for the thermos flask and then poured out a cup of tomato soup. He could feel the tension in Sean's diminutive body as a giant Catherine wheel exploded into life. If he hadn't been here he told himself, participating in this colourful pandemonium, he'd be at home, dosing fitfully over Scotch.

He was dog tired, he had to admit it. For the last two weeks he and the team had been monitoring a house in the Earlham Road. Two Chinese students from the University had been operating a cannabis factory in one of the large houses there. Ketch believed they'd been part of the Triad and that there were several houses like this right across East Anglia. They had rented the house using headed notepaper from the University in order to supply fake references. Someone must have tipped them off, for on the Sunday night prior to the planned arrests, a large plume of smoke had been seen issuing from one of the bedroom windows. When the team broke down the front door and entered the property they discovered that the first floor of the house was a blazing inferno and that one of the residents had already succumbed to smoke inhalation and the other was severely burned. The two had tried to destroy all evidence of their scheme with tragic results.

There was a loud explosion, followed immediately by oohs and aahs from the crowd. Sean squealed again and struggled in his arms, wanting to be let down.

"Let me take him," said Carol, handing him the thermos flask. His left thigh started to vibrate. He delved into his trouser pocket and, pulling out his phone, answered it.

"Sorry to disturb your bonfire celebrations, sir," said DS MacKenzie. How familiar those words were, and how trite the apology.

"Where are you?"

"I'm at the Saddlebow Industrial Park in Kings Lynn."

"What's up?"

"A security guard here noticed banging sounds coming from a container about half an hour ago. We just managed to break the main door open. 20 occupants inside –illegals, we suspect, probably from Afghanistan. 15 of them dead, three comatose and badly dehydrated, two compos mentis though they speak only a few words of English. They're being attended to by the ambulance crew at present."

"Have you contacted a translator yet?"

"I've done that – a Mr Khan. He's meeting us at the Lynn A and E in about an hour's time."

"What about Stoppard?" Stoppard was the pathologist who had largely replaced Carol when she undertook her maternity leave. A large, pompous man with an appetite for expensive living, he annoyed Ketch intensely and was renowned for the carelessness of his method.

Fortunately for him, his errors were often covered up by friends in high places, not least the chief constable.

"He's just arrived though I suspect there's not much for him to do."

"I'll see you in half an hour." Ketch pressed the off key on his phone, then rang for a taxi. The first attempt and the second failed which, given the date, was hardly surprising. On the third attempt, he was promised a waiting time of 15 minutes.

"Do you really have to go?" asked Carol, after he'd explained the circumstances.

"Yes, I really have to go."

"Then you'd better the phone for a taxi for us too – or had you forgotten?" she added, caustically.

Ketch's cab arrived 30 minutes later. Carol and Sean had already left the park and returned to their flat by the riverside and Ketch had been left to stand at the entrance to the park. By now it began to rain heavily and he was feeling decidedly bad tempered. Conscious of his soaked trousers and coat, he reached into his pocket for his packet of cigarettes. The taxi drivers face loomed in the rear view mirror.

"Sorry, no smoking," he instructed.

Ketch cursed and put away the fags. For the remainder of the journey he remained silent and amused himself by staring out into the darkness. The cab sped through the city where groups of intoxicated revellers spilled out onto the streets, clutching their bottles of lager. Then westwards through Taverham where the roads were engulfed in darkness and he glimpsed through the trees bright constellations of fireworks peppering the night sky.

Ketch was familiar with the Saddlebow Industrial Estate. Three months ago a similar scenario had been acted out when a container from the Netherlands had been discovered containing nine illegal immigrants from Somalia. All were alive but much emaciated and exhausted from their intercontinental journey and all were subsequently repatriated. Suspicion had fallen on a Russian Mafia organisation known as the Bratva (thief in law), a disparate network consisting mainly of ex-KGB personnel who were behind a large proportion of the sex slave industry in Britain and France and who also had links with the heroin trade. They had bases in Latvia France and Sweden. Much of this information has been provided by Interpol but when it came to proof, that was an altogether more difficult challenge.

One name, in particular, had come up: Sergei Vasnev. Vasnev was an importer of Oriental goods and, trading under the name of Rainbow, had a distribution centre in both Cambridge and Norfolk. The firm's main Norfolk office was situated in Kings Lynn.

Ketch peered out of the car window as the taxi slowed to a halt. In front of the tall buildings he could make out the container and a collection of uniformed officers, straddled by the familiar barrier tape. He got out, paid the driver, then pulled the lapels of his damp coat tight around his neck. He wished that he'd brought a hat. As he greeted MacKenzie, a corpulent figure emerged from the back of the container, his face bathed in sweat. It was the pathologist, Mike Stoppard.

"Well?" asked Ketch.

"Fairly routine. They all died of natural causes as far as I can ascertain. A combination of hypothermia and lack of water. There's no sign of foul play."

Ketch climbed up into the container and was met by the stench of faeces and urine. He put a handkerchief to his nose and looked round the interior. Crumpled clothes, blankets, cigarette packets, a few books and the remains of takeaway meals were strewn across the floor.

"They've probably been in here for weeks," said Stoppard. "I'm not surprised so many died, given the overnight temperatures recently."

Ketch turned to MacKenzie. "Where are the survivors?"

"They've been taken to the Oakington Immigration Centre in Cambridgeshire."

"By whose authority?"

"By my authority." A short grey-haired man in a dark suit stepped forward. "John Sims. Chief Immigration Officer for NOREAST. I don't think we've met, inspector."

"Chief Inspector. No, I haven't had the pleasure," Ketch replied somewhat testily. "Couldn't transportation have waited an hour or so?"

"Regulations I'm afraid. It's out of my hands."

"I find that hard to believe. What about the container?" he asked MacKenzie who had been standing awkwardly observing this interchange.

"The vehicle is the property of a Latvian haulage company. I ran their head office in Riga but there was no reply – probably too late in the day. I'll try again in the morning."

The following morning found Ketch trudging his way through fogbound city streets to HQ where he had arranged to meet DS MacKenzie. As the car sped through the outskirts of Norwich and headed for the Cambridge Road, Ketch wound down his passenger window and lit his third cigarette of the morning. He was not in the best of moods. He had travelled back from Kings Lynn at around ten pm with MacKenzie and asked to be dropped off in Tombland so he could stretch his limbs. When he got to the flat he found it in darkness. Carol and Sean had long since retired. There was a note on the kitchen table which read: 'Dinner in the oven. If cold, suggest you microwave it. C.'

He'd opened the oven door, stared down at the chicken and congealed gravy, then decided not to bother with it. He'd opened the fridge, taken out a can of real ale, and downed it in one go. Then he'd reached for the whiskey bottle and poured himself a generous measure. The offering in the oven had been one of those pre-packaged, instant meals.

Carol was not the best cook in the world and Ketch himself had a culinary range which consisted of three meals. At around midnight and feeling somewhat intoxicated, he turned in, trying not to wake his partner. For a long while he lay there, sleep evading him, pondering his mismanagement of the Earlham Road cannabis affair. Of course, he had done nothing to jeopardise the mission, but that was not how DC Batarde had perceived the affair. Someone in his team was an informant, of that he was certain. He sincerely hoped that drugs money was not at the bottom of it. The question was: who exactly? Certainly not DS MacKenzie – he was far too straight. Then there was DC Thomas – not likely. And Willis? What about Willis? Willis had once confided in a reporter and suffered the consequences but Ketch didn't think he was corruptible. Still, you never knew...

He finished his cigarette, threw the butt out of the car window, then shut it. A strong odour of cigarette smoke now filled the car.

"I'm sorry about that," he apologised to MacKenzie. McKenzie smiled.

"No problem, sir."

They were now on the notoriously dangerous A10, in a queue of traffic and hemmed in by large articulated lorries.

"Any luck with the Riga phone number?" Ketch enquired.

"As a matter of fact, yes. The driver was one Alex Belinsky. Apparently, there were two drivers. The first driver took the container from Riga to Prague. Belinsky then took over and completed the journey after an eight-hour stop at Rotterdam. I have liaised with the Suffolk HQ. They have an address for him at a boarding house in Lowestoft."

They turned off onto a slip road and soon they were heading along a narrow, tree-lined road which then gave way to flat barren fields on either side. After about 15 minutes the car took a sharp left turn and a sign marked: 'HM Oakington Immigration Services' loomed into view.

"Looks just like an open prison," McKenzie commented.

"Ketch nodded. "It's a bit less open than you might imagine," he replied. The car slowed to the barrier and Ketch showed his warrant card to the security officer.

"I believe we are expected." The man nodded and raised the barrier. As they approach the main doors to the prison, a dark haired woman in her early 20s approached them.

"Belinda Gray. I'm the liaison officer. Come this way gentleman." She led the way down a series of corridors which gave way to a large room containing rows of tables and chairs. "Our visitor room," she explained. "There are five of them but I'm not sure how you want to handle this."

"We'll see them individually," said Ketch.

"Oh, this is Nasir, our translator. He will be assisting us."

By lunchtime Ketch was weary. None of the men could tell him much, even with the assistance of the translator who spoke the language fluently. It transpired that each of the men had paid the equivalent of £1000. For that, they were provided with a forged passport and passage across Eastern Europe. They did not know the names of their accomplices and had no idea of the route they had taken. Each one of them gave a detailed description of a man in his mid-50s who had interviewed them prior to the journey, but they had no idea of who he was.

By the time they had reached their first destination – probably Prague – another man had appeared – possibly a Russian. This second man had talked extensively to the lorry driver but then had disappeared. After that, they had not seen the light of day for over a week. When the container had reached its final destination, they had already run out of food and water. Those who were still able, had banged on the wall of the container in order to summon help. This had gone on for two days but no one had come to their assistance. After that, they had become too weak to persist further with pleas for help and were convinced that they would die like their companions.

On the way back to Norwich they stopped at a dismal roadside cafe near Huntingdon. MacKenzie brought Ketch a cappuccino and an atrophied sausage roll. Ketch looked round at the customers in the service station cafe. To his left, a group of six overhung looking men in their mid-20s stared at plates containing indigestible food. To his right, sat a young mother and her two young children were eating burgers. It seemed to him that service station cafes had much in common with Dante's vision of hell. His phone leapt into life in his trouser pocket and he answered it. It was DC Thomas

"Thomas here, sir. Something has come up."

"Then explain it to me," said Ketch, reaching for his coffee.

"There's been a shotgun incident – a fatality."

"Whereabouts?"

"Felthorpe Minor."

Ketch remembered the place – a small village adjoining the grand estate of Felthorpe, a large National Trust property set in extensive woodland near to Cromer.

"Who's the victim?"

"A Russian by the name of Sergei Vasnev. His wife returned to the house just after lunchtime to find him dead in the study. Most of his head has been blown away by a shotgun."

"Any witnesses?"

"None so far. The place is called The Vicarage. It's a detached villa on the edge of the village and there are no immediate neighbours here."

"Who's attending the incident?"

"I'm here with Willis. I've contacted Dr Stoppard and the SOCO team are on their way now."

"Very good. We should be with you in about an hour."

Turning to MacKenzie, who was halfway through his sausage roll, he said: "We have to go – you'd better take that with you."

"What's up?"

"I'll tell you on the way, but first I need a pee."

Back in the car, MacKenzie put the siren on and they sped down the A10 heading northwards. Vasnev... The news of his death had not come as a surprise to Ketch. His name had come out in connection with the Somalian immigrant incident some while back and it had been long suspected that his oriental import company served as a front for his nefarious trade in trafficking. Only a month ago, a jeweller's shop in Kings Lynn had been burgled by two men who were both Russian. They were wanted by the Czech police for the murder of a man in Prague and it was considered to be a gangland murder. Vasnev, Kings Lynn, Prague – they were all somehow connected.

By the time they reached Felthorpe Minor, a dank mist had once more descended and darkness was already encroaching. Under the dense canopy of trees which lined the road that darkness seemed even more profound than usual. Beyond them stood a tall, opulent looking Victorian mansion built in the Dutch style, common to Norfolk. On the top of the steps facing the front entrance stood a rather apprehensive looking DC Thomas.

"Mrs Vasnev is in the lounge," he explained. "WPC Simmonds is with her."

"And the body?"

"This way."

Thomas led the two men down a dark terracotta painted hallway, lined with oil paintings, depicting a series of hunting scenes. Ketch detected a strong odour of Russian tobacco – probably sobranie. They entered a large room, lined from ceiling to floor with antiquarian books which were in a variety of languages.

Behind a Regency style writing desk lay the body of a man. He was dressed in an expensive striped suit and a pink shirt which had been stained with blood. On the desk in front of him were strewn numerous bloodstained papers and behind him, one of the bookcases was peppered with gouts of blood and brain matter. His head must have exploded like a pomegranate with the impact of what Ketch imagined must have been a shotgun blast. Taken by surprise by the grotesque nature of the scene, DS MacKenzie raised a handkerchief to his mouth.

"Not a pretty sight is it?" commented Mike Stoppard who had been bending over the body and was examining the shattered remains of the victim's head. He turned and grinned at Ketch as if such sites

142

were routine to him.

"I can think of better," Ketch replied.

"Most of the back of his head is on the bookshelf yonder," Stoppard went on as if he were describing a scene at sunset. "The problem will be extricating it from the complete works Ovid and Tacitus. Pity about the books - they are worth a bob or two."

"Shotgun blast?"

"Certainly – both barrels, judging by the state of him, and discharged at point-blank range I should imagine. The shot residue is also somewhere among those antiquarian volumes – most of it in the Walter Scott volumes. I don't envy SOCO's job quite frankly."

"Time of death?"

"Can't be sure at present – I need to get what's left of him on a slab to determine that more precisely. But at a rough guess, I should say about 4 to 5 hours ago, no more than that."

Ketch turned to DC Thomas who had been hovering in the doorway. "Who found him?"

"Mrs Vasnev. She returned home after a shopping expedition in Cromer. She's in quite a state – understandably."

Ketch looked round the room. At the far end was a set of French windows leading onto the lawn and beyond it an ornate garden with mature trees and bushes, still shrouded in mist. He walked over to the windows, trying the handle with his gloved hand and found them unlocked.

"We need to check for prints," he remarked to MacKenzie. "Okay, let's go and see the wife."

Irina Vasnev was sitting on a large basket chair in the conservatory at the back of the house, surrounded by a collection of exotic plants. Although middle-aged, she was still a woman of remarkable beauty. Long straight hair framed a pale face with high cheekbones and prominent blue eyes. She was dressed in an expensive black dress, the neckline of which was decorated with precious stones. As Ketch and MacKenzie approached she stood up and it was then that Ketch realised how tall she was, probably 6'3". Irina Vasnev extended her left hand in greeting and for a split second, Ketch wondered whether he should kiss it as one might feel appropriate in a scene from a Tolstoy novel.

"Chief Inspector," she addressed him in a strong Russian accent. "welcome to my house. I'm only sorry the circumstances could not

143

have been more amenable."

"I quite agree, Mrs Vasnev."

"Please call me Irina."

"Do you feel able to answer some questions?" She waved the officers to a chaise longue. Ketch glanced round the room. The walls were lined with Victorian watercolour landscapes and he was sure that he recognised a Turner among them. This was quite clearly a very prosperous household.

"I have already told your officer here, Mr Thomas, of the circumstances," she said, turning to acknowledge DC Thomas who all this while had been standing somewhat embarrassedly by the fireplace.

"Mrs Vasnev arrived back here at approximately 11 o'clock," Thomas offered. "Her chauffeur found Mr Vasnev in the library and told her what had happened. When she realised her husband was beyond help, she telephoned the emergency services."

"When you left your husband early this morning, how did he seem to you?"

"He was preoccupied – but that was hardly surprising."

"Why's that?"

"My husband was one of the directors of a wholesale import business. There had been some problems recently concerning the Board of Directors. He was concerned that he might not be able to overcome these problems without the support of the other board members."

"Perhaps you could be more specific?"

"I'm afraid that I can't. Sergei very rarely divulged details of such matters to me and I have never been a board member, so I am unable to help you in that regard."

"Had your husband ever talked of any animosity between himself and other members of the Board of Directors? Anyone in particular?"

Irina Vasnev opened a silver cigarette case and lit a cigarette. "Only once. Artem Dernov. The two were not especially fond of each other. His name was mentioned a few times by my husband, though I'm not sure what the source of their animosity exactly was."

"Had you noticed any change in your husband's demeanour recently? Did he seem at all worried or concerned about his safety?"

Irina thought for a moment.

"He had been talking about taking some measures to upgrade the security here at the house. He mentioned the possibility of having video surveillance though he had not got around to having it installed. He seemed very preoccupied – that is all I can tell you, inspector."

"Have there been any visitors to the house lately? This man Dernov that you mentioned, for example?"

"My husband had entertained a number of visitors – business clients in the main. Their names are in my desk diary – I can give you a list of them if you wish. Some of them were business contacts from Czechoslovakia and Latvia."

"Before you left the house this morning did your husband mention he might be receiving a visitor?"

"He told me that he had a number of business calls to make and some paperwork to attend to but no, no mention of any visitors."

"One further thing – can you recall if the French windows in the library were unlocked before you left the house this morning?"

"I have no idea if they were locked or unlocked, inspector. They would certainly have been locked last thing at night though."

"Was your husband in the habit of unlocking the windows when he worked in the library?"

"Sometimes he would go outside in order to smoke. On those occasions he would often open the windows. He was more particular about smoking than I am." She inhaled from her cigarette.

"Your husband smoked a pipe I believe?"

"Yes, how did you know that?"

"The tobacco he smoked, a fine cut sobranie, is known to me."

"My husband allowed me to smoke cigarettes in the house but he would only smoke his pipe out of doors. The only exception to this was when he was sometimes under pressure of work."

"I see. Thank you, you've been of considerable help. Of course, we shall need to look at your husband's business papers and his computer before we leave today."

"By all means."

"And if you think of anything further, any detail, no matter how seemingly insignificant, regarding your husband and his affairs, please don't hesitate to contact me."

By the time Ketch and MacKenzie left The Vicarage, it was already growing dark and a mist had risen, making the work of the SOCO team and the six accompanying uniformed officers more difficult. Two large floodlights had been mounted, providing an arc of illumination over the extensive lawns.

"Any sign of a murder weapon yet?" Ketch asked DC Thomas.

"Not yet – we've sectioned up the area and are making progress though. There's quite a large area of woodland yonder which forms part of the grounds, so we may have to resume tomorrow morning at first light."

"What about the flower beds which adjoin the French windows at the back of the property? Has anyone checked yet for footprints?"

"There were two sets of prints, one a man's, the other smaller, quite possibly a woman's. SOCO have taken casts of them both."

"Good – keep me up to speed if anything else shows up."

They made their way to the driveway where they got back into the squad car. For some moments, Ketch sat in silence. Then, lighting a cigarette, he said:

"Tim, I want you to check out this Artem Dernov for me. Look through Vasnev's correspondence, business papers etc., and see if you can find anything relevant. Do we have an address for him?"

"Yes, he lives in Fakenham."

"Good, give him a ring and let him know we want to see him – sometime tomorrow morning will do."

"I'll see to it."

"Is there a village local in the vicinity?"

"The Estate Arms – we passed it on our way here."

"I could murder a pint and a bar snack – let's see what's on offer."

Ketch did not return to the flat until late that night, having spent two hours in the Estate Arms with DS MacKenzie. He consumed copious quantity of alcohol whilst MacKenzie, Ketch's eternal ferryman, had to content himself with non-alcoholic beers. As he turned the key in the lock he noticed that the hall light was on. Carol was standing in her dressing gown looking as if she was ready to do battle with him.

"You realise, I suppose, how late it is?"

"I hadn't noticed," he replied defensively.

"It's past midnight and you've woken Sean. It took me nearly an hour to get him to sleep and now this!"

"Look, you know how it is Carol."

"Do I? As a matter of fact, I don't think I do. Plus you stink of booze. Maybe you should make an appointment with the AA. It might do you some good." With this she retreated to the bedroom, shutting the door behind her.

Ketch took his coat off and poured himself a glass of water, then made for the couch in the lounge. For some minutes he lay there, listening to the far-off sounds of drunken youths as they careered their way round the streets of the old city.

Carol was right about him. Up until six months ago he had managed to wean himself off drink completely but in recent weeks, his drinking had slowly increased. He really needed to do something about it. Of late, he had felt increasingly disconnected both from his job and from his new family. Part of him wanted to chuck it all in and take a road trip somewhere for a few months – North Wales perhaps, the land of his paternal ancestors. But the Protestant in him told him to stay put and shoulder his responsibilities He reached for the iPod Carol had given him for his birthday, a piece of kit he found that, unlike other inventions of the 21st-century, he could actually understand, and pressed the play button. The soaring retro strings of the Electric Light Orchestra soon lulled him into a profound sleep.

The following day dawned fair and the mist, which had clung to the fields from the previous evening, was slowly relinquishing its spectral grasp. MacKenzie and Ketch took the ring road south of the city and were soon on the A146, heading for Lowestoft. It was an attractive stretch of country, passing through the ancient villages of Bergh Apton and Loddon where thatched cottages huddled around ancient Saxon churches.

"I did some digging earlier this morning regarding the Rainbow Trading company," McKenzie informed Ketch as the latter lit his second cigarette.

"And?"

"Vasnev's business has links both with Czechoslovakia and the Netherlands."

"I think I knew that."

"It also has connections with two haulage firms, one in Prague and the other in Riga. Last year, two drivers were arrested in connection with drugs seizures but the authorities there were unable to establish a link with either Vasnev or Rainbow."

"Any luck with Dernov yet?"

"None I'm afraid."

"Let's check the customs and see if we can find a trace of him."

Ketch hadn't visited Lowestoft for some years and had forgotten its broad esplanade and Victorian seaside villas with their bed and breakfast signs. They checked in at the Suffolk police HQ and were introduced to a young fresh faced DS called Wilson.

"Belinsky's in interview room three," he explained. "He speaks only a few words of English so we got an interpreter in for you."

Belinsky was a short, squat man with a protruding beer belly and muscular, tattooed arms. He explained that he had picked up the container in Prague where he worked for a haulage firm called Azarov's. At Rotterdam, he checked into the holding bay by the docks where he was met by a man who paid him in cash before he took his obligatory rest period.

Ketch asked Belinsky to describe the man and then produced photographs of Vasnev and Dernov. No, it was neither of them. The man that he had met was young, no more than 30 or so with long black hair, tied in a ponytail. He had been smartly dressed and wore a black suit with patent leather shoes. He had a Russian accent. He didn't open the container and no, he hadn't heard any sounds coming from the container. He wouldn't have done so anyway because of the noise of the lorry.

He had done the same job several times before and never once suspected he might be carrying a consignment of illegal immigrants. How long were they going to detain him? He needed to phone his wife and tell her what was happening.

When Ketch exited the interview room he found MacKenzie waiting for him outside.

"The port authorities have no record of Dernov passing through immigration controls," he explained.

"You tried the airports?"

"I'm waiting for a response."

"Then let's get back to HQ. There's nothing more that we can do here."

The rest of the day proved to be equally fruitless. Ketch was still waiting for the autopsy report and SOCO 's findings but was told that they wouldn't be available until the following day. He decided not to hang around and, before leaving his office, he rang Carol. There was no reply and he left her a short message.

When he got back to the flat at six pm he had a surprise waiting for him. An envelope lay on the kitchen table which he opened. It read: Have taken Sean to mum's place for a few days. Needed a break. Have stocked up the fridge for you and left a quiche – just reheat it. Ring me if you need to – love Carol.

Ketch crumpled the note in his hand then threw it in the wastepaper bin and subsided onto the sofa. For a few moments his mind was clouded with thoughts about his own inadequacy as a father and partner to Carol. Then he got up and, putting his coat back on, left the flat, heading in the direction of The Grapes where he intended to drown his sorrows.

He woke around 4 AM. His head felt as if it had been cased in cotton wool and his throat was parched. He went to the sink and poured himself a mug of water, downing it in one go. He really must not make a habit of this he told himself. He took a quick shower, washing away yesterday's sweat, dressed, then ate breakfast, consisting of muesli and bananas. Then he put on his coat, left the flat and made his way along the banks of the River Wensum, taking advantage of the new footbridge. There were few pedestrians about at this early hour and a low mist shrouded the riverbanks, making the bare trees looks skeletal and otherworldly

 By the time he had returned to the flat, taken a nap, then glanced at his wrist watch, it was already eight o'clock. He wondered whether to ring Carol's mobile, but then thought better of it. What she needed from him at this moment was space, otherwise, things could become claustrophobic. He knew that.

In the first few months of their relationship, he had been rather cloying with her, overprotective, and she hadn't much liked it. Carol was fiercely independent and beholden to no one. She'd always been that way and it wasn't up to him to try and change her.

By 8.50 he was at his favourite coffee stall in Norwich market and by nine o'clock he'd entered the sliding doors at Bethel Street. On the first floor he found Tim MacKenzie waiting for him.

"Morning Tim. Anything to report?"

"The autopsy is just in. I left a copy on your desk. And also the prelim from SOCO, though there's nothing very surprising in it."

"What about the findings of the autopsy?"

"Much as we expected – cause of death was loss of blood caused by the gunshot blast. One curious thing though – apparently Vasnev was wearing a pair of size 6 leather shoes."

"What's curious about it?"

"He took a size 8."

"That's odd."

"Exactly my reaction. Maybe he enjoyed feeling the pinch. Something else I managed to dig up about him by the way."

"Oh?"

"He'd taken out two life-insurance policies in recent months – one of £60,000 and the other £70,000."

"Intimations of mortality…"

"Perhaps. I contacted Interpol. They're sending me everything they have on both Vasnev and Dernov."

"Still nothing more on Dernov?"

"Not a thing."

"You got the search warrant for his house?"

"Came through yesterday night."

"Then I suggest we take that trip to Fakenham."

Ketch had largely forgotten Fakenham, a once prosperous town, now showing signs of the ever encroaching recession where charity and discount shops had driven out the more traditional retailers. The Dernov residence was one of a series of large Victorian villas situated on the outskirts of the town where once, prosperous merchants had resided. On a wide tree-lined street, MacKenzie parked the car and the two climbed some stone steps to the front door. There was no response to their summons.

There isn't a mortise lock," McKenzie declared. "I think I can slip the lock with my credit card."

For a moment he jiggled his card, then the lock yielded under pressure. Ketch and MacKenzie entered a long hallway, carpeted with a huge Afghan rug and lined on both sides by sumptuous Oriental furniture. There was a smell of beeswax. At the end of the hallway, two doors led off and the first of these yielded to a large, airy sitting room which had been converted into a spacious office. On a long walnut desk sat two laptops, a printer, a mobile phone and a large pile of papers.

Ketch leafed through the papers as MacKenzie left to explore the other rooms. The files were mainly in Russian so he soon gave up. When MacKenzie finally returned, he said:

"The fridge is full and there's washing up in the sink. Looks like he just popped out for a bit."

"Let's check his most recent phone calls," Ketch replied. Reaching for the mobile phone, he paged through its memory, writing down several numbers.

"We'll check these later," he said. He sat down on the office chair and began pulling out the drawers. More files, pens and a dictaphone. He pressed the play button on the dictaphone and a voice in Russian could be heard.

"I guess we'll need an interpreter," commented MacKenzie. Ketch made no comment. He had noticed that the top drawer was locked.

"Pass me that paper knife will you?" Inserting the blade into the drawer, he gave it a quick sideways movement and the lock gave way. In the drawer was a large black file which he took out and opened.

"This might be of interest," he said. He turned the pages and a series of shots of well-endowed women presented themselves. Maria, Tanya, Pasha, Yaria and others.

On each of the plastic sleeves containing the photographs were details of vital statistics and mobile phone numbers.

"Dernov's personal harem?"

MacKenzie mused. "So it seems."

"We'll take this and the laptops. Any sign of a passport yet?"

"No, not yet."

"Well keep looking then."

Back at HQ there was a fax from HM Customs. Artem Dernov had left from Norwich airport six hours ago on a flight headed for Prague. Ketch contacted the Czechoslovakian police HQ in Prague and asked if the border police could be alerted and that he be detained. By lunchtime, he was beginning to show signs of fatigue and had developed a headache, a sure sign of his previous evening's alcohol abuse. Leaving his desk at Bethel Street, he made his way to the Grapes where he indulged in a largely liquid lunch. For half an hour he sat in the lounge bar, musing over the case.

It was evident that Rainbow Imports was a smokescreen for illegal immigrants and quite possibly drug-trafficking. The existence of the folder they had picked up at Dernov's house also suggested to him that Dernov and Vasnev had been importing sex slaves, though as yet there was no definite proof that they had been connected to the

Somalian immigrant affair.

Ketch believed that the lorry driver was innocent of the true nature of his human freight. The idea of using different drivers was part of the system which prevented a causal link being discovered. How much Vasnev's wife knew of her husband's

affairs remained an enigma but he had high hopes that the two laptops would yield them useful evidence.

When he got back to the office, his headache had largely disappeared and he found MacKenzie waiting for him.

"The interpreter finished checking the phone messages for me," he said. "The majority were business calls to the main warehouse in Kings Lynn but there were three calls which might prove useful to us, the first one to someone called Tanya – a mobile number - the other two were from Irina Vasnev. They were both timed for the evening prior to her husband's death and came from her mobile."

"Interesting – any luck with the Czechoslovakian police yet?"

"I had a call about 20 minutes ago from a Captain Smetana. Dernov has a flat in central Prague. They've issued a search warrant. They will ring us if they manage to pick him up."

"I take it you tried the numbers in the call girl folder?"

"I did. They're offering a mobile massage service at a hundred pounds an hour."

"Right – ring one of the numbers back and arrange for a session. We can use my Earlham Road address as a venue."

An hour later Ketch and MacKenzie were sitting around the two bar electric fire in Ketch's flat off the Earlham Road. He'd always intended to have central heating installed but never quite got round to it. On this cold November day, he regretted his tardiness. The flat seemed barer and more forlorn than he had remembered and bore the marks of his previous solitary bachelor existence.

Faded photographs of holidays spent with his father in Snowdonia graced the flock wallpaper, whilst a long oak table which had been a family heirloom was strewn with junk mail and unanswered correspondence. There was a real open fireplace here which, on winter days, he often used, piled high with coal and logs while comforting himself on long winter evenings with a bottle of good malt whiskey.

In many ways, his reluctance to sell the flat was an indication that

152

he had not quite surrendered his soul to a perpetual and lasting relationship with Carol. Despite his recent entry into fatherhood, there was within his soul something of the Rogue Male and the wanderer. Of late, he had entertained notions of early retirement from the force but had not gone through with these tempting thoughts partly because he didn't want to give satisfaction to some of his detractors – people like the soulless managerial despot, ACC Batarde, who was always looking for an excuse to pillory him.

Ketch's role as a dinosaur detective in a newspeak, dumbed down police force was what kept him going. Sometimes he would find an excuse to come here to the flat on his own and spend an hour or two after a job had been concluded, looking through old photograph albums or just staring into space as he played vinyl albums from the 60s.

Today, however, was not one of those tranquil occasions. There was work to be done. The doorbell rang and Ketch looked at his watch.

"Let's meet Tanya," he said.

He opened the door to reveal a tall, dark haired woman in a fur coat. "Mr Price?" she asked in a strong Russian accent.

"The same. Please come up." Ketch was struck by the woman's appearance. Judging by her stylish clothes and the expensive perfume she was wearing, she was a high-class prostitute.

They entered the lounge where Tanya caught sight of Tim MacKenzie.

"How do you want to do this? Both at once or maybe your friend would first like to watch, then take turns?"

She spoke in matter-of-fact tones. Ketch showed her his warrant card. "We have some questions to ask you," he said, "but not here. We want you to come down to the station with us."

At first, Tanya would not give her second name, was uncooperative and sat with arms folded over capacious breasts, staring at Ketch and MacKenzie. But when Ketch explained the process of immigration control and her repatriation, she began to look very concerned.

"It might be better for you if you were able to answer some of my questions," he explained.

"What do you wish to know?"

"How many girls are there?"

"Six girls."

"Where do you live?"

"There is a house in Kings Lynn where we share rooms."

"Who set you up there?"

"I can't tell you that."

"Why not?"

"Because we have all been told not to talk"

"You've been threatened, is that it?"

"I can't say."

"Have you ever seen this man or had dealings with him?"

He showed her the photograph of Dernov.

"Yes, several times – he is a client of mine."

"And this man? What about him?" He showed her a photograph of Vasnev.

"Yes, him also I know."

"What about this woman?" He showed her a photograph of Irina Vasnev. She looked away.

"I can't say – maybe."

"How do you get paid?"

"In cash. We are paid 40% of the fee for each client – the rest goes to pay for our upkeep and admin costs. We keep ourselves to ourselves."

"Who brought you here to England?"

"I don't know his name – he came to our village six months ago."

"Where was this?"

"Near Riga. He was asking for girls who wanted to come to England in order to find work in the tourist industry."

"Doing what?"

"As guides, escorts – three of us volunteered. We were told we would be looked after, found a place to live and paid well. Of course, we agreed."

"Then what?"

"We were given food and water and put into the back of a container. There was a big journey. We knew we were here in England. Men put us in a car and we were taken from the docks – I don't know where – to a place in Kings Lynn. For two weeks we were told not to leave the house. One of the girls disobeyed and she was beaten badly."

"By whom?"

"I don't know."

"Would you recognise this man?"

"Maybe – there were several men – Russians. One in particular I remember – he was the worst of all – his name was Anton. For how long are you going to detain me, please?"

The following morning, Ketch organised a raid on the Kings Lynn house and by lunchtime all of Tanya's co- sex workers had been arrested. At the premises, a file containing clients' phone numbers and a mobile number for Irina Vasnev was also located.

By lunchtime the same day and armed with an arrest warrant, Ketch and MacKenzie travelled to Felthorpe Minor. The chauffeur answered the door.

"We'd like to see Mrs Vasnev," said Ketch. "Is she in?"

"I'm sorry sir but she isn't. I've just come back from the airport."

"Where was she headed for?"

"Prague."

"When will she be back?"

I'm not entirely certain of that. You're very welcome to come in though."

It turned out to be too late to intercept Irina Vasnev who had passed through passport control at 8 AM that same day. Ketch and MacKenzie, therefore, spent the rest of the afternoon searching through the files and correspondence at the Vasnev residence before packing up several box loads to take away with them for further investigation.

Over the next few days nothing more was heard of Irina Vasnev. The files taken from the vicarage revealed that both Irina and Sergei had been responsible for the Kings Lynn brothel, drafting in the girls from Eastern Europe on false passports. They had employed four men, all of them Russian nationals, to act as their procurers and enforcers and of these two were known members of the Russian Mafia.

A week passed, then two months. During this time nothing more was gleaned about the Vasnev affair. Then, one brilliant sunny morning in late February when Ketch had taken Carol and Sean to Earlham Park for a quiet stroll among the trees his phone rang. It was MacKenzie.

"Something rather odd has come up about the Vasnev business," he explained

"Enlighten me, Tim."

"You recall that I've been liaising with captain Smetana of the Prague police?"

"I do."

"Apparently they have some CCTV footage of a man entering a bank in Prague where he asked to empty a safe deposit box. His name was Sergei Vasnev."

"I suppose you're telling me it was Dernov?"

"Here's the thing. He e-mailed me the video clip as an attachment. Judging by the photographs we have of Vasnev, I'd swear that it was him and not Dernov."

Shocked by the revelation, Ketch found a bench and sat for several minutes before Carol returned with the buggy. Then he rang Stoppard. "Mike, can you do me a DNA check on Vasnev's body?"

"Why should I want to do that?"

"Because I have a hunch that the body in the morgue isn't Vasnev's."

"Right, I'll see to it."

When the results came back later that day confirming Ketch's suspicions, it all began to fall into place. From a hairbrush at Dernov's residence, Stoppard was able to confirm that the body in the morgue was that of Artem Dernov.

It was now clear what had happened. Between them, the Vasnevs had managed to lure Dernov to their home in Felthorpe Minor where Sergei Vasnev had killed his colleague, dressing him in his own clothes. That explained his shoes which were a size too small for Dernov. His wife had claimed on three life-insurance policies taken out on her husband's life before leaving for Prague where she had been reunited with her husband. They had emptied the contents of the safe deposit box and then promptly disappeared.

Ketch subsequently discovered that the vicarage had been rented and was in fact owned by a company in Switzerland where, no doubt, the Vasnevs had a Swiss bank account.

No more was heard of the Vasnevs and Ketch expected to hear nothing more, now philosophical in defeat. But then, one morning in early June, he received a phone call from Prague. Two people had been found in a car which had been set on fire and left on an area of wasteland in the eastern sector of the city. Though badly burned, DNA and dental records proved that they were the bodies of Sergei and Irina Vasnev. Ketch could only assume that their luck with the Russian Mafia had finally run out.

THE ELM HILL CORPSE

He left the pub on Fye Bridge some while after closing time, his head befuddled with drink. It was pitch black outside and there was a cool easterly wind blowing, which threw gusts of leaves into his face.

Drawing the lapels of his threadbare coat about his neck, he made his way over the bridge, pausing momentarily to gaze down into the murky waters of the River Wensum.

To the left, behind the pub, was a small public garden. He decided that he might spend the night there. Despite the lateness of the tourist season in Norwich, the three B and B's he had tried that afternoon had proved to be fully booked and he had no intention of spending his limited cash on a hotel. Besides, he had a rendezvous to fulfil.

In his rucksack was a warm blanket. That and the half bottle of whiskey would provide him with the warmth he needed. Anyway, it looked like a sheltered spot. In the morning he would find somewhere to break his fast, then set about sorting out his personal affairs. By all accounts, it would be a momentous day, a day of reckoning and a day of surprises, not all of them welcome for those he was about to visit.

Dropping down through the alleyway at the back of the pub, he found a park bench situated under a large oak tree. He started to make himself comfortable. He was out of the wind here and with the aid of the whiskey and the blanket pulled over his legs, he had begun to feel warmer.

He must have drifted off for a few minutes, for when he awoke, he was aware of voices. Three youths stood round him, all wore hoods and smelled of alcohol. The tallest of the three was holding his rucksack and digging through its contents. He stood up.

"That's mine. Give it back!" he demanded. The youth smiled, then tipped up the rucksack, his possessions dropping onto the damp grass.

"Nothing worth nicking," the youth declared to his companions. He lunged at the youth who threw the empty rucksack at him, then drove his fist into his face. He reeled, then fell sideways onto the concrete path, banging his head.

By the time he had recovered and picked himself up, the youths had disappeared. He felt the side of his head. In falling, he must have gashed it for it was damp with blood. He took out a small handkerchief and dabbed the wound. It appeared to be only superficial.

He stood up, feeling groggy, and began to collect his few belongings from the grass. He had almost finished this task when he became aware of a figure standing behind the tree. He turned and the figure advanced towards him, but he was unable to see the face clearly. He called out a name, then stepped back, aware of imminent danger. It was not who he had expected. There was a glint of steel, then he felt a sudden sharp pain. He fell to his knees, hands flailing. He was coughing blood. The figure advanced again, driving the blade into his neck. He groaned, then his legs folded under him. He blacked out.

Detective Chief Inspector Huw John Emrys Price, known to his friends and colleagues as 'Ketch', sat by the open window, smoking a cigarette. It was 4 AM on a cold, blustery, autumn morning and he felt like a reanimated corpse. He drew on the cigarette, inhaling a large lungful of smoke then coughed as he exhaled. He really must give up the weed. It was ruining his health. The question was when to do it. Not now, certainly not now under the present dire circumstances. There were three of them, living in Carol's bijou apartment and it had become a kind of sleepless hell. He couldn't recall the last time he had slept properly and stress was now beginning to show.

Since Carol, his partner, had given birth to a baby boy some six weeks ago, he had discovered just how hard it was being a 50-year-old father. Of course he had been through it all before when his wife Anne was still alive but he had been in his 20s then and was more robust. In those days, he could go without sleep for long periods and still maintain his strength and concentration. These days it was completely different.

Twice in the past week, DS MacKenzie had entered Ketch's office to find him asleep on the desk. It looked bad and it felt much worse. He didn't know how long he would be able to survive like this. Carol, who up until eight weeks ago, had been pursuing her career as a pathologist, was now on leave, but for Ketch there was no remission. He had just completed a lengthy and complex investigation into a drug ring, involving a gang of Latvians in West Norfolk, a case which had dragged on for months. It had not ended well, since there had been insufficient evidence for the DPP to proceed against the gang leaders, a fact which had not impressed the ACC. All in all, this last month had proved to be an unmitigated disaster.

He finished the cigarette, then peered in the bedroom. Mother and child were finally asleep. He decided he'd take a walk along the riverbank in order to clear his head. Outside, a low mist had risen, giving the river bank a ghostly hue. The air was still at this hour and the city still slumbered. He found the bench and, sitting down, lit another cigarette.

When he awoke, it was broad daylight and an orange sun had risen in the east. He glanced at his watch. It was 7 AM. He must have slept for at least two hours. His throat felt like parchment. He must get back to the flat and fix himself a coffee. Carol would be wondering where he was.

His mobile leapt into life. At first he was tempted to ignore the summons. How he hated all things digital. But when he glanced at the caller's ID and saw that it was DS MacKenzie, he thought better of it.

"Sorry to call you so early sir." How many times had he heard that?

"Go ahead."

"We have a body in Elm Hill Gardens. An unidentified male."

"Okay Tim. Give me 30 minutes, will you?"

He walked back to the flat where he found Carol still fast asleep, took a shower, and changed into a fresh shirt and trousers. Then he left a brief note on the kitchen table, explaining his absence.

Outside, the sun had now risen, dispersing the mist. It was a fresh, sunny autumn morning.

He knew Elm Hill Gardens well, a quiet, tranquil spot between the art college and River Wensum, a spot he'd often used when courting his wife in the days when he'd been a humble DS. He recalled those times with great affection. How much simpler the job had been then – or so it seemed to him. Perhaps it was a case of rose tinted glasses. Or perhaps he was right after all. These days, the job was hidebound by procedure and paperwork and the business of pure detection was often obscured. But Ketch often refused to play by the rules, earning him opprobrium from the higher echelons. It mattered not. He was too far near the finishing line now to worry about such concerns. He felt sorry for the likes of his sidekick, DS MacKenzie.

As he reached Fye Bridge, he saw the familiar barrier tape and nodded in greeting to the uniformed copper.

"Nice weather for it sir," the man said.

He passed down a short alleyway by the side of the pub and entered the gardens. By the tow path stood Tim MacKenzie and, crouched next to him in the familiar SOCO suit, was a man who Ketch often likened to a large walrus – Dr Michael Stoppard. Ketch would have preferred doing business with Carol, for Stoppard, an overweight and pompous pathologist who was known for his careless methods, was not one of his favourite colleagues. Sensing his approach, Stoppard heaved himself to his full height and greeted Ketch with a hand like a flipper.

"Glad you could make it," he remarked sarcastically. Ketch ignored the comment and looked at the body. A bearded man in his mid-40s lay spread-eagled on the path. He was conventionally dressed in a leather jacket and denim trousers and his blue shirt was stained with blood. Near the body lay a brown rucksack.

"Who is he?" asked Ketch.

"No idea, old son," Stoppard replied in his slow Norfolk drawl. "If he was carrying a wallet and ID, someone must have removed it before they stabbed him."

Ketch knelt to examine the body. He noticed that there were abrasions on the knuckles of the left hand and scuff marks on the trouser legs.

"Two wounds to the chest and one to the heart."

"He put up a fight," said Ketch.

"Looks like a mugging," said MacKenzie. Ketch peered at the adjacent grass where there were several depressions and grooves. He stood up and stared up at the pub wall.

"There's a camera up there," he told MacKenzie. "Look, on the edge of that wall. Let's see what it can tell us. What about the contents of the rucksack?" he asked.

"Nothing of much use sir. A paperback, a map of the city, a thermos flask, tobacco, a National Express timetable, oh and a small pocket diary."

"You checked the diary?"

MacKenzie nodded. "No name in it unfortunately."

"Estimated time of death?" he asked Stoppard.

"Around midnight I would guess – that's approximate of course."

"What about the murder weapon?" MacKenzie shook his head.

"Not yet. Of course there's the river."

162

Ketch frowned. Something told him this wasn't going to be at all easy.

When Ketch reached HQ later that morning, the desk sergeant hailed him.

"Morning sir. The ACC has asked to see you." Sergeant Travis, something of a comedian among his colleagues, grinned broadly. His delight grated with Ketch. The animosity between Ketch and ACC Batarde (known affectionately among the lower ranks as "Bastard") was well known at the Norwich HQ. Their tete a tetes always left him feeling less than adequate. "Thanks Travis," he mumbled and took the lift to the third floor.

Batarde was sitting behind his newly installed stainless steel desk, finishing a phone call. He waved Ketch to a seat.

"Morning, Huw."

"Morning sir." Ketch hated the false camaraderie of Christian names.

"I'm guessing you know why I have asked to see you."

Ketch nodded. "The Latvian drug ring?"

"Precisely. Anything to say about that matter?"

"Nothing which springs to mind, no."

"Are you aware of how much this operation has cost the force?"

"Not entirely, no."

"I've been examining the figures. With overtime factored in, we're talking about a sum not far short of £200,000. And with little to show for it. Any comments?"

There was a pause. Ketch felt his face redden with rage. "My team acted with total professionalism."

"I daresay. But at the end of the day I'm interested – we are all interested, and that includes the chief constable I might add – in concrete results. And in this case results, like any other case, means convictions. Which in this case you failed to arrive at, Huw."

"Point taken."

"I'm glad it is. I understand you've become a father?"

"I have."

"How are Carol and the baby doing?"

"Fine, thank you."

"That must be quite a responsibility at your stage in life?" Ketch didn't reply. There was another awkward pause. ACC Batarde gave

Ketch a fixed smile. "Good, good. Anything coming up I should know about?"

"A John Doe. Body found in Elm Hill Gardens this morning."

"I see. Keep me informed on the progress of that matter. Keeping well are we?"

For a moment, Ketch wondered whether to retaliate to this parting shot which was a veiled reference to his former problem with alcohol. Instead, he stood up and, moving to the door, replied: "Very well." It was not entirely true. He was feeling old and crotchety.

Back in the safety of his own office, he found a large evidence box on his table. He took off the lid and, slipping on a pair of forensic gloves, examined its contents. A packet of mints, an apple, an edition of Baudelaire's poems, a small A5 notebook with dates and times, a National Express timetable, a thermos and a red cloth bound diary. Dates and times plus some entries in French. He turned to the back pages which were headed "notes." His door opened and Tim MacKenzie entered, carrying two cups of coffee.

"This diary," said Ketch. "You said there was no name on it?"

"I couldn't see a name."

"Then you didn't look far enough. See this?" He pointed to an inscription on the back page of the diary.

"A la mere – by the seaside."

"Look at it again and what do you see?"

"The number."

"Not the number, Tim. There's a dot after the a. It's a name. A. La Mere. Have you tried ringing this phone number?"

"No."

"Then do so."

MacKenzie put down the coffee and left, his face red. Ketch looked at the National Express timetable. Tuesday morning's departure from Victoria coach Station, an express coach to Norwich, underlined. Arrival time – 11:45 AM. What was a French tourist doing in Norwich? Maybe one of the hotels had a booking for him with an unpaid bill. It was worth checking out.

He gazed at the small neat hand. His French was not bad. He turned the diary again and looked at some of the longer entries. August 28:

'Today has been a revelation. 10 years and now the truth is clear to me. Must act immediately. Have started to make preliminary arrangements already.'

'September 3rd. Took leave owing to me – 10 days in all. Still cannot believe it's true. Have decided that surprise is by far the best strategy. Booked the ferry this afternoon. Will travel light. Much depends on this. Must act carefully and proceed with some caution. This morning I recalled more of the circumstances. Proving it will be difficult enough. Now full of intense anticipation.'

There followed a series of times but there were no more extensive entries in the diary. He put the diary aside and sipped his coffee which tasted disgusting as usual.

Maybe the CCTV would yield something significant. His mobile rang. It was a text from Carol which read: 'When you finish, can you pop into Boots and get some stuff for the baby.' There followed a list of items. He folded the phone and sighed.

The following morning Ketch and MacKenzie visited the AV suite at HQ. A large, windowless room, it was situated on the fourth floor of the building and was equipped with state-of-the-art digital hardware and software. They found DC Dave Thomas sitting in front of a large widescreen television.

"What have we got here?" asked Ketch. His abrupt manner was proof positive of his three hours' sleep the night before. This had led to a blazing row with Carol and resulted in him wandering the bank of the river Wensum at the ungodly hour of 3 AM. The silence of the scene had been impressive. There was something both eerie and beautiful about a city in the dead of the night which appealed to the poet in him. He had spent a good half hour thus before returning to the flat where he found both mother and child sound asleep. Exhausted, he had spent the rest of the night on the sofa.

"Two cameras," DC Thomas replied. Ketch and MacKenzie sat down and turned to the screen. "One situated on the edge of the Fye Bridge Arms, trained on the alleyway which leads on to the gardens. The other camera is up on the arts building. This one is at a greater distance and the view of the gardens is partially obscured by two large oak trees."

Thomas clicked a button on his console. "This is from the second camera, time 11:15 p.m. on the night our John Doe was murdered. You can just make out his figure on the bench." Ketch looked at the screen. It was a side view, somewhat blurred. The figure did not appear to be moving.

"Now watch this," said Thomas. He clicked, frame by frame, and the outlines of three figures could be seen approaching the man on the bench. For a few seconds, they stood in a huddle, apparently talking, then approached the seated figure. There followed a struggle, then one of the figures emerged from the huddle, holding the seated man's rucksack and upended it onto the tarmac path. His two companions gathered round, examining the contents of the rucksack. And then the seated figure stood up and ran towards the three attackers. There was a short struggle, then the tallest of them appeared to knock him down. He fell backwards and disappeared beneath the tree where only his feet were now visible. The three muggers fled in the direction of the art college buildings where there was a small cut through to the next street.

"Let's look at the footage from the first camera," Ketch instructed. Thomas changed the disc and scrawled forwards to 11:20 pm. The officers watched as the three figures emerged from the alleyway. One of them, the tallest, stopped abruptly, then turned and reached into his jacket pocket, pulling out a packet of cigarettes.

"Stop it there," said Ketch. "Can you enlarge the image for me?" Thomas obliged. There was a face but it was blurred.

"Can you use digital enlargement on the face?"

Thomas nodded. "I can try and sharpen it up for you."

"Let me know what you get."

Ketch was not in the best of moods. The phone number in John Doe's diary had proved to be out of service. He had discovered it was a Paris landline number and accordingly contacted his old friend, Commissionaire Vance of the Surete. Instead of speaking to Vance, he found himself talking to a junior officer who was less than helpful and insisted on carrying on the conversation in French. Vance would have been a lot more considerate Ketch told himself. Besides, he spoke English. It was agreed that he would give his colleague the message.

Following a largely liquid lunch at The Grapes, Ketch and MacKenzie proceeded to the mortuary where they found Stoppard in a robust mood. Whichever mood Stoppard adopted, Ketch found him irritating and boorish.

"I'm far from finished, gentleman," was his opening shot. "The victim certainly died from a single stab to the heart which severed the left ventricle but there are other wounds and abrasions. A second stab wound narrowly missed the left lung and shortly before death he'd been struck on the nose. Age approximately 50, has good teeth with some expensive dentistry work and he last ate about half an hour before he died. I can't tell you very much beyond that."

"What about contact traces? His fingernails, for example?"

"We're analysing what we have, but I wouldn't bet on it."

At two pm, Ketch received a phone call. It was Vance. They chatted for a while. Vance was recovering from a recent divorce, after 23 years of marriage These days, he told Ketch, the job was all about crime originating from Eastern Europe. Drugs and sex trafficking held centre stage. Ketch decided not to tell his old compatriot about his new role as a father. He didn't feel up to it.

"We checked the number for you and we have an address in the Rue Saint Michelle in Montmartre. The subscriber was one Marie La Grande. She used the number until about a year ago. We've been able to track her to a new address though. I'll give you the number."

Ketch thanked Vance, finished the conversation, then rang the number he'd been given. He got the answerphone and left a message.

By six pm that evening no one had run back. The office was hot and stuffy. Feeling claustrophobic, Ketch opened his office door and called MacKenzie.

"Any luck with that digital enhancement yet?"

"Just got it. Not a bad result."

"Fancy a pint at the Fye Bridge Arms?"

"I can think of nothing better."

Ketch had forgotten the interior of the pub. He had visited it often in his youth before the advent of Sky TV and gaming machines. In those days, the pub had served real ale to a discerning clientele. Now all those features had disappeared and the oak interiors had given way to plastic and Formica.

Ketch glanced at the menu board as they took their seats at the bar and saw that it was entirely blank. The barman, a large, greasy fellow with acne arms, approached Ketch and MacKenzie.

"Any food available?" Ketch quizzed.

"I can do sandwiches or crisps," came the laconic reply. They ordered their pints and sandwiches. A few minutes later, two tired looking cheese and onion sandwiches of desiccated white bread and stale cheddar duly arrived. Ketch ate his in grim silence before returning to the bar. As he waited for the barman to return from the public bar, he glanced round at the clientele. Two old soaks sat glued to the widescreen television while, in the far corner, sat a huge woman with peroxide hair and double chins, staring into space. It was one of those end of the world pubs thought Ketch, a place of lost souls queueing for oblivion. He took the CCTV photo from the envelope, placed it on the bar, then showed his warrant card to the barman.

"We are investigating an incident," he explained.

"You mean the murder the other night?"

"That's it. Do you recognise him?" The barman stared at the photograph.

"I recognise him all right. He gets in here a lot. In fact..." He broke off abruptly and stared across the bar to the far corner. "That's him." Ketch followed his gaze. A tall youth had pushed back his chair and was now making his way with alacrity towards the side door of the pub.

"Quick," Ketch instructed MacKenzie. MacKenzie leapt from his chair and bolted for the exit. Ketch finished his pint, put the photograph back into the envelope, then calmly followed his colleague.

Outside, in the alleyway, he caught up with MacKenzie who had pinned the prostrate youth to the ground and was now applying the handcuffs. The youth was growling and cursing. MacKenzie pulled him to his full height.

"Get your fucking hands off me!" the youth shouted.

"Don't I recognise you?" asked Ketch. "Yes, the face is familiar to me. It's Freddy Cole as I live and breathe. We need to have a chat down at the station, a long intimate one. Keep a tight hold on him, Tim."

Interview room four was hot and stuffy. Ketch and MacKenzie sat opposite Freddy Cole, a tall, gangly youth with severe acne. Ketch remembered him well, not only from the slightly blurred photograph. His career as a criminal had begun at the age of 13 when he'd been part of the drugs gang operating from the Earlham Road estate. By the age of 15 he'd graduated to burglary and muggings. Now he'd formed his own gang which used a method known as 'steaming.' This

168

involved a team of youths moving through a large department store, snatching items at high speed.

Ketch switched on the recorder. "Interview with Frederick Cole. Tuesday, September 15, seven thirty pm."

The youth stared back at Ketch and MacKenzie, his arms folded in defiance. "I guess you know why you're here, Freddy."

"Don't have a clue."

"Let me take you back in time then. Sunday night, the Fye Bridge Arms. Who were you drinking with?"

"I don't remember."

"Let me make things clearer to you. Is going to be a lot easier for you if you cooperate. We're talking about a murder charge, Freddy, not your common or garden mugging. Do you get my drift?"

"I don't know anything about a murder."

Ketch produced a photograph of the John Doe and placed it on the table. "Bad luck, Freddy. You were picked up on the CCTV footage attacking this man on Sunday evening."

"The guy on the bench, I remember now."

"Good. At last we're making some progress."

"We were just having a bit of fun, that's all. Craig started it."

"Craig?"

"Craig Sutton, my best mate. He grabbed the guy's rucksack to see if there was anything in it worth nicking. The geezer got a bit stroppy so I thumped him one."

"You stabbed him."

"No, I thumped him."

"You stabbed him twice and one of those wounds proved to be fatal. Where did you stash the knife, Freddy? In the river?"

"Don't know nothing about a knife or a stabbing. When we left him he was alive."

"You're sure about that, are you? Perhaps it was your mate Craig who stabbed him?"

"No one's stabbed him, I keep telling you. Just thumped him, that's all." There was a pause. "When can I see a solicitor?" Freddy asked at last.

"Let's go over the events of Sunday night again shall we?" Ketch insisted.

By eight thirty pm no further progress had been made, except that

Freddy Cole had revealed the name of his second accomplice and had confessed to emptying the victim's wallet before throwing it into the river. Ketch decided to wait until morning before requesting warrants for their arrests and returned Cole to his cell.

He had just decided to call it a day when his phone rang. It was a woman and she was speaking in French. "Give me your number along with the international code and I'll call you straight back," Ketch instructed her.

The woman's name was Marie La Grande. She was the former occupant of the flat in Montmartre and had been asked to phone him by Vance. Fortunately for Ketch, she also spoke fluent English. She was now living in Normandy but had spent a year cohabiting with Alain La Mere. What could she tell him about her former lover?

"What you want to know precisely? We met at a bar in Montmartre. He was waiting tables there. He was charming and also very handsome. At that time, he was living in a kind of squat in one of the poorer areas of the district and sharing the place with a couple of artists. One thing led to another, and we found ourselves living together. "

"Did he tell you much about his past?"

"Alain had no past. That was one of the odd things about him. He appeared to have lost his memory entirely. I'm not sure how it happened to him. He was of the opinion that he might have been involved in some kind of accident, but he wasn't even sure of that. The only thing he did recall clearly was finding himself on a beach near Dunkirk. He didn't know how he got there, and had no ID on him."

"What about his name?"

"He was convinced that his first name was Alain. The surname was chosen because he believed he had come from the sea."

"Can you tell me why you decided to part company?"

"He was not very easy to live with. He had a drink problem and was subject to frequent fits of depression. In the end, I just couldn't cope with him. About a year ago, I got an offer on a job in Normandy, so I decided to take it. Since then I haven't seen him."

"You didn't stay in touch?"

"About two weeks ago I got a phone call from him. He sounded exuberant. He told me he had discovered something about himself. He said he'd started to remember certain events in his former life. He told me that he was planning to go back to England to sort out his affairs.

He wouldn't be more specific about it than that."

"I don't suppose you have a current address for Alain?"

"I don't, though I believe he was sharing a squat with his old friend, Pierre Duchamps, somewhere in Montmartre. I only have his mobile number. Pierre used to loan him his ID card for employment purposes."

The following morning dawned clear and bright. Mist had risen over the riverbank, a sure sign of the approaching Equinox. He showered early and, feeling benevolent, cooked Carol a full English breakfast before walking across the city to HQ. The air was crisp and the early autumn sun threw long shadows over the covered market where the stallholders were already busy, setting out their produce. When he reached the office at 9 AM, the first person who greeted him was DC Thomas.

"Can you spare a few minutes?" he enquired. "Something I think you should see, sir." They took the lift to the fourth floor and Dave Thomas switched on the VCR.

"I've been checking the footage from both of the CCTVs," he remarked. "What I hadn't realised is that after he was attacked by the youths, our John Doe staggered to the path, gathered up his belongings, then returned to the bench and collapsed."

"Where subsequently he died."

"That's where I think we got it wrong." He pressed the play button. "See here, he's moving. Look at his arms."

"Go on."

"If you look carefully you can see a dark shadow beneath the tree directly behind him. "

Thomas enlarged the picture. Ketch could dimly discern the outline of a figure.

"And if you look at this sequence, you can see what looks like an arm being raised. Now watch. See how the victim convulses? Then he slides off the bench onto the ground beneath."

"The second attacker," said Ketch.

"Exactly. And that's when he received the blow that killed him."

When Ketch returned to his office, he found Tim MacKenzie waiting for him.

"I've got Freddy Cole's mates waiting downstairs, sir."

171

"Don't bother Tim. There's been a new development." He updated McKenzie about the CCTV. "Get Stoppard on the phone for me, will you?"

Luckily for Ketch, Michael Stoppard was just about to leave the premises when his phone rang.

"Mike, what's happened to those dental records for our John Doe?"

"I'm hoping to hear back this afternoon. By the way, I have some DNA evidence from the victim's fingernails which we sent for testing. That also might prove useful for you."

"Good, keep me informed."

Three days followed, during which nothing much happened. In Paris, Vance managed to track down Pierre Duchamps, but the result was less than helpful. La Mere had moved out of the squat a month before his arrival in England and his friend had little information to add, apart from the fact that Alain seemed to be troubled.

On the Sunday morning, Ketch, Carol and little Sean took a walk on Mousehold Heath where they were able to command a view of the great city. It was a fine, clear day and the early mist had cleared. The spire of the ancient cathedral was lit by golden sunlight and the bones of the city could be picked out in great detail.

It wasn't until late on Monday that the first break in the case came. Ketch had just returned to his office from the nearby coffee shop, armed with a takeaway latte when his phone rang. It was Stoppard. " I have a result for you from the forensic science unit at Wymondham. The dental impressions provided a match. Your John Doe is one Eric van Linden."

Ketch thanked Stoppard and put the phone down. Eric Van Linden... Van Linden. The name was well known in Norwich. The Van Lindens were a wealthy family who had made their fortune through the manufacture of mustard and Linden mustard was a household name in East Anglia. The father and founder of the firm, Jacob Van Linden, had died in an accident at the Linden factory some years back. Eric Van Linden was the youngest son and Paul was the elder.

Ten years ago, Eric Van Linden had disappeared in what was thought to have been a boating accident in the channel. His body had never been discovered. Not, that is, until now... Ketch recalled the incident well, hardly surprising, since it had been in the national press.

Paul Van Linden had inherited the business since Jacob had not left a will, and had divorced his wife Janet.

He started up his laptop and began trawling through the archive pages of the Eastern Daily Press in order to refresh his memory on the family. It made for interesting reading. The Van Linden Empire was worth a cool £50 million. Clearly, mustard was big business. Jacob Van Linden had fallen into a mustard vat at the company's main factory, a colossal warehouse situated on the banks of the river Wensum. There had been no witnesses to his death, the body having been discovered the following day by a worker. What Jacob was doing in the factory at that late hour remained a mystery.

The details of Eric's disappearance were equally intriguing. Eric, his girlfriend, Sarah Buxton, and brother Paul had set out on a yacht from Dover on an evening in September, ten years ago. Somewhere near Dunkirk, Eric had gone overboard in the middle of the night. Paul and Sarah, who had been asleep in the cabin, had awoken to find him missing. They contacted the coastguard but despite extensive searches by helicopter and lifeboat, his body was never found.

On Tuesday morning, Ketch and MacKenzie drove to St Stephens Road, a wide thoroughfare situated on the southern boundary of the city. Sarah Buxton's residence was a large, six bedroomed property, set well back from the busy main road and one of a number of mansions sporting high-performance cars in their driveways. A tall, regal blonde in her mid-30s answered the door and ushered them through an ornate twenties style hallway into a lounge with leather armchairs and a marble fireplace with a roaring fire. Feeling the heat, Ketch removed his jacket, placing it next to him.

"I'm glad you're here," said Sarah. "This is a very disturbing business and it helps to talk to someone about it."

"You were very close?" She nodded.

"We'd intended to marry. Then the accident happened and after a while, I just gave up hope. When Eric phoned me on the Sunday and told me what had happened to him I couldn't believe it. He said he wanted to meet up on the Monday morning but of course, he never turned up at the house. And he didn't phone me again. Now, of course, I realise why. Who could have done such a thing to him?"

"That's what we hope to discover. You live here alone?"

She smiled.

"Goodness, no. This isn't my place. It belongs to Paul, Eric's brother. After the accident on the boat, Paul was very kind to me. He suggested I moved in here. I occupy the lower part of the house and I pay him a nominal rent. It works out well, especially since we work for the same firm."

"Tell me, Miss Buxton, can you think of anyone who might have wished Eric harm? Did he have any enemies you can think of?"

"I honestly can't. He was such an easy-going fellow – not at all aggressive, and very easy to please. He had a lovely nature and he was very forgiving. Of course, he and Paul both had quite a deal to put up with from their father."

"Jacob Van Linden?"

"Yes, he was not an easy man to please, a martinet you might say. I'm not surprised that their mother left him. He was a driven individual – which is why the business was so successful, I guess."

"And what actually is your position in the Van Linden firm?"

"I am now the company secretary. I've been doing the job for about five years. I used to be a lowly clerk but my efforts were rewarded – Lucky old me." She laughed.

Outside, there was the sound of car tyres on gravel. Sarah Buxton went to the window. "It's Paul. I told him you were coming, inspector."

Paul Van Linden was the kind of man you would notice in a crowd. Well over six feet in height, his broad, Anglo-Saxon face resembled those which Ketch had once seen in the paintings of the old Dutch masters. Square-jawed and with penetrating blue eyes, he stepped forward and shook Ketch firmly by the hand. "I'm so sorry I couldn't have been here earlier, Inspector," he explained. "I was tied up in a board meeting. This is very sad news indeed. It has been a double shock to both of us. Can I offer you anything to drink perhaps? Some tea or coffee?"

"No thanks. It would be very helpful if you could give me some background."

"By all means – what would you like to know exactly?"

"What sort of a person was Eric?"

"Eric was very much his own person – wayward, you might say, and very artistic. Father wanted him to go into the business of course, but Eric made it clear to him that this wasn't his intention. When he left school, he took a fine arts degree here in the city and left with a first-class honours. Much good it did him I'm sorry to say. After

174

several years spent in the wilderness, he reluctantly relented and was given a job in the office at our headquarters here in Norwich."

"Which is where we subsequently met," said Sarah.

"Tell me more about the boating accident."

"There's not much more to tell if truth be known – not much beyond what appeared in the newspapers at the time, that is. We'd intended to take a short break in France, a short holiday. Our family has a villa there in Normandy. It was to be a treat prior to Eric and Sarah's forthcoming nuptials. Anyway, we set sail from Dover. Eric had been drinking rather too much as I recall. That wasn't uncommon for him."

"He had a severe drink problem?"

"Pretty much, yes. A habit he'd picked up in his days as an undergraduate. Anyway, Sarah and I retired around midnight, and Eric decided he would finish his whiskey before coming down to the cabin. We'd all had rather a lot to drink on that particular evening, so Sarah and I slept deeply. I woke up around dawn and found him gone. The conditions were good, there was hardly any wind to speak of. It seemed that he'd simply slipped overboard and drowned, or so we thought. Of course, we alerted the French coastguard and a search was conducted, but he was never found. What I don't understand is how he could possibly have survived and then ended up in France. As you probably know, Sarah waited for him but Eric never showed up. We both thought it a bit odd, but we imagined there was some perfectly rational explanation. Now, of course, we know why. I understand that you have made an arrest, Inspector?"

"We did, although the case is by no means closed."

"You mean you have more than one suspect?"

"Quite possibly. The investigation is still at an early stage. We're following up several leads at present."

Finnegan's Irish bar was situated at the end of Princess Street, a large rambling pub standing opposite St Andrew's Church. Ketch often drank here mainly because of the real ale and the Irish groups which played in the evenings. He found that Irish traditional music appealed to his Celtic soul. It was lunchtime, the bar was crowded with students from the city art college and he was staring at a large, appetising ploughman's lunch which had just been delivered to his table.

"Did you notice anything odd about Sarah Buxton's flat?" he

asked MacKenzie. The latter paused over his pint and put down his glass to consider this.

"She seemed well britched, judging by its contents. No, can't say that I did."

"There were no photos of Eric van Linden, not a single one. Several of Paul Van Linden though."

"More than just a lodger then?"

"Yes, more than just a lodger. I looked up the report on Jacob's accident at the factory by the way. There are some interesting features to the case."

"As I recall there were no witnesses to the event."

"None, though Paul Van Linden was on the premises on the evening prior to the discovery of the body. There was a point about the rails which formed the circumference of the vat into which he fell. It came up at the inquest. The rails had become loose. That's the reason he fell."

MacKenzie looked thoughtful. "How much was the business worth at the time of Jacob's death?"

"Nigh on £15 million."

Ketch dug into his ploughman's lunch. "Food for thought," he said.

Ketch had just got back to his office when his phone rang. It was Mike Stoppard.

"You'll be pleased about this," he drawled.

"Try me."

"Those contact traces under Linden's fingernails. The DNA analysed by SOCO came up with a match on the CRO computer. They belong to one Bert Speer. He has form for GBH. Thought you'd like to know that."

Speer, a short squat man with a bald head, sat in interview room three, facing his inquisitors. Ketch opened a manilla folder and placed two photographs of Eric van Linden on the table in front of them. "You recognise this man?"

Speer leaned over the table. He smelt of stale sweat. "I recognise him, yes, he was causing trouble outside the club on Sunday night."

"You're a bouncer at the Butterfly Club in the Prince of Wales Road?"

"I'm part of the security team there, yes."

"You had an altercation with this man, is that what you're telling us then?"

"That's it."

"What time on Sunday night did this happen?"

"I don't remember the precise time, I guess it was around ten pm. He wasn't a member of the club, so I refused to let him in. He became violent and struck me so I dealt with him. He was very drunk."

"What happened to him then?"

"He went off up the road."

"You followed him?"

"I stayed on duty until ten thirty pm. On Sundays I do an earlier shift."

"So you are telling me you didn't follow him?"

"That's what I'm saying, yes."

"You have a conviction for GBH."

"What's that got to do with anything?"

"You have a problem controlling your temper. I'm suggesting that when you left the club at ten thirty pm, you made your way across the city and saw this man coming out of the Fye Bridge Arms. There was an altercation and you then stabbed him. What did you do with the knife?"

"I don't know what you're talking about."

Speer remained in the interview room for the next hour, but despite going over his story several times, he refused to add anything further or make an admission about the death of Eric Van Linden.

That night, Ketch slept fitfully. For once, the baby did not disturb them. At 6 AM he rose, dressed, and made his way down by the riverbank where the trees were veiled in early-morning mist. He sat on a bench down by Pull's Ferry and tried to marshal his thoughts. He believed that Speer had stabbed Eric van Linden, but there was much more to it than that, he was sure of it.

By 9:30 AM he was back in his office with DC Thomas.

"Dave, check the CCTV coverage for the stretch between Magdalen Street and Fye Bridge, will you? See if you can find anything."

"What exactly am I looking for?"

Ketch produced a photograph of Speer. "You're looking for this man."

At 10 AM, MacKenzie appeared at the office door.

"Do me a favour, Tim. Find out who the owners of the Butterfly Night Club are."

"Sure."

When Ketch returned to the office later with his skinny latte, he found both MacKenzie and Thomas waiting for him.

"Well?" he asked.

"The Butterfly Club is owned by a consortium," said MacKenzie. "But one of the directors will be familiar to you. His name is Paul van Linden. And another thing – Speer formerly worked as a security guard for the Linden Empire."

"And what about the CCTV?"

"I have a result," said Thomas. He placed two grainy photographs on Ketch's desk. The first of these showed a side view of a figure who resembled Speer, talking to someone through a car window. The second showed the back of the car as it proceeded down the road in the direction of the city centre. "Can't quite make out the number plate," said Ketch. "BMW isn't it?"

"Digital enhancement will get us the number plate," said Thomas confidently.

It was three pm on a blustery March day of bright sunshine. Ketch sat on a bench overlooking the river, smoking a cigarette, the hum of conversation at his back as the personnel of the Norwich Crown Court reached their appointed vehicles in the car park.

In the end, it had not really been a long or protracted case. Paul van Linden had admitted to the charge of conspiracy to murder and received a sentence of 15 years for his part in the killing of his brother Eric. When Ketch had examined the CCTV photograph of the car in Magdalen Street, it proved to be Paul van Linden's BMW.

It transpired that he had not gone on a business trip to London on Sunday but instead had instructed Speer to follow Eric from the nightclub to the pub where Ketch believed he had arranged to meet Sarah Buxton. Sarah had been in on the whole affair of course, but there was no way of proving her part in the conspiracy. Fortunately, Speer's confession had been enough to prove the case against Paul van Linden.

Under questioning, the latter had broken down and made a formal statement confirming his part in the murder. Ketch felt certain that Paul had murdered his father. However, proving that would be an altogether more different matter and one which he knew would prove fruitless. As for the knife which killed Eric, it was never found. Shortly after Paul made his confession, Sarah Buxton left for America and had not been heard of since no doubt fulfilling her role as bounty hunter elsewhere. The van Linden mustard empire carried on, regardless of the cause celebre which had darkened its reputation.

Ketch stared down at the waters of the River and smiled. For the first time in months he had begun to feel happy. Ketch junior had now moved on from his role as a mewling, puking monster and was a delight to behold. And when Ketch was not on duty there was nothing he enjoyed more than to play with the little one. All in all, life wasn't so bad especially now that normal conjugal rights had been established between him and Carol.

He ground his cigarette beneath his heel and stood up, the sun now full on his face. Maybe he'd take a short walk along the riverbank before returning to HQ. After all, no one was indispensable, especially at his age. He might even drop into his favourite local for a swift pint. On the other hand, maybe not...

A DOG IN THE NIGHT

For the fourth time that summer morning, Roland Jenkins climbed the stairs to the room at the front and sat behind the telescope which he had trained on the living room of the house opposite in Romany Road, Norwich.

A squat, obese man in his early 50s, he had found the stairs increasingly difficult to negotiate, especially since his release from prison twelve months ago. As he adjusted the lens, memories of his incarceration flooded back to him.

From the moment that he had entered the gates of Peterborough prison, he had been targeted. He was not alone in this: paedophiles were easy prey for the harder cons and word soon got around about the new arrivals.

Although he was subjected to daily attacks of the verbal kind, far worse were the physical degradations. By month four, his existence had turned into a state of hell. A prisoner called Jackson, who headed a gang in the jail, had decided to target Jenkins for his entertainment.

One morning, he had gone down to the showers and had almost finished his ablutions when he was confronted by three of Jackson's Confederates. They had tossed him about like a piece of paper, then beaten him with broken chair legs.

This attack had resulted in surgery and the consequent loss of his left testicle. It had taken him a month to recover in the prison infirmary. But far worse than the physical damage had been the psychological scars.

Jenkins peered through the telescope. The young couple living opposite him had only moved in a few months back. He had been excited to learn that they had a young baby. Although he had never seen the infant, it was the custom of the mother to take the pram from the house every morning up the road and onto the broad expanse of Mousehold Heath, a great common, overlooking the city. And each morning, for a very brief period, the mother, a girl in her late 20s, was in the habit of leaving the child in the pram outside the property as she popped inside to collect her handbag.

Jenkins had begun to fantasise about snatching the child from the pram. It was a quiet road whose residents were, in the main, commuters, and at this early hour, it was often quite deserted. It was all a question of timing, of course, but so far he had not been able to pluck up sufficient courage to carry out the deed.

Jenkins never thought once about the possible and devastating consequences for him of such an action. Like all paedophiles, he was consumed and obsessed by the idea of the act itself and would spend hours fantasising about what he might do with his defenceless captive.

In a perverse way, he could understand the mentality of those men who had beaten him senseless with the chair legs. They could never understand how he felt, never comprehend the strong urges that compelled him to do what he had done.

At times, he was haunted by the memories of his deeds and cries of those two girls whom he had attacked on a piece of waste ground in Norwich often came back to haunt him. But such considerations were overridden by his desperate need for consummation. By others' standards, he was a freak of nature but by his own, he was perfectly normal.

Jenkins gave a sharp intake of breath. The door of the house opposite had opened and the pram was being wheeled out. The young woman, dressed smartly in a red jacket and matching red shoes, leaned over the pram to tuck in her diminutive charge, then looked about her. She had a long, pale face with dark eyes. Jenkins thought there was a sadness to the face, a sense of tragedy.

She opened the gate, wheeled the pram through it, then engaged the wheel lock and went back into the house for a few moments. Jenkins glanced at his watch and waited for the young mother to return.

This routine was a regular occurrence and he had estimated that the pram was left alone for an average of one minute before the mother returned. The problem, however, was the presence of passers-by. On six separate occasions he had left his house at the exact moment when the pram had been left unattended, but on each of those occasions there had been either cars or pedestrians in the street who might have seen him snatching the child. He had begun to keep a daily diary and had discovered that of all the days of the week, Wednesday was the day on which they were hardly any passers-by to impede his plan.

He adjusted the lens of the telescope and watched as mother and pram made their way up Romany Road towards the Heath. He had even thought of intercepting the pram on the Heath itself. Indeed, once on a Sunday, he had passed the pram and said good morning to the mother. At that point he knew he could have overpowered the woman and grabbed the child, but that would have meant losing his anonymity.

Jenkins was on the sex register and would have been a prime suspect. Providing an alibi would not have been a problem since his younger brother would vouch for him, but that wasn't really the issue. No, he needed to proceed with stealth and cunning if he were to succeed.

He had never seen the child, never seen the mother take the infant from the pram, but that had not stopped him from fantasising. It was the fantasies which drove him on and fuelled the obsession. Sooner or later, he must act and the sooner the better he told himself. But for now, he had the Internet and the thousand or more images he had stored on his memory sticks.

He looked at his watch. 9:05 AM as usual. There was nothing more he could do. Tomorrow was Wednesday. Now, more than ever, he must bring matters to a head.

DCI Huw Emrys Price, aka. Ketch, of the Norwich police, sat down on a bench in the Castle Gardens and reached inside his jacket pocket for a packet of cigarettes. Although it was a fine July day and the sun was shining overhead, for all he cared, it could have been overcast and raining. For Ketch was a troubled man and had been cloud-girt since the previous evening when Carol Hennessey had broken the news to him. Of course, he had feigned cheerfulness, but inwardly it was as if a great chasm of despondency had opened up and threatened to annihilate him. Unlike Carol, Ketch, as he was known to his friends and colleagues in the job, was far from young. In November last year he had chosen to ignore the big five O and these days he avoided looking in the mirrors.

He'd even taken steps to remove a large mirror in his bathroom. The jowls, the deep lines etched on his forehead, the receding hairline, all these signs bore witness to the fact that he was no longer the man he once was. They were the stigmata of old age he told himself.

Excessive drinking had expanded his midriff and he could no longer sprint when pursuing criminals, often leaving the job to his patient sidekick, DS Tim MacKenzie. Realistically, Ketch knew he had only a few years left now in the force and with the prospect of retirement looming, this was no time to enter into fatherhood for the second time. Carol had broken the news to him the previous night. He'd taken a shower in her luxurious bijou flat and returned to the bedroom, his sagging stomach swathed in a towelling robe.

"Aren't you pleased?" she said, her face exultant.

"Pleased? I'm over the moon," he replied. But inwardly, he wasn't at all pleased. He was terrified. Yes, he had to admit it, he *was* terrified. By the time the infant had become a teenager, he'd be 65 years old and, at the rate by which he'd been abusing himself with fags and booze and cheap takeaways, probably decrepit if not completely deceased.

But Carol, the forensic pathologist who he'd fallen for over a year ago, Carol who was 20 years his junior, young, athletic and sexy, clearly hadn't thought through their joint prospects.

"I'm totally delighted," he affirmed, his robe slipping from his waist with the shock. Carol had glanced at his nakedness and smiled but when Ketch glanced down at his drooping sex organs and his protuberant stomach, he couldn't imagine what she saw in him. He told himself he was like a father figure to Carol. That was what she saw in him. After all, it wasn't uncommon among some young women.

One thing was certain about this sorry affair. He could never tell her the truth about how he felt. He would just have to accept his fatherhood as a sort of vengeance from the gods. Ketch was feeling angry about the gods. His wife Annie had died after a prolonged struggle with cancer and his son had cuckolded him, a fact which he'd never quite managed to come to terms with.

He finished his cigarette and coughed spasmodically, aware that a young woman sitting on a bench opposite him was watching his convulsion. He felt embarrassed and ground the fag under his left foot. Just then, his mobile phone rang.

"Sorry to interrupt your lunch hour sir."

"No problem Tim. What's up?"

"Missing person, missing infant to be precise. The mother rang it in about 45 minutes ago, very distraught."

"Where was this precisely?"

"At the end of the Royal Arcade, adjacent to Gentleman's Walk in the middle of the city. Apparently, she had gone into a sandwich bar and when she came out again the child was missing from the pram."

"Where's the mother now?"

"Back home. Number 253 Romany Road. WPC Davis is with her."

"Okay, I'll see you there in 20 minutes."

Romany Road. He remembered it well from the time when he and Anne used to park at the top of the road and walk their golden Labrador, Jake, on Mousehold Heath. Romany Road, named after the Romanies who used to camp there in the 19th century, immortalised by the Norfolk painter, George Borrow. When he needed air and space, the Heath was still a place where Ketch went to unwind and gain a perspective on his existence, a great high expanse of common land which commanded a view over the surrounding city.

The Heath had enjoyed a chequered history. In 1144, a boy had been found murdered there, a crime blamed on the Jews who had, so rumour had it, ritually murdered him. In the late Middle Ages, it had seen the final battle of the Peasant's Revolt and in the 16th century, had provided a place to camp for the followers of the ill-fated William Kett. These days, it was a favourite place for joggers and dog walkers. Ketch liked to walk in the city and rarely drove, having an aversion to cars, but this morning his lassitude got the better of him and he hailed a cab.

Number 253 Romany Road was one of a number of typical 1930's properties which had seen better days. WPC Davis, a fresh-faced recruit who'd been in the force only for a year, stood at the front door as Ketch paid the taxi driver his fare. "How's the mother doing?"

"Holding up, sir."

She stood aside to let him pass into the hallway. "A pot of tea would be good," he said quietly, entering a sparsely furnished room with dark red wallpaper and closed curtains. Ketch was struck at how gloomy and claustrophobic the room was. Tim MacKenzie stood up.

"Mrs Atwell," he said. "This is Chief Inspector Price." The woman was short and dark haired with hollow cheeks, stained with mascara. She extended a thin hand which Ketch shook . He glanced at the husband next to her. Tall and fair-haired, he looked as if he worked out and was possibly younger than the woman.

"Lucy," the woman said, "and this is my husband, John."

WPC Davis returned with the tea which she began to pour.

"Mrs Atwell has already described what happened this morning,"

185

MacKenzie explained to Ketch.

"That's fine. Nevertheless, I'd like you to go over it again - if you feel up to it, that is."

The woman nodded, dabbed her cheeks with a tissue and reached for her husband's hand. "By all means, inspector. As I told your officer here, it was a sunny day, so I decided take Phoebe down into the city. I needed to do a bit of shopping."

"And you walked down."

"Yes."

"When you set out, did you notice anything unusual?"

"In what way?"

"Was there anyone about? Did you notice anyone following you, for example?"

"One or two people I guess. The paperboy, and the guy who lives opposite, he was in his front garden. He said good morning."

"Okay. What time did you get to the sandwich bar?"

"I'm not entirely sure. Does it matter?"

"It matters."

"Let's see… I went to the cashpoint at the Halifax and took out some money. I checked my mobile for messages. There was one from my sister Mary which I then deleted."

"And why was that?"

"Lucy has a problem with her older sister," said John Atwell. "She suffers from schizophrenia. Last year we had to get a restraining order against her."

"And why was that?"

"She's abusive and has been violent towards Lucy. She resents what she has, resents the fact that she's had a child." Lucy Atwell glanced at her husband.

"She has a thing about John. She thinks she's in love with him and that I was responsible for taking him from her."

"And this is all fantasy, I take it?"

"Absolute fantasy. John never did anything to encourage her."

"Mary and I used to be fellow students at the UEA. That's how I met Lucy – a few years ago now."

"I see. What was the context of the text that she sent you?"

"It was the usual threatening stuff, incoherent really."

"The problem with Mary is that she often refuses to take her medication," said John Atwell. "That's when she becomes potentially dangerous. Last Thursday she turned up at the house at around 2 AM, demanding to see her child. She'd got it into her head that Phoebe was her child and that we'd had an affair."

"I see. At what time did you get this text?" he asked Lucy.

"At 9.15 or thereabouts, I remember that."

"Then what did you do?"

"Then I made my way up Gentleman's Walk to the sandwich bar on the corner. It was such a nice sunny day I thought I'd get a sandwich made up and send a text to John, suggesting that we meet for lunch in the Castle Gardens after I'd done a bit of shopping."

"So where did you leave the pram exactly?"

"As I told your colleagues here, I left the pram right outside the shop. It has a big plate glass window, so you can keep an eye on the pram from inside."

"And you gave your order, then you waited for your sandwich to be made up. How long did that take exactly?"

"About 10 minutes I would guess."

"And when you were waiting, did you keep an eye on the pram?"

"I looked around at least three times, I remember."

"And you didn't notice anything unusual?"

She shook her head. "No, nothing. Just people passing by, it was very busy."

Ketch nodded.

"Lucy told the officer all this earlier," said John Atwell.

"I'm sure she did, but sometimes it helps to go over the events again in some detail. It can jog the memory, Mr Atwell."

There was a pause.

"Do you have a photograph of Phoebe that we could use, Mrs Atwell? Something fairly recent perhaps?"

"We have some framed photos in her bedroom," said Lucy. Ketch accompanied her upstairs. They entered a back bedroom and Lucy Atwell took a framed photograph from a collection which had been carefully arranged on a small dressing table. Ketch glanced round the room. It had been recently painted a shade of bright pink and was immaculately tidy. There were colourful mobiles hanging from the ceiling and an expensive looking cot. Everything in the room was neat and orderly as if the contents had just come from a catalogue and there was a smell of cleaning fluid and freshly laundered sheets.

Ketch took the photograph out of its frame and looked at the small, round, smiling face. "How old is Phoebe?" he asked.

"Just 18 months."

He placed a reassuring hand on her shoulder. "Don't worry, we shall do everything in our power to find Phoebe for you."

By the afternoon, the team swung into action. Ketch placed Tim MacKenzie in charge of the CCTV surveillance with a group of three other officers who examined material from three of the shops which adjoined the market and Gentleman's Walk. He also contacted the media and e-mailed Phoebe's photo to both local and national press contacts, together with a brief statement.

After a liquid lunch accompanied by an indigestible pork pie at The Grapes, he returned to his desk where he examined the sex offenders register for the area. Two names came up but the most significant of these geographically was one Roland Jenkins. Jenkins, who had served a prison sentence for molesting two teenage girls on a housing estate in Hellesdon, had been released only six months ago and had taken up residence in Romany Road. Ketch decided he was in line for a visit.

The next day was cloudy and misty, all traces of the hot summer weather having given way to an intense humidity. MacKenzie drove Ketch to Romany Road where the two discovered Jenkins' house was directly opposite that of the Atwell's.

"Déjà vu," said MacKenzie as they got out of the car. They rang the doorbell and a short, fat man with small eyes appeared, wiping his mouth with a dirty napkin.

"Mr Jenkins? Police. We'd like a word with you please." Ketch put his warrant card back in his jacket pocket and Jenkins led the way through a dingy hallway into a small, poorly furnished lounge where Ketch and MacKenzie sat in two faded armchairs. Jenkins placed himself opposite them and crossed his legs defensively. He looked distinctly ill at ease.

"What's this about?" he asked nervously.

"I'm DCI Price and this is my colleague, DS MacKenzie," said Ketch. "We are investigating the disappearance of a small child."

"I see. And what has this to do with me inspector?"

"It has to do with your neighbour, a Mrs Atwell. She lives opposite you."

"I'm afraid I can't help you at all in the matter. When exactly did this take place?"

"Yesterday morning. Can you tell us exactly where you were yesterday morning?"

"When exactly?"

"Around 9 AM."

Jenkins steepled his fingers, then lowered his head as if he were an actor preparing to perform.

"Certainly. I left the house at around 8:30 AM and made my way down to the city via Ketts Hill. I arrived in the centre at approximately 9 AM and proceeded to the cashpoint machine at the Royal Bank Of Scotland where I took out £50. I then went into the market where I purchased fish and some vegetables before returning home by foot." Jenkins smiled and unclasped his hands. "Is there anything else I can help you with?"

"You live alone here, Mr Jenkins?"

"I do. This was my mother's house. She passed away some months ago."

"Mind if we take a look around?"

"I have no objection at all."

MacKenzie remained seated while Ketch made his way into the dining room and kitchen. Everything was immaculately clean, neat and orderly, the mark of a meticulous man.

He climbed the stairs. At the back of the property was a small bedroom which had been turned into a study. It was lined with books, many of them relating to British history. On a table stood a small laptop and a printer. He moved across the landing into the front bedroom, where there was an overpowering scent of lavender. A small single bed, a round oak table with a vase of flowers and a telescope, mounted on a tripod.

He stood by the window. From here Jenkins had a bird's eye view of the Atwell's front room and garden. He opened a wardrobe, but there was nothing of importance except a rail of well-arranged shirts and trousers and a small black holdall. Inside this, neatly packed, was a selection of pants and socks, and beneath them a small video camera. He turned it on and pressed the replay button but there was nothing more significant than shots of Mousehold Heath and the River Wensum. Clearly, if Jenkins had something to hide, he had been unusually careful. He returned to the lounge.

"Thank you Mr Jenkins. That will be all for now."

Outside, in the car, MacKenzie said: "Anything sir?"

"Nothing. He's good, I'll say that for him. Get Thomas to keep a watch on the house, will you? Meanwhile, let's see what the CCTV might yield. Do we have an address for the sister?"

"She lives in a bedsit in Heigham Road." Ketch knew the road, a small turning of the Earlham Road and not far from his own flat.

"Good, let's pay her a visit, shall we?"

Heigham Road was a short stretch of modest Victorian cottages which had once been elegant and respectably trim, but was showing signs of wear and tear. These days, the villas had been largely given over to student accommodation.

Ketch surveyed the intercom, then pressed the button marked M. Robinson. They waited but there was no response. He pressed it again and the front door opened. A tall, emaciated youth with dreadlocks stood in the doorway. Ketch detected a whiff of marijuana.

"Yes?"

"We're looking for Mary. Is she in?"

"She's at the nursery where she works. Who might you be?"

Ketch showed his warrant card. "And who might you be?" he asked.

"I'm Kevin, her flatmate."

"When will she be back?"

"She gets in and around three pm."

Ketch handed him a card. "When she does return, ask her to give me a ring, will you?"

The youth nodded and shut the front door. They walked to the car.

"Drugs?" MacKenzie asked.

"Oh certainly. He has that reanimated corpse complexion of the heroin addict. I'm sure you noticed it." MacKenzie nodded.

By lunchtime, the skies had cleared. Ketch decided that, since he was feeling unusually cheerful, he'd offer to take MacKenzie to lunch at one of his favourite watering holes, the Adam and Eve pub, a hostelry set by the river and well-known for its selection of real ales. They sat outside in the hot summer sunshine where Ketch could indulge his nicotine habit.

"Anything yet from the CCTV?" Ketch enquired.

"No, nothing yet. There were three cameras, one above the

Halifax, one adjacent to Smith's and the third was above the marketplace itself. Only the marketplace camera shows the pram and then the image is indistinct, been partly blocked by a news vendors' van."

"What about digital enhancement?"

"Limited effect from that distance. One thing though. The pram was outside the sandwich shop longer than Lucy Atwell claimed. She must have lost track of the time when she recalled the incident."

Ketch paused as his Ploughman's arrived, then finished his pint.

"What about this character Jenkins?"

"He's kept a clean sheet since his release from prison. I looked over the report from the psychologist."

"And?"

"He has a particular obsession with very young children –female children. When his computer was seized, the investigating team found over 1000 abusive images. He'd been downloading material from a paedophile ring which operated from the Netherlands."

"Let's get a search warrant and see what we can find."

Ketch's mobile rang. "Yes, speaking. Okay, right. We'll see you at five pm then."

"Who was that?" asked MacKenzie.

"Mary Robinson. Finish that pint and I'll get you another one."

MacKenzie placed his hand over the glass. "One's enough for me thanks."

By four thirty pm there was still nothing concrete from the CCTV. The best the team could come up with was an image of Roland Jenkins, visiting the Halifax bank machine at the time he had indicated. For 10 minutes, the image of the pram had been obscured by a group of youths who stood chatting in Gentleman's Walk so that it would have been entirely possible during that time for the perpetrator to have snatched the child and, given the number of passers-by, little notice would have been given to such an event.

By five pm the intense July heat had begun to abate and a thin layer of cloud covered the sky. Ketch, who didn't do well in sticky conditions, was glad of the relief that it afforded him.

Mary Robinson was a tall, thin individual whose blond hair had been crafted into dreadlocks. She answered the door shoeless, wearing a worn green T-shirt and a pair of faded denim shorts. As they passed through the hallway, Ketch immediately noticed the needle marks on her forearm. They entered a large living room, furnished with two battered second-hand chairs, a scratched pine table and several stained floor cushions. There was a smell of stale wine and cannabis. Ketch sat down on the chair and it creaked beneath him.

"I guess you have come to ask me about sis?"

"We have."

"What do you want to know?"

"You sent your sister a text early yesterday morning. Will you tell us what the content of that text was?"

"Yes, I can tell you. Sis owes me money. When I quit the house in Romany Road, I left behind some jewellery which I subsequently found out Lucy – or John more probably – had sold. Three times I've asked for the cash value of the jewellery but she just ignores me."

"You lived with them?"

"We all shared the house the year before I left uni, when John and me put down a cash deposit. John coughed up the lion's share which was a legacy from when his mother died. I was in love with John then. Lucy lodged with us. We were both doing the same psychology course. When John was in his final year at teacher training college, big sis moved in on John."

"Which is why you resent her?"

"Which is why I shall never forgive her for what she did to me. And what's equally unforgivable is the fact that I never got my £5000 back. It was an arrangement between us but I had nothing on paper to prove it. We'd planned to buy the house together, have children –"

She paused, her eyes welling with tears. Then she reached for a tobacco tin and began rolling herself a cigarette. "Then I fell ill," she continued. "Very ill. But I'm getting over it," she added. She lit a cigarette and the room filled with the pungent aroma of cheap tobacco. "Now they won't allow me to go near the house. I've never seen Phoebe. They won't let me near her, they treat me as if I'm some sort of freak. They even took out a restraining order against me."

"Why was that?"

"Because I messed up John's car."

"Messed up?"

"I poured bleach over it." She stared across at Ketch and chewed her bottom lip.

"Can you tell me what you were doing at 9 AM yesterday

morning?" he asked.

"I was here as usual."

"Alone?"

"Yes, alone. Kev had gone into town to see someone he knew."

"Kev?"

"My partner. I got up around 8 AM, had a wash, then went for a short walk. That's when I sent a text to her."

"You didn't walk into the city centre then?"

"No, just down the Earlham Road and back. I got a few things from the 24-hour shop, then I came back here."

Ketch woke early the next morning, his head full of a vivid dream. He was sitting on Mousehold Heath with Carol who'd been rocking a large Victorian pram. The pram squeaked every time it moved. When he complained to her she stood up, reached into the pram, then took out a hideous old doll which she presented to him. "Here you are, you can change his nappy. It's the least you can do," she said.

He found that he was unable to speak and when he finally awoke, his mouth was as dry as parchment paper. He rolled over to the side of the bed, trying not to wake Carol, then went into the bathroom to get himself a glass of water. When he returned, Carol had turned over, revealing her ample breasts. How beautiful she looked in the early morning sunlight. He glanced down at her swelling abdomen and then thought of his forthcoming responsibilities as a father. It filled him with abject horror. There was no way he could tell her. He just had to keep it to himself. He hoped he could maintain the pretence. God forbid if he dropped his guard.

By 9 AM when Ketch left Carol's flat, the sun was already hot on his head and shoulders. He removed his suit jacket and made his way up Pull's Ferry Lane towards the city centre, his thoughts still preoccupied with that odd dream.

He had to face facts. He couldn't keep stumm much longer about the matter. He resolved that he would talk to Carol about how he felt and he'd better do it tonight.

By the time they got to Romany Road, the day was blisteringly hot, despite the fact that it was only 10 AM. Ketch was convinced that when he was a boy, summers were nowhere as hot as this. DC Thomas got out of the unmarked car which had been parked some way down the road and approached Ketch and MacKenzie.

"Anything?" Ketch asked.

"He's been to the Spar shop down Ketts Hill, then he walked up onto the Heath, that's all."

The door opened to reveal Jenkins, clad in a long blue dressing gown, his hair glistening. There was a strong smell of bath oil.

"Inspector. How pleasant to see you again – and your friend. How may I help you this morning?"

"We have a warrant to search these premises," came the curt reply.

While MacKenzie searched the downstairs rooms, Ketch took an extendable ladder and opened the loft hatch. Aided by a powerful torch, he searched it from end to end but without success. Plastic bin liners littered the area, stuffed full with old clothes, bric-a-brac and pornographic magazines of the hard-core variety.

By now Ketch was sweating profusely, drops of perspiration pitter - pattering on the bin liners as he made his way methodically through the chaos of Jenkins's effects. Satisfied that he had found nothing of any significance, he climbed down the ladder and, pausing to mop his forehead, joined MacKenzie in the lounge where Jenkins stood to attention, his back to the window. MacKenzie was clutching Jenkins' laptop.

"I hope you're going to return that to me," said Jenkins, pointing to the computer.

"In good time," Ketch replied.

"Only it's my absolute lifeline, you see. It helps me keep in touch with distant friends. It's part of my support network you might say."

You mean your paedophile support network thought Ketch.

"Any luck with your investigation yet?" he continued. Ketch didn't reply. "If you've done here, let's go," he instructed MacKenzie.

Outside, in the car, MacKenzie closed the windows and switched on the air conditioning.

"Let's see what we can get from the laptop," Ketch said.

"Oh, I should have mentioned it earlier," said MacKenzie. "I put Mary Robinson's name into the system."

"And?"

"She has previous. Possession of cannabis. Also, a GBH when she was a student. It took place when she was in the third year of her psychology degree at the UEA. She attacked another female student with a knife. Quite a vicious attack. Got a suspended sentence owing to her psychological condition." Ketch nodded.

"Contact the Psychology Department at the University. Let's see if we can talk to somebody about it. No word from the Atwells yet?"

"No, nothing. We have set up the record device on the telephone in case of ransom calls, but there's been nothing yet."

Professor Pilbury, their contact at the UEA, was tied up with lectures all that morning, so Ketch and MacKenzie, having an hour or so to spare, took advantage of the fact. They found a small catering van in a layby next to Earlham Park Road and, armed with beef burgers, found a seat overlooking the River.

Ketch ate half of his burger. It was greasy and tasteless and he threw the rest of it in a bin. When he returned to the bench, MacKenzie said: "Do you think Jenkins has abducted the child, sir?"

"I'm not at all sure what I believe, MacKenzie. He has means, motive, and opportunity, that's for sure. I don't believe the front he put up for one moment. Let's see what his laptop can tell us shall we?"

"What about the sister?"

"A distinct possibility. She has no alibi."

"Oh, by the way, that crowd of youths who were captured on the CCTV, standing outside the cafe."

"What about them?"

"DC Thomas recognised one of them – Wayne Doyle."

"The boy off the Hellesdon estate?"

"The same."

"Now there's a possibility... Let's get him in for questioning. He may not have had anything to do with the abduction itself but nevertheless, he might prove to be a useful witness."

Professor Pilbury was much younger than Ketch had expected him to be. Smart and urbane, he had the manner of a TV presenter about him. Hardly Ketch's view of what an academic should look like.

"So you want to know about Lucy and Mary Robinson, Inspector?"

Ketch nodded.

"I must first tell you that Lucy was the brightest of the two students."

"They both took a psychology degree course?"

"That is so. Though Mary found it impossible to complete her

195

third year. That was hardly surprising, considering her overwhelming mental difficulties at the time."

"You mean her schizophrenia?"

"Yes, though the term is a very approximate one you must understand. And during her first and second years here she had not yet been diagnosed with the condition. She also suffered from paranoid delusions."

"And attacked a female student when she was in her final year?"

"Indeed she did. Which is partly why she was not able to proceed with her course. You know quite a bit about her I can see."

"A fair amount."

"It was a tragic case, inspector. A ménage a trois you might say. She'd fallen in love with a third-year student – one John Atwell. They'd set up house together and had, according to Mary, intended to marry. But then John Atwell turned his attention to Mary's sister. Absolute dynamite, considering Mary's fragile psyche. You know about her obsession with having children I suppose?"

"Enlighten me."

"She was always talking about the idea. She even took the child psychology unit as part of her degree course. She'd intended to train to become an infant school teacher when she finished her degree. Of course that never happened as things turned out in the end. It was probably for the best."

By the time they left the Psychology Department at the UEA and made their way to the visitors' car park, the main concourse was full of students. As Ketch got into the driver's seat, MacKenzie asked him: "What's next then? Do we re- interview Mary Robinson?"

"Softly softly, MacKenzie. No, I think not, we wait and see what happens."

"Don't you think that she abducted the child?"

"Let's not theorise without the facts. As someone once said, it's a very destructive habit, so perhaps you'd desist."

When he finally got back to Carol's flat, there was a delicious smell of spices. Carol was in the kitchen, presiding over a curry. She'd gone to considerable effort, laying the table with candles and linen napkins. She'd turned the lights down and on the CD player, 'Enigma' was playing softly.

The place resembled a love nest he thought. Carol was wearing a loose fitting green dress with a plunging neckline and smelt of perfume. His resolve crumbled. Now was not the time to bare his feelings towards her. It would just have to wait until the morning.

When morning did come his resolve was dealt a further blow. A bout of early morning love-making was followed by tea and toast in bed. At 7.30, Carol announced that she would shower and make tracks, having an autopsy to perform. Ketch tried to say something to her but his throat dried and all he could say was: "I'll see you later than."

When he got to HQ at 9 AM, MacKenzie was waiting for him. "There's been a development," he told Ketch.

Lucy Atwell had clearly been crying. She sat opposite Ketch and MacKenzie, pale-faced, her husband trying to comfort her. He handed Ketch the envelope. "It came in this morning's post," he said. Ketch slipped on a pair of forensic gloves and opened the envelope.

"You both touched the contents?" he asked. John Atwell nodded. The note had been computer printed in a large, Gothic font. It read: 'Your baby is dead.'

He replaced the note in the envelope as Lucy Atwell wept again.

"I shouldn't put much store by it," he told them. "It could be from a crank. We will get it tested for prints. You have had no communication by phone, I take it?"

"Only from Mary," said John Atwell.

"And what was that about?"

"She accused us of pointing the finger at her as she put it. She didn't much like being interviewed by the police. She got quite abusive, so I hung up on her."

"When was this?"

"Yesterday evening."

Ketch remembered the youth from the Hellesdon estate. Wayne Doyle was a tall gangly teenager with dyed blonde hair. His arms, which were muscular, sported a series of tattoos and on the knuckles of his left hand were letters, spelling the word hate.

A much plumper and older version of Wayne sat next to his son, arms folded over a protuberant stomach.

"What's all this about Wayne?" he demanded.

"We need to ask him a few questions about where he was on

Wednesday morning."

"What's he done, then?"

"As far as we know, he's done nothing. Wayne, you and some friends were caught on CCTV in the city at the end of the Royal Arcade. This would have been around 9 AM. Do you remember that?"

The youth grinned and nodded. "Yeah, I remember, me and a few mates went into town to look in HMV."

Ketch produced a photograph of Roland Jenkins and laid it before Wayne on the table. "Do you remember seeing this man?"

"Maybe. There was a geezer by the bank machine further down the street – maybe he looks like him – not sure – could be."

"Did you notice if there was a person standing outside the cafe where you were?"

"Yeah, I remember, an old-fashioned pram thing. It made us all laugh cos Johnny pushed one end of it and made it rock."

"Did you notice if there was a child in the pram when your friend was rocking it?"

"Nah, there wasn't a child. We thought it might belong to some old bag lady. Made us all laugh."

Ketch showed him a photograph of Lucy Atwell. "Do you remember seeing this woman?"

"Yeah, she come out of the cafe and started shouting. Looked kind of crazy. We legged it into the market. Didn't want no trouble. That's all that happened."

"Is that it, then?" asked Mr Doyle, frowning.

"Yes, that's it," replied Ketch.

"So he can go now?"

"Yes, Wayne is free to go."

When the Doyles had left, there was a long silence. MacKenzie said: "What do you make of it, sir?"

"It's rather like the incident of the dog in the night-time," said Ketch.

"I don't follow you."

"The dog did nothing in the night-time, that was the curious incident."

"I still don't quite follow you," said MacKenzie, who was no reader of crime fiction.

"I mean that there was no baby in that pram. There wasn't a baby that morning and there never has been one. That, Tim, is the curious incident."

Lucy Atwell sat in interview room six, her face stained with tears. Her husband sat next to her. Ketch showed her the letter again.

"You sent this to yourself I believe?"

She nodded. "I thought it would be right."

"Right so you could keep up the pretence?"

"I had to go through with it, once we had committed."

"And whose idea was it?"

"It was my idea. I persuaded John to go through with it."

"It started when Lucy's baby died," said John. The baby lived for only five days – that was 18 months back."

"You have a death certificate I presume?"

"We don't have one. The baby was born at home and I helped to deliver it. Lucy hates hospitals and she refused to see a midwife. She wanted to have the baby at home."

"And what happened to the baby?"

"We buried Phoebe in the back garden – it seemed the right thing for us to do. We kept her room just as it should be, and the pram. That helped Lucy a great deal. It kept Phoebe's memory alive you see." John Atwell looked apprehensively at Ketch. "Will we be charged?"

"With wasting police time, yes, certainly. We had best go back to Romany Road and see the grave but first, I shall need you both to sign statements."

Ketch sat in the saloon bar of The Murderers, in Timber Hill, supping a pint of its excellent real ale. The pub was one of three watering holes in the city where he often retreated to console himself. And tonight was one of those occasions.

He should have trusted his instincts and kept his feelings private. Instead, he had let reason prevail and told Carol the truth about how he had felt. The results had been devastating.

He finished his pint then reached for the whiskey chaser. The golden whiskey burned his throat and it felt good. He tried to blot out the events of the previous evening but they persisted. Carol's tear stained face, the broken crockery, the demands that he pack his things and leave the flat. He had returned to his own flat off the Earlham Road to find a heap of junk mail and bills. The place was more austere and cluttered than he had recalled and it smelled of unwashed clothes and stale whiskey bottles. A bachelor paradise...

It was boiling hot so he opened the windows, surprised at the accumulation of dust and spiders' webs on their surfaces. And so he had walked across the city in the cool of the evening and ended up here in The Murderers, so-called after the landlady's daughter, one Mildred Miles, had been done to death in 1895 by her mother's partner. A fitting watering hole for DCI Ketch.

They had dropped the charge against Lucy and John Atwell. Ketch had read the psychologist's report and discovered that she was suffering from Asperger's Syndrome. It was a sorry tale. Both daughters had been brought up on a farm near Dereham, the mother having died from cancer when the two girls were quite young. The father had kept his abuse of his two teenage daughters a secret until the older daughter, Mary, had attacked a fellow pupil at her school and had undergone a psychological assessment. Then the truth had come out. The father had been abusing them for four years and the mother had been complicit in the horrors that had taken place at Danvers Farm.

As a result, a terrible, and unending rivalry had ensued and both of the daughters had developed unfulfilled fantasies about child-rearing. When Ketch and two constables were led into the garden at number 253 Romany Road, they discovered a small unmarked grave next to a derelict shed. It had been a sad and poignant experience staring down at the tiny body.

Ketch finished his chaser, put out his cigarette and left the pub. He made his way down Timber Hill past the great Norman castle where the soft evening sunlight illuminated its smooth facade. Years ago, the likes of Lucy Atwell would have been brought here to spend time at Her Majesty's Pleasure but these days, the justice system was a tad more lenient. Thank God for that anyway.

He passed a young mother, wheeling a buggy, and glimpsed the tiny face and hands. Tomorrow, he told himself, he would give Carol a ring and try to resolve matters. Although the prospect of being a father again filled him with apprehension, maybe it was the right thing to do. Just maybe he could get used to it.

THE FENLAND MURDERS

The little village of Gedney Bridgewater lies some 5 miles west of Long Sutton in an area of East Anglia known as the Fens. Once a vast area of marshland, the Fens has always enjoyed a reputation of being a place remote and cut off from the rest of the county. In winter, a peculiar feeling of desolation and otherworldliness clings to this great flat land, where the soil has been trained to form deep dykes. And because there are no fences or boundaries by the roadsides, each year the dykes claim their victims, whose cars plunge into the dark depths.

Older denizens of the Fens say that the land hereabouts demands a yearly sacrifice, a theory which is scoffed at by members of the younger generation. Even so, the belief remains and is borne out by the annual road traffic accident statistics in this desolate and sparsely populated region.

Peter Oliver was but 15 years old when he fell victim to the Fens. Some of the inhabitants of Gedney Bridgewater described him as the 'golden boy', not least because of his golden, glossy, shoulder-length hair and deep blue eyes.

Those who were close to Peter often remarked that there was something otherworldly and troubled about the boy. His piercing blue eyes seemed to examine your soul and his gaze was unwavering. But he didn't speak, not that is, until shortly after his 15th birthday. For Peter Oliver was an elective mute. No one in Gedney Bridgewater, not even Anne and Frank Cushing , his foster parents, knew what trauma had closed a wall of silence around the growing boy, no one it later transpired, save one person, who was determined to keep his silence a secret from the world.

Despite his silence, in all other respects, Peter Oliver was a normal, healthy boy, an excellent athlete and academically gifted, according to his teachers. Like many other boys of his age, Peter loved cycling and, in the summer months, travelled the length and breadth of the flat roads around the Fens, equipped with a pair of high-powered binoculars, for he was a keen birdwatcher. He also relied on his bicycle to accomplish his daily newspaper round and it was this chore which was to prove his undoing.

On the morning of 30 June, 2003, several residents of Gedney

Bridgewater phoned the small newsagents in the village to complain that they were without their daily newspaper. By 9:30 AM on that same morning, Alice Cushing also phoned the shop to enquire as to Peter's whereabouts.

At 10 AM an early commuter, setting off for Kings Lynn, noticed a bicycle, lying beside the road, adjacent to the Great Dyke. Newspapers lay scattered across the road and, stopping to investigate, the driver spotted what appeared on first sight to be a bundle of clothes lying in the murky brown waters.

At 10 AM on that same Monday morning, DCI Huw Price, a.k.a. Ketch, woke abruptly. For a brief moment, he wondered where he was. As his eyes grew accustomed to the high-end finish of the bedroom with its stainless steel lamp and glass table, the reality then dawned on him. He was in Dr Carol Hennessy's apartment. In fact, he had been in Dr Hennessy's bed since the previous evening. That in itself was slightly disturbing, since he had no clear recollection of the events which preceded his arrival here.

Slowly, his memory assisted him. It had started with a dinner date at an Indian restaurant in Norwich, a favourite place of Ketch's where he knew the staff well. The date had been the culmination of several promising encounters with the young pathologist, who was 20 years his junior. Several times, matters had almost come to a head, but there was in Ketch a hatred of consummation probably fuelled by his awareness of his advancing years. For one thing, he had never believed that he was intrinsically attractive to women, a belief which his former wife Annie had tried to persuade him was not true. Nevertheless, the doubts remained.

Ketch pulled back the bed covers and, realising that he was naked, grabbed a towel from the chair opposite to conceal his sagging, gravity challenged body. He caught sight of his gaunt, lined face in the bedroom mirror. Deep grooves etched his forehead, the blue eyes surrounded by a lattice of creases, the chin already sprouting a two day accumulation of stubble. How could anyone make love to someone with a face like that? To him, it was an enigma. He felt an urgent need to pee and made his way to the bathroom. Through the shower screen, he could make out Carol's shapely back and buttocks as she showered, apparently oblivious to his presence. He tried urinating on the side of the pan, embarrassed by her close proximity and the sounds that he was making. Brief snatches of last night's lovemaking crossed his mind. It was an activity he had to admit he just was not very good at. Hopefully, she would have made allowances for him. The shower door opened and Carol smiled at him. He glanced at her athletic form, the large pert breasts glistening with beads of water, the slender waist and prominent mons Veneris.

"Is that your mobile ringing?" she asked, "or is it mine?"

"Both," he replied.

After a brief breakfast and two welcome cigarettes on Carol's balcony, they drove north from the city in the direction of Kings Lynn. Though he was slightly uneasy about sharing the car with Carol, it seemed the practical thing to do, though it might raise some eyebrows when they arrived at the scene of the crime.

He was glad that Carol was driving. Ketch rarely drove these days. Though he had had a licence for 30 years or more, cars were, along with much other modern technology, complete anathema to him. With Carol's permission, he wound down the passenger window and indulged in his third cigarette that morning.

"They'll kill you in the end," she advised him.

"Life kills you in the end," was his riposte.

He had forgotten what the terrain looked like this far west of Kings Lynn, the broad, flat fields, interspersed with lines of poplar trees and the occasional, scattered hamlets, each one with its small church and red brick pub. It was a quiet, almost forgotten land, far from the hustle and bustle of Norwich, his home city. Strange to think that once, much of this area, up until the 13th century, was covered in dense forest.

The car passed through a small village with an ornate sign, marked Gedney Bridgewater and a large church with a flat topped bell tower. Onwards the car sped, past two scattered terraces of houses, until, on one side of the road was a broad swathe of early oil seed rape crop and on the other a deep dyke. Then ahead, Ketch spotted a huddle of police vehicles and the familiar barrier tape.

"This is it," he said, as Carol slowed the car to a halt.

From the edge of the dyke, the familiar face of DS Tim MacKenzie loomed into view.

"Morning Sir, morning Dr Hennessy." Ketch thought he detected a slight grin.

"What do we have here?" asked Ketch.

"Body of a local boy, one Peter Oliver."

Ketch and Dr Hennessy got out of the car and began donning their obligatory white suits.

"Who found him?"

"Delivery driver. He noticed the abandoned bicycle about 9:30 AM this morning and went to investigate. He found him lying face down in the dyke."

"Did he move the body?"

"Yes, onto the edge of the bank over there. He thought he might still be alive. No one has since touched it though."

Ketch waited on the bank as Carol carried out a preliminary examination of the body.

"It appears that he sustained a heavy blow to the back of the head, then was dragged into the Dyke," she told Ketch. "You can also see marks in the earth here and here. There are two sets of marks, the first where the body was pulled into the dyke, the other where the driver dragged the body out."

Ketch looked at the boy. Golden hair, matted with the detritus of the Dyke, framed an angelic face. The lips were full, the features chiselled. It was a Pre-Raphaelite face with a deathly pallor.

"What was he doing here?"

"He was on his paper round, in fact, he was on the last leg of it when he must have been attacked. That farmhouse yonder would have been his last delivery."

"Have the parents been informed yet?"

MacKenzie nodded. "Foster parents. Anne and Frank Cushing. They have a cottage by the church. WPC Atkins is with them now."

"Foster parents you say. What happened to his real parents?"

"The father deserted them some years back. The mother was murdered about eight years ago."

Ketch trawled his extensive memory. Diane Oliver...He recalled the case... It also explained why the name Gedney Bridgewater had been nagging at him during the journey here. In the summer of 2001, a young woman had gone missing in the village. At the time there were rumours that she had gone off with her former lover in Suffolk, being at that time estranged from her husband, a soldier who had fought in Afghanistan. However, despite extensive searches and enquiries, she was not found. Not until that is, over a year later, when her body turned up in the Bridgewater Dyke. Although greatly decayed, forensic examinations revealed that she had died in the August of

2001 as a result of a knife attack. The blow which killed her had hit the carotid artery. All ID had been removed from the body before the murderer pushed it into the Dyke, filling the coat pockets with stones to weigh it down in the murky waters.

"Okay," said Ketch, "we are more or less done here. Let's have a word with the foster parents. Where do they live?"

"It's a short walk from here. You'd have passed it on your way through the village. The large thatched cottage right by the church."

Frank Cushing answered the door to them. A tall, studious looking man in his mid-50s, he led Ketch and MacKenzie down a long hallway into a large, airy sitting room. On the sofa sat a tearful looking Anne Cushing. Dark haired and petite, she was younger than her husband and dressed in a Bohemian, artisan way. Ketch smiled at her, then surveyed the room whose walls were covered in large landscape paintings, mostly sea views of the Norfolk coastline. There was a touch of Seago about them, he thought, but they were bolder in style and more expressionistic. On a large table by the window was a sculpture of a woman's head which bore a strong likeness to the woman who stared back at him.

"WPC Atkins, how about a cup of tea?" Said Ketch. He and MacKenzie settled in the two easy chairs situated either side of the fireplace. "I'm sorry for your loss," he continued, somehow aware of the triteness of that phrase which he had so often used in cases like these. Frank Cushing nodded, then put his arm around his wife. She said nothing.

"We're sorry too," he said.

"Would you mind answering a few questions?"

"Anything to help the investigation."

"Okay then. Firstly, do you know of anyone who might have wished harm to Peter? Someone at school, for example?"

"Frank Cushing shook his head. "Peter was popular among most of his school friends. Good at sports, excellent at his studies. He had a number of friends and no enemies, at least know one that we knew of, of course."

Anne Cushing nodded in agreement.

"And what about here in the village itself?"

"There are very few children of Peter's age actually living in the village. It's a mixture of second home owners, commuters to Lynn and some agricultural workers."

"How long have you actually lived here, Mr Cushing?"

"About 15 years now. As you probably can guess, inspector, Anne and I are both artists. We got to know the place when we met Philip Valence whilst we were on a holiday here. That was about 18 years back."

"Philip Valence?"

"Another local artist. Actually, he's a well-established landscape artist. He and his partner Susan live about half a mile away in the Big House. Diane, Peter's birth mother, was the sister of Philip's partner. It was how we got to know Peter in the first place."

"I see."

"When Diane died, Philip and Susan looked after Peter for a while. That's how we first met Peter, when we came up here on holiday and stayed with them."

WPC Atkins brought in the tea. There was a prolonged silence. "Peter had been doing so well," Anne Cushing offered at last in a quiet, quavering voice. "Only a few days ago, he had begun to speak again."

"Speak again?" asked Ketch.

"Peter was an elective mute," Frank Cushing explained. "He'd been like that ever since the day his mother died. I take it you're familiar with what happened to his mother?"

"Refresh my memory," said Ketch. Frank Cushing clasped his wife's hand.

"On the day that his mother disappeared, Peter was found sitting on the doorstep of number 27 Tunn Road. He was terribly distressed and quite unable to speak. What had happened to him even now remains a complete mystery."

"Who found him?"

"Susan found him. She took him to her place. He was clearly traumatised but could speak to no one. Philip and Susan decided to look after him. When Diane's body was found, Anne and I decided that we would offer to foster him. "

"Tell me, Mr Cushing, did you notice anything different in Peter's demeanour this morning? You tell me he'd begun to speak again." Frank Cushing nodded.

"He told us that he had confused memories of the day that his mother disappeared. Certain bits of the jigsaw puzzle were falling into place, but he couldn't recall the whole sequence of events."

"He seemed preoccupied when I went in to see him early this morning," said Anne Cushing. "I asked him what was wrong, but he didn't want to tell me."

"Okay. Could we take a look at Peter's room?"

"Of course," said Frank Cushing. He led the way upstairs to a small bedroom at the back of the house whose walls were lined with paintings, mainly oils. On the back of the bedroom door, Ketch instantly recognised a reproduction of Munch's The Scream. However, the painting which really intrigued him was a small canvas, painted in dark colours. It showed a large 17th-century country house. In the foreground stood three figures on a yew lined footpath, the first a young man, holding a bloodstained knife, the second an old man, lying on the ground, his face averted, and the third, half concealed in shadows, a daemonic looking individual with a red face who appeared to be grimacing at the young man. At the bottom of the painting, the artist had written: 'Richard Dadd at Cobham Hall.'

"Peter painted this?" asked Ketch.

"He was an accomplished artist, despite his age," said Frank Cushing. "these are all his own work. He'd hoped to go to art school and we didn't discourage him in that ambition."

Ketch thought for a moment. Richard Dadd. The name was somehow familiar to him. DS MacKenzie showed Ketch a diary and a small laptop.

"We should like to have a look at these if you have no objection, Mr Cushing."

"By all means."

They had barely left the house when Ketch's mobile rang. It was Tom Evans, the lead . SOCO Ketch put the phone on speaker mode. "Couple of things to interest you, sir."

"Go-ahead Tom."

"We noticed a flattening of the bushes and undergrowth about 5 yards from where the body was discovered. Looks as if someone may have lain in wait for the victim. On that side, adjacent to the dyke, the onlooker wouldn't have been spotted from passers-by on the road."

"Interesting… The other thing?"

"We found a mobile phone in the lad's pocket. Several phone calls, but only two on the morning he was attacked."

"Let's find out who he was talking to," Ketch instructed

MacKenzie.

Back at HQ, Ketch found time to study the SOCO findings and got MacKenzie to dig out the file on Peter Oliver. Invigorated by his liquid lunch at The Grapes, he soon made light work of the SOCO report. Nothing of much use here. Fibres found in the bushes which might provide a lead of sorts, but then maybe not. No contact traces on the boy's body, either. He turned to the file on Diane Oliver.

"Autopsy report on female, approximate age 28, height 5'10". Body affected by advanced adipocere. Cause of death: heart failure caused by knife wound to left ventricle of the heart. Seven supplementary wounds, 3 to the abdomen, one rupturing the bladder, approximately 3 inches deep. Defensive wounds to both the arms. Weapon, probably a thin bladed kitchen knife, 6 inches in length. Time of death: from insect and other evidence, (see below) late July or early August 2001. Decomposition has also been accelerated by the presence of phosphates in the water where the body was discovered."

He skipped the footnotes and turn to other information in the file. Six photographs of the deceased. He paused, noting a distinctive tattoo on the left forearm, which looked like the eye of Horus.... Unusual... He moved on.

'Information by SIO Jack Spector on Diane Oliver: The deceased is one Diane Oliver, according to dental records. This woman was discovered in the Bridgewater Dyke by a passer-by, Jackie Goodman, who believed the corpse to be a bundle of clothes. Diane Oliver was reported missing in August 2001 by her twin sister Susan, who lives in the village of Gedney Bridgewater. Diane Oliver and her son Peter had lived in a cottage about a mile east of the village itself since she separated from her husband the previous year. Peter Oliver was found on the morning of his mother's disappearance and was unable to help with our enquiries. According to Dr Smith who examined the boy, he appeared to have suffered some kind of trauma. The deceased was something of a loner and like her sister, was also a trained artist. From some of the correspondence we examined, it transpires that she worked for a modelling agency, situated in Kings Lynn and also she worked part-time as a waitress in a local pub. Earnings were supplemented by Social Security benefits. A total of 21 local residents were interviewed regarding her disappearance, but no one remembered seeing her on the morning that she disappeared. Her son is still unable to speak and was not able to communicate in writing about his mother. He is now living with Mr Philip Valence, the partner of Susan Oliver.'

Just then, Ketch's office door opened. It was MacKenzie. "Traced those phone numbers for you, sir."

"Go on."

"One was from Susan Oliver, the other was from a John Proctor."

"Who is John Proctor?"

"A pupil in Peter's form at the local secondary school. Oh, and something else in connection with this John Proctor."

"Yes?"

"I took a look at Peter's Hotmail and Facebook accounts. It appears that he was being bullied by this boy. And guess what? They share the same paper round."

Bridgewater High was a collection of ugly modern buildings, casting concrete and steel, situated between Kings Lynn and the village of Gedney Bridgewater. Like many modern comprehensives, it was a soulless, dreary place with a perpetual air of impending chaos and disorder. Ketch and MacKenzie were ushered into a small office in the lower school, an equally unattractive building from the 1930s, where they were greeted by a woman with a thin face and bulbous eyes. Ketch thought she looked rather like a rabbit in a car's headlights.

"Stacey Richards," she explained. "Head of year. I understand that this is about Peter Oliver."

Ketch nodded. "Were you aware that he was being bullied?"

"I wasn't, no."

"He had not complained about being bullied then?"

"As you know, Chief Inspector, Peter didn't speak but he was quite capable of communicating his thoughts by the written word. No, nothing like that. How did you find that out?"

"Through his laptop. We have a name – John Proctor."

She frowned. "It doesn't come as a surprise to me to be quite frank with you. John has already been in trouble for bullying other boys. And for extorting money from younger boys."

"We'd like to talk to him."

"Of course." She disappeared from the office, returning in a few minutes with a large, fat boy, with dark, shoulder-length hair.

"What's this about?" he demanded in a sullen voice.

"Sit down John," Ketch instructed. The boy sat down, arms folded, staring directly at the two detectives.

"These gentlemen are from the police and they have some questions for you."

"About what?"

"About Peter Oliver," said Ketch

The boy smiled. "He's dead, ain't he?" There was a silence. Ketch stared back at the youth.

"You were bullying Peter?"

"So what?"

"You called his mother a whore?" The head of year looked shocked. For a moment Ketch thought she might break into tears.

"It's true, she was a whore."

"What you mean by that? Explain it to me."

"She went with other men. You know? Everybody in the village knew about it. Besides, Peter was gay."

"How do you know that?" asked Ketch.

"Being gay is nothing to be ashamed of, John" interjected the head of year. "You should know that."

"How do you know that he was gay?" Ketch repeated.

"He did stuff with the younger boys. It was well known about in our year."

"And so you persecuted him for it?"

"Not just me, others did it too."

"In your year?"

He nodded.

"I shall need their names."

"You can have them." The boy shrugged nonchalantly.

"You did a paper round yesterday I believe?"

"Yes."

"Same area of the village as Peter Oliver?"

"No. I do the east of the village. He did the western end."

"And when did you end your paper round? What time exactly?"

"About nine o'clock I should think."

"You use a bicycle?"

"We all use bicycles. There are four of us, me, Oliver, another boy and a girl."

"All in your year group?"

"All in my year, yes."

"We shall need to speak to them," said Ketch to the head of year. "You made a phone call to Peter yesterday morning at 8:03 AM. What was it about?"

"It was a reminder."

"A reminder of what?"

"Of the money he owed me."

"Money? Money for what?"

"Money to keep my mouth shut about what he got up to."

"Blackmail money then?"

"You could say that. I waited at the end of my paper round for him but he never turned up."

Colney House was a large, red bricked villa built in the Dutch style and hidden from the road by a long driveway, on either side of which stood ornate, tree stocked gardens. It had been Philip Valence's home for over 25 years

Ketch and MacKenzie parked in the drive and pulled the antiquated bell pull. A tall, distinguished looking man in his late 50s answered the door. Although his face was lined, it was a strong face with dark, penetrating eyes, a broad forehead and a bushy white beard. He shook Ketch's hand and said in an accentless, well-cultivated voice: "DCI Price, I presume? And this is –?"

"DS MacKenzie."

"Do come in, gentleman, and make yourselves comfortable. The drawing room is this way. I'll fetch Susan."

They passed through a dark hallway, lined with framed paintings and entered a spacious room, furnished in the Victorian style. While they waited for their hosts to return, Ketch surveyed the interior. The walls, which were lined with ornate wallpaper in the style of William Morris, displayed a number of large paintings in oils, mostly large, bold landscapes of the Norfolk countryside. On the wall opposite him however, were four smaller life studies, each one of a female model, lying on a chaise longue. From the poses, Ketch gained the impression that the model was on intimate terms with the artist. He also noticed a small reproduction, about 10 x 12", in a dark frame, an intricate study of faeries, entitled 'The Faery Fella's Master Stroke.' He was sure he had come across a copy of it before, a Victorian painting by Richard Dadd.

The door opened. His suspicions about the model in the paintings were immediately confirmed.

" Susan, my partner," said Philip Valence. Susan stepped forward and shook Ketch's hand. It was the woman in the paintings. Tall and elegantly dressed in a colourful caftan, her face was long and fine featured. Blond haired, she looked as if she might be of Danish descent he thought. The hand offered to him was decked with intricately wrought silver rings.

"I am pleased to meet you," she said. "Would you care for some tea inspector?"

"Tea would be good." Valence nodded and left the room.

"You've come to ask me about poor Peter?" she asked.

"Indeed we have. When Peter Oliver was found, we discovered that you had spoken with him about an hour before he was killed. Can you tell me what the phone conversation was about?"

"Certainly. I'd phoned to congratulate him about finding his voice again. We'd heard that he'd started speaking again from neighbours in the village. They have a daughter who attends Peter's secondary school."

"I see. I understand that Peter lived with you here for a while shortly after his mother died?"

She nodded. "It seemed the proper thing to do at the time. Diane and I were very close you see. Besides, she only rented the house where she and Peter lived so it wasn't possible for Peter to have stayed on there – not on his own. He was only too glad to stay with Philip and me. He was very close to Philip, you know. They shared a common interest."

"Painting?"

"Yes. Peter was a very talented student. His art teacher believes he was so good that he might have been able to take his GCSE in art a year earlier. He had such an intuitive gift for the medium of oils. It's such a terrible tragedy."

Philip Valence had entered, holding a tea tray. "A tragedy indeed, inspector. During the time Peter spent with us, we often painted together. He had an extraordinary eye for detail. And a deep interest in the history of art. He used to devour my books on the subject. He was especially fond of the 19th century period – Richard Dadd in particular.

"I notice that you have one of his paintings."

"Ah yes, you spotted the little reproduction. It is thought to be his finest painting, though I would personally dispute that."

"I must admit I've never heard of him."

"No, he's not as well-known as Constable or Millais of course."
He paused to drink his tea.

"Tell me, Mr Valence, during the time that Peter spent with you,
were you conscious that he was especially unhappy at school?"

"Peter was something of a loner, an isolate – he didn't mix well
with other children of his own age. He had one good friend at primary
school, a boy called Ray, but the family moved away when Peter was
in the top juniors. After that, he was very much on his own. Why do
you ask me that?"

"We have evidence that suggests he was being bullied at his
secondary school."

"I'm sorry to learn that. Let me guess – it wasn't a boy called John
Proctor by any chance?"

"It was."

"He has quite a reputation in the village I'm afraid. An utter ne'er-
do-well. He's bullied other boys, I believe, but there is little the school
are prepared to do to stop him – that's the story I got, anyway. You
don't think that –?"

"We haven't ruled out the possibility."

"It wouldn't surprise me if it was so," said Susan. "The father was
extremely violent but he no longer lives with them, thank God."

It was around six pm when Ketch and MacKenzie finally arrived back
at HQ. Ketch spent a while going through what little forensic evidence
SOCO had submitted on the Peter Oliver case and half-heartedly
examined the autopsy report, but there were no more useful leads.
MacKenzie's notes on John Proctor were equally inconclusive. It
would have been impossible for him to have interrupted his paper
round, cycle to the other end of the village and kill Peter Oliver, then
complete his own round, but the timing would have been very tight,
though technically possible. Door-to-door enquiries had proved to be
unhelpful. Most of the village residents who worked used cars to
commute to King's Lynn and would have seen no one along the stretch
of road where the murder had occurred at that early hour in the
morning. Neither had there been any pedestrians using the road at that
time. Peter Oliver had been heading for the last cottage on the edge of
the village when he was attacked and beyond that cottage was open

land, stretching for 10 miles without another habitation insight.

It was around eight pm when he left his office. Carol had rung him at seven-thirty pm asking if he had eaten, which he hadn't. He made his way across the city, heading for the river in the direction of Carol's flat, a neat, two bedroomed apartment adjacent to the River Wensum.

Neither of them spoke about the case over the meal, Ketch being quiet and somewhat introspective. Shortly after 11 o'clock, they retired to bed and then made love, Ketch slipping afterwards into a profound sleep. He awoke around three am with a strong desire to pee. As he completed his task in the bathroom, the image of Peter Oliver drifted back into his mind, the boy who had lost the power of speech, then regained it. He recalled the drawing that he had seen in the boy's notebook and painting in Philip Valence's house – Richard Dadd...

Moving quietly now so as not to disturb Carol, he walked into the lounge and opened Carol's laptop then googled Richard Dadd. Dadd, a gifted painter, had murdered his father on an estate near the Kent village of Cobham after hearing voices, instructing him to kill the Devils who inhabited his father's spirit. He had been found guilty of murder and spent the rest of his days in the madhouse at Bethlem where he continued to paint. He had simply knifed his father to death.

Ketch closed down the laptop and returned to bed where he found Carol still sleeping. What was it that had troubled young Peter Oliver so much that he had lost the power of speech? And why, shortly after regaining his speech, had someone then attacked and killed him? And what was his connection with Dadd?

When Ketch woke the next morning, it was already gone nine o'clock. He ate a small breakfast with Carol, gave his apologies to her, then made his way across the city. Already the sun was high in the sky. It was a bright morning with a light westerly wind blowing, a day to be anywhere but stuck in his office he thought, pondering the enigma of the teenage murder.

He had no sooner reached the lobby at HQ when the desk sergeant called out to him. "Visitors for you, sir."

"Who?"

"A Mrs Proctor and her son. It seemed urgent. The woman said she needed to speak to you personally, so I put them in room 6."

"Thanks."

He took the lift to the upper floor where he met McKenzie.

"There's a visitor for you, sir, a Mrs –"

"I know Tim. On my way."

Mrs Proctor sat solemn faced next to her large offspring. The latter sprawled back on his chair, arms folded. Mrs Proctor looked worried. "Thank you for seeing us, Chief Inspector."

"Not at all. Clearly, you have something of importance to tell me Mrs Proctor."

The woman stared at her son fixedly. "Tell the policeman what you told me, John." The boy grimaced.

"All right, it's about Mr Sutton and Peter Oliver."

"Who is Mr Sutton?"

"Mr Sutton is the art teacher at the comp," explained Mrs Proctor.

"And what about Mr Sutton?"

"He and Peter had a thing going between them."

"What do you mean – a thing?"

"You know…"

"You'll have to explain in more detail to me."

"All right. Sutton's gay. Everyone knows about it in our year. Fact. Peter Oliver used to go to Sutton's house for one-on-one sessions. Fact. Mind you, he wasn't the only one."

"This was a regular occurrence – is that what you're telling me?"

The boy put his hands behind his head, clearly enjoying the spotlight. "That's what I'm telling you. They were gay boys. I put the pressure on Peter, got him to admit it Not that he said anything because he couldn't." He laughed, a short hollow laugh but he wasn't smiling.

"You said other people knew about this affair. How many people?"

"Most of our year group knew about it, probably more. Someone put a post on his Facebook page about it but he deleted it. Sutton used to invite boys round to his place for what he called portrait sessions. He's been doing it for years. He lives in the old vicarage. He asked me once, said he'd pay me to sit for him, but I refused – I've been told about him."

There was a pause. Then Ketch said: "All right, Mrs Proctor, leave this with me."

"What are you going to do about it then?"

"We shall take the appropriate action, I can assure you."

"Disgusting, I call it. The filthy pervert."

After Mrs Proctor and her son had left, MacKenzie appeared at the door of the interview room. "Thought you should know immediately sir, SOCO think they've found the murder weapon."

"Prints?"

"Not yet, they're going to check it. It was half submerged in a ditch, so we may not be lucky."

"I shall need you with me this afternoon, Time – around five pm."

"A break?"

"Possibly... I need you to telephone the comprehensive school, try to get hold of a John Sutton."

The old vicarage lay on the edge of the village, not that far from the place where Peter Oliver's body had been found. An elegant, late Victorian building with stucco pillars at its entrance, its lichened, red brick frontage gave it an air of faded opulence.

Ketch and MacKenzie pushed their way through overgrown bushes until they reached the porch. The door opened, revealing a short, stout man in his early 50s with a rounded face and full red lips. He was dressed in a loose fitting, linen suit and a pale green shirt with matching green cravat.

"I got the message, inspector," he said. "What is this about exactly?"

"May we talk inside?"

He led the way down the dark corridor to a sparsely furnished room containing the battered sofa, two battered chairs and a large easel on which stood a half-finished portrait of a young boy in oils.

"Can I offer you both tea? Or coffee perhaps?"

Ketch shook his head. "We're here to ask you some questions about Peter Oliver." Sutton raised his eyebrows, then sighed.

"Such a fine pupil. He's a great loss to the school."

"I understand that he sat for you?"

"That's correct. Principally I'm a portrait painter as you can see – that's when I'm not school mastering. And subjects are hard to come by. I got to know Peter through his mother many years ago now. She also sat for me, like her sister, Susan. I was introduced to the Oliver sisters through Philip Valence. We met at Goldsmiths College together, way back."

"So Peter came here on a regular basis?"

"Yes, that's right inspector."

"Up until fairly recently?"

"Yes that's right. Until shortly before his untimely death." He paused.

"With Mr and Mrs Cushing?" Sutton licked his lips and hesitated for a moment.

"No, he came alone."

"But with his foster parents' permission?"

"I should imagine so, yes. Just what are you getting at, inspector?"

"We have reason to believe you may have had a relationship with Peter Oliver." Sutton stood up sharply.

"Who told you this?"

"Sit down Mr Sutton."

"Who told you?"

"Is there any truth in this assertion?"

Sutton was red-faced. "None whatsoever. It's a preposterous assertion. My relationship with Peter was wholly professional."

"That's not what we've been told by one of our informants at the school. Presumably, you paid his foster parents for the sittings?"

"No, I paid the sitter in cash."

"And he offered you no other favours in return?"

Ketch was trying to determine whether Sutton's indignation was fabricated. "Then you have no objection I presume, if we take a look around at some of your work here?"

"None whatsoever, if that's what it takes to convince you. Most of my completed work is in the back room. This way gentleman." He led the way into a dingy, large room at the back of the house, lined with canvases and piles of drawings. Ketch and MacKenzie began to sort through them as Sutton stood, arms crossed, in the doorway. Ketch noted several head and shoulders studies of young boys, executed in pastels and charcoals. Among these were two of Peter Oliver and a number of other young boys. He continued rummaging and, behind a stack of landscapes, discovered three nude life paintings of Susan Oliver. However, when he looked more closely at them, it became apparent to him that one of them was Diane Oliver.

The only way he could determine this was because of the distinctive tattoo on her arm. All three of the studies were realistic and faintly erotic.

"I trust that everything is as it should be, Chief Inspector?" said

Sutton, a hint of triumph in his voice.

"So far, yes," replied Ketch. He glanced at MacKenzie who shook his head.

"As you can see I am no sexual pervert, I am an artist. There is a difference, though that may not be apparent to you and your colleague." Ketch ignored the taunt.

"We're finished here for now, but we may wish to speak with you again."

"I'm not going anywhere."

When they had left the house, Ketch paused before getting back into the squad car. The spot where Peter Oliver's body had been discovered was only 200 yards from the house he noticed and was clearly visible from the window of Sutton's front room. He wondered... Was it possible that Peter Oliver had blackmailed the man with dire consequences? He couldn't discount it altogether.

Two weeks passed without much incident, although further enquiries regarding Sutton revealed that there had been a complaint made against him in his previous school by the parents of a 15-year-old pupil who had, like Peter Oliver, agreed to sit for the artist.

However, after a brief investigation by the school's governors, the complaint had been withdrawn. The proximity of Sutton's house to the murder scene continued to vex Ketch but, despite a further appeal to the public, no eyewitnesses came forward to supply further information to the police. The case was beginning to look like a complete nonstarter.

The lack of forensic evidence was lamentable. Despite finding what was most likely to be the murder weapon, there were no prints or DNA traces to be found on it, the brackish water having removed everything that might have proved vital to the investigation.

It was early on a Saturday morning that the break finally came, though the conclusion to the case was not dependent on the fruits of the police investigation, much to the chagrin of Ketch and his colleagues.

Ketch had been sleeping at Carol Hennessey's flat when his mobile rang early. It was MacKenzie. "There's been an incident, sir. Philip Valence has been murdered. Susan Oliver phoned it in about 15 minutes ago. I'll send a car round to your flat shall I?"

There was a pause, then Ketch said: "Don't bother Tim, I'll make

218

my own way. Just give me half an hour with you?"

By the time Carol Hennessey's car pulled up outside the Valence household, a dense mist had arisen, lending the surrounding flat fields and roads a strange, ivory luminescence.

As they passed the Ops van, Ketch noted Susan Oliver, sitting inside, being comforted by a WPC and noted the blood stains on her blouse.

MacKenzie took Ketch into the bedroom where the body of Philip Valence lay, slumped on the floor. Carol Hennessey, who by this time had donned her forensic suit, left Ketch and McKenzie at the doorway and shifted the body.

"What's the verdict?" asked Ketch.

"Single knife wound to the heart. The weapon is still in him."

Ketch cast a cursory glance around the room, noticing that the bedside lamp shade was crooked. Someone had obviously tidied up. "What's Susan Oliver's story?" he asked.

"She says she heard a cry earlier this morning, then came into the bedroom and found him like this."

"Any idea when he died exactly?" Ketch asked.

"The body is cold– sometime in the night I should guess."

"We need to interview her – let's get SOCO in here and see what we can find out Tim."

Susan Oliver's initial statement explained that she had woken early in the morning when she had heard Philip Valence cry out in the adjoining bedroom and that when she entered the room, she found his motionless body slumped over by the side of the bed. She also claimed to have moved him and that was when she had touched the handle of the knife. However, SOCO 's report on the angle of the incision made by the blade indicated that Philip Valence could not have stabbed himself.

Susan Oliver sat in interview room five next to her solicitor. It was 10 AM on a hot July afternoon and she had been in police custody for six days now. At first, she had been detached and inscrutable, but for whatever reason, on this particular morning, she had informed the duty officer that she wished to make a full statement about the circumstances of Philip Valence's death.

Though he had only circumstantial evidence that Susan Oliver had killed her partner, Ketch didn't have enough for a conviction without a confession. He looked across the table at her as she began to speak but she avoided his intense gaze and seemed distant.

"I want to make a full statement about what exactly happened."

Ketch turned on the tape recorder. "Go-ahead."

"I killed Philip. I'd planned to do it days ago but didn't have the courage to go through with it."

"You attacked him with a knife?" She nodded.

"And why did you do that?"

"Because of what he did to us – all of us."

"And what did you do to you?"

"He destroyed us – me, Diane, Peter."

"Perhaps you could be more specific?"

"Philip was a charming man, everyone who met him said as much. But there was a side to him that people didn't know about. He was driven by his sexual obsessions. When Diane and I first came to Gedney, we got to know him through a mutual acquaintance, John Sutton. The two of them had been to the same art school years ago. I fell in love with Philip and became obsessed with him. But so did Diane. Philip, being who he was, took advantage of us and set up a ménage a trois. I was fairly innocent sexually until I met Philip, but soon that all changed for me."

"In what way?"

"He was into all kinds of things – unspeakable things. We both went along with him at first, but then he demanded more and more from each of us. He claimed it was necessary in the course of his art. And we were both stupid enough to believe him. What's more, Diane encouraged him. She enjoyed the sadomasochism, revelled in it. She used it as a weapon to shock and alienate me. Pretty soon, I began to loathe what my sister had done to me and even more, detest who she was. And then she became pregnant with Peter.

"For a while after the birth, things reverted to relative normality, but then, when Peter was quite young, Philip and this man Sutton corrupted him. So when Diane introduced him to the so-called 'sessions' at the house, I felt I had to do something. I knew that, despite the monstrous nature of his acts, Philip loved Diane – more than he ever loved me.

"That morning, I followed her and Peter and confronted her with what she had done to us. She just laughed in my face. I lost my temper and when she turned away from me I stabbed her. I stood there, not knowing what to do next. It was then that I realised Peter was so traumatised by what he had seen that he had lost the power of speech. I was consumed by guilt and, as a recompense, I decided I would look after Peter until suitable foster parents could be found."

"And when you found out he'd regained his speech, you followed him on his paper round and attacked him."

"I didn't intend to kill Peter you must believe me. He told me he had remembered everything that had happened to Diane. He told me it had all come back to him. He said he was going to inform the police. That's when I lost my temper, that's when it happened."

"And what about Philip?"

"He was corrupted, tainted. I wanted nothing more than to expunge the past and obliterate what had happened to us. But I knew that the past could not be wholly laid to rest until I'd dealt with Philip. At first, I thought I could change him, despite his ways. But as time went on I realised that it was completely hopeless. There was only one avenue left to me. I confronted Philip, told him he had to atone for what he had done to all three of us, but he laughed in my face. It was then that I snapped. No matter how much you love somebody, inspector, ultimately it's a question of survival."

She paused. Ketch said: "We will need a more detailed statement from you, including dates and times. This will do for now."

On the day that followed – Sunday – Ketch decided he'd take a walk in Earlham Park. It was one of his favourite parks in the city, a place of tranquillity where he could wander through ancient oaks and beeches and ruminate.

On such occasions he made sure his phone was turned off. It was a cool, overcast day, a pleasant change to the blisteringly hot weather that they had had to endure of late and he was glad to be in the open air and away from the confines of HQ.

Yet, as he wandered across the long grass in the direction of the stream, he found he couldn't shake off the feeling of oppression that had overwhelmed him in Gedney Bridgewater. Perhaps it wasn't the case at all. May be it was the Fens themselves which had made him feel like this. It was impossible to say, yet wasn't it true that some people were influenced by landscape more than others?

He found a bench and sitting down, smoked a cigarette, reflecting on the case. Outwardly, Philip Valence appeared charming and urbane, but behind closed doors, he was a monster. Following Susan Oliver's confession, Sutton was taken in for interrogation, and when under pressure, admitted that he and Valence had corrupted Peter Oliver, claiming that they had done so with the cooperation and approval of Diane Oliver – a story which could not of course be corroborated.

Nevertheless, the search of Sutton's attic produced photographs and drawings of the young boy and the two men which left nothing to the imagination. And throughout the whole ghastly business, Susan Oliver had kept her secret until at last she had decided to wreak vengeance on both her sister and her lover.

And what of Peter Oliver? He had been the victim of circumstances. What if he had never been able to speak again? It begged a question...

The sun had come out and the leaves of the oak tree above him shone with a green iridescence. Far off, two families sat having a picnic together by the river. It was a charming, pastoral scene which gave him comfort. He looked at his watch. In another hour The Grapes would be open for business. Thank God for this other, parallel universe. It was balm to the soul.

He finished his cigarette and headed back to the park entrance, a great weight lifted from his shoulders, the sounds of children playing still ringing in his ears

A CROMER CONUNDRUM

It started with a frozen shoulder, a condition which he'd experienced before. This time though, it lasted for six months. Whenever possible, DCI Ketch avoided doctors because he had little faith in the medical profession.

His wife Annie, who died of cancer, had been misdiagnosed with diverticulitis. By the time the tumour which killed her had been picked up, her condition was terminal.

Ketch finally relented after he chased a suspect through the city's market – a strategy which ended in failure. Reaching out to grab the thief's jacket, he experienced a sharp shooting pain in his shoulder and arm. The man eluded capture for another six months.

The GP, who was overweight and seemingly disinterested, gave him a steroid injection which proved useless.

"Come back to me if it doesn't improve," he told Ketch blithely. Ketch returned after a fortnight, but this time he noticed something else. The thumb and forefinger of his right hand had started to quiver.

One morning at a briefing, he found DS MacKenzie staring at it. Ketch returned to the surgery and pointed it out to the doctor. This time a flicker of interest passed across his podgy features.

"We'd best send you to a neurologist and get it checked out," he said.

"What d'you think it might be?"

"It could be Parkinson's," came the damning reply.

Ketch had to wait another month before he was seen at the Norwich Hospital during which time he researched Parkinson's disease. The most alarming thing he discovered was that the condition was non-curable and progressive, though thankfully, it seemed, the older you were, the slower it advanced. Unlike cancer, Parkinson's didn't kill you, it just slowly disabled you. And since it affected each person differently, it was impossible to predict its exact progress.

The interview at the hospital took just 15 minutes. He sat in the small waiting-room, trying to spot who had the condition, but it was impossible to be certain. When his time came, he was asked to walk up and down, raise his arms, answer numerous questions. The examination seemed rather cursory. Then came the final judgement.

"I'm afraid, Mr Price, that you have Parkinson's disease."

A statement of undeniable and brutal fact, like a judge giving sentence – something he'd heard many times in court but this time it was personal. Carol, his partner, who'd come with him, was supportive and positive but the truth was that it didn't make much difference. From now on nothing would be the same again.

He began to wonder just how long he had got to live but soon realised this was absurd. Sometimes people lived for 20 years with the disease – even longer, so he was told.

He decided to tell no one at work about it – not even his trusted colleague, DS Tim MacKenzie, not even his own son. There were groups he could have joined for support, but he somehow couldn't yet face it. The thought of sitting with a band of fellow sufferers, though fine in principle, just failed to inspire him.

Two months after the initial diagnosis, he had parted from Carol and his new son Sean. Life at the riverside flat had become intolerable. He had been unable to stop his drinking. Indeed, the diagnosis had had the effect of increasing his intake. This, plus the continual antisocial hours he worked as a DCI, had proved to be the straw that broke the camel's back. Besides, the flat was far too small to serve their needs. Sean, who was now two years old, was a hyperactive child and rarely slept through the night – a contributory factor to the split up.

So, on a grey morning in mid-March, DCI Ketch, aka Huw Price found himself staring out of one of the grimy windows of his bachelor flat off the Earlham Road in Norwich at the falling snow. The winter, which seemed to have lasted for an eternity this year, had tested his primitive heating arrangements to the very limit. His heating costs, derived from three electrical storage heaters plus an open fire, had driven up his bills to 100 pounds a month, despite the fact that he was living in a small flat. Not that he had any double glazing of course. When the wind blew from the East as it had done continually for the last two months – or so it seemed – the curtains at the window overlooking the street visibly moved a fraction.

No wonder that most days he kept his coat on in here. The one small compensation was that he had rediscovered what it was like to feel completely independent again. But he missed Sean and Carol more deeply than he was prepared to admit.

The last time he and Sean had met was over a month ago. As he poured milk over his bowl of morning muesli, his mobile sprang to life on the kitchen table. It was Tim MacKenzie. Ketch glanced at the clock. 8:30 AM.

"What's up?"

"A double homicide sir."

"Where are you?"

"I'm at Warren Wood, just outside Cromer." Ketch knew the place well, a patch of old woodland which had once served as the grounds of the Royal Links Hotel. The hotel itself had burned down sometime in the 1940s, a once fine building which had flourished in the days of the Edwardian tourist boom. It was here in the 1900's that Arthur Conan Doyle had hatched his plot for the Hound Of The Baskervilles whilst on a golfing break. When Ketch was 20 years younger, it had been one of a number of places he had walked his dog with his late wife Annie. A winding path straddled the cliff, high above the town of Cromer and then on to Happy Valley and the woods themselves. The woods here had, at times, a feeling of enchantment or so it seemed to his Celtic sensibility.

"Okay," Ketch replied. "I'll see you in half an hour. Who are the victims?"

"We found two dead – a couple - and a young girl, barely alive. The latter looks like the couple's daughter. She has a chance of pulling through though she's sustained two gunshot wounds, one to the chest and the other to the abdomen. The bodies were found only a little way into the wood, lying to the side of the path. They were spotted by a man walking his dog who heard the girl's cries."

"Their names?"

"The man's driving licence is made out to one Vladimir Vetochkin. The dead woman's presumably his wife and the girl his daughter though they carried no ID on them."

"Are SOCO there yet?"

"Just set up."

"Very well."

"I'm afraid the media are also here – someone must have tipped them off."

"Well make sure the crime scene is well secured – I'll see you soon."

Ketch dialled for a taxi, then finished his bowl of muesli. He rarely drove and when he did so it was under sufferance. Like most

Luddites, he had an aversion to most inventions of the 20th and 21st centuries, though secretly he admitted that the mobile phone had been a boon to police work because of its speed and convenience. But when it came to cars, he had a very strong resistance. It wasn't that he was a bad driver. He passed the advanced driver's test years ago. His perpetual drinking had a lot more to do with it. These days police officers no longer had the immunity from prosecution that they once enjoyed way back in the late 70s when he was a raw recruit.

He washed his dish, dried up, then enjoyed an after breakfast pipe. Recently, he had alternated between pipe and cigarettes under the misguided illusion that pipe tobacco was less likely to produce throat or lung cancer. This was based on the premise that he inhaled less smoke. Of course, it was all utter nonsense and he knew he was fooling himself.

The journey to Cromer was a pleasant one, especially since the sun had risen into a clear, almost cloudless sky. Much of the route to the old seaside town alternated between stretches of woodland and open, rolling fields.

The car wound through part of the once stately Edwardian town where tall and ornate villas lined the wide streets. Once these had housed wealthy merchants, but many of these solid residences were now given over to flats and B&Bs.

The car climbed a winding hill, then pulled in on the side of the road where he spotted the familiar barrier tape, sealing off the entrance to Warren Wood. He stepped out of the car to greet DS MacKenzie. The air here, imbued with sea breezes, was fresh and bracing.

"Crime scene is just up here, sir," said MacKenzie.

"And this presumably is their car?" asked Ketch, pointing to a large range Rover which had been parked several metres away and where two SOCO officials were examining the interior.

"It is."

"This year's model – they were well britched then."

MacKenzie nodded. "I did some initial checks while I've been waiting for you. Vladimir Vetochkin was a well-established businessman. He owned a number of shops across North Norfolk, supplying food to the Latvian and Polish communities. He also ran an import business whose headquarters are in the Netherlands."

"Good – you can tell me the rest later. Which way?"

"Up here," said MacKenzie, pointing to a winding path leading off to the left. The two officers pushed their way past a large overgrown beech tree which was partly blocking their path, until they entered a small clearing, surrounded by ancient yew trees. Ketch spotted the rotund shape of Dr Stoppard, the senior pathologist. He was crouching over the body of a large middle-aged man, dressed in an expensive suit. Stoppard turned, grinned at Ketch, then stood up.

"Best not come any closer," he instructed them. "The fewer feet here, the better."

"I was told there were two bodies," said Ketch.

"You were told right. The second is over here in these bushes. If you walk around the perimeter you won't disturb the evidence."

Ketch and MacKenzie dutifully complied. The body of a woman lay face down beside the edge of the path, a crimson pool of blood oozing from her head.

"How did they die?"

"Gunshot wounds. The man probably died from exsanguination following a shot to the chest at close range. The woman died from one shot to the back of the cranium which appears to have exited via the carotid artery."

"And the young woman?"

"She's in Norwich at the A and E at present in a critical condition."

"Any witnesses?"

"Only the dog walker I mentioned to you earlier. I took a preliminary statement from him. A Mr Abel White. He lives in a bungalow just along the coastal path."

"He saw no one else apart from the victims?"

"No. By the time he came onto the scene, the murderer must have been long gone. He's a St John's ambulance man so he was able to staunch the girl's wound while he waited for the ambulance to arrive."

"Do we know what type of weapon was used?" Ketch asked.

Stoppard stepped forward, ducking under the barrier tape and presented him with a small evidence bag.

"One of our SOCO team dug this out of a pine tree over there," he gesticulated." Ketch looked at the bag which contained a cartridge shell.

"There are several of these dotted around the murder scene. My guess is – and I'm not a ballistics expert – that he used an automatic weapon."

"Probably an assault rifle, wouldn't you agree, sir?" asked MacKenzie.

Ketch nodded. "We'll see what ballistics have to tell us. You have the male victim's effects?"

Stoppard waved to a SOCO team member who presented Ketch with the second evidence bag. MacKenzie handed him a pair of forensic gloves. Inside the bag were a silver cigarette lighter, pocket notebook, diary and a driving licence. Ketch opened the latter, then stared at the face. He thought it was familiar to him, but from where exactly?

Darya Vetochkin lay in bed in the Norwich Hospital enmeshed by tubes, an oxygen mask clamped over her mouth. To one side of her bed stood Ketch and MacKenzie, to the other the presiding doctor.

"What are her chances of recovery?" Ketch asked the doctor, a shaven headed man with eyes which had weathered many sleepless nights.

"Not too good I'm afraid to say. She has suffered major trauma and she has a bullet lodged to the left of her spinal cord. Removing it would require a complex surgical procedure." Ketch frowned and pursed his lips.

"Did she at any time regain consciousness?"

"Once only in the ambulance. She said something in Russian but neither of the medics speak the language, so..."

Ketch turned to MacKenzie. "Let's get uniform to post an officer outside her room – just in case."

"Right, sir."

"You'll let us know if there's any change?"

"Of course."

Ketch handed the doctor a card and turned to MacKenzie.

"Let's grab some air."

At the front of the hospital complex, they found a seat where Ketch sat and lit a cigarette.

"So – what do we know about Vladimir Vetochkin?"

"He and his wife lived in a large mansion between Cley and Burnham market."

Ketch knew the area well, a prosperous hinterland of North

Norfolk, populated by second home owners and TV celebrities.

"DC Thomas checked out the place this morning," MacKenzie went on to say. "He spoke to the cleaning lady there. The house has a large perimeter with security cameras. Thomas also talked to a neighbour who confirmed that the Vetochkins had been living at the address for the last 10 years and apparently pretty much kept themselves to themselves apart from having the odd party."

"Any other relatives?"

"Yes, Vladimir has an elderly mother who lives on the outskirts of Cromer."

Ketch looked at his watch. "This afternoon then. We'll take WPC Blaze with us."

Ketch was glad the following day was a Sunday. Sunday was his access day for seeing Sean, his youngest son. This was an unofficial arrangement with Carol. Each Sunday morning Ketch would pick up Sean from Carol's riverside flat near the river and take him up to Mousehold Heath, a broad expanse of common land whose height enabled them both to glimpse a vast vista of the old city of Norwich.

Today, the spring weather had settled in and all trace of the early morning mist had disappeared. As he and Sean kicked a ball about, Ketch was able to see the tall spire of the ancient mediaeval cathedral, glinting in the morning sun. As Sean squealed and laughed, Ketch recalled the events of the previous afternoon.

Irina Vetochkin lived in a large five bedroomed house on the northern edge of Cromer, a mansion she had one shared with her husband Peter. They sat in a large, ornately furnished lounge made darker by a set of heavy velour curtains. A frail 70-year-old with bright red hair like her son's, Irina stared at Ketch and MacKenzie with penetrating blue eyes. Despite the news of her son's death, she seemed composed, resigned to what had happened.

"I must apologise for the fact that the media notified you of your son's death before we were able to do so," said Ketch.

Irina shrugged her shoulders. "It is of no consequence. Somebody had to tell me. How is my poor Darya?"

"Still critical I'm sorry to say. We can arrange to take you to the hospital if you..."

"I shall be arranging my own transport. So – you have come also to ask me some questions – yes?"

"If you feel that you're up to it."

"I am up to it. What exactly do you want to know?"

"Can you think of anyone who knew your son and who might have wished him harm?"

"Vladimir was a businessman but his work was largely beyond my sphere of interest. Besides, he rarely spoke about his business affairs to me. He inherited much of the business along with his brother Boris, from my husband Peter. It was Peter who started up the import business many years ago. That was in the early 1980s when this country was booming."

"What sort of import business is it exactly?"

"Mainly objects d'art, fine art, rugs from the Orient, sculptures, glassware and jewellery. Originally Peter handled the business from his depot in Rotterdam. My husband started when he was in his 20s, shortly after the conclusion of the Second World War. He purchased a number of works by the artist Kandinsky. When we settled here in Britain, he was able to sell the paintings and this money he used as an investment for the import business. His first operation was in Kings Lynn but later we opened one here in Cromer."

"Tell me – when did you last see your son?"

"He came here a couple of days ago to pick up some papers."

"And how then did he seem to you?"

"Preoccupied – but that was not unusual for him. He often had a lot on his mind."

"What was his relationship with his wife?"

"Ania and Vladimir were a very devoted couple. And now there is only Darya..."

The old woman's face was suffused with grief.

"You mentioned some office premises here in Cromer – perhaps you could give me the address?"

Irina Vetochkin stood up, went over to a writing bureau and produced a business card.

"Thank you. I'm afraid we shall have to ask you to make a formal identification for us. I realise that maybe rather painful for you."

"So be it then."

By lunchtime on Sunday, Ketch had returned Sean to Carol at the riverside flat in Norwich and then walked back to his own bachelor flat off the Earlham Road. As soon as he got past the front door, he could make out the odour of French manufactured cigarettes. There was only one person he knew who smoked them and that was his son James, who still had a set of keys to the flat, despite the acrimonious nature of their last encounter. James, who had last year graduated from a Northern University, was now pursuing his postgraduate certificate in education from the University of East Anglia and had been renting a flat in Cromer, just off the Cromer Road, a stone's throw from Warren Wood.

Ketch opened the lounge door and saw James supporting himself with a crutch. His left hand was bandaged.

"What on earth happened to you?" asked Ketch.

"I got knocked down by a maniac in a car. I was cycling down to the railway station in Cromer when it happened.

"When was this?"

"Early Saturday morning. I had just come out of Ellen Hill when this maniac in a 4x4 overtook me down the hill. The car was in such a mad rush he caught my handlebars and I ended up on the other side of the road. No permanent injuries I'm happy to say. I wondered if I could spend a day or two recuperating here in your flat – I should be on teaching practice this week but at the moment that's an unlikely prospect."

"That's fine James. Give me the details again?"

"I'd just turned out from Ellen Hill and was parallel with Warren Wood. I turned round because I could hear a vehicle accelerating towards me at some speed."

"What time was this precisely – can you remember?"

"Yes, I can remember - it was 8.30 – my usual time. I know because I catch the same train each weekday – the 8.55 to Norwich."

Ketch looked thoughtful. "Can you describe the car to me in much more detail?"

"Is it important?"

"Yes, it's important."

"Okay... A black 4 by 4. Possibly a range rover. Last year's reg. I'm pretty sure of it though I didn't see the entire number plate. AZ something or other. Will that do?" James laughed. "Any chance you might be able to do the driver for dangerous driving?"

"Probably not, though the information may prove very useful to me."

He laughed again. "How very enigmatic!"

"Sit down and I'll make us both a brew."

Ketch woke and looked at his wristwatch. It was 8:30 AM. He went to the window and discovered the cause of his rude awakening. Outside the flat he could see James being helped into a dilapidated looking Renault estate by a tall young woman with long blonde hair – presumably James's latest conquest. There was a banging of car doors, then the car accelerated towards the junction with the Earlham Road, leaving a trail of black exhaust fumes behind it.

He quickly dressed, washed, then made his way to the kitchen to face a scene of devastation. Frying pan and greasy plate had been left on the kitchen table and there were fat stains on the cooker hobs. As Ketch, cursing under his breath, poured a bowl of hot water and submerged the frying pan and dish, the trace of a dream came back to him.

What must have informed that dream was the smell of frying bacon. He had been staying at his auntie Maisie's house in North Wales where she and his uncle Jim often played host to him and his father. The old farmhouse possessed an ancient Welsh range, fuelled by anthracite. This black beast operated as the downstairs heating system and its back boiler warmed the rooms upstairs. During the day his aunt would cook a variety of dishes including delicious meat and fruit pies, the evidence for which could be seen in her vast figure.

When he stayed in Wales with his father during the summer and Easter breaks, he would always recall the early morning smell of frying bacon as it drifted up into his bedroom in the ancient farmhouse.

He finished washing and drying, then decided he would grab his breakfast from one of the many food outlets in Norwich covered market on his way to HQ. Just before he left the flat he checked the fridge. It was as he suspected. The milk had gone and the bread and margarine needed replacing. It was ever thus when James came to stay with him. He was like a wind of chaos.

Ketch reached Bethel Street armed with a coffee and croissant. It wasn't a proper breakfast in his opinion but it would just have to suffice. He met MacKenzie in the main lobby.

"Morning, sir. The autopsy reports are in. And Dr Stoppard asked if you wanted to examine the bodies."

"Yes – when I finish this coffee – give me 10 minutes and I'll see you in the mortuary."

Stoppard was his usual pompous self. However, this morning he was looking slightly liverish as if he had rather overdone the spirits at the Norwich gentleman's club which he was known to frequent. It was a venue attended by local businessmen and reputed to be part of the city's gay scene though Ketch had never been able to confirm this. Stoppard was of that previous generation of homosexuals who were not entirely happy with the business of 'outing.'

Stoppard nodded to his young male assistant, a tall thin youth who rarely spoke, and the bodies were unceremoniously wheeled out of the refrigerated drawers.

"As you can no doubt see," said Stoppard as if he were addressing a roomful of first-year undergraduates, "both victims have sustained a number of gunshot wounds. In both cases however, the bullet wounds to the heads have been the cause of death. Here," indicating Vladimir Vetochkin, "the bullet has entered the left eye socket and exited from the cranium. In the woman, as previously indicated to you, the bullet entered just below the ear and exited through the back of the neck, severing the carotid artery. There are additional and less severe wounds in the thorax and abdominal areas of both corpses."

"What kind of bullets were used?"

"All were identical and all from a single weapon, a Russian assault rifle, an AK101 Kalashnikov to be precise. They probably both died in under a minute. The female was dispatched whilst attempting to flee with her back to the murderer, the male was killed as he faced his attacker probably from a distance of a few feet. You'll get SOCO's report later this morning, confirming the rest of the ballistics, I should imagine. How is the girl doing?"

"She is still critical – and unconscious."

"If you want my opinion, it's probably a professional job – but of course you may not want my opinion." Stoppard smirked.

"We'll just have to wait and see," replied Ketch.

On his way to the lunchtime media briefing, Ketch past ACC Batarde's office and the door opened. "Word if you please, Huw."

Ketch entered the immaculately tidy office with its black laminated surfaces, stainless steel lamp and framed photos of the assistant commissioner's holiday in Switzerland with his two daughters, both of whom bore an unfortunate resemblance to their father, with the trademark prominent noses and bulbous foreheads. Ketch sat down on the proffered chair which swung back at an alarming angle. Batarde sat opposite him, steepling his fingers.

"This Cromer shooting... Any leads yet?"

"Early days I'm afraid. We might have a witness trace on the car used by the perpetrator."

"How come the media got to know the details so early on?"

"I'm not entirely sure of that."

"This is not the first time that this has happened, Huw. See if you can determine the source of the leak. It strikes me that someone in this outfit may be taking a backhander from the press."

Ketch nodded. "We'll be putting out an appeal for additional witnesses who may have been walking in Warren Woods around the time of the murders."

"What about the daughter?"

"She hasn't yet regained consciousness and is in a critical condition."

"What do we know about the family?"

"Not a great deal. The father ran an import business with his sons. Precious objects, paintings etc. They have two warehouses, one in Kings Lynn, the other in Cromer."

"Any links with the Russian Mafia?"

"At this stage I'm not sure. The weapon used was a Russian assault rifle – a Kalashnikov, popular among the Mafia, so that may be a possibility or it may not. We don't yet have a motive for the killings."

"Then keep me up to speed with the case – oh and another thing Huw.."

(Only Batarde used his Christian name, a mark of the distance between the two men.)

"Your department's overtime expenses for last month – they seem somewhat excessive."

"Necessary surveillance. Especially regarding the Roughton cannabis raids."

"Then try to get a grip on it – use fewer officers if necessary."

"If I can."

"Just make an effort – that's all."

The press conference concluded just after one pm. It was the usual affair, comprising a room full of journalists and cameramen facing the investigating team. Ketch sat in the middle and fielded most of the questions, the majority of which he was unable to answer – questions about the Russian Mafia were legion but Ketch wasn't prepared to endorse the theory though privately his thoughts were turning in that direction. He appealed for witnesses to come forward and gave a brief description of the vehicle that James had seen.

The Cley Marshes had particular resonance for Ketch. Six years ago the body of a young woman had been discovered here lying in a ditch. She was a Polish immigrant who had been employed like many of her compatriots at a large book wholesalers in Kings Lynn. The last that was seen of her was at a beach party near Wells Beach where she had been photographed dancing with a group of her friends. Despite appeals for witnesses and extensive research into her background and social connections both in Norfolk and in her home country, her killers were never found, although two young men who she had been seen drinking with on the night of the beach party were arrested and interrogated by Ketch. However, because of the lack of any real DNA evidence he could prove nothing, though he continued to suspect that they had raped and killed her.

The Vetochkin house lay at the end of a long driveway some way inland from the marshes, the latter being the domain of the wildlife trust. The Myrtles was a large Victorian mansion which had had an extension added onto it and, as DC Thomas had initially discovered, it had a high perimeter fence, stout iron gates and several security cameras. Adjacent to the property was another large thatched house much older than the myrtles.

As Ketch's car drew up to the gates, a middle-aged man came out from its front door and waved to them. Ketch wound down his window and the man smiled.

"I'm David Sloan, the Vetochkin's next-door neighbour," he explained. "I read what happened to them in this morning's paper. Thought I might be able to help."

Ketch got out of the car and glanced briefly at the assortment of reporters and photographers waiting by the gate. "You're very kind, Mr Sloan. Perhaps you'd like a word with one of my colleagues."

Ketch and MacKenzie made their way up the drive to the front door where a uniformed constable was standing guard. They entered a long high hallway with an elaborate ceiling, beautifully restored in art nouveau fashion. Along the walls were paintings by artists who Ketch

235

immediately recognised. At first glance, they looked like originals by the artists Mondrian and Kandinsky and there were other abstract pieces that he was less familiar with.

The two men turned left into a room which had once served as a library and was lined with leather bound books. The interior had been partly modernised and possessed a number of filing cabinets. Two laptop computers had been placed on a long mahogany desk and behind this sat DC Thomas. The latter was well-known for his IT skills and had in the past been instrumental for Ketch in turning up evidence relating to computer fraud.

"How long have you been here?" Ketch asked.

"Just over an hour sir," Thomas replied.

"Found anything useful yet?"

"Early days. One of the laptops he kept for private and personal use, the second was devoted to his business affairs. It appears that Rainbow Imports has a depot in Amsterdam and another in Toulouse. Both of these were operated by Russian colleagues. The accounts are interesting though."

"How is that?"

"Vetochkin had four different bank accounts, two of them lodged with Swiss banks. In the last six months, very large sums of money were transferred from the UK bank accounts."

"How large?"

"We're talking about millions. There is also a link with a business in Iran. I need more time to investigate this but my immediate suspicion is that he wasn't just importing objects d'art and paintings. He was also exporting though I can't yet say what it was which yielded such large sums of money."

"Firearms?"

"Possibly – there are a number of e-mails from individuals in Russia. One name in particular crops up, and Andrei Datsik. Unfortunately, I don't understand much Russian."

"We'll get someone who does to take a look at the laptops. When you finish with them, back them up. Have you looked in these filing cabinets?"

"Mainly accounts though I did find a pistol and a bottle of vodka in the second drawer down to the left there."

Ketch walked over to the cabinet and pulled open the drawer. Inside was a small weapon of the type often used by the KGB. He had seen one of its kind some years back when investigating a murder at Swaffham.

"So maybe Vetochkin had something or someone to fear. I guess you checked the answerphone for messages?"

"Again all in Russian. A woman's voice mainly and three other messages by different men."

"Ring Golovkin. Get him to do the translations for you."

"I already did. He's in court in Ipswich this morning but he's going to rendezvous with me here this afternoon."

"Good work."

"I'll finish off going through these filing cabinets then. Oh just one other thing. There's a Mrs Greengage in the kitchen. I said she should hang around in case you wanted to speak to her. She's the family's general factotum."

"Fine. I'll have a word with her – hopefully not Russian."

"Not at all Russian – in fact very old style Norfolk."

"Tim – try and get hold of the brother."

"Boris Vetochkin."

"Yes – he lives in Cromer."

MacKenzie nodded.

"Try to fix up a meeting with him for later on today – failing that, tomorrow morning will do. Oh, and speak to the neighbour – a Mr Sloan."

Mrs Greengage the housekeeper was a short, stout woman in her early 60s. She had a florid face and a disconcertingly owlish expression caused chiefly by the strong prescription glasses which were perched on the end of her nose. When Ketch entered the kitchen, he found her sitting at one end of a long pine table on which she had set a tray with two bone china cups and a large teapot and jug of milk. She extended a stubby hand in Ketch's direction.

"I thought you might appreciate some refreshment, Chief Inspector. I'm sorry to say that this might be one of the last pots of tea that I shall be making for visitors here at the big house."

"I'm sorry to hear that, Mrs Greengage. I presume you knew Mr and Mrs Vetochkin very well. How long had you been their housekeeper here?"

Mrs Greengage poured their tea. "Ten years this autumn it would have been. Yes I knew them well. Mrs Vetochkin did not speak much

English so most of my instructions used to be written down for me by their daughter."

"Darya."

"Yes – how is the poor girl? This has been such a terrible business." She paused to dab her eyes with a small handkerchief.

"I'm afraid that she is still critical and has not yet regained consciousness."

"Such a lively and fun loving girl."

"What can you tell me about the family, Mrs Greengage?"

"What exactly would you like to know? They were a good family – Mr Vetochkin was a very respectable man and his wife was extremely sweet natured - she doted on her daughter."

"Did they have friends or visitors to the house?"

"Not that often, no – but I only worked here mainly in the mornings. I believe that they used to hold a number of big parties because quite often I would have to come and clear up in the mornings. Of course, they paid me extra for that – they were very kind – very generous indeed. They gave me jewellery. This is a gift that Ania gave me." She pointed to a large amber necklace set in a gold mount. Ketch examined it.

"Very fine. Would you say that in the last week or so you noticed any difference in Mr or Mrs Vetochkin's demeanour?"

"Mr Vetochkin was always a very tightly controlled man – serious I would say. He rarely showed much emotion though he was always very considerate to me. One thing I did notice was that he had started to drink quite heavily recently. I think it was about a week ago that he and his wife had a blazing row. I have no idea what it was about though."

"Did Darya have a boyfriend?"

"I'm not sure that she did actually. She had just got a place at the local university when this dreadful thing occurred – she was such a very studious girl."

"What had she hoped to study?"

"Business studies I believe." She paused. "Perhaps I ought not to mention it."

"Go on."

"Well, is just that there was a sadness about Darya, a sort of melancholy. I often wondered what that was about. After all, she wanted for nothing and her parents provided for all her material needs.

I asked once why she seemed so sad but she wouldn't say. There was something not quite right I'm sure of it..."

Boris Vetochkin's house was a large redbrick Edwardian villa in Grove Road, a tree-lined avenue which formed part of the eastern perimeter of the old town. At the front door, Ketch and MacKenzie were met by a tall bald-headed man in a black suit who reminded Ketch of one of the bouncers employed at the nightclubs on the Prince of Wales Road in Norwich.

"Mr Vetochkin is in the lounge, gentleman," said the flunky in a broad Russian accent. "This way if you please."

He led the way down a dark, wood - panelled hallway to an equally dark lounge with a high ceiling and red flock wallpaper. Boris Vetochkin, a small compact man in his mid-50s and wearing a pale green velour suit, rose to greet them.

"Boris Vetochkin. I'm pleased to meet you both. Can I offer you some refreshments?"

"No thanks."

"Then do both take a seat. How may I help you?"

"Mr Vetochkin – can I start by asking you the nature of your relationship with your brother?"

"Certainly – we were very close – always we have been. This came as a terrible shock to me you must understand."

"As well as being brothers you were also business partners?"

"Vladimir handled the business here in Norfolk whilst I dealt mainly with the European and Asiatic outlets."

"You have a connection with a business in Amsterdam I believe?"

He nodded. "And much further afield – France, Germany and Mombasa."

"And also Switzerland?" He looked blank.

"I was not aware of it."

"Your brother has a Swiss bank account – perhaps you were not aware of this?"

"I was certainly not aware of it – it's the first I've heard of it, I must say."

"It seems then that Vladimir was not entirely open with you in his business dealings."

"Perhaps so."

Boris Vetochkin looked thoughtful.

"Tell me, during the last few days, had you noticed anything unusual in your brother's behaviour? Did he express any concerns about his safety?"

"He spoke about a rival – Andrei Datsik."

"A business rival?"

"Certainly. Vladimir and Andrei had a history extending back over a decade. Andrei has something of a reputation."

"In what way?"

"In Russia, he was part of the Soin Tsevskaya Bratva."

"The Russian Mafia?" Boris nodded.

"His people had been operating across the county for some years before Vladimir and I took over the business from our father, Peter. In 10 years we expanded the business, providing it with an international base in a number of European capitals. Unfortunately, Datsik became aware of the extent of Rainbow's trade and its continued expansion."

"So what? He threatened you? Is that it?"

"Not me. He threatened Vladimir. He was the senior partner. At first he was offered protection money but my brother refused. Then we had a couple of fires, one here in Cromer and the other in Kings Lynn. The first of these was put down to faulty electrical wiring but when the second fire occurred we began to have our suspicions. Following the fires my brother kept getting a number of anonymous e-mails and phone calls threatening him. None of them were traceable to Andrei of course but they were undoubtedly sent by his people."

And were you threatened?"

"Not directly. Twice I was sent viruses to my PC but nothing more than that. However last year my brother was attacked outside a nightclub in the city – he was badly beaten by a couple of youths. The police looked into it but were unable to find the perpetrator. Since that time the threatening e-mails and letters have continued unabated. I'm convinced that Andrei is behind the murders of my brother and his wife. That's why I employed Ilyish here to keep an eye on me." He motioned towards the bodyguard.

"This man Datsik – do you have a contact address for him?"

"More than that – I have a file on him. Just one moment, it's in my office."

Ketch stood up and strolled around the room. On a small mahogany occasional table by the window, he noticed two framed photographs, the first of Boris and a woman of similar age whom he guessed was his wife, the second a group photograph of Vladimir, his wife, Boris and two teenage girls, one of them being Darya Vetochkin. They were framed against a modern apartment block and travel resort which might have been somewhere on the Black Sea. Ketch turned towards the minder.

"Who is this other girl?"

The man smiled. "Kata – Boris's daughter. That photograph is a few years old. Kata is no longer with her father."

"She left home?"

"No, she is dead."

The door opened and Boris Vetochkin walked in clutching a large file.

"Here, this will provide you with all you need to know about Andrei." He handed the file to Ketch.

"I'm sorry to hear about your daughter," he replied. "Do you mind me asking you how she died?"

A shadow passed across Boris Vetochkin's face. "She committed suicide."

"I'm sorry to hear that."

"Not as sorry as I was, Inspector. It was a year ago and still, I am unable to come to terms with what happened to my beloved it Kata."

"She and Darya were friends?"

"They were great friends. Darya found it impossible to overcome the loss."

Ketch did not return to his flat until later that same day, having decided to enjoy a meal and several pints of beer at one of his favourite watering holes, The Murderers, a real ale hostelry set in the heart of the city. When he opened the front door he could smell it: the distinctive and acrid odour of cannabis. Ketch felt a surge of anger. He had specifically instructed James not to indulge his habit when in the flat. He opened the lounge door but there was no trace of his son, only a pile of discarded newspapers littering the floor, a used ashtray and a half-consumed cup of coffee.

Over in the kitchen sink was a pile of unwashed, greasy plates. He opened the fridge and discovered that his double pint carton of milk had been consumed. James hadn't bothered to replace it. He took a tumbler, half filled it with one of his favourite malt whiskeys, then sat on the sofa and lit a cigarette. In the morning he'd best have words

241

with James and find out exactly how long he intended to stay at the flat - redefine a few ground rules.

As the golden liquid trickled down his throat, he thought of the group photograph and of Kata Vetochkin's unhappy demise. He reached for his briefcase and took out the file that Boris Vetochkin had given him regarding Datsik. According to Boris's information, Datsik had an import business operating from Dubrovnik, dealing with high-quality Russian optical instruments. It appeared that he used this as a cover for drug importation - according to Boris. There was a photo of Datsik in the file, a heavily built man in his late 50s, shaven headed and with cold blue eyes.

The account also claimed that Datsik operated a protection racket in both Cambridge and Norwich, offering protection to several of its nightclubs and supplying them with bouncers, a workforce recruited by him and drawn mainly from the Ukraine area.

Weary, he closed the file, then his eyes. He slipped into a shallow dream where he was a boy again, walking the hills and mountains of North Wales with his father. Though the dream only lasted for a few seconds it offered him considerable comfort. He would not have woken at all had he not heard the sound of James's key unlocking the flat's front door.

For the second morning running Ketch found himself staring into the toilet bowl at the contents of his stomach. The new medication, a dopamine agonist, was no better than the first that he had been prescribed. The drugs diagnosed for his Parkinson's were aimed at boosting the dopamine in his brain, thus counteracting some of the symptoms, including his stiffness and slight shuffling gait. But they also had side-effects: dizziness, sleepiness, nausea, vomiting and in some cases, increased sexual arousal and addictive behaviour.

Ketch wiped his mouth, stared at the packet of tablets then consigned the contents to the waste paper bin. He had read recently that regular exercise helped combat the symptoms of the disease. Perhaps he'd do that and meanwhile continue with the drinking. It wouldn't do his liver any more harm than it had already done.

By the time he got back to the bedroom his phone was ringing. It was MacKenzie. "Darya Vetochkin's dead, sir. I received the news from hospital just 5 minutes ago."

"How did it happen?"

"Apparently someone turned off the ventilator."

"I thought we had an officer on the door 24 seven?"

"We did. He says he must have nodded off somewhere around 5 AM."

By the time Ketch got to HQ, the officer in question was waiting for him in his office. PC Atkins had only been in the Force for six months and was clearly embarrassed by the dereliction of his duty.

"All I can remember was a male nurse went and got me a coffee from the vending machine down the corridor. When I drank it I began to feel sleepy. The next thing I knew the alarm was sounding in the room. You know the rest – I'm very sorry sir."

"This nurse - can you describe him to me?"

"I didn't really take much notice of him. Average build, middle-aged. It was only a fleeting moment."

Ketch put his head in his hands. "Just shut the door behind you Atkins and on your way out ask DC Thomas to see me."

"Any luck with Vetochkin's computer?" asked Ketch.

Thomas nodded. "Several e-mails from Datsik. They confirm what the brother has suggested. Some of the e-mails are abusive in tone. It seems that Vetochkin owed Datsik a large sum of money for goods that he'd received but never paid for. He doesn't say precisely what the goods were but they were a shipment from Russia. The sums owed were up to about half a million. There seems to have been no love lost between the two."

"When was this exactly?"

"About a month ago."

"Okay, we'll see what Datsik has to say for himself."

Just then MacKenzie appeared at the door. "Sir, there's been a development. A member of the public telephoned. She reports having seen the black 4x4 on the morning of the shooting."

"I don't suppose she caught the license plate number?"

"Actually she did. The car belongs to Andrei Datsik."

A short, pugnacious man with bulbous blue eyes, Andrei Datsik sat in interview room six alongside his solicitor, a young man who looked slightly bewildered by the task which had been foisted upon him. Opposite them sat Ketch and MacKenzie, the former looking fatigued. Ketch had not slept well previous night, one of the acquired blessings of his Parkinson's. He must see his GP about getting a prescription for some sleeping tablets. He spoke into the machine, stating the time and persons present at the interview.

"Before we start, Mr Datsik, do you wish to tell us anything about the murders of Vladimir Vetochkin, his wife and daughter?"

"I do not wish to comment."

"But you admit to being the owner of a black Range Rover, registration number A 212 SAB?"

"That is my vehicle registration number, yes."

"This vehicle was seen by two independent witnesses near Warren Wood, in Cromer, at the junction of the Cromer Road, on the morning of 21st of March. Do you admit to driving the vehicle?"

"I do not. My vehicle was stolen – a fact that I reported to the police on the afternoon of the same day."

The solicitor leaned forwards. "Mr Datsik can corroborate that."

"You have had several communications with Mr Vetochkin."

"I knew both brothers as business contacts – that is quite true."

"Vladimir Vetochkin received a number of threatening e-mails from you prior to his death. Do you admit to sending these e-mails?"

"Vladimir owed me a considerable sum of money, a debt which his firm had not paid. I simply requested that he pay the debt by the end of the financial year – not an unreasonable request."

"This is an e-mail you sent him four days ago."

Ketch passed a printout across the table. "As you can see it is a threatening letter – pretty strong language, wouldn't you say?"

Datsik read the contents. "I did not write this message."

"But it has your e-mail address at the top."

"Nevertheless I did not send it."

"There are others of a similar nature," said Ketch, laying them out on the table.

"I did not send them," he repeated.

The interview which lasted another half an hour proceeded much along similar lines. Datsik remained imperturbable, simply denying the accusations that were thrown at him by Ketch.

By 11 o'clock Ketch terminated the interview and Datsik was released without charge. That evening found Ketch and MacKenzie in the saloon bar of the Murderers. It had been a long and largely unproductive day and Ketch was not in a very good mood. An examination of Datsik's clothes had yielded no forensic evidence regarding gunshot residue. His report of a stolen car had also checked out correctly. Moreover, the alibi he had given Ketch later on in the interview of his visiting his local newsagents at 8:30 AM on the day of the murders had checked out with the owner of the shop where he was a very regular customer.

"Datsik must've employed one of his henchmen to take the car and do the shootings," said MacKenzie when the latter had returned from the bar with their drinks.

"Though we can't prove it," Ketch answered. "In the morning ask Thomas to go through those e-mails again and see if he can turn something up."

By 11 pm Ketch had returned to his flat. The place was in the usual chaos, discarded newspapers lying on the floor, empty beer cans and a stale smell of smoke. Pinned to his noticeboard, Ketch found a note from James. It read: 'Dad, thanks for everything. Leg much better now. On the mend. Best, James.'

That night, having cleaned the debris into two plastic bin liners, Ketch slept badly. This was the third night in a row that he had found himself awake in the small hours. He decided now that he really had no option but to see his doctor and get those sleeping tablets. He was beginning to feel severely fatigued.

The following morning he found he had overslept. His watch told him it was already nine o'clock. He cursed, washed and dressed quickly, then made his way by foot into the city.

When he got to HQ he found Mackenzie waiting for him in the lobby. " PC Atkins is waiting to see you," he said. "He seemed rather anxious."

The young PC was standing awkwardly outside Ketch's office.

"What you want to see me about now?" Ketch asked him.

"I was in the incident room this morning – passing through – when I noticed a photograph on the display board."

"Which one?"

"This one," he explained, pointing to a photograph of Boris Vetochkin.

"What about it?"

"I recognise the face – though the man who brought me the coffee at the hospital had black hair. Then I realised – the features were identical – he must have been wearing a wig."

"Why didn't you tell me this earlier?"

"I just hadn't made the connection – I'm sorry."

"PC Atkins, making the right connection is part of our job. Very well – leave this with me."

Unfortunately for Ketch, MacKenzie and the rest of the team, confirmation of Boris Vetochkin's complicity in the Cromer killings was far from the end of the matter. When a squad car arrived at his property in Cromer, they found no one at home. In fact, Boris had taken the ferry from Harwich to the Netherlands on the previous evening.

Six months elapsed before the Dutch police eventually found him, operating under a pseudonym in the Haarlem district. So it was that on a grey November morning Ketch and MacKenzie found themselves sitting in interview room three at the Bethel Street HQ with Boris Vetochkin and his solicitor. Boris looked older and seedier than when Ketch had last seen him. The solicitor, a young man whom Ketch had encountered on numerous previous occasions, leaned forwards with an air of confidence which belied his cherubic countenance.

"My client wishes to make a deal," he said.

"We don't do deals here but get on with it anyway - state the nature of your request."

"He will confess to the manslaughter of Mrs Vetochkin and the killing of his brother Vladimir, but with mitigating circumstances."

"What about the daughter?"

"He had nothing to do with that."

"Unacceptable. Murder on all three counts but we're willing to listen to the case for mitigation and the DPP may take it into account."

"Acceptable," said Vetochkin.

"Then if your client is willing to make his statement..."

"You do not know what my brother was like – few people did," he told Ketch. "Outwardly a respectable businessman – personally not so. He had the most depraved sexual appetite of anyone that I have ever met. Since he was a child he was like this. When we moved to England I hoped he might seek counselling for his condition but it was not so. He continued to hold parties at his house. From an early age, Kata and Darya were close friends. What I did not know was that at the age of 15, Vladimir had corrupted his daughter. I discovered this soon after Kata returned home from one of his parties much distressed. She told me that Vladimir and three other men in the party had raped both of them. For two hours, they were forced to endure his

246

bestiality. About a month after this my beloved daughter took her own life. I could not endure it. I confronted Vladimir but he simply denied it. My pleas to his wife also fell upon deaf ears.

"I decided then and there that I would take my revenge for what he had done. I had borrowed a considerable sum of money from Andrei Datsik and he had issued threats against my life. I decided I would find a way of settling my account with him. I stole his car and followed my brother to the Warren in Cromer. When Vladimir tried to escape, I shot him. I had resolved that his wife should also be punished for failing to control his behaviour. Shooting Darya however, was a terrible mistake. I had not intended that she should be so badly injured.

"After the shooting, it occurred to me that Darya remained a vital witness to what I had done. Reluctantly I decided to terminate her life. The chances are that she would never have fully recovered from her injuries anyway so I viewed this as a mercy killing. That is all I have to say about the matter."

The Vetochkin trial took place in the February of the following year at Norwich Crown Court. Boris Vetochkin received three concurrent life sentences for the murders he had confessed to, with a minimum of 15 years. But his stay in prison was a short one. On February 10 he was discovered in his cell. His throat had been slashed from ear to ear and prior to his death he had been partially garrotted. Although there was no proof, Ketch was convinced that Boris Vetochkin had died as the result of a direct order from Datsik, for his death bore all the trademarks of a Russian Mafia killing.

After his murder, Ketch received a file from Interpol, confirming his suspicions about the brothers. They had both been members of an infamous Russian Mafia organisation. Moreover, their import business had served as a cover for extortion rackets and money-laundering.

In late February, Ketch returned to the flat by the River Wensum and resumed his relationship with Carol, though he was in many ways a changed man. The disease which now plagued him had forced him to reduce his drinking and moderate his diet. These days he found he was easily fatigued and relied much on his younger colleagues for support in his day-to-day investigations. However, one thing above all had made him a much happier man. He had his family back with him again. It was a redemption and a source of great comfort to him.

THE BURLESQUE CLUB

For the third night in a week, DCI Ketch, aka. Huw Price, lay naked on his bed. It was hot, unbelievably hot. Temperatures in the thirties had melted the tarmac on some of the city roads, caused deaths among elderly residents and killed fish which were seen gasping for oxygen in the River Wensum down by the Norwich law courts.

Ketch had never seen a summer as hot as this. He had taken measures of course. He'd draped heavy curtains across his windows to shut out the sunlight, bought a giant fan, applied ice packs to his forehead at intervals during the hot afternoons when he was here off duty and plied himself with ice cold beers. He'd also taken to walking around the flat naked, a habit which provided some embarrassment when his new neighbour from the ground floor flat below him came up to borrow a pint of milk. Her name was Cheryl and she was an extremely attractive blonde in her early 30s, a young solicitor whom he had encountered recently when she'd represented a client at the Norwich HQ in Bethel Street. Fortunately for Ketch he had the foresight to wrap a bath towel around him before opening the door, but as he answered the summons, he was only too aware of his bulging midriff and moobs, the legacy of a lifetime's indulgence in bad food and excessive alcohol.

After she'd gone, Ketch had fallen into a sexual reverie about his new neighbour, then laughed at himself, realising how absurd he had become. Since the split up with his partner Carol, he had become aware of his need for sexual stimulation. He had even thought of employing the services of a prostitute but then discarded the notion.

He looked at his watch – 4 AM. He got up, went to the sink and poured himself a glass of water. Streets away, in the Prince of Wales Road, he could hear the shouts of drunken youths as they fought their pitched battles outside the nightclubs. It was Saturday morning. Since the Blair era, the clubs had managed to extend the licensing hours to 6 AM which meant that the drunks could drive themselves into a state of enraged intoxication. The police could now barely contain the numbers in these mass conflicts which spread out down the street and often involved innocent bystanders. The situation was virtually ungovernable and although the ACC had advised the residents of

Norwich that the city was still a safe place to live, there were some residents who did not believe him.

Ketch downed the water, then moved to the window and pulled back the heavy curtains. On the other side of the road lay a drunken youth attended by his equally intoxicated friend. It was a typical Saturday morning in Norwich.

Sometime after six o'clock, he woke again, this time from a vivid dream involving the new downstairs neighbour. He reached for his mobile. It was his sidekick, DS Tim MacKenzie.

"I'm sorry to disturb you so early sir. "

"No problem. I was already awake."

"There has been a development at Bawsey Pits."

Bawsey Pits was a large area of connected lakes in the West of the County. Once a gravel pit development, it was a favourite spot for locals who swam in large numbers here, despite the clear warning signs which the company had placed prominently by the edge of the waters about the dangers of swimming here. Over the past two decades, no less than six people had drowned, several of them trapped by thick weed which lay submerged beneath the waters. On the Friday morning, local police had been alerted to an incident at the pits. Two young men had been diving into one of the lakes at the far end of the development, a place called Greenbottom, which was notorious for its depths. When one of the pair failed to return to shore, his friend alerted the emergency services, but by the time the police and ambulance staff arrived, it was already too late to save him. The unfortunate swimmer had become trapped in weed and drowned.

"What sort of development?" asked Ketch.

"They've found a second body," MacKenzie explained, "- a female. One of the divers found her whilst he was searching in the weed."

"Any ID?"

"None so far. You want me to send a car?"

"Give me 30 minutes, will you?" Ketch took a shower and washed himself clean of the detritus of the previous day, then downed a large plate of muesli and mashed banana.

By the time he had dressed, the squad car had arrived. Mackenzie smiled at him as he got in but they said nothing. Such silences were not unusual between the two men. Ketch had known Tim MacKenzie now for nearly 10 years. In many ways, they were a perfect match.

Ketch was by nature grouchy, introspective and inclined to be short tempered. MacKenzie, who was 15 years younger, was outward going, equable and infinitely patient. He also possessed the ability to work independently and methodically, qualities which did not go unnoticed in his older compatriot. Ketch also admired MacKenzie because he was both punctual and a very good driver. Ketch could drive of course, and like many policeman, had passed the advanced driver's course, but he chose not to drive. In truth, he was something of a Luddite who had taken five years before finally purchasing a mobile phone. The notion of texting had seemed abhorrent to him. Indeed he preferred whenever possible to leave the technical aspects of police work to his junior colleagues.

By the time they had driven 20 miles west of the city, the sun had already risen in the east. Like a giant fireball, it hung on the edge of the flat landscape, throwing the scattered copses into sharp relief. Ketch had a particular fondness for this part of the county with its vast open skies and long, deserted beaches. It was one of the least claustrophobic places he had ever visited. The car swept onwards, touching the outer edge of King's Lynn, then passed a large crematorium, a place which held painful memories for Ketch. It was here that he had said farewell to his wife Annie many years ago. Since her untimely death from cancer at the age of 43, his life had never been the same. It was as if part of his soul had unravelled and he had lost direction. Only the job held him together and provided him with a focus. In the intervening years, his addiction to drink had proved to be almost uncontrollable and was the main cause of his breakup with his partner, Carol Hennessy, the young pathologist who had given up her career to raise their son Sean. Now he lived in a dingy flat, not far from the city centre, once more alone, surrounded by memories and burdened by the early onset of Parkinson's disease.

"Here we are sir," said MacKenzie, breaking his reverie. "Bawsey Pits."

With the early morning sun shining through the trees and casting its light on the placid waters of the wide lake, the place possessed an eerie feeling. Ketch could imagine Sir Bedivere casting the sword Excalibur into the waters and a hand as white and smooth as marble, rising from its depths.

MacKenzie parked the car. They walked along a rough track where a sign warned visitors about the dangers of swimming in the lakes. About 20 metres ahead, Ketch spotted the familiar barrier tape denoting the crime scene. Behind it, he recognised the portly form of Dr Stoppard, the pathologist, a man who over the years Ketch had grown to tolerate, despite his exasperating manner.

"Such a beautiful spot, don't you think?" Dr Stoppard observed. "Such a pity that no one takes the warning sign seriously. I have two bodies for you. The first presents no problem at all." He beckoned to the two officers, then knelt down, unzipping a body bag, revealing the white face of a dark haired youth, dressed only in a brief pair of swimming trunks. "Ashley Smith. It's the usual story I'm afraid. Got tangled in weed about 20 yards from the middle of the lake. His friend summoned help but by the time they got him back to the shore, he had already drowned."

"His friends are giving their statements to WPC Atkins," explained MacKenzie, indicating a police van parked next to the lake about 30 yards away.

"Straightforward then," said Ketch.

"Precisely. The other one is more problematic, however. Let me show you."

Stoppard unzipped the second body bag and Ketch stared down at a bloated white face.

"How long?"

"I estimate at least six weeks – it could be longer. I can't be entirely sure until I get her out and onto the slab."

"Did she drown?"

"She did not. See these marks around the neck? "

"Murder."

"No doubt about it."

"Any ID on her?"

"I'm afraid not. A couple of receipts in her pocket. Illegible – but there is this card." Stoppard handed Ketch an evidence bag. Though faded from exposure to water he could still make out the lettering. It read: The Burlesque Club, Norwich, followed by a phone number. The legend rang no bells for him.

"The Burlesque Club. What is that?" he asked MacKenzie.

"A nightclub which specialises in burlesque dancing," replied MacKenzie.

"Never heard of it."

Stoppard smiled. Ketch handed back the bag.

"The body was weighted down with a sandbag," Stoppard added. "It was attached by a rope to her midriff."

"DNA?"

"Maybe - though she's been rather long in the water."

"Keep searching the lake – see if anything else turns up," said Ketch. "And check the missing persons reports for the past two months."

Back at HQ, Ketch realised why he felt so lousy. In the rush to leave his flat, he had forgotten to take his Parkinson's meds. These days he took a combination of drugs to control the symptoms of the disease. If he got the timing wrong, not only would the tremor on his right side increase to a noticeable level, but he would also be played by fatigue and stiffness in his joints.

It had taken two months to find the drugs which best suited his physiology. Some of them, especially the dopamine agonists, had distressing side-effects. One, in particular, had caused an increase in sexual desire. Since he now led an almost monastic lifestyle, this had become a problem. He'd also found that drinking excessive amounts of alcohol only served to heighten his symptoms and he now restricted his intake to a couple of glasses of malt whiskey each evening.

By the time he left the building and made his way across the city towards his Earlham Road flat, the sun was already high in a cloudless sky and he found himself sweating profusely. It was the middle of July and the city streets were packed solid with locals and tourists.

Back in his flat, he pushed open the kitchen window, downed his pills, then checked his landline for messages. The first was from Carol, reminding him that he was due to spend the forthcoming Saturday morning with his son, Sean. The second message gave him pause for thought. It was from Rachel, a 50-year-old blonde whom he had spent an evening with two nights ago. So frustrated had he become with his monastic existence that he had joined an online dating bureau. For the first time in his life, he had been required to prepare a video profile of his personality, an experience which filled him with trepidation. The task had taken him over two hours to complete and was made all the more difficult by his horror and distrust of technology. So bland and uninteresting was the result that it came as a shock when found someone matching his profile. Rachel, whom he had met in the saloon bar of The Murderers in Norwich, turned out to be a lively and engaging woman with obvious physical charms which she had done her best to cultivate. She was a librarian at the University, a mother of two, grown-up sons and a divorcee.

For one hour they chatted, consuming a great deal of red wine, discovering that they had several interests in common including theatre and music. This was followed by an invitation to coffee at Rachel's flat which Ketch interpreted as a metaphor for sexual congress. His analysis proved to be correct. However, in the cold light of day and on the receiving end of a hangover, he started to have misgivings.

Although Rachel was physically very attractive, he dreaded the possibility of yet another complicated relationship which might well end in disaster. There was also the job to consider, which was often all consuming. Now that he had his Parkinson's to deal with, this provided him with additional stress. If only, he told himself, relationships with the opposite sex could be conducted purely on the basis of sex, life would be so much easier. It was a Hedonistic and utterly unrealistic viewpoint, he knew that.

He picked up the phone but then put it down again. Maybe he'd ring Rachel later about the offer of dinner. Or maybe he'd think about it instead.

When he got back to Bethel Street, he found ACC Batarde waiting for him in the Ops room.

"A moment of your time please, Huw," said Batarde. Ketch sighed. Batarde, whose profile bore a strong resemblance to Gilbert and Sullivan's Modern Major General, was the bane of Ketch's life. Obsessed by PR, he had a habit of interrogating Ketch whenever the image of the force seemed to be under threat. Today was no exception to the rule. He waved Ketch to a seat and stood by the window, his arms crossed before him. He had an irritating habit of scratching his head when he spoke which made Ketch wonder whether he was afflicted by dandruff.

"The Prince of Wales Road rioting," he began in his familiar clipped tones. "I don't see much progress being made on that front. Have you anything positive to report?"

"We had a meeting with most of the nightclub managers last Tuesday evening. They have agreed to set up an instant texting network when trouble sparks. Also, we have put another two riot vans on Friday nights."

" Why don't I hear of this in the local press?"

"We sent out press releases to that effect to both the local and national press."

"Let's hope we see some results from that quarter then. This second body at Bawsey Pits - what do we know about the victim?"

"A female in her 20s – no ID as yet. We will be putting out an appeal to the public for information later on today."

"Very good. How is Carol by the way?"

"Well, I believe."

Clearly, word had got round about his separation. Still, he had no intention of giving Batarde an accurate update of his situation.

"Is there anything else, sir?"

"No, that's it. Just make sure you keep me up to the mark. It's not one of your better qualities."

Ignoring the remark, Ketch shut the door and returned to his room where he found MacKenzie waiting for him.

"Autopsy report is in, sir."

"That was quick."

"Dr Stoppard dropped it in personally."

Ketch sat down and waved MacKenzie to a chair as he scanned the report. Cause of death: manual strangulation. Hyoid bone broken. Several contusions around the neck. Also around the stomach, indicating rope marks approximately one centimetre wide. Stomach contents suggest the victim consumed a large meal an hour prior to death. Adipocere renders facial recognition difficult. Larval insect evidence indicates that death occurred around the middle of May. There was no other data which Ketch found indicative.

"Have you checked the missing persons register for May?"

MacKenzie nodded. "Three reports. Two teenagers and a woman in her mid-20s from Norwich. The latter was reported missing by her husband, a Dr John Hunter on May 30. I checked the report. Hunter is a lecturer at the University. His wife left the home at Hellesdon on May 15 and has not contacted him since."

"What about The Burlesque Club?"

"The club is in St Margaret Street. It specialises in burlesque dancing."

"Remind me. Burlesque dancing – what exactly is that?"

"Burlesque dancing is a fairly recent form of striptease. Some people believe it dates back as far as the comedia de l'arte as an art form. The dancers dress in ornate costumes intended to arouse erotic feelings in the audience. Some people claim that burlesque is a legitimate art form in its own right."

"You can spare me the lecture, Tim. Have you contacted the club yet?"

"I rang them while you were out. The club opens this afternoon at two o'clock. I spoke to the manager there."

"Ring him back and fix us an appointment will you? And while you're at it, see if you can contact this Dr Hunter."

Ketch looked at his wristwatch which told him it was already one o'clock. "Fancy a pint and some lunch at the Murderers? Then we'll drop in on the club." MacKenzie nodded. It was a routine he was familiar with which involved Ketch quaffing a pint and whiskey chaser while MacKenzie consoled himself with a diet Pepsi and the inevitable steak pie. 'Lubricating the synapses,' was the phrase Ketch used to describe this almost daily ritual. MacKenzie had found his superior to be a creature of ingrained habits, of which drinking was the most sociable.

The Burlesque Club was a small, dark premises set ironically between a Methodist church and a betting shop in the older part of the city. On the side panel of the front door was a selection of photographs of women dressed in blue corsets and stockings, adopting a variety of erotic poses. Ketch pressed the intercom button and the door was opened immediately by a tall, bald headed bouncer, dressed in an ill-fitting dark suit. Ketch showed his warrant card.

"We would like to see your manager – is he in?" The bouncer led them down a dark corridor where there was an overriding smell of sweat and stale alcohol. The hall gave way to a small auditorium and stage and on the left of this was a hallway behind which rose a flight of stairs leading to a tiny office, sparsely furnished with a desk, two chairs and walls lined with more photographs of erotic dancers. A tall, ugly man of Eastern European origin stood up to greet them.

"It's the police," explained the bouncer. The man grinned, exposing a row of white teeth with gold fillings.

"DCI Ketch. And this is my colleague, DS MacKenzie."

"Ivan Kropotkin. I'm the manager here – how can I help you?"

"I understand that you employ a number of female dancers here at the club."

"That is correct. We have three full-time artistes and a number who work here part-time."

"Have you had an employee go missing in the last six weeks or so?"

"Why do you ask that?"

"We are investigating a missing person. She may have worked here."

"I would have to check. Certainly, all our full-time staff are accounted for. Part-time staff are by nature more sporadic. They come and they go."

Kropotkin strolled over to a filing cabinet and took out a wad of brown folders which he then placed on the desk.

"These are all out temporary girls."

"May I?" asked Ketch.

"By all means – help yourself."

Ketch opened the top file. A dark haired, buxom girl, clad only in bra and panties stared back at him. The legend read: Sweet April.

"Do these girls also have real names?" he enquired.

"You will find the names and contact details at the end of the file," Kropotkin explained.

"And how many of these girls still work here?"

"All of them except two if my memory serves me correctly." Kropotkin leafed through the pile. "This one and this one I have not employed for a couple of months or so." He pulled out two files, both of them tall blondes with rather similar faces. Ketch made a note of the names, addresses and phone numbers.

"And you say these are the real names?"

"As far as I can determine, yes."

"How exactly do you pay them?"

"In cash of course. As I said, they are employed here on a strictly casual basis, filling in for my permanent dancers whenever necessary."

"What about National Insurance?"

"They pay their own National Insurance."

"I'd like to borrow these files – I can let you have them back some time tomorrow."

"That's no problem." The man smiled back at Ketch like a crocodile approaching its prey. "Anything else I can help you with? A drink perhaps?" Ketch declined the offer.

Back at HQ, MacKenzie phoned the mobiles of the two girls. He then walked into Ketch's office.

"Any luck?"

"I got a reply to the first number – she's a student at the UEA, alive and kicking."

"And the second?"

"Voicemail only. I got Dave to check out the mobile number though. It's a Vodafone. The subscriber was an Alice Hunter."

Dr John Hunter had just finished his lecture on the late prose works of Charles Algernon Swinburne in room C 21 at the University when he received the phone call from DS MacKenzie. He agreed to meet Ketch and MacKenzie at four pm in his room at the English faculty. A tall, lean Scot in his early 30s, with dark eyes and an aquiline nose, he looked distinctly uneasy as he ushered the two police officers into his small seminar room. Ketch thought he detected an odour of patchouli oil. Unusual for a man. Then he dismissed thought, surprised by his own naiveté. Times had changed since he was in his 30s. He had even noticed one or two male students wearing makeup and nose studs as they made their way across the main concourse. What was the term MacKenzie had used? Metrosexual. That was it. Nowadays anything goes.

Hunter removed his jacket and placed it around his chair. He was wearing a short sleeve shirt. Ketch noticed that his left forearm had a tattoo in the shape of an ankh.

"Do sit down, inspector. Your sergeant here tells me you may have found my wife Alice."

"At this stage of our investigation, we can't be entirely certain. I believe you reported your wife as a missing person in mid-May?"

"That's correct. May the 16th to be precise. I understand that you found the body of a woman at Bawsey Pits? Is it Alice?"

"As I've said, we are not certain of anything at this stage while our investigation's proceeding. The body we recovered from the lake was unrecognisable and could only be identified from dental records or DNA tests. I am going to show you a photograph of the dress the deceased was wearing when the body was recovered. Perhaps you could tell me if you recognise it as one belonging to your wife."

Dr Hunter leaned forwards over the desk and a shadow passed across his gaunt features.

"It's one of Alice's dresses. I remember it. What about her other belongings?"

"I am afraid we only recovered the body itself and clothes that she was wearing. There was one other item however which we found in one of the pockets."

MacKenzie produce the evidence bag containing the Burlesque Club visiting card.

"Does this ring any bells?"

Hunter nodded, then held his head in his hands. There was a moment's silence. Then he said in a hollow voice: "Alice worked there on a part-time basis as a burlesque dancer. It was one of her passions. She had trained as a dancer you see, was part of a ballet company when I first met her here in Norwich. We met in the Maddermarket Theatre during the show's interval. That was some four years ago."

"You didn't object then, to your wife's part-time occupation as an erotic dancer?"

"Alice and I had what you might describe as an open marriage. We both tried to live independent lives. She was also studying for a master's degree in English here at the uni. She was a bright girl."

"You speak of her in the past tense."

"Shouldn't I?"

"At the moment we can't be certain the body recovered is that of your wife, Dr Hunter. What we would like you to do is to give us something which belongs to your wife. A personal item like a hairbrush would suffice. We can use that for a DNA match. That would help us to eliminate her from our enquiries."

"Certainly inspector."

"You said earlier that you reported your wife missing on 16 May. Can I ask you when in fact you last saw her?"

Hunter thought for a moment. Then he said: "It was a Saturday when I last saw her. The 12th of May. I'd come home from the University library to find her in a buoyant mood. She was excited because she had just put the finishing touches to her MA thesis. We had a meal together around midday. Then she slept for a while before preparing for the evening shift at the club. She was due to perform there around eight pm. She never returned. I rang her mobile around 1 am but I just got voice mail. I spent the next two days waiting to hear from her but there was nothing. A couple of days later I contacted the police and reported her as a missing person."

"She never mentioned to you that she had problems?"

"No nothing like that."

"What about other men?"

"As I told you, we had a fairly open relationship. To be honest, I suspected she might be having an affair."

"You knew the identity of this person?"

Hunter nodded. "Stephen Goddard, one of the junior lecturers here at the University. He joined the department about two years ago. He was supervising Alice's MA work. Consequently, they spent a deal of time together. Stephen was a frequent visitor to the club. In fact, I introduced him to the place – a decision which, on reflection, I must say I now regret."

"Did you confront her about your suspicions?"

"Oh certainly. She admitted that they were close but that it wasn't serious. She was quite upfront about that. I told her that I was quite happy for her to carry on – how could I not be? We both had had lovers over the time we'd been together. We didn't see that as a problem. Unlike many other couples, we enjoyed an adult relationship"

"Is there anyone you can think of who might have wished your wife harm?"

"I can't think of anyone in particular. Alice was a vibrant, vivacious, friendly woman. She didn't make enemies. In fact, it was impossible not to like her. I'll go and get one of her hair brushes, shall I?"

Ketch nodded. "And if you have no objection, we'd like to take a look at some of her personal belongings. Do you have a photograph of your wife that we could have?"

"I do."

"Did she keep a diary?"

"She kept a journal, yes. I'll get it for you."

As Ketch drifted backed into consciousness, he realised with horror that he was not in his own bed. Slowly, the events of the previous night cascaded into his memory. He opened his eyes to find Rachel's naked form slumbering beside him. She was snoring loudly. As he shifted from beneath the duvet and reached for his pants, the episode reconstructed itself. It had started with a meal in an Italian restaurant near the Bridewell. This was followed by drinks at The Murderers. Then they had gone back to Rachel's flat in Timber Hill, where a bout of vigorous lovemaking had occupied them until well past midnight.

He finished dressing, then quietly left the flat. He hadn't washed, not wishing to wake Rachel. He was consumed by an overwhelming feeling of disgust at his lack of self-control. The lure of Rachel's body had overwhelmed him. Yes, he liked her, but there was certainly no spiritual empathy between them. With Rachel it was pure carnal desire and he was not content with that. Deep down he knew he was looking for a life partner and Rachel did not fit the bill. Perhaps that was unreasonable and unrealistic. He stopped off at a stall in the covered market where he equipped himself with a latte, then made his way to HQ. Having showered on the third floor, he then returned to his office where he found MacKenzie already waiting for him.

"Rough night sir?" said MacKenzie. Ketch glowered back at him.

"Don't even ask ."

MacKenzie placed a folder on his desk. "The DNA from the hairbrush gives us a match. I've been checking through the CCTV footage from the camera which overlooks the Burlesque Club."

"And?"

"On the evening she disappeared we have a clear shot of her arriving in a car at seven thirty pm."

"Did you get a look at the licence plate?"

MacKenzie nodded. "The car belongs to one Stephen Goddard. The same car picks her up later at 11 pm."

"Good work MacKenzie. Let me look at that journal."

"What about Goddard, sir?"

"Let's get him in for questioning – this afternoon will do. And I shall need another coffee."

Alice Hunter's journal was a curious mishmash of academic observations relating to her doctoral thesis on Victorian pornography and comments about fellow students. There were a number of entries dealing with academic enquiries, including some observations on a Victorian book entitled The Pearl. This meant nothing to Ketch. Among the more or less fortnightly intervals in the diary there also occurred a number of what appeared to be grid references, followed by the initials of what might have been names. He turned on his PC and googled Ordnance Survey, then fed into the search bar one of the grid references. Foxley Woods. Then the second and third references: Felthorpe Woods and Blickling Woods. He frowned. Why woods? A nature lover, perhaps? He googled The Pearl. There were several Pearls listed. Online jewellery sites, a novel by John Steinbeck and a magazine of erotic literature, now available at last online in PDF format. He downloaded it and decided to examine it later.

Dr Stephen Goddard stared nervously at Ketch and MacKenzie. A short, balding man in his early 30s, he resembled a typical academic. Myopic and slightly stooped, he was dressed in a pair of corduroy trousers and a tweed jacket patched at the elbows. Ketch, himself a heavy smoker, detected a whiff of roll ups.

"How exactly can I help you, Chief Inspector? I suppose you want to know about Alice Hunter."

"Indeed we do. Try to relax, will you? This isn't a formal interview – you are simply helping us with our enquiries."

Goddard sat back in the chair and attempted a weak smile.

"I'm relieved to hear that. What precisely do you wish to know?"

"We understand that you gave Alice Hunter a lift to the Burlesque Club on the evening of May 12."

"Indeed I did so. She had visited me the same afternoon and wanted to discuss an aspect of her doctoral thesis."

"This would have been at the University?"

"No, at my flat in Hillside Road."

"And were such visits a common occurrence?"

"They were not uncommon. I was mentoring Alice, giving her guidance in her studies. It's a fairly normal procedure," he added patronisingly. Ketch ignored the deflection.

"In her diary, we found a number of map grid references along with the initials of people's names, yours included. Perhaps you would like to enlighten me about that?"

Goddard smiled. "Indeed I can. Alice, her husband and me are part of a walking group. We all share a love of nature and like to explore the wooded areas of East Anglia. We have been doing that for a couple of years now. Several of us are also keen photographers so our expeditions have a dual purpose really."

"We know that you picked up Alice from the club at 11 pm. Where did you take her then?"

"We went back to my place for a nightcap. She stayed with me for a couple of hours and then she left."

"What time was that?"

"Around 1:30 AM I guess."

"You went back to your house and had sex?"

"You put it rather bluntly."

"But that's what happened wasn't it?"

"Maybe."

"You argued, things got out of control. Is that how it was?"

"Certainly not. We parted on perfectly amicable terms."

"You then gave her a lift back home."

"No. She said she wanted to walk across the city. She wanted to clear her head."

"What was her husband's view of your relationship?"

"John and I are the best of friends. He and Alice had an open relationship. He didn't object to it."

"You're sure about that?"

"I'm certain about it."

"Okay. We shall have to examine your car, Mr Goddard. Is that a problem for you?"

"Not at all."

By that afternoon, the sun had retreated behind a dense bank of cloud and the temperature in the city had dropped by 5°. Since it was one of his access days, Ketch had taken time off from the investigation and was up on Mousehold Heath , spending a few precious hours with his son Sean. After a short but vigorous game of football, the two found a bench, where they sat gazing at the vast expanse of the city beneath them. It was a favourite spot for Ketch, the place where he could shed his feelings of claustrophobia. Though light rain had now begun to fall, the two remained on the bench for a considerable while, listening to the birds and the distant hum of the city. The spell was only broken when Ketch's mobile sprang into life. He cursed. He had forgotten to turn it to mute.

"MacKenzie here sir. Sorry to disturb you."

"Let's hope it's important."

"Stephen Goddard has been found dead."

"Where?"

"At his home in Hellesdon. The cleaning lady found him. He'd hung himself. I am at the premises right now."

"Suicide?"

"It looks very much like it. He left a note."

"Very well. Give me the address and I'll be there in an hour. SOCO there yet?"

"They're on their way."

Having dropped Sean back at Carol's flat, he took a taxi to the address, a large three bedroomed semi backing onto the churchyard.

"He's in the study," said MacKenzie, showing Ketch down a long hallway, lined with Victorian paintings. They entered a spacious, highly ceilinged room, sumptuously furnished with oak bookcases. Goddard's body was suspended from the ceiling rose above a long mahogany writing desk. To the left of it, was a straight-backed chair which had toppled over. On the face of it, MacKenzie's suicide theory seemed convincing.

"Let me look at the note," said Ketch. MacKenzie passed him a folded sheet of paper. It read: I am unable to bear this burden any longer. Alice's death was a terrible accident but I cannot reconcile myself to it nor live with it on my conscience. My will and other instructions can be found with my solicitor." There followed a name and address. The letter had been computer printed and given a brief and almost indecipherable signature.

Ketch's reading of the note was interrupted by a voice emanating from the doorway. "Time we cut him down I think." It was Stoppard, accompanied by two SOCO assistants. "How long has he been hanging there?"

"The cleaning lady found him when she entered the house at two pm. She's in the other room with WPC Atkins," MacKenzie replied.

The two SOCO stood on the writing desk and carefully severed the rope. Stoppard leaned over the now prostrate body of the academic.

"Well?" asked Ketch. "Is it suicide?"

"It's certainly death by asphyxiation, that's for sure," Stoppard replied. "There are some contusions on the forehead which probably occurred shortly before he expired which have interesting possibilities though."

"You mean that he was attacked?"

"They may have been self-inflicted. It's not possible to be exact. I need to examine the body in greater detail."

When Stoppard had left the room to get his medical bag, MacKenzie said: "There's something else I think you should see sir."

"Oh yes?"

"There's a cellar."

"Show me."

They walked into the hallway. MacKenzie opened the door under the stairs, then the two men descended a steep flight of steps into what once had been a large wine cellar but was now kitted out as a photographic studio with lamps, several expensive looking cameras and a laptop with a tray of memory sticks. Around the walls hung a collection of framed photographs showing a nude model reclining against a selection of sumptuously furnished Victorian interiors. Ketch peered at one of them and at once recognised the face of Alice Hunter.

"Let's get this equipment packed up for further examination," he instructed MacKenzie.

As MacKenzie set about his task with a fellow officer, Ketch made his way back upstairs to the study where he found the SOCO officers in the process of finalising their investigations. He began checking the bookshelves. There was a wide selection of 19th-century prose classics and volumes of poetry by the likes of Wordsworth, Keats, Shelley and Byron. Among the shelves he came across an altogether more unusual selection whose names were less familiar to him with titles like 'My Secret Life,' and 'A Night In The Harem.' After a little searching, he found what he had been looking for: a small, leather bound edition of 'The Pearl.' He opened it and began scanning its pages. An anonymously edited magazine, it contained a number of narratives which described in explicit detail scenes of sexual domination and depravity. He placed it in an evidence bag and made his way back downstairs to rejoin MacKenzie.

When Ketch awoke it was not quite dawn. He had slept badly, partly owing to the intense humidity, but mainly because of the insomnia triggered by his Parkinson's medication. He decided he would shower early, breakfast, then take a walk by the River Wensum in order to clear his head. As he wound his way along the misty riverbank, he mused on Stephen Goddard's suicide. Clearly, he had been obsessed with Alice Hunter. The photographs in his studio made that apparent. But why strangle her and conceal her body in the lake? What had been his motive for murder? Had she refused to leave her husband perhaps? Or had Goddard forced her into performing acts of depravity which she had denied him and he had then strangled her? Then there was the letter of confession. It seemed genuine on the face of it but the signature would need to be compared with some of his other correspondence.

By nine o'clock and fortified with coffee, Ketch was back at his desk at Bethel Street where he found MacKenzie waiting for him.

"Any developments?"

" SOCO report is in sir. They examined Goddard's car where they found rope fibres in the boot. They are a match with the rope used to bind Alice Hunter."

Ketch nodded. "What about the laptop and the memory sticks?"

"You might want to take a look yourself. It seems that Goddard had a pretty extensive collection of erotic shots, some of them of Alice Hunter, some using other models. Dave is in the IT suite, going through them now." (Dave Thomas was one of the IT specialists at Bethel Street.) "One thing we did find though –?"

"What is that?"

"Those grid references that you found in her diary..."

"I remember."

"It appears that Goddard was employed as a photographer for a group who met at woodland sites around Norfolk. They would dress up in Victorian costumes and act out scenes of seduction and sexual congress. The participants often used masks so it is not easy to identify them in the photographs."

Armed with fresh coffee, Ketch made his way to the IT suite where he discovered DC Dave Thomas hunched over a widescreen computer.

"It's pretty tame stuff – well most of it, anyway," he explained. "There's a good deal of bondage and simulated flagellation."

"Let's take a look, see if we can recognise anyone," said Ketch. Thomas began downloading the images. Alice Hunter dressed as a maid, tied to a tree. Alice Hunter as red riding hood pursued by a figure dressed as a wolf. Alice Hunter lying naked on an improvised stone altar, surrounded by figures in cloaks and hoods, one of which featured the mask of the Green Man. There were at least 200 shots but they had been taken in such a way as to disguise the identities of the male participants and the fact that none of them featured Goddard himself suggested to Ketch that the photographer was always behind his camera and not involved in the action. There were also other shots – portraits of Alice Hunter dressed in regal costume or as an angel. Her seraphic pose gave Ketch an insight into Goddard's obsession with his subject.

"Put these on a separate memory stick, will you Dave? I'd like to examine them in more detail."

As he was leaving the IT suite he found Stoppard entering the lift.

"Have you finished the autopsy on Goddard?" asked Ketch.

"Indeed I have," replied Stoppard. "And I can tell you categorically that he did not commit suicide. I found a clear ligature mark around his neck indicating that he had been strangled prior to the hanging. There were also a number of defensive wounds to his hands and arms. There were some traces of DNA under the fingernails of his left hand which will undoubtedly prove very useful."

"When can I read the report?"

"As soon as I have completed it," Stoppard replied snappily. "I'm on a busy schedule."

After a brief liquid lunch at the Adam and Eve pub, one of his favourite watering holes, Ketch walked back to Bethel Street via the old part of the city, winding through its ancient cobbled streets, ruminating on Goddard's murder. The evidence of the rope fibres indicated that he had killed Alice Hunter but who would have a motive for killing Goddard and then faking his suicide?

By one pm he was back at his laptop, scanning the collection of photographs again. Apart from the shots of Alice Hunter, they were mainly close-ups of the participants, a back, a thigh, a pair of buttocks. About halfway through the shots, he paused, then enlarged the image. It was a forearm with a tattoo of an ankh.

Dr John Hunter was nowhere to be found on the university campus. Neither was he at his home address when Ketch and McKenzie called on him that same afternoon. It was as if he had completely disappeared.

On a cold, frosty morning in mid-March, DCI Ketch sat on a bench overlooking the waters of the river Wensum. It had been a long, seemingly endless winter and an equally unsatisfactory trial. For six months Hunter had eluded capture, having sought sanctuary in northern Spain. It had taken three months to track him down to a small villa in a remote region of the country and another month to complete the extradition order. He had been indicted on two counts: the murder of Stephen Goddard and the murder of Alice Hunter. However, he had only admitted the first of these charges. When presented with the DNA evidence taken from underneath Goddard's fingernails, he had made a full confession to the murder. He had visited Goddard and his flat and confronted him, strangled him, then faked his suicide. Hunter had been jealous of Goddard's relationship with Alice. It had started when he had offered Alice a portfolio of photographs to assist her in her career as a burlesque dancer. He had invited the couple to participate in a series of sexual exploits with a group known as 'The Erotic Club,' a collection of ageing swingers who he had made contact with through the Internet.

Hunter had been persuaded to go along with the notion by Alice who had more liberal ideas about sex than her husband. The group met at a series of remote woodland places throughout the county where they enacted scenes of mythological and Victorian seduction, many of them wearing ornate costumes and masks. Goddard acted as their photographer. As time passed and Hunter realised the extent to which his wife was being exploited by the other participants he demanded that both Alice and Goddard withdraw. Both of them refused. Hunter claimed that on the night that Alice disappeared, he and his wife had rowed and she had left him, telling him that she intended spending the night with Goddard. She never returned. Believing that Goddard had murdered his wife, Hunter claimed he then set about exacting his revenge.

Ketch knew that this was a tissue of lies. He believed the couple had rowed after her return that night from the club and that Hunter had attacked his wife, strangling her in the process. When he realised he had killed her, he set about concealing the body, then, after her discovery at Bawsey Pits, he had exacted his revenge on Goddard. It had been Hunter who had placed the rope fibres in the boot of Goddard's car. Hunter denied this vigorously both in the interviews and throughout his trial. He was found guilty of Goddard's murder but innocent of his wife's murder.

Ketch reached into his overcoat pocket and, pulling out a packet of cigarettes, lit one. It had been a bizarre, unsatisfactory and drawn out case, one that he was glad to finally get shot of. It seemed that there was no limit to the extent of human depravity lately and he had had a surfeit of it. It appeared that Alice Hunter had found inspiration in The Pearl and other works of erotic fiction and shared her interest with Goddard. The two had then acted out many of the narratives. Then matters had got out of control and her husband's jealousy had caused him to snap with disastrous consequences.

Ketch finished his cigarette and was now staring fixedly at the placid waters of the River Wensum. A flotilla of swans and cygnets had come into view, skirting the riverbank. It was an image of grace and beauty which he found both inspirational and comforting. Thank goodness for the natural world he thought. He stubbed out his cigarette and rose to leave.

A SEASON OF MELANCHOLY

It had been a cold, dank night, the coldest for many weeks. In Aylmerton Woods, a dense mist had arisen, the early morning light throwing the great oaks and beeches into sharp relief so that they stood either side of the rough track like ghostly sentinels. Though the woodland canopy was still plunged into semidarkness, the 4x4 vehicle had not used its headlights, wary of being glimpsed by those in the few cottages that lay on the perimeter of this large swathe of woodland.

At the end of the narrow track, the vehicle stopped. The driver got out and, opening the boot, lifted out a large sack with some difficulty, then dragged it along the uneven ground under a stand of tall pine trees, where loose brush and bracken was used to conceal it.

By now, the cloud-wrack above had cleared, revealing a bright, full moon. Conscious of the sudden visibility, the driver returned to the vehicle and, removing gloves and boots, got into the driver's seat, reversing back up the track to the junction with the main road.

In the cottages beyond the great wood, no one stirred. This was an isolated spot, not much used by walkers even in the height of the tourist season, mainly because the track itself led to a dead end where it backed onto part of the royal estate and from the main road it was not waymarked. Largely unmanaged, the trees here had formed a cluttered canopy, shutting out the sunlight and the dense, lichen covered interior dissuaded most hardy walkers from penetrating the trees. In fact, it was the perfect spot to dispose of a body.

DCI Ketch stared out across the mist - shrouded waters of the River Wensum and lit his second cigarette that morning. It was 5:45 AM on a chilly autumn day. This was one of his favourite spots and he wanted to sit and think. The sun was slowly rising in the east, tinting the clouds with orange and pink. Overhead, a flight of geese gave their mournful utterances as they made their way out towards the Norfolk coast.

There was a primeval beauty to the scene which comforted Ketch and this was matched by his complete isolation. He had been here for 20 minutes and during that time, not a single person had appeared

271

along the riverbank path.

The last week had been difficult for Ketch. His personal life had provided him with little comfort. Estranged from his partner Carol, he had now returned to his shabby bachelor quarters at his small flat off the Earlham Road in the less desirable quarter of the city. Over the last year, he had been struggling with the symptoms of Parkinson's disease and some of the medicines he had been prescribed had unfortunate side-effects, not least of which was an increased sexual appetite. This had encouraged him to join an e-dating agency.

His first encounter had been with a woman called Rachel with whom he had enjoyed vigorous sex but whose company he had found dull and uninspiring. Two other equally unsuitable matches had followed and, in despair, he had given up with the project. There was also the problem with the young and very attractive resident of the ground floor flat, a 30-year-old solicitor called Cheryl who had shown a keen interest in her older upstairs neighbour. Ketch had spent several hours in her flat hoping to sort out her plumbing problems and had developed a strong attraction to her. However, since he often encountered her in a professional capacity, he feared yet another disastrous relationship might develop and if this also ended in disaster he would feel greatly compromised.

He had also encountered a problem at work. In January ACC Batarde, his old foe, had finally retired. This came as a relief to Ketch, for Batarde and Ketch had never seen eye to eye. In fact, Batarde had been a constant thorn in Ketch's flesh, especially since he was a man obsessed with the public profile of the Force. The fact that he was also a leading Freemason also infuriated Ketch who was intensely suspicious of secret societies. Batarde had always looked upon Ketch as a dinosaur who should have taken early retirement years ago, an opinion shared by some of Ketch's colleagues. Ketch had grown to loathe their weekly meetings where he would do his utmost to provide obtuse answers to Batarde's direct questioning. But at least the man was predictable. The new ACC, Diane Fletcher, was altogether more difficult to predict. Outwardly pleasant, even affable, she possessed a forensic mind and an antenna which immediately spotted sham.

Within minutes of their first meeting in February, she had instantly got the measure of Ketch, classifying him as an old guard Luddite, stuck in his ways and carrying the additional baggage of alcoholism. She had also figured out that he was suffering from the early onset of Parkinson's disease, a condition which he had shared with no one at HQ. There was no doubt about it: ACC Diane Fletcher had his number and would not stand for any of his obfuscations.

Unfortunately, things had not got off to a good start under the new regime. In the month following her appointment, Ketch had headed a task force aimed at arresting a gang of Irish gypsies who had been stealing rare objects from the museums in Cambridge and Norfolk and shipping them to Eastern Europe. An early-morning raid on a caravan site in Swaffham had ended in the arrest of one of the gang leaders. The other seven men had already left and disappeared without trace somewhere in Bulgaria. Ketch was convinced that someone in the Force must have given them a tip off. This fiasco did nothing to impress ACC Fletcher.

Ketch lit his third cigarette and glanced at his watch. He had been sitting here for well over half an hour and during that time he had seen only three people walking along the riverbank. As he stood up to leave, his mobile rang. It was MacKenzie, the young DS who Ketch regarded as his most reliable ally.

"Sorry for the early call, sir."

"Go ahead."

"I'm in Aylmerton Wood with the SOCO team. We had a report of a body here about an hour ago. A local out walking her dog found it some way off the main track about a quarter of a mile from the King's Lynn Road."

Ketch was familiar with the place. Aylmerton Wood was a dense stretch of ancient deciduous woodland which once had served as a private hunting ground for King John. Although it was still part of a royal estate, these days it was managed by the Woodland Trust. It was a popular spot with locals and tourists alike and about a year ago had served as the backdrop to a series of illegal raves. On the northern perimeter were a number of Edwardian cottages which served as holiday residences but large stretches of the wood were directly accessible from the two main roads which adjoined it on either side.

"Any ID on the body?"

"Not yet. Female, but it looks as if she's been here for a considerable while."

"Give me an hour."

Ketch terminated the conversation then phoned for a taxi.

273

Although he had passed the advanced motorist's test many decades ago, Ketch had not driven for years. He usually relied on MacKenzie to drive him but this morning he had chosen alternative transport.

Within minutes, his cab had arrived and he was travelling west from the city via the suburbs of Hellesdon and Taverham out onto a landscape of lush green fields and isolated copses of ancient oaks and beeches, straddling low hills. The car sped onwards through the scattered villages of East and West Rudham, then it turned on to a small B road which skirted the perimeter of Aylmerton Wood. Soon after this Ketch spotted the familiar barrier tape.

"Just here," he instructed the taxi driver. As he got out of the car he saw MacKenzie looming out of the mist.

"Body is just down this track sir," said MacKenzie, pointing the way between a line of gnarled yew trees. "Dr Stoppard arrived about 15 minutes ago," he explained as they approached a huddle of white-suited men. The tallest of them, a corpulent figure with long grey hair and beard, waved at them.

"Nice spot for a murder," he joked. Ketch sighed. Stoppard's graveside humour always left him cold

"What have we got?"

"Not much I'm sorry to say. Female, probably in her early 20s.She's been here since Midsummer, I'd estimate, judging by the state of the body. Not only has there been rapid putrefaction, she's also been predated by woodland scavengers. We are missing part of a foot and a hand. And there's not much left of the face either. Identification isn't going to be easy."

"Cause of death?"

"Probably a gunshot wound to the head. I'll be able to tell you much more later on."

"What about her possessions?" Ketch asked MacKenzie.

"We did find a small handbag some yards from the body. In it a purse with £10 in cash and a business card which might possibly give us the lead of sorts." He showed it to Ketch. 'The Bay Tree Restaurant,' it read. 'Stanton Road, Kings Lynn.' There was a phone number and website.

"No other significant traces yet?"

"Not yet sir. The footpath is used extensively by local walkers. A local woman discovered the body by pure chance. She'd let her dog off the lead and it started digging in the clearing here."

Ketch frowned. "Let's check missing persons. See if they have anything that might help us. There's nothing more we can do here at present."

When Ketch returned to the HQ in Bethel Street, he found a note on his desk. 'Please report to my office on your return – ACC Fletcher.'

Fletcher's office was on the second floor. Supplying himself with a cup of instant chemical brew from the machine in the corridor, Ketch took the lift and rapped on the door where he noticed the shiny new sign bearing ACC Fletcher's name and rank. "Come!" a voice barked from the interior. Ketch entered. The room reflected the new ACC's personality. The once cream walls were now an institutional white and the landscape paintings of the Norfolk countryside had completely disappeared. The furniture had also been upgraded in a contemporary minimalist style with high backed stainless steel chairs and a leather sofa. Diane Fletcher sat with head down, absorbed in her paperwork. She was wearing a tight fitting black suit and her hair, also black, was pulled back in a tight bun revealing sharp cheekbones, thin lips and a hawk like nose.

"I'll be with you in just a second, DCI Price," she said. She shuffled the papers, stapled them, then placed them in a tray marked 'Processed.'

"I've been examining your file," she said, fixing him with an unblinking stare. "You're not far off retirement are you?"

Ketch nodded. "That's correct."

"Thinking of retiring?"

"Not yet, no."

"Then I should do so. Frankly, your medical report suggests to me that it is an option you might seriously consider. "

"If you are referring to the Parkinson's, that is something I am learning to deal with."

"And the alcohol problem? What about that?"

"I no longer have a problem with it. It's not an issue."

"Really?"

"Really."

"There's also the question of clear up rates. I conducted an analysis, year on year. Your rate for last year was 50% down on the rate achieved five years ago when your team was actually smaller.

Your overtime rates are now significantly higher also."

"And the crime rate has also risen."

"That's not relevant."

"I think it's relevant. You have to take into account..."

Fletcher gave him a withering look and interrupted him. "Then we must disagree. Anyway, bearing these factors in mind, I'm putting your name down for a motivational course at Ipswich HQ. It's a three-day course. I think you would benefit from it."

"You think I need motivating?"

"I didn't exactly say that. It's not uncommon for senior officers like yourself to attend courses like this."

" When does the course begin?"

"The end of next month." She gave him the dates. Ketch said nothing further and left the room.

The following morning he was awoken by heavy rain beating on his windows. He had not slept well. He'd spent the evening drinking alone in The Murderers where he'd imbibed far too much malt whiskey. When he got back to the flat he'd fallen into a deep sleep during which he had a vivid dream about an erotic encounter with his downstairs neighbour, Cheryl Stanton. In the dream, he had somehow regressed to his early 30s and was endowed with immense sexual athleticism. When he awoke at 3 AM the patent absurdity of the dream depressed him even further and he then dozed fitfully until falling into another, more shallow sleep.

He got up, took an aspirin for his hangover, downed his Parkinson's meds, then breakfasted before taking a walk across the city by its ancient mediaeval quarter to Bethel Street. On entering the reception area he encountered MacKenzie.

"Stoppard's autopsy report is on your desk, sir," MacKenzie observed. "Also the last month's crime stats." Mackenzie exited. Ketch grabbed himself a coffee, then glanced briefly at the crime figures before turning his attention to the autopsy report. They did not make very comfortable reading.

According to the autopsy report, the victim was in her mid-20s. She had died from a small caliber bullet which had been fired at close range, entering her cranium and exiting through her left cheek. She had not been sexually molested and, prior to death, had eaten a large meal. There were two tattoos, one on her left buttock with the initials

S I and AD either side of the heart shape, the other showing what appeared to be a Madonna shaped figure. There was considerable decomposition and part of one arm was missing, probably through predation by foxes. Larval evidence suggested that the body had been concealed beneath leaves sometime in late July but curiously death most likely occurred in the April or May preceding the month. It was obvious that whoever had shot her had somehow preserved the body for some weeks before disposing of it in Aylmerton Wood. Apart from the restaurant visiting card, there were no other clues as to her identity although there was a small label inside her dress which bore a Russian brand name.

MacKenzie entered, interrupting his reading.

"Ask forensics to check out the bullet for us. We're probably looking for a small revolver. And let's see if we can get a trace from the missing persons file for March to April this year on anyone with the initials SI or A.D."

"Right, sir."

"Did you contact the restaurant in Kings Lynn?"

"Rang them just 10 minutes ago. I got the answer phone."

"Then we'll pay them a visit this afternoon after we've checked missing persons."

MacKenzie passed him a file.

"What's this?"

"The dog walker's statement."

"Anything useful?"

"Not especially."

"Okay. Leave it with me."

MacKenzie's check on the missing person's list for the months of April and May proved to be useful to the investigation. During these two months three people had been reported missing in the North Norfolk area. Two of them were male but one was a female by the name of Alise Ozols, a part-time student at the University of West Anglia who lived in Hunstanton. She was reported as missing by one of her flatmates after she failed to return from her job as a waitress at a restaurant in Kings Lynn. The restaurant was called the Bay Tree. That could not be a coincidence.

By two pm it had begun to rain heavily and heavy fog had cloaked the old streets of the town. Ketch had been here on numerous occasions but was always intrigued by its strange atmosphere of world weariness. The modern shopping precinct sat oddly amongst its Georgian and late Victorian houses and its population which comprised both commuters and agricultural workers, many of them from Eastern Europe, provided an unusual mix. Once the Hanseatic centre of eastern England, the town had seen times of former glory but these days it was exhibiting clear symptoms of urban decline.

The Bay Tree Restaurant was situated in a side street some way from the town centre. Housed in a tall Georgian building, with bow windows, it had been sympathetically restored by its owner. A short, weasel faced man in a chef's uniform answered the door and Ketch showed him his warrant card.

"How can I help you?"

"Are you the owner?"

"I'm not the owner. I am Pierre, the manager."

Ketch detected a French accent.

"Mr Beckett is the owner. What's this about?"

They entered the restaurant. It had been decorated in a mock Victorian fashion. On the walls hung a number of 19th-century paintings showing landscapes of Norfolk.

"We are investigating the disappearance of a woman called Alise Ozols. We understand that she used to work here?"

"Yes, she was a waitress here. She worked on a part-time basis with two other girls. They were all students at the University of West Anglia. They shared a flat together in Hunstanton. She left us in the earlier part of the year. I assumed that she had gone back to her family in Latvia."

"When exactly did she leave?"

"I think it must have been in late April. It was a little odd. She gave me no warning that she was leaving. Didn't appear to tell her flatmates either."

"What was she like as a person?"

"A bright girl. Extremely attractive. And popular with the customers – especially the male customers. I always thought that she would go far. She was doing some course connected with the hospitality industry, so she told me. I couldn't figure out exactly what it was. She was so good at the job that the boss offered her a full-time job here but she declined it."

"Do you have any more details that you can give us? A photograph perhaps?"

"I have a couple of old photos of the three of them here in the restaurant. They were on a hen night. I remember one of them was celebrating her engagement. I'll go and dig it out for you."

He fetched the photos and Ketch studied them. They showed three young girls, all blonde and in their early 20s, sitting at a table behind a collection of wine bottles.

"Which one of these is Alise?"

"Here on the left." He pointed to the most attractive of the three, a girl with fine, chiselled features and brilliant green eyes.

"Do you still have their contact details?"

"Alise's friends no longer work here. I don't know what happened to the flat they shared. Hang on though, I do still have a mobile number for Sarah, the oldest of them. I'll go and fetch it for you."

As Ketch waited for him to return, he examined the second photograph. It showed the three waitresses again but this time they were sitting at another table with a dark haired man in an expensive suit. Alongside him was a short, athletic looking woman with short blond hair. She was dressed smartly in a low-cut black trouser suit and her neck was adorned by an ornate gold torc.

"Who are these people?" Ketch asked.

"That's Mr Beckett and his wife Janet. Alise used to work for them on a part-time basis. They lived in the Manor house in Old Hunstanton. Here is the mobile number you asked for."

Sarah Trimble had just left her lecture when her phone rang. She agreed to meet Ketch back at her flat in Hunstanton, a ground floor apartment in one of a row of Edwardian terraced houses not far from the promenade. A short, petite girl with cropped blonde hair, she led Ketch and MacKenzie into a large airy sitting room on the second floor, painted in vivid mauve.

"I last saw Alise at the Bay Tree," she explained. "When she didn't turn up the following day we thought she might be at Sean's flat."

"Sean?"

"Sean Isaacs, he was her boyfriend. Well, he was her boyfriend for a while until she ditched him. Frankly, Debbie and me weren't surprised at that."

"Debbie was your flatmate?"

"That's right."

"Why weren't you surprised?"

"Because he's a lowlife. And because he knocked her about when he was high on booze and crack. It was because of Sean that she started taking the stuff."

"The cocaine?"

"Yes, Sean was a dealer. He supplied half the student population at the college. It was common knowledge there. But Alise could not help herself. She was an emotional butterfly. Things were always complicated for her. Then there was Boris to deal with."

"Boris?"

"Boris Bardzecki, an old flame from Latvia. When Alise first arrived here in Britain, she and Boris were an item. They shared a flat in Wisbech for a while when they were doing agricultural work there. But Alise left him when he started bringing other women to the flat. I think she still secretly held a torch for him though."

"You contacted the police when she went missing."

"I did. It seemed odd because she'd left all her belongings here – even her passport. We rang her parents in Latvia too but unfortunately, neither of them speak English."

"What made you move here?"

"Alise was the named tenant and when she didn't return, Debbie and me could no longer afford to pay the rent. We didn't have much of an option since the rent was £600 a month. We could only manage a hundred pounds each so we could never figure out how she managed to stump up the rest. We always had the impression that she might have had help from another source."

"Her boyfriend?"

"Hardly likely."

"Ketch finished his coffee which was a disgusting dark brown colour. There was a taste of sour milk.

"Do you have any contact details for Isaacs and Bardzecki?"

"I'm sorry but I can't help you. Alise kept her contact numbers on her phone. I can't believe that she's been murdered. I'm just sorry that I can't be of more help to you."

"On the contrary, you have been most helpful Miss Trimble."

It took three days before the Aylmerton Woods body was finally identified as Alise Ozols. Using Interpol's resources, MacKenzie contacted the Latvian police and a DNA sample from Alise's parents in Riga was flown over for examination by SOCO Boris Bardzecki proved to be more of a problem, having returned to his native Russia over a week ago but again, using his international connections, MacKenzie put in a request for the police in Moscow to track him down.

Finding Sean Isaacs, Alise's boyfriend, was a much easier task. He already had form from the possession and supply of cocaine and had also served a nine-month prison sentence for a serious assault in Thetford two years ago. He was brought in for questioning on a bleak October morning. Ketch was not in a good mood. He had been sleeping badly of late, partly because of the effect caused by his Parkinson's meds, and partly because he seemed to be haunted by past memories, especially of his late wife Alice.

A short, squat, hirsute figure casually dressed in jogging trousers, a grubby T-shirt and scuffed trainers, Sean Isaacs sat opposite Ketch and MacKenzie, his face twisted into a sneer. He had the air of someone who had become used to interviews such as this.

"Tell me about your relationship with Alise Ozols," said Ketch.

"What is there to tell?" Isaacs replied superciliously.

"You've visited her frequently at her flat in Hunstanton and you supplied her with drugs?"

"No comment."

"Why did she end the relationship with you?"

Isaacs shrugged.

"Because you used to beat her, Sean. Isn't that right?"

"I used to slap her about a bit. I don't deny that. I do that to all my bitches. It does them no harm. Some of them even like it. That isn't the reason that we split though."

"Tell me what the reason was then."

"Turned out she was a slag."

"Explain that to me."

"When I came back to the flat, I found her with this Russian creep. They were hard at it on the kitchen table. After that, I decided I would move out."

"Exactly when was this?"

Isaacs shrugged. "Around the end of May, I think. I don't exactly remember the date. It was a Saturday."

281

"And did you see her after that?"

"No, I did not."

"But until that point you supplied her with crack and cannabis?"

"No comment."

"I put it to you that after Bardzecki left the flat you lost your temper with her. You killed her. When you realised that she was dead you waited until after dark, then you removed her body. You waited a while before taking the body to Aylmerton Woods. How did you do that? Perhaps you put her in a chest freezer."

"You can say what you like. I'm telling you the last time I saw her was at the end of May. Why don't you question the Russian? Look, are you going to charge me with murder or not? Make your mind up."

There was a long pause. Then Ketch said: "You're free to go now but we may need to question you further."

Isaacs stood up and smirked back at his interrogators.

"As I thought – bullshit."

After Isaacs had left the interview room, Ketch turned to MacKenzie.

"These two security cameras at the end of Bank Street – they were adjacent to the flat, weren't they?"

MacKenzie nodded. "One above the Hunstanton Post Office, the other above Lloyds Bank."

"Let's see if they kept the tapes for the end of May and we'll also check the vehicle registration numbers. Then we can determine whether Isaacs is telling us the truth or not."

The following day was a Saturday. Ketch had been woken early that morning and called to a murder in The Prince of Wales Road. Around midnight on Friday, a gang of drunken youths had come out of a nightclub and spotted a Muslim couple on the other side of the road, getting out of a taxi. Following a succession of racist taunts, three of the youths, two male and one female, attacked both of them and then punched the man to the ground where they proceeded to kick him to death. Fortunately, two nightclub bouncers had intervened, making a citizen's arrest. Ketch had spent two hours in the interview room with the attackers, all of them in denial of what they had done. Three separate statements from three shaven headed youths, with a below average IQ level, boozed and witless, each one contradicting the other. It was a depressing experience.

By 9 AM Ketch had developed a pounding headache and had just

282

downed two paracetamols with his morning coffee when MacKenzie appeared at his door.

"There have been a few developments in the Ozols case, sir."

"Tell me."

"I checked the CCTV records that you mentioned yesterday. There's a list of about 50 registration plates – one of them belongs to Isaacs. He visited Alise Ozol's flat on 29th of May but after that his vehicle doesn't reappear. The angle of the cameras doesn't include the entrance door to the flat itself, it's too far away, unfortunately."

"Not especially helpful to us then."

"No sir."

"What are the other things then?"

"The contact I made with the Latvian police –"

"I remember."

"He e-mailed me earlier this morning. Boris Bardzecki was killed in a street brawl last night in Riga."

During the next few weeks the investigation came to a standstill. With Bardzecki out of the frame and no further evidence to implicate Isaacs, there were few other leads to follow. The weapon which killed Alise Ozols turned out to be an old German Luger which had been fired at the victim at a distance of approximately 6 feet.

Over the next few weeks, Ketch spent two days attending the motivational course in Ipswich. And he found himself in the company of a group of young, aspirational officers. Some of them he had encountered previously and had little in common with them. He spent most of his time filling in boxes, drifting through the endless lectures and reluctantly participating in 'bonding sessions.' The food was terrible, the course presenter an anorexic looking blonde in her late 20s and there was little opportunity for serious drinking. He was therefore relieved to get back to his desk in Norwich despite the onset of a gale which beat at his window at HQ like a madman trying to gain entry.

He had just opened his desk diary when MacKenzie entered.

"How did it go, sir? he asked cheerily.

"Don't even ask," growled Ketch.

"I have been looking into Alice Ozols' background and contacts. It turns out that the flat in Hunstanton was owned by Richard Beckett."

"The Tory councillor – the restaurant owner?"

"The same. He is also the owner of a chain of East Anglian mini supermarkets. But here's the thing – the flat in Hunstanton where Alise lived – turns out that it was purchased for her by Beckett . She worked for Beckett and his wife for a year after she left Wisbech. And I also discovered that Sean Isaacs was employed at the Manor House by the Becketts and that he was there when Alice was working for them."

"We need to speak to Beckett."

"I phoned the Beckett's half an hour ago. The wife confirmed that both Alise and Isaacs had worked for them. The husband is away in Birmingham on a business conference at the moment."

"Never mind. Let's see what the wife has to say."

The Manor House lay on the eastern edge of Old Hunstanton. A large 18th-century limestone building, it stood at the end of a winding driveway and was quite invisible from the main road because of the dense woodland which surrounded it. It had once been the seat of the Creake family, a wealthy dynasty who made their money through cotton and the slave trade and who settled here in the 1770s. The extensive grounds, landscaped by Inigo Jones, included two Gothic follies and an ice house. Beckett had purchased the property 10 years ago when it was in a state of disrepair and renovated much of the interior, although the grounds themselves had been left undisturbed.

MacKenzie parked the car and the two officers walked up to the grand portico entrance, their footsteps echoing on the ground like pistol shots. MacKenzie rang the bell and the door opened, revealing a short, squat man smartly dressed in a dark suit.

"Police officers," explained Ketch, showing his warrant card. "Here to see Mrs Beckett."

"This way sir," the flunkey replied, ushering them through a grand hallway whose walls were lined with 19th-century landscapes of the Norfolk countryside. There was a smell of wax and polish.

They entered a library and were introduced to Sarah Beckett, a tall redhead in her middle years. Ketch was struck by her statuesque appearance.

"I'm sorry that Richard is unable to see you, Chief Inspector," she explained. She spoke with a strong French accent. "He is attending a business conference in Birmingham and will not be back for some days. How may I help you?"

"We are investigating the murder of Alise Ozols. I understand that she used to work for you?"

"That is correct. She was employed here as one of our domestic staff. She worked here for about 18 months I recall."

"Why did she leave?"

"We discovered that she had been stealing. Certain valuable items from our collection went missing. After a short investigation, we discovered that two of these items were in her possession. I had no real option but to get rid of her. It was a choice between doing that or calling the police."

"I understand that you also employed a man by the name of Sean Isaacs."

"That is correct. He worked here as an assistant gardener. Mr Isaacs was dismissed after an incident involving the head gardener."

"What was that?"

"He and Mr Skipton did not see eye to eye. There was a dispute and Isaacs attacked him. He suffered some unpleasant facial injuries. My husband would not tolerate it."

"Alise Ozols was subsequently employed as a waitress at your husband's restaurant in King's Lynn. Why was that?"

"Richard left the hiring of staff to the restaurant manager. He had no idea that she had been given a job there. By the time he did find out there was little he could do about it."

"Were you aware of the fact that she was also a tenant in a flat in Hunstanton owned by your husband?"

There was a long pause. Sarah Beckett folded her arms and her head lowered as she answered.

"Initially I was not aware of the fact."

"He didn't mention it to you?"

"No."

"Didn't you think that was rather odd?"

"Indeed I did."

"How often did he visit the restaurant?"

"On a regular basis as I recall. He liked to keep an eye on the management."

"Did you visit the restaurant with him at all?"

"He never invited me. We lead fairly separate lives inspector. As an artist, I tend to be rather antisocial. I don't care much for eating in public."

"You are a painter?"

"A sculptor. I also collect paintings – landscapes mainly. It is one of my interests. Are you suggesting inspector, that my husband was having an affair with this woman?"

"I wouldn't rule it out."

"That would not surprise me."

"Really?"

"Richard was not especially faithful to me. He had several affairs. I learned to tolerate them. In more recent years we have led rather separate lives."

"You suspected there was something going on between them?"

"It had occurred to me, yes. I was not unhappy when she left us. I didn't much like her."

"Why was that?"

"I found her somewhat predatory. She had an unnerving habit of staring at you when you were unaware of it. There was also the business of the cannabis."

"She smoked cannabis?"

"One of the staff told me about it. It later transpired that she was being supplied by one of the gardeners."

"Sean Isaacs?"

"Of course, when we found out what was going on, we had no option but to dismiss him."

"But you continued to employ Alise?"

"For some while after that, yes. It was then I noticed that several objects had gone missing from the Manor House. Mostly small things – a silver inkwell set, a snuffbox which used to belong to my father, a couple of 18th-century candlesticks and two pieces of jewellery. I had my suspicions of course, but could never prove that it was her. Not until the day that is when I went into the bedroom and found her at it."

"Your husband agreed about the dismissal?"

"He agreed that she would no longer work at the house but he argued that it shouldn't affect her work at the restaurant. I was not happy about the decision."

"You suspected at this point that he might be having an affair with her?"

"No, the idea didn't then occur to me. As I explained to you inspector, Richard and I have always lived very different lives. The nature of his business means that he is away for a lot of the time. And my vocation means that I spend a great deal of my time in isolation. I need space to think and to create. The Manor house provides me with that. I leave it to the staff to look after the day-to-day minutiae."

"When is your husband due back here?"

"By Wednesday evening if all goes well."

"Then will you please ask him to contact me?" said Ketch, giving her his card.

"By all means. Do you have a suspect?"

"We are exploring a number of lines of enquiry. By the way, do you or your husband own any firearms?"

"My husband has two antique shotguns which are kept in a secure cabinet in the library. Do you wish to examine them?"

"If you would.".

After they had returned to Bethel Street, Ketch phoned Beckett's mobile. He got voicemail. He rang again an hour later, then several more times that same evening. Still no reply. Exasperated, he rang the hotel in Birmingham and asked to be put through to his room. The hotel receptionist explained to him that there was no one staying there with the name of Richard Beckett. Realising that Beckett had lied to his wife, Kettch issued on all points alert to all of the UK police divisions to apprehend Beckett.

A month passed without incident. Beckett's passport had not been checked at any other UK airports and there had been no sightings of his car on any of the major highway cameras. It was as if he had never existed.

During those long weeks of frustration, one useful piece of the jigsaw came to light. On the CCTV tapes which covered Alise Ozol's flat in Hunstanton, Beckett's vehicle was logged coming and going on the last two days of May. Ketch reinterviewed Sean Isaacs. He admitted supplying cannabis to Alise Ozols and two other members of staff at the Manor House during his employment there but stuck to the rest of his story with a dogged determination.

Beckett's motive for murdering Alise remained a problem for Ketch. Had she attempted to blackmail him, threatening to reveal their affair to his wife? Or was there another reason? He began looking into Beckett's background. Beckett was the child of an Irish traveller, one of a family of 8. He had left school at 16 without formal qualifications and was then employed as a retail clerk in a shipping firm in Kings Lynn. Over the next 10 years, he worked his way up the ladder, gaining the position of marketing director at the age of only 30. It was then that he married his French wife, Sarah. Over the next 10 years, his growing fortune enabled him to invest in a series of businesses including the restaurant trade and it was then that he purchased the Manor House. Ketch could find no links with the underworld and there were no shady financial deals which might provide a clue to his sudden disappearance. It remained a complete enigma.

On a cold morning in early November, Ketch woke from a vivid dream in which he was floating down an icebound river and slowly capsizing as the waters engulfed his face. So vivid was this dream that he woke gasping for breath. He realised what had provoked the nightmare. The duvet had slipped from the bed and he was freezing. When he checked the thermometer on the bedroom window it registered only 2° above 0.

He got up and, donning his dressing gown, made his way into the kitchen to brew tea. While he was waiting for the kettle to boil, his mind began to make connections.

What if Beckett had never made it to the conference in Birmingham? Why had his vehicle not been found? And what would have been his motive in killing Alise? He finished his tea, then checked the alarm clock. 8:30 AM. Then he picked up the phone and rang MacKenzie.

By the time they reached old Hunstanton, it had started to snow and an icy wind was blowing snow flurries across the windscreen of the police Range Rover. Halfway along the road to the Manor House, Ketch pointed to the left and MacKenzie parked up in a small layby.

The ice house lay in a small hollow beyond the circle of ancient yew trees, a solid, limestone structure placed here in the early 1800s.

Ketch tried the handle of the peeling door but it refused to budge.

"Force it," he instructed MacKenzie who returned from the Land Rover holding a crowbar. As the door gave under pressure, Ketch shone his torch into the dark interior. There, encased in ice and wrapped in a plastic sheet, lay the body of Richard Beckett, his face bloated from the onset of decomposition. In the centre of his forehead was a large gunshot wound. Ketch reached into his overcoat for his mobile.

It took two days before Sarah Beckett finally made her statement, admitting to the deaths of Alise Ozols and her husband. Throughout the interrogations, she remained composed, sitting with her arms folded and staring straight ahead like some prim headmistress.

"When did the idea of shooting Alise first occurred to you?" Ketch asked her.

"You should understand that what happened was not something that I had planned in advance. When I visited the restaurant that night in May, I had intended only to talk to her, to plead with her to leave Richard alone, to leave us both alone. Alise Ozols was a parasite. Soon after Richard employed her at the Manor House, she began to inveigle her way into his affections. Richard was highly susceptible to women. It was his Achilles heel. He had had three previous affairs during our marriage, all of them with women half his age. I had told him I would not tolerate another. Neither was I prepared to have a divorce. I believe in the sanctity of marriage which is a commitment for life. I told him that if he betrayed me again I would kill him. I pleaded with Richard to stop the affair but he would not listen to me. Then in the library one morning I found them together. Neither of them seemed concerned. That enraged me. I also discovered that Richard had purchased a flat in Hunstanton and had been renting it to her at a subsidised rate.

"And you dismissed her from your service?"

"I found out that she had been taking drugs, supplied to her by the assistant gardener."

"Sean Isaacs?"

"Yes. She had also been steadily stealing some of the small objects d'art which belonged to the house. That was the main reason that she was dismissed."

"On the night of the murder, you took your husband's car and drove to the Bay Tree?" She nodded.

"As I said I had intended to reason with her, to bring her to her senses. She refused to listen to me. She mocked me and told me that she and Richard had planned to start a new life in Europe together and that Richard intended selling the business and the Manor House to fund their escapade. I believed her. That's when I shot her. I really had no alternative."

"You must have had plans to kill her. You had taken the gun with you. It was a calculated act."

"Yes, I took Richard's Luger but I had intended only to threaten her with the gun. When I produced the gun, she merely laughed at me. She continued to mock me, she even spat in my face. That is when I shot her. She opened the car door and I fired at her. There was so much blood. On the windscreen, the car seat, on my face and dress. It took me most of the rest of the evening to clean it up. By the time it was getting light, I hit on the idea of putting her body in the ice house. I packed it in plastic bin liners and filled it with ice cubes and packs of frozen food from the freezer. After about a week I went back and retrieved it. You know the rest."

"And your husband – he never suspected anything?"

"Not at first, no. He was away that weekend when I transferred the body."

"But he came to suspect you?"

"In time – yes. At first, he couldn't understand what had happened to her. After a while, he began asking me questions. Then, one day, when he was cleaning the car he found traces of blood. It was then that he confronted me and it ended in a blazing row."

"And that's when you shot him?"

"He attacked me, knocked me across the room. Richard had a nasty temper when he was roused. He'd done it once before in our marriage and I swore after that that if he laid hands on me again I'd not take it lying down. I must have lost consciousness for a few moments. When I woke up, he was sitting in a chair opposite me, smiling. I had no option but to act. He kept a small gun. It was in the bureau. I took out the gun. Richard laughed at me.

"Now I suppose you're going to shoot me," he laughed. I didn't believe I had it in me. But I shot him anyway, straight through the forehead. I shall never forget the expression of surprise on his face. He didn't believe that I could do it. He never understood how much he had hurt me over the 10 years of our marriage."

"You said he had been unfaithful to you before on several occasions?"

"On three occasions – all with younger women. He used to describe his affairs as 'mistakes.' As if they were merely errors of judgement."

"And after you had shot him?"

"It was in the early hours of the morning before the staff arrived. I got a wheelbarrow from one of the outhouses and took his body to the ice house. The rest you know. That is all I have to say."

The trial of Sarah Beckett was concluded on a bright afternoon the following May. Ketch had found a bench facing the river Wensum and was indulging himself in yet another cigarette, his third since lunchtime.

The verdict had not been entirely satisfactory for him. Sarah Beckett had pleaded guilty to the murder of Alise Ozols and to the manslaughter of her husband. Ketch believed that it should have been murder on both counts but the DPP thought that the evidence was not sufficient to warrant this. Ketch thought entirely differently. He had discovered that, prior to her marriage to Richard Beckett, Sarah had been married to a wealthy businessman in Donegal. He had died under questionable circumstances whilst on a walking holiday with Sarah in the Wicklow Mountains. Three years prior to that marriage, her first husband, a leading Dublin art dealer, had died in a car crash. The vehicle he was driving was discovered to have faulty brakes. His death had made Sarah a very wealthy woman. Ketch believed that only part of Sarah Beckett's testimony was true. Richard Beckett was a serial womaniser – that much was true. And Alise Ozols was certainly ambitious. But Sarah Beckett was an opportunist. She claimed she had shot her husband whilst in extreme distress, she claimed that killing him had been a reflex action, it was something she had not intended to do. Ketch believed that she had planned the whole thing in advance. Richard Beckett's business investments would have yielded her a huge inheritance – millions.

As Ketch finished his cigarette, the sun came out from behind a cloud, illuminating the surface of the river. His phone rang but he chose to ignore it on this occasion. Outside the court, here in the fresh air, it felt good to be alive. For the next half-hour, the world could just wait. Right now solitude, the trees and the river were what he most required. And besides, in another half an hour, the pub would be open again.

A GOLDEN DAWN

The case had started out as a coincidence. What followed might have been regarded as an act of the gods.

DCI Ketch slipped quietly out bed and pulled back the heavy velour curtains. It was 7.50 am on a cold winter morning in Norwich and the sun was rising, revealing an azure and pink sky. Here, at Cheryl Brandon's bijou flat you were sufficiently high above the city to gain a broad vista of its familiar landmarks: the old castle with its Victorian limestone façade, the tall spire of the mediaeval cathedral and the long, winding river Wensum, banked on either side by ugly contemporary buildings.

When he had first moved here with Cheryl, he had missed his old retreat off the Earlham Road, a dismal flat where he endured a lonely bachelor existence. Yet, for all its shortcomings, the proximity of the flat to the very heart of the city made Ketch feel more comfortable. It was perverse of him, he knew that. His flat was old and single glazed, uncomfortably cold in the winter months, blindingly hot in the summer and near enough to the centre of the city to disturb his sleep with its echoes of late night drunken voices and the wail of ambulance sirens, especially on Friday nights when the clubs on the Prince of Wales Road turned out their clientele at 3 and 4 in the morning to roam the city streets.

Yet Ketch eventually tired of his monkish life and had fallen for the charms of a woman twenty years his junior. Somehow, though God knew why, Cheryl, a tall, buxom, dark haired woman from County Wexford, with a razor sharp brain, had fallen for a crumpled wreck of a man in his mid-fifties. There were times when Ketch woke in the night and could not believe his good fortune about this new relationship. No less than on this crisp winter morning.

He remained at the window for several more minutes, staring across the riverbank opposite as a group of swans glided down the fast flowing waters, the sun glinting on their feathers, considering the concept of coincidence. Was there really such a thing as fate? He wondered.

It had been a cold afternoon in January, so bitter that he had decided he would drive to the AA meeting in Brewer Street. Though he had been abstinent for the last six months, he still had to acknowledge the fact that the demon that had stalked him for so long was not dead but merely sleeping.

Although it had not snowed for the last 24 hours, he had driven back from the meeting slowly, conscious of the fact that some of the B roads had not been gritted. Half way down Magdalen Street he saw the girl. Striking in appearance, with an hour glass figure, long, black waist length hair and a smooth olive skin, she was standing next to a white van and a mini cooper. The van had mounted the pavement and there was a dent in its side. A red faced man stood opposite her, over six feet high, with a bald and pugnacious bristle bearded face, jabbing his forefinger at her. Ketch drew up alongside them and wound down his window.

"Is everything OK?" he asked. Hearing these words, the balding man spun round and looked uncertain. He began to back away, cussed, then got back in his van and drove off towards the city centre.

"He didn't hurt you?"

"No, I'm fine. Just a bit of road rage, I'm afraid. He was overtaking me and we collided. He blamed me of course." She spoke with a strong Greek accent. Close up, she seemed even more striking. She possessed an unusual face with high cheekbones and large dark eyes. She extended a long, delicate hand to him. He glanced at the trimmed fingernails and clasped the hand.

"You have been most kind. Thank you."

"It was no trouble. What about the damage to your car?" he replied, glancing at a long scratch in the paintwork.

"Too insignificant to make a claim," she said, smiling at him.

"I got his licence number though, just in case."

"That won't be necessary but thanks anyway. What's your name?"

He saw in her face a single mindedness, a fixed concentration.

"Huw."

"Maria."

That unlikely meeting in Magdalen Street had led them to a small cafe in Tombland where they chatted over coffee for the next hour. Her full name was Maria Marinos. She told him that she was working as an English teacher at a language school in the city and that her father ran a Greek restaurant in the large shopping complex. As she talked, Ketch found that he was becoming attracted to those large, lustrous eyes.

Ketch shivered. He reached for his dressing gown, pausing briefly to glance at Cheryl's sleeping form. It had always seemed to him quite bizarre that an attractive woman in her thirties would even consider him as a suitable partner, given his physical condition. Ketch was in the twilight of a long career in the police force and was declining rapidly. Having more or less conquered the lure of the demon drink (his phrase) he had then received a diagnosis for Parkinson's Disease. This had occurred 18 months ago just before his consummation with Cheryl.

Since then, the disease had progressed slowly but surely. The tremor in his right hand and arm which had started as a twitch in his thumb, was now clearly discernible to his colleagues and he could no longer hide it. ACC Batarde, his loathsome superior, had called him into his office.

"Considering the nature of your condition, Huw, should you not be thinking of early retirement?" he quizzed Ketch.

"I don't have any intention of retiring yet," Ketch answered rather shortly. Batarde was right of course but he dare not admit it.

"What about the physical limitations, though?"

"It's not predictable. I should be able to carry on for some years."

"Isn't that a tad unrealistic, Huw?"

Batarde gave him an unconvincing smile which reminded Ketch of a lizard.

"Not at all."

The conversation then moved on to more pressing matters.

Hearing Cheryl cry out, Ketch turned from the window. Bleary eyed, she sat forwards, the bedclothes falling from her, revealing her ample form.

"Bad dream?" he asked her. She nodded, then reached for a glass of water and gulped down its contents.

"Yes, a nightmare. It was about the Kaplinski brothers."

Although the Kaplinski murders had occurred over fourteen months ago, its horrific details still continued to haunt Cheryl. It had been widely reported in both the local and national press.

Stefan Kaplinski and his brother Ivan had originated from Latvia where, unbeknownst to the Norfolk police, they had both served terms of imprisonment for aggravated burglary. Stefan was the older brother.

Tall and powerfully built, his jet black beard gave him a menacing appearance. Ivan, though much smaller, was by far the more deadly. Both were addicted to crack cocaine which fuelled their crime sprees.

Their infamous career in East Anglia reached its peak one autumn afternoon when high as kites, they travelled north from their squalid flat in Norwich to the town of Wisbech, ostensibly to collect a consignment of drugs from a major supplier. Short of cash, the brothers decided to burgle two bungalows on the outskirts of the town on the assumption that they would meet with little resistance from its elderly residents.

Their hunch had been correct. Their first victim was Dorothy Smith, a frail 82-year-old widow, their second a World War Two veteran aged 90, but still relatively fit and active. Between the hours of four and six pm, the brothers not only murdered but also tortured their victims with sadistic pleasure. Their bodies were discovered only after six days had elapsed, both being solitary in their habits.

Cheryl Brandon remembered the case in vivid detail for she had been the duty solicitor the day after the brothers had been arrested. Apart from the horrific nature of their deeds, there was another element that had disturbed her but which she found difficult to define.

Both men possessed a primal strength and appeared to mock the investigating detectives as they stared across the table in the interrogation room. Neither admitted to the crimes but after 24 hours had passed, they eventually confessed.

Cheryl could never forget the horrific details of their confessions and those details had haunted her ever since. Two days ago their trial at Norwich Crown Court concluded and they had both been given life sentences because of the appalling barbarity of their crimes and utter lack of remorse.

Cheryl pulled on her bra and joined Ketch at the window.

"I try not to think about it," she said, cuddling up to him. He pressed into her, feeling her smooth skin.

"That's exactly what you need to do," he replied. "It's something I've learned to do in the job. Otherwise, it might drive you crazy."

His phone rang. It was DS Mackenzie.

The body lay on a green chaise longue in an apartment in Magdalen Street, a cosmopolitan area of the bustling city which had once seen better days but, with the modernisation of the nearby riverside, was becoming increasingly desirable by young middle class professional couples.

Number 23B was no exception, since the landlord had renovated the original interior to a contemporary finish. There was a preponderance of steel and pine and, though only a two bedroom flat, the light cream emulsion walls and tall sash windows made it appear much larger.

Ketch observed the room. In one corner stood a guitar, there was an expensive looking hi-fi system, a large flat screen TV, two small basket chairs covered with ethnic looking throws, an original Victorian fireplace with alabaster mantelpiece and, on a coffee table, two wine glasses, one of which had been knocked over, spilling its contents onto a white rug adjacent to it.

"Ah, there you are, Ketch. Better late than never." The voice came from the entrance to the lounge. Ketch turned and saw the portly form of Dr Michael Stoppard. In his white forensic suit he rather resembled a large porpoise, it occurred to Ketch. Behind Stoppard and rather pale-faced, stood the ever efficient Mackenzie. Mackenzie looked as if he hadn't slept.

"The victim is one Maria..."

"Maria Marinos, yes I know her," Ketch replied. "A Greek English teacher."

"Yes, a Greek citizen but she had a British passport. She rented this flat with her sister Helena."

"You spoke to the landlord I take it."

Mackenzie nodded.

"Cause of death?" asked Ketch, directing his question at the Pickwickian Stoppard.

"Manual strangulation, if these marks on her throat are anything to go by. The lividity of the face and the protruding tongue are also clues. She appears to have put up quite a fight, judging by the condition of her fingernails. Should offer some DNA traces."

Ketch interrupted him. "Who found her?"

"A colleague," Mackenzie replied. "They were both teachers at the language school."

"The time?"

"About 7 am. Apparently, they often went jogging along the riverbank before work."

"A boyfriend? Husband?"

Mackenzie shrugged.

"Nothing as yet."

"You've informed the father?"

"No, not yet. His name is Aaron Marinos. He owns a Greek restaurant…"

"I know it. The Socrates, in Chapelfield. "

He looked at Maria's face. Though distorted by the manner of her death, it still retained a certain radiance. The lifeless dark eyes stared back at him. She was taller than he had remembered. She was wearing a low cut t-shirt and tight faded denims which emphasised her figure.

"Any sign of sexual molestation?"

"No, nothing that's obvious," replied Stoppard. "I'll be able to give you more detail later."

Ketch nodded, then looked on as three SOCOs entered the room and began the usual forensic procedures.

"Where's the sister?"

"We haven't yet been able to trace her," Mackenzie informed him.

"Then let's start by interviewing the father. We'll make that our next port of call."

"You said you knew the girl?" asked Mackenzie tentatively.

"I met her purely by chance only yesterday. She was involved in a road rage incident in Magdalen Street not far from here. She took the licence plate number of the man who confronted her. Let's see if we can find it."

By the time Ketch and Mackenzie reached Chapelfield shopping mall, the Greek restaurant was already half full with customers, mainly due to the policy of offering cheap lunchtime business courses from 11 am onwards. Half the tables had been taken up by young business types in immaculate suits. Ketch recalled the place well from some months ago when he had visited with Cheryl. He had especially enjoyed the main course, a gemista, consisting of baked, stuffed vegetables with a rice and herb filling.

Ketch spoke to the head waiter and the two detectives were ushered into a small, windowless office at the rear of the building where a grey haired, short man with prominent eyes sat, hunched over a table. He rose and, extending a large hand, said:

"Aaron Marinos. What's this all about?"

Ketch introduced themselves.

"It's about your daughter, Mr Marinos."

"I have two daughters."

"Is this your daughter Maria?"

Ketch showed him a photograph. Marinos nodded.

"Yes, why do you ask me this?"

"I have some unpleasant news for you."

"Why, has she had an accident? Has she been injured?"

"It's more serious I'm afraid. I have to inform you that she died yesterday. We suspect she was murdered."

"Murdered? By whom?"

"We don't know that, not yet."

Marinos was clasping and unclasping his hands in agitation. He muttered something to himself in Greek.

"When can I see her?" he asked, despairingly.

"We'll take you to see her, to identify her."

After they had visited the mortuary and Marinos had completed the identification, Ketch ushered him into a small room at the Bethel Street HQ. Marinos looked pale and drawn.

"I need to ask you a few questions," Ketch explained.

"Go ahead."

"Can you think of anyone who might wish to have harmed Maria?"

Marinos shook his head.

"Maria was loved by everyone who knew her. When she was little I used to call her my angel. Sadly over the last two years, we had grown apart."

"Oh, why was that?"

"A number of reasons. She is - was a very headstrong person. Always knew her own mind. She could never be told – especially not by me. After she went to the University, Maria seemed to be more introspective, almost secretive. It's my view that while she was a student she met up with some rather odd people."

"In what way odd?"

"I mean odd political types. Activists. When she graduated, she took a variety of part-time teaching jobs here in East Anglia. Eventually, she ended up in Norwich, teaching at a language school. She was fluent in Greek, Polish and English. It was while at the language school that she met her most recent boyfriend."

"His name?"

"Andreas Bajorek. He's also a teacher who came to Britain a couple of years ago. We did not get on."

"You referred to him as Maria's most recent boyfriend. What happened?" asked Ketch.

"Maria turned up at my restaurant about a week ago. She had a large bruise to her left eye. When I asked her how she got it she wouldn't tell me. At last, I got her to admit that Bajorek had attacked her in a fit of rage. Apparently, he'd suspected that she'd been having an affair."

At this point, Mackenzie left the room and made a short call to HQ.

"What about other boyfriends?"

She never talked much about them. And I never used to ask."

"Where can we find Helena, Mr Marinos?"

"At present, I have no idea. Last time I spoke to Helena was some while ago. She was the elder – five years in fact. We did not get on very well. I rarely see her now. I have her mobile number."

"Thanks."

Marinos examined Ketch quizzically.

"Don't I recognise you?"

"Perhaps."

"You were at the restaurant – about a week ago."

"I was."

"I never forget a face."

As Ketch and Mackenzie left the restaurant, the sun came out from behind dark clouds and the snow was already turning to slush. Ketch noticed it had turned a few degrees warmer. His mobile rang. It was DC Thomas.

"I checked out this guy Bajorek, guv. Mackenzie asked…"

"Well?"

"Moved here from Krakow two years ago. Applied for a teaching post at Colman Street Language School. But he has form. Before he left Poland he was done for GBH. Beat his wife up. Apparently, he has a drink problem."

"Anything else?"

"Just the one conviction."

The language school in Colman Street was smaller than Ketch had expected, each room full to the brim with attentive multi-racial students. The school's proprietor was a tall, smartly dressed South African.

"It's terribly sad," he said, lugubriously, after Ketch explained the reason for their visit. "Maria was one of our most gifted teachers. She was motivated, very intelligent. She had strong views of course."

"About what?"

"About politics – especially Greek politics. She used to say that the Greek people had been betrayed by their politicians. She was especially critical of the far right. She used to go back to the motherland frequently during the recesses."

"And how did she get on with other members of the teaching staff?"

"Very well I believe."

"She was friendly with this man, I believe?"

Ketch showed him a photograph of Bajorek.

"Ah, Andreas. Yes indeed, I think they were probably having a relationship. Unfortunately, I had to let him go."

"And why was that?"

"I found out he was in a sexual relationship with one of our students – highly unprofessional. You don't think that -"

Ketch shook his head. "We are still in the early stages of our enquiry."

"Of course. Forgive me for my presumption, inspector."

"Did Maria ever mention her sister Helena?" asked Ketch.

"I didn't know she had a sister."

A phone rang on the director's desk.

"You must excuse me," he said, picking up the receiver. "A problem with a student." He raised his eyebrows and made a weary face. Ketch nodded and he and Mackenzie made their way out into the sunshine of the bustling city streets.

As soon as he got back to his office in Bethel Street, Ketch's phone rang.

"This is Inspector Dudek. I'm calling you from Krakow."

"Good morning to you, inspector. Thank you for getting back to me."

"Yes. Regarding Andreas Bajorek. We have a file on him which may be of interest to you. I'm sending you an email with an attachment."

Ketch thanked his Polish colleague and, after exchanging a few pleasantries, turned to his computer. Mackenzie entered the office holding a brown file. "Autopsy report on Maria Marinos, sir."

"Thanks. Any luck locating Bajorek yet?"

"No luck so far. He's not answering either his landline or mobile."

"Keep trying. Has the search warrant been issued?"

There was a ping from Ketch's PC.

"Ah, this looks like it."

As Mackenzie left the room, Ketch peered at the screen. He was never easy with computers, being something of a Luddite, but was grateful for the translation.

'Andreas Bajorek,' he read, 'Born 1989. Convicted of shoplifting 2003, and ABH, 2010. Member of the right wing political group, Golden Dawn, since 2012. Suspected of involvement in the murder of two students from Krakow University in May 2013. Arrested but later released through lack of sufficient forensic evidence. Emigrated to the UK in late July, 2013.'

Golden Dawn...Wasn't that some kind of esoteric society? Something to do with the black magician, Aleister Crowley? No, clearly this was different. He clicked on the attachment.

'Golden Dawn. Founded by Niko Laos Khakos in 1980. Registered as a political party. Campaigns for the return of the right wing in Greek politics and for a military dictatorship, also the expansion of Greek territory into Southern Albania. In 2012, Golden Dawn ran a campaign during the Greek elections on the themes of unemployment and immigration. Party members have been accused of violence and hate crimes against Moslems both in Greece and Macedonia. In the 1990's, Golden Dawn was complicit in assisting a number of war crimes against Bosnian Moslems. Regarded by many as a neo-Nazi group, Golden Dawn has campaigned for the 'National Rebirth of Poland. Other groups linked to Golden Dawn include the British BNP, British Voice and New Dawn.'

The door opened.

"Just had a call from Border Force," Mackenzie explained. "Bajorek's been picked up at Heathrow Airport. And we now have our search warrant."

"Excellent news. Before we interview Bajorek, let's check out his flat."

Bajorek lived in a small, one bedroomed flat in Reepham, a sleepy village some miles north of the city. The flat yielded little of consequence. Housed in a Victorian semi, the place possessed few furnishings, comprising a battered black leather sofa, a small, tired easy chair, a single bed and two large bookcases, containing books in both Polish and English, correspondence files, an old analogue TV, and, in the dated kitchen, several half empty bottles of Vodka and Schnapps. Clearly, Bajorek was a man of Spartan habits.

Outside the flat was a small fiat bearing a Polish registration plate.

"This might prove useful to us," observed Ketch to Mackenzie.

Ketch sighed with frustration. He had now read both the autopsy report and the SOCO report. The former revealed that Maria Marinos had died from asphyxiation caused by manual strangulation. There were two large bruises, one on her left cheekbone, and one on the right collarbone. There were also traces of skin under the fingernails of her left hand, suggesting that she had put up a fierce resistance to her assailant. The report also stated that she had died at around 11 pm on Sunday evening. The SOCO report informed him that several prints had been discovered on items of furniture, some of which proved a match to those of Bajorek and others belonging to Maria and another, unknown person.

That night, Ketch slept fitfully, waking just as dawn broke. Since the onset of his Parkinsons, he rarely enjoyed an unbroken sleep. And tonight was no exception. Over the last few years, he had experienced a slow, insidious decline in his health.

It was not just the physical effects which tended to blacken his mood these days. The increasing tremor in his hand – a hand that no longer allowed him to button up his shirts – added to his frustration. His former sprightly gait had now deteriorated into a slight shuffle and he had started to stoop as he walked. Worse were the vivid and often disturbing dreams, often of a sexual nature.

He pulled on his dressing gown and, sliding out of bed, walked over to the window. It had been a clear, frosty night and the sun was rising resplendent, above a long patch of wispy cloud. He began reviewing the events of the previous day. Things had started well enough but had not ended satisfactorily. Bajorek had stood his ground when interviewed and proved tougher than Ketch anticipated. A large, simian looking man with raven black hair and beard, he sat facing his interrogators with a look of grim determination.

"You admit that you visited Maria on Sunday evening?"

"Correct."

"You say that you left the flat an hour later."

"Yes, I left around 10.30."

"And you say she was alone when you left?"

"Yes."

"Her sister Helena wasn't in the flat?"

"No."

"So where was she?"

"I didn't ask."

"I believe you had feelings for both sisters."

"Yes, I don't deny it."

"When you left the flat, were you on good terms with Maria?"

"I wouldn't say that."

"Oh, and why was that?"

"We had an argument."

"About what exactly?"

"About lack of loyalty."

"Another man?"

"She had been unfaithful to me."

"Which she admitted?"

"Yes, she admitted it."

"Then you became angry and struck her?"

"It wasn't like that."

"So what was it like then? You tell me."

"We had a row. You must understand that Maria was hot tempered. We often had disagreements.

"About what?"

"About politics."

"You are a member of a group called Golden Dawn?"

"I am."

"A right-wing neo-Nazi group."

"That's how we are described by the socialists."

"And Maria – she was a socialist?"

"Yes, she had very left-wing views."

"You served a prison sentence in Krakow for attacking a man."

"I don't deny it."

"And therefore you would not hesitate in attacking your girlfriend, if she provoked you. You lost your temper, isn't that the case, Andreas?"

"I told you. We had a disagreement. Then I left the flat."

"And where did you go after that?"

"I went for a drink."

"Where?"

"The Murderers."

Ketch knew of it, an old pub near the castle. In the past, it had served as one of his haunts.

"Can anyone vouch for you?"

"The landlord – the barman."

"And you left there at what time?"

"At closing time."

"When did you last see Helena Marinos?"

"About a week ago, at the flat."

"Not since then?"

"No."

"You're sure?"

"I'm sure."

Bajorek had to be released without charge. There was still no concrete evidence, only circumstantial suspicion. Neither had there been any indication of the present whereabouts of Helena Marinos. He had reached a dead end. Even Bajorek's alibi had proved sound. The landlord of The Murderers remembered him because of his striking appearance. Bajorek had told Ketch that he had been attempting to fly back to Krakow to attend his uncle's funeral when he had been arrested – a claim which had been verified.

Maybe he would take a look at the crime scene again to gain a fresh perception.

The sun had now risen above the cloud, casting a golden glow over the old city. He opened the window, then lit a cigarette, blowing the smoke out. Cheryl did not approve of his smoking. It was admittedly a disgusting habit and he wished he could give it up, but he'd found it impossible.

By the time he got to the flat it was approaching midday. He ducked under the barrier tape and climbed the narrow stairs to the first floor. The loud strains of Beethoven's 9th rose up the stairwell as reached the landing. The occupant of the ground floor flat was an elderly pensioner who had been of no real help because she was deaf and had heard nothing on the night of the murder, telling Mackenzie she had been watching TV. Ketch glanced downwards and glimpsed an ancient face peering up at him.

Inside, the flat was surprisingly warm. Clearly whoever was last here had left the central heating turned up. He turned the dial to the 0 position, then stood in the middle of the lounge for a moment, looking about him. There was the sofa where Maria's body had lain, there the guitar and coffee table with the wine glasses, one overturned. There was an oppressive feeling of melancholy here which he found to be not uncommon at crime scenes. It was a reaction which was decidedly unscientific but which had served him well over the years. He became aware that his hand was now shaking uncontrollably and moved on to the bedrooms. The first of these was Maria's, judging by the photos of her on the wall. Maria standing on a rock probably in Greece. A much younger Maria, in a group, shot, probably taken on a school trip. Maria with her sister Helena in a nightclub. Helena had long blonde hair, Maria equally long, luxuriant dark hair, and they closely resembled each other. They might even have been twins. And this was Helena's bedroom. Unlike Maria's room, it was quite devoid of clutter, containing a small single bed, an equally small wardrobe and an antique easy chair. But what drew his eye were three large paintings. They were all unframed and had been executed in thick oil paint. The style of each painting was what might be described as expressionist.

The first showed the crouched figure of a peasant woman. Behind her stood the ruins of a building. The figure had her hands clasped. They were thin and veined, expressing the woman's anguish.

The second painting was a landscape. In the background was a dark mountain range. It was dusk, the sky illuminated by a crescent moon. In the foreground were three figures, indistinct, huddled, not entirely human. He found it disturbing.

The third painting was very different in mood and subject matter. It showed the naked figure of a woman who resembled Maria Marinos. She was lying on a sofa, her head thrown back, her legs apart. The painting had clearly been executed to arouse a mood of erotic pleasure. He examined the painting more closely. It had been done with heavy brush strokes and a palette knife and was technically accomplished. Unlike the other two paintings, in the bottom right hand corner the initials HM and the date 2012 had been inscribed.

A sound disturbed his ruminations. He turned round to see a young woman. She was dressed in a thin, figure hugging velour jacket, pink scarf and tight blue jeans. She gave him a broad grin.

"I'm Annie. I guess you must be a policeman."

"DCI Ketch. You realise you've trespassed on a crime scene?"

The girl blushed and looked slightly embarrassed.

"Gosh, I'm so sorry. Of course, forensic evidence and all that. Actually, I just came to collect my guitar."

"That's OK. You can take it. So you knew Maria, then?"

"Actually, we met through Helena. We were both in the same year at the art school."

"I don't suppose you know where Helena is at present?"

She shook her head.

"That's really why I came by. Of course, I knew what happened to Maria. I saw it on the news. A terrible thing. I wouldn't have come up without permission but there was no one about and I noticed that the door was open..."

"Quite. Tell me, how close were the sisters?"

"Very close, although they quite often disagreed. Maria was very politically aware but Helena was artistic. The best in our year. I see you've been admiring her work. What do you make of these paintings?"

"Intense – and rather disturbing."

"I agree. But all of Helena's work is like that. It must have something to do with her Mediterranean temperament." She laughed.

They chatted for a while, then the young woman picked up the guitar and left. Ketch remained at the flat and looked again at the portrait of Maria Marinos. Intense, passionate. He had sensed that when he'd first encountered her. If both sisters had shared that passion, what then...? There was a piece of the jigsaw he still had to find. And Bajorek was part of the picture, he was sure of it.

Sunday had started well but it was not to last. It was usually a special day for Ketch, offering him a break in the continual onslaught of police work.

Today was no exception. After a long breakfast, he and Cheryl had strolled along the riverbank, through the ancient cobbled streets of the mediaeval quarter until they reached the shining glass and steel structure known as The Forum, aptly named since on Sundays it was a popular meeting place for local residents.

Ketch had just settled down with Cheryl to a latte and croissant, when his work mobile rang. It was Mackenzie. Bajorek's body had been discovered after a visit to his flat by the landlord. He was lying on the kitchen floor and there was a deep stab wound in his chest. Whoever had attacked him had used a long bladed kitchen knife, then dropped it in the sink where an attempt had been made to clean it. Judging by the long, attenuated blood spatters on the wall, his attacker would have been comprehensively bloodstained.

The landlord, a short, bald, rotund man in his 50's, proved a useful witness.

"He had a visitor last night. I heard the car pull up outside. I'd been decorating next door."

"You own both properties?"

"I'm a property developer. I own a number of places here and in Norwich."

"Can you describe the driver to me?"

"A woman – young, long fair hair. I only caught a glimpse. Tall- she was wearing a black sweater and jeans. Is that enough?"

"What sort of car?"

"An old red Citroen – a 2CV. I remember because it was a bit unusual. These days you don't see them often."

"You don't recall the licence number?"

"Sorry, I don't remember it."

The landlord's testimony seemed too good to be true. Ketch felt an initial sense of elation since it confirmed his suspicion that Helena Marinos had been Bajorek's visitor and his nemesis.

When the autopsy had been completed, traces of DNA had been discovered which matched those extracted from minute epithelial fragments from Maria Marinos's fingernails. But whose DNA was it? That was a matter for speculation and over the years Ketch had learned not to speculate.

A week passed. There was still no sign of Helena Marinos,

despite a careful watch being kept at ports and airports. Helena Marinos had simply gone to ground.

Finally, after three more weeks of frustration, there was a breakthrough. A member of the public had wandered into a yard adjoining a shop premises just off Timber Hill in the city. There, parked under a lean-to, with its car cover half off due to the cold winter winds, was a red 2CV.

The manager of the shop, a delicatessen serving the local Greek community, was very helpful. He told Mackenzie that he was an employee of Aaron Marinos and the 2CV had been parked there by him several weeks ago.

Ketch brought Marinos in for questioning. At first, he was uncooperative, but after two hours of close interrogation, he relented.

"I will tell you the truth," he told Ketch. His eyes were now bloodshot and he blinked in the harsh light of the angle lamp. "You must understand that this man Bajorek was no better than an animal. Maria was besotted with him. I warned her that he would be trouble but she refused to listen. I guessed that he knocked her about, I had predicted it. So when I realised that you weren't going to charge him, I decided to take matters into my own hands."

"You killed him."

"He attacked me and I retaliated. I picked up the kitchen knife which I saw lying on the table and I stuck it in him. Men like him are only too common now in my homeland, inspector."

"What do you mean?"

"Fascists. The same as those tyrants who killed both my grandparents in Athens in 1941. Nothing changes. History just repeats itself. Don't you agree?"

Ketch didn't respond to this observation. Instead, he replied:

"Where is your daughter Helena, Mr Marinos?"

But Marinos said nothing.

A week later Helena was discovered. She had been offered a place of sanctuary by her friend, Annie Styles who rented a one bedroomed flat in Hellesdon. Two members of Ketch's team had spent a week watching the premises.

Helena, as vivacious as her sister, displayed a studied defiance, sitting with clasped hands, staring directly at her accusers. The effect was somewhat disturbing.

"I need you to answer one question, Helena. Why did you murder Bajorek?"

"I know nothing about that."

"Then how do you account for the fact that your DNA was found on his body?"

She had removed her dark glasses now and was playing with them with her long, thin fingers. Her stare was direct and challenging.

"If a dog went crazy and attacked you, wouldn't you fight back?"

"You're saying you killed Bajorek in self-defence?"

"After I heard that Bajorek had been released I went to see him at his flat to confront him. He attacked me, tried to strangle me. Fortunately, I took classes in self-defence last year so I was able to fight back. Then he picked up the knife and swung at me. We struggled and somehow the blade turned on him. I didn't intend killing him. It's just the way things worked out."

"You and Maria were close?"

"We were soulmates."

"And more than that?"

"What are you implying?"

"That you were lovers."

"Why should I deny it?"

"Perhaps you can explain why we found your DNA under her fingernails?"

There was a pause.

"Very well. We had a row. It used to happen between us."

"About Bajorek?"

She nodded.

"Maria was besotted. She couldn't see him for the lying, violent fascist he really was. I implored her to give him up but she wouldn't listen to reason. So I lost my temper with her. I told her that if she carried on with him much longer, he'd end up killing her."

"But instead you ended up killing her?"

Helena's eyes filled with tears. She buried her head in her hands and was silent. Mackenzie stopped the recorder and Ketch sat impassively for a while, staring across at her. A line from Oscar Wilde's *Ballad of Reading Gaol* came back to him: 'And each man kills the thing he loves...'

It was a bright September morning. Ketch and Cheryl were sitting by one of the large windows in the Forum. It was Sunday, the weather unusually warm. By the river where they had walked, the air was fresh and the golden leaves of the waterside trees lay in a thick, rustling carpet. Of late life had been good to him. After consulting his neurologist, Ketch had been put on a new type of medication, one that had fewer side effects. And he had found a buyer for his bachelor flat in the Earlham Road, thus releasing much needed funds to augment his forthcoming police pension.

The trial of Helena Marinos had taken place a month ago but the case seemed to him remote now. She had admitted to both killings on the plea of manslaughter and in court revealed much about the details of her relationship with Maria. The two sisters had enjoyed an incestuous relationship since the age of 14 and their father had suspected it but failed to intervene. Charged with obstruction, he admitted he had concealed Helena's car and persuaded her friend Annie Styles to offer her refuge. He also admitted trying to mislead the police by claiming he had murdered Bajorek in order to protect his daughter.

What was it about the Greeks, Ketch mused as he drank his latte and gazed out of the window at the tall tower of St Peter Mancroft? All that passion, tragedy... and incest. Zeus and Hera, Cronus and Rheas... How the gods do mock us.

If you have enjoyed reading this collection, why not try some of the other Cunning Crime titles:

www.cunningcrimebooks.co.uk

Printed in Great Britain
by Amazon

86005594R00180